THE
BEAUTY
OF
TRUTH

DUALITY

Book I of
An Epic of Metaphysical Existence

ALWYN

BOT Publishing LLC
PO Box 62
Mt Pleasant, SC 29465

Copyright © 2004 by G. Alwyn Zittrauer

First Edition published by BOT Publishing LLC in 2005

Library of Congress Control Number   2004096210
ISBN 0-9759493-0-6

Printed and bound in the United States of America
Typesetting by Dom Roberti
Edited by James T McDonough, Jr., Ph.D.

www.thebeautyoftruth.com

Contents

Book I is dedicated to my parents

Author's Notes

This book will challenge your beliefs,
no matter what they are.

The philosophy within these pages evolves.

The politically correct should not venture further,
for those who rely on division cannot grasp the whole.

This book is organized to be read in small doses.

Try to read what is actually written;
preconceived notions will definitely lead to misunderstanding.

Within is an expanded metaphysics,
intended to replace the present one, rapidly failing.

When old age shall this generation waste,
  Thou shalt remain, in midst of other woe
Than ours, a friend to man, to whom thou say'st,
  Beauty is truth, truth beauty,—that is all
  Ye know on earth, and all ye need to know.

Final lines from *Ode on a Grecian Urn*
by John Keats

Day I _____

06:00

TIME appears in faceless MIND
as the turbulent slumber of night is abandoned for day.
Cold pale fake stone still imprisons my body;
the same light washes it in a world of color gone gray.
Lights on and lights off, with darkness on both sides;
why should TIME matter at all when it is beyond control?
No matter what I do, it will repeat and it will end;
whether I move or stew in stained sheets, TIME goes on.
TIME on this earth is limited for all of us,
yet that does not affect this moment, right now.
Shuffle out of bed and put my bare feet upon a bare floor;
this moment in TIME gives me a contact that is cold as hell.
A dissonant reprieve from the dull sustaining reveries
which make entombed LIFE so stupendously estranged.
As if walking over a grave, I feel shivers attack my spine;
though they are from a physical cause, not mental.
In here there is no longer any use for it—this TIME;
floating along from day to day in endless repetition.
Lungs cycling in and out, and heart pump-pump pumping;
my external existence now simulates my internal one.
What is the use for existing in this placid fashion;
could there be anything more routine than timeless LIFE?
Like my morning exercises, a natural coffee substitute;
though now I'm as addicted to this healthful alternative.

1

A mortal drum unjustly held to rhythm without a melody;
no probability that tomorrow will not be the same as today.
My stomach growls with an abnormal post-SLEEP rumble,
likely because I refused to eat the previous evening.
What use is food when its consumer is dead to the world,
deserted by justice; a repast offered to the greedy masses?
I've always been possessed of a healthy appetite,
but now I make myself sick with the jest foisted upon me.
IDEA! It strikes Zen MIND wide awake into a brilliant alert:
turn last night's depression into this morning's inspiration.
Refusing to eat won't right any legally induced wrongs;
I'll still remain trapped within this square x square.
If right and wrong mattered, this situation would not exist;
what is left is to make LIFE have meaning here and now.
There is no point in living if I only seek to find DEATH;
the result of LIFE isn't something I desire to advance.
The point is to have a goal, to protest this wild injustice,
to withhold from them LIFE they do not own.
Anything is better than this BRAIN-numbing repetition,
and the likelihood it will end has been stamped DENIED.
Fast to the point where they think just desserts are done,
not realizing it has been snatched from their bitter bite.
A fast unto DEATH seems so final, so vastly unhelpful;
still, there seems to be no other way to resist omnipotence.
As doubt wrestles with resolve for control of twisting MIND,
neither one is able to force it into a neat contained box.
So now I just sit here with no immediate prospects,
not even 3 squares a day amidst the rumbling herd.
An action has been initiated, which will inspire reaction;
authorities desire to control everything, even TIME.
This prison doesn't entrap me to the extent TIME does;
if I were outside these walls, I would still be limited.
Yet TIME did not seal one more block into permeable stone;
the absence of TRUTH has made our TIME seem irrelevant.
TIME is fundamental QUANTITY within this universe;
TRUTH is just another failure rightly attributed to man.
How is a gem known but through each of its surfaces;
if one is pierced, will another not be there to replace it?

A gem is known by the nature of how it does exist;
if I know TRUTH only by its facets, then I've no use for it.
Hold TRUTH to the light and see its ordinary smudges,
then immerse it in a spring where illusion is washed away.
TRUTH by its nature is the material of facts,
accurate and commonly defined for ubiquitous use.
It still cannot be put into our hands to manipulate at will;
TRUTH is a puddle of water on asphalt waiting to dry up.
I want to know TRUTH, for without it I know nothing;
knowledge is nonsense unless founded in TRUTH.
It is a simple question to ask, with no solid purchase:
what is TRUTH?
It's that by which it is represented;
knowledge of facts will give me complete access to TRUTH.
Spinning meaning in Ouroborous circles—what is a fact?
What facts do we truly know without a shadow of doubt?
I know quite a few facts: my former address;
I'm a male; Columbus sailed the ocean blue in 1492.
Yet these facts are defined by their nature as true;
is there no possibility they could be false?
There is no supernatural existence for known facts;
all of them have been agreed upon as mutual knowledge.
Does that mean they are true, or facts;
is TRUTH dependent on, or can it be beyond, agreement?
I agree with the government what my address is;
historians have agreed on some of their facts; I acquiesce.
Ascribing attributes of TRUTH numbering to INFINITY
will allow it to find a home among many possibilities.
But TRUTH found through the application of facts
is limited in the number of suitable options to pursue.
CONCEPTION of TRUTH faces out in one of three directions,
all of which allow observers to see out as well as in.
TRUTH can change, TRUTH can't change,
or TRUTH is beyond the notion of change.
TRUTH will not be found limited by its termed distinctions;
a waterfall does not stop because of a downstream dam.
But those are the only notions of TRUTH I can understand;
even if it's an absolute, my THOUGHTS aren't.

How can TRUTH exist in a world where it miserably fails;
why strive toward something that seems unattainable?
It's much easier to believe in an absolute degree of false;
at least that would be easier to reconcile with my fate.
If TRUTH exists, it should eventually rear its head;
how can it function at the whim of imperfect humanity?
So far, in my case, there doesn't appear to be any TRUTH;
people only believe what they see, never what really is.
A white dove of failing heart, dying within;
faith is only as strong as the hope which sustains it.
Day after day of endless drudgery pushes hope away;
enough of me remains for 1 last battle to end the war.
To resist with limp power is worse than futile,
only weakness can defeat overweening strength.
They can take my freedom and offer bitter sustenance,
but no man can make me consume the dregs of injustice.
A path can be lit with steadfast guidance, see by TRUTH;
fast along the unseen road where TIME is interference.

06:49

Hunger seems to have awakened my sense of smell,
or maybe I'm imagining breakfast cooking this morning.
MEMORY of food makes an unwelcome appearance,
obscuring TRUTH when subject to sensory deprivation.
I normally think I know what is real, my TRUTH,
but fasting has already put my PERCEPTIONS of it in doubt.
Imagine TRUTH can change, it is endless putty;
no universal mold makes its existence real.
There is nothing I can point to as being absolutely true;
only unison among varied observers allows facts to exist.
Is it possible OBJECT cannot be itself;
how can a chair be a chair unless it is first a chair?
I agree with other observers which OBJECTS are chairs,
and the definition changes based upon who is defining.
Thus a chair is sometimes a chair, and sometimes it is not;
so what are we to do when two observers disagree?

If observers don't agree about the nature of OBJECT,
then a definition can't be applied; so, no chair.
Thus it does not matter what someone else conceives,
individual CONCEPTION allows us to find form for function.
No. It's always possible 1 party can be wrong,
such as if my address is claimed to be other than it is.
TRUTH seen as mutable has this unwavering fallacy:
what is real can be wrong if someone has that belief.
If what I recognize as a table is what another calls a chair,
then obviously at least 1 of these 2 observers is wrong.
Exactly the point: how do we determine which
is truthful, if TRUTH by its nature should never be wrong?
Identifying something as true means it can't be false,
and if it's possible it can't be true, then it's not TRUTH.
It is not a tangled web to separate TRUTH from false,
yet it is one to separate it from arbitrary applications.
I regularly confuse TRUTH with what is identified as true;
a chair is a chair, unless when I define it I'm wrong.
Place an arbitrary wall between TRUTH and OBJECT;
then they can adequately fit within defined boundaries.
Any definition can be wrong depending upon PERCEPTION,
so anything capable of definition is actually not-TRUTH.
Whatever is TRUTH behind the presence of the chair
will exist as itself whether or not it is defined as a chair.
That which I define as being true doesn't ensure TRUTH;
I and others agree on facts only to avoid trivial arguments.
The putty of TRUTH does not harden within sure MIND;
it remains more like unfinished wood than sculpture.
The appearance of TRUTH may be a changeable essence,
but only because anything defined as true can be false.
It is too early to harden TRUTH into an ill-timed mold;
its form will be revealed as excess REALITY is chipped away.

07:09

Bob the pan-fried shuffling guard tells me I'm gonna fry;
my case has been adjudged and a penalty has been applied.

Casting doubt on Wisdom in a legal system,
leaving Truth in the hands of those who cannot detect it.
I know what Truth is in my particular case,
a platonic absolute no 1 else can seem to find.
Then try to imagine Truth cannot change;
Reality is subject to its fixed and unyielding boundaries.
But I have just yielded to Truth that can't be defined,
and it's a definition to assert it can't change.
A bubble is only a barrier between air and air;
note the difference in discerning the air and the bubble.
So Truth exists beyond the meaning a definition gives to it;
I'm only trying to imagine a characteristic of its nature.
Conceive of how its essence could not change,
how the air is the same within and without.
Then I'm still not trying to determine the nature of Truth,
only reflecting on how I'm able to know of its existence.
A bubble does not change the air within, only defines it;
contrast an unchanging Truth to its changing Perception.
There is no difference to me between 1 and the other;
awareness of Reality arrives only through my senses.
Although Perceptions are tied to Conceptions by necessity,
there will always be a barrier between one and the other.
I don't understand how to find Truth unless it's examined,
and I see no way of examining it unless my senses limit it.
Verity of Perception is according to an observer's views;
how can one Truth be its Perception if no less must shift?
If Truth can't change, or be limited by Perception,
then its essence is such that I can't define it.
Yet how can we acknowledge Truth does exist,
and at the same moment propose it as insensible?
I have leapt too far past what I'm able to discern;
maybe it's more probable that Truth doesn't exist.
Parse Truth into a unicorn that has never breathed;
thus making Reality known only bestride this mount.
If Truth exists, then I have only murky Concept of it;
what it is seems like hope held just out of reach.
Submit to Truth's existence, and a not impossible point:
all of it may not be gained through sensual Perception.

I wish to know TRUTH laid bare, but for comprehension,
I must believe in REALITY existing beyond my senses.
To believe a bubble can hold air, or it does not,
means grasping empty TRUTH, or cold sensual impulses.
If that is the choice I must make, then I choose my senses;
while not perfect, they are still better than blind faith.
So we temporarily leave the grand possibility of TRUTH
for the chance to fill in an ample babble of facts.
I can't acknowledge TRUTH that doesn't change;
nothing I can bring to bear will establish the framework.
Only outside of sensation might an absolute be obtained;
bubbles are only blown with a suitably slick surface.
But that is merely a choice, not an observation of fact;
I could just as easily have chosen uncompromising TRUTH.
It is a choice to accept any interpretations of fact;
CONCEPTION chooses definition by way of circular TRUTH.
I stand by my choice to know what comes to my senses,
the source of the minimal facts of which I'm aware.
Understanding of TRUTH comes with a choice;
we are free to choose, whether it ends up good or bad.

07:34

Bob the guard may know something I don't,
but his access to TRUTH surely can't be greater than mine.
Can two self-gratifying fools possibly be right,
or maybe two views can both be inordinately wrong?
I know my TRUTH exists, and they have missed it;
what happens is real, not just imagination.
Two leaves have been blown off of the three-leafed tree,
leaving one attached, yet to be sundered from TRUTH.
TRUTH can't change, it lacks attachment to definition;
and TRUTH can change because my senses demand it.
One leaf is left, colored beyond the notion of change;
is an essence possible that neither changes nor does not?
That's asking me to believe something *<is>* and *<is not>*;
though the absence of both is a little more believable.

Pure absence beyond the notion of existence;
why is this more possible than a basic paradox in REALITY?
Both <*is*> and <*is not*> qualify as defined CONCEPTS;
I only have to imagine VOID where neither could exist.
That analysis only makes <is> *and* <is not> *into an* <is>;
VOID *becomes nothing more than another* <is not>.
So there is no practical way to see TRUTH beyond change;
it's like trying to prove it both <*is*> and <*is not*>.
The problem lies in trying to make TRUTH *solely* RATIONAL,
while its eventual emergence makes it also seem irrational.
I accept IDEA that TRUTH is beyond mutable CONCEPTS,
but there is no RATIONAL way to further pursue this option.
Only using a RATIONAL *perspective in pursuit of* TRUTH
leaves IDEA *lost in a thicket that does not exist.*
One of my steps follows another until a goal is reached;
there is no other way for me to see what underlies it.
For now, a sufficient beginning in this search for TRUTH;
as yet just a Sisyphus log, not worth the effort and TIME.

07:43

There are 4 walls around me and this hasn't changed;
I can see anything to their limit, but not 1 little bit further.
Still trapped inside a secure cocoon waiting for freedom;
a new world within which facile MIND *tries to find itself.*
These walls are no less part of TRUTH than my situation,
but how I hold them in my head seems quite different.
Is TRUTH *submissive to rule by dominant* MIND,
safe at the top, master of all that is perceived to conceive?
I rule—I'm the master—of all I know;
senses produce PERCEPTIONS forming neural CONCEPTS.
Yet they gain us no substance, a specter haunts them;
within, a light tightly transfixes knowledge with a guess.
A union of neural signals raises distinct CONCEPTS;
this is how my BRAIN becomes a structure for my THOUGHTS.
Ghostly MIND *forever cajoling and biding* TIME *for* TRUTH;
a snare that cannot be escaped, forever attached.

However my MIND may exist, it's a part of me;
some insubstantial piece charged by my BRAIN.
It gives its body no rest, its body gives it no peace.
How does it bind? Is it a moment like no other?
I'm bound to my MIND by the structure of my BRAIN;
therefore when it ceases to let TIME go by, so do I.
MIND is a hard ghost to bear, hiding from TRUTH'S burden;
it has no existence without us; do we exist without it?
MIND is only hidden by unknown neural processes;
the burden is held by my BRAIN'S struggle to form THOUGHTS.
Can MIND plant THOUGHT, a passionate sweeping seed,
from which will grow perfectly resolved CONCEPTIONS?
An intention to grow my understanding of TRUTH
by levering it against my MIND'S prearranged CONCEPTS.
Only by seeing MIND as it truly is, not a ghost or master,
not the hills seen through a shear on a cloudy day.
I can't know or comprehend anything, including TRUTH,
until I expand the notion of what it is that turns in my head.
Is full MIND really here? Is it not here if it is not there?
Where is that part held with which we most identity?
It must be within me, somewhere;
my THOUGHTS don't originate from outside myself.
No THOUGHTS pass except bidden by unexposed MIND;
no actions result save initiated by its furtive influence.
I see no MIND in others, it isn't an animal trait;
only by my actions does my MIND even claim existence.
Swipe a clean finger through dust and claim it;
every piece of what makes MIND comes here, as it is there.
There is no part of me not considered part of my essence;
from soles to bald spot, all of it is mine.
A rose smells divine because delicate MIND wills it so;
thus honey is nectar to tongue; thus silk smoothly caresses.
Sights and sounds all begin and end with me,
whether it's the most brilliant color or the bluest note.
The light sought is greater than any ability to see it;
the realm each of us may claim is all, only by half.
There does seem to be an independent aspect to my MIND,
how THOUGHTS arise there unconnected to anything else.

Ruling MIND is master of MATTER when attached to LIFE;
only looking within will bend its knee to another.

08:10

Growing by the side of the yard is a spindly cactus,
sitting patiently in the sun, waiting for water.
It is an easy distinction between "cactus" and "observer;"
what is it that knows various OBJECTS are "out there?"
I can touch the cactus and know it's not me;
even the cactus detects that it's different from the ground.
Yet how does the "observer" know the "cactus"
beyond the simple capacity for creating its definition?
It's another thing, another OBJECT, what I perceive it to be;
though my MIND and I both conceive it the same way.
Does earth possess cactus, or cactus possess earth,
or are they separate, each to its own unique nature?
The cactus can't be the same thing as I am,
just as I must be the same thing as my MIND.
Can a plant exist outside of its own boundaries,
possessing what it touches as well as where it lives?
The notion I could exist somewhere outside of myself
is nonsense, it makes no sense, I'm only me.
There is the seed which must be planted—who is in here?
Give it TIME and ENERGY and see what grows.
I'm a thinker of THOUGHTS, which originate with my senses;
THOUGHTS arising from within me, not from without.
Do a plant's roots know the ground in which it grows,
alkaline or acidic, it gives as it gets?
These THOUGHTS I own are dependent upon my senses,
but there must be more to me than just my PERCEPTIONS.
Could MIND be only senses reacting to repeated pinpricks;
does any planted seed arise just from reflex?
No. That I'm only my senses is more nonsense;
they give me noise and light, but they aren't who I am.
Dare we say who we are, and still believe it;
can a cactus know more of itself than that it is a cactus?

I can only define who I am in relation to what others are;
whether living or lifeless, some of both is required.
Basking in the sun or bathing in cool springs,
neither of them violate "the who" actually in here.
If everything is subject to my own personal interpretation,
then who I am depends on who I think I am; nonsense.
A cactus likely knows what it as well as any man;
try another unknown seed—what is in here?
This is easier—I'm BRAIN in a body, fully formed,
able to think tall THOUGHTS in multiple bounds.
Is BRAIN the source of its varied THOUGHTS,
or is manifold MIND the source of them, fully grown?
My BRAIN can exist whether I do or not;
animals have them without recognizing themselves.
Does a cactus flower open because it is the plant,
or does it open because it comes from this source?
I must come from my BRAIN because it exists before me;
there can be no creation of "I" before this fact.
How can ephemeral THOUGHTS arise from gross matter;
where in the material realm can they possibly exist?
There is only 1 realm I know:
that which I touch and hear and see.
Yet everything is not within that sphere of influence;
usual MIND is not just its THOUGHTS, yet they belong to it.
Everything within my body is me, as are my THOUGHTS;
they conceive of me as I conceive of them.
More than one seed is required to grow proper THOUGHT,
so another question is pertinent—why is anything in here?
I am here because I must be, this is my nature,
just as the cactus must exist as a cactus.
Is order required for chaos to exist,
if there is no rationale for existence other than chance?
I can find no REASON within me why I shouldn't exist;
it's ludicrous to suggest I'm only possible, or probable.
Yet why are THOUGHTS attached to an existence;
what given law mandates one OBJECT to have firm MIND?
My existence flows with my THOUGHTS,
though there is much within me still beyond my ken.

Is there a disconnect between self and Reality;
how can Thoughts *control a formed external existence?*
Nothing of me will exist unless I can sense and feel myself,
and I logically know Reality exists beyond me.
A paradox in the making, the biggest seed;
how is Reality *known to continue beyond* Perception?
I can look everywhere around me and see bodies dying,
yet Reality is unshaken—no yawning paradox.
Oh . . . that all could be spared from sorrow yet to come;
only solitary growth will bring forth the flower of Truth.

08:41

I sit watching my fingers make a fist and then uncurl,
adding something to my body, and then it vanishes.
Who is watching, and what is making the fist;
is anything new there outside of creative Mind?
I'm sitting here thinking, but I'm also existing;
some combination of the intangible and the physical.
Each man creates his own Mind, *he gives it structure;*
yet is his Purpose *and* Life, *his own* Mind, *with him?*
Mind formed by coalescing Concepts is phantom Brain,
nothing more than a symptom of delusive Thoughts.
How does Matter *wake except through a sentient*
ghost; what knowledge can exist in pulpy gray Mass?
This is minimal awareness: I think, I exist, cogito ergo sum;
Descartes endowed me with the minimum beyond doubt.
It is not doubt that exists in the universe between Space;
self-knowledge is insufficient to create alert Mind.
If I have Thoughts, then <. . .> must have them;
if I'm convinced nothing exists, <. . .> must be convinced.
It is this mystery that substitutes Mind *for* Thoughts,
connecting the immaterial to the material.
A demon could deceive me into believing nothing exists;
<. . .> must exist in order to be deceived.
Is it possible to look past the reflection of any one Mind,
if it only shows that the mirror must be the observer?

I can't think I'm nothing
as long as I think that I'm <. . .>.
Yet what fills SPACE expansive MIND fits into; is it limited
to fit in the volume within hollow bone?
Since I know I exist, either I exist and all else is illusion,
or I exist and all else is real.
Could we not exist, with some parts of REALITY as illusion,
and some other parts still known completely real?
Certainly possible,
but my REALITY is based on knowing 1 from the other.
We may be phantoms in a world made up as a nightmare,
or its mate shifting through wall and flesh alike.
I discredit the former because I've already discovered I'm not
aware of myself without BRAIN to aid me.
Is any man just a ghost attached to awareness
even as he demands dualistic degrees of definition?
Real am I,
and there is more within this realm of REALITY that is real.
Yet REALITY must fold upon itself to see that it exists;
one is present, a neatly creased self touching itself.
There can be no doubt there is doubt;
it's part of that which I own, belonging to no other.
From where does a stinging doubt arise;
is it an electrical signal which fears its own validity?
I see doubt within myself; I'm capable of doubt;
it seems doubt and I shall ever be found together.
Does doubt arise from THOUGHT given LIFE
in MIND or in BRAIN or together or somewhere else?
Doubt can be little else than THOUGHT;
it comes and goes like the others I don't possess.
THOUGHTS ricochet in wide MIND like a bounding boulder,
crashing into one location and another, stop then go.
Each THOUGHT I have stops, and departs;
then races on until another 1 feels the need to attend.
Is one of those passengers a doubt without doubt;
does each boulder stop on one, or is it one itself?
My THOUGHTS bounce along the recesses of my MIND;
each could end in a doubt, but only 1 does.

Energy producing Thoughts of doubts seems unstoppable,
a ghost which makes a solid appearance.
A member of my Thoughts which isn't bounded by them,
doubt must arise within me, but I know not wherefrom.
Wherefrom do Thoughts causing doubt arise?
Unfold each self so that it can no longer see itself.

09:07

Bob the guard has begun to entertain me with his Wisdom:
"Only a nut would demand the right not to eat!"
Any path set upon is usually validated by another;
although not always in the way in which an ego intends.
It pisses me off that he could be right about something;
there is no Rational Reason to go on a fast.
Do Rational Thoughts not have other siblings;
is there doubt as to where anger is made manifest?
Emotions are irrational, I don't think them;
their effect upon my existence makes no earthly sense.
We taste, yet why should anyone prefer a peach to a pear?
We smell, yet why should anyone prefer a rose to refuse?
Physiological reactions suggest feelings,
but these aren't the same as Emotions themselves.
Sights, sounds, and touch are mere sensations
without pleasure or joy—is joy felt or sensed?
I assume feelings use felt and sensations use sensed;
1 can lead to the other, but they aren't synonymous.
Life can be given to feelings, although not to sensations;
a feather touch inspires different reactions.
I can define them and consider them, totally formal,
but never can I state that I have actually felt senses.
Even some Thoughts show a preference over others;
how unlike Rational products to be so irrational.
But Thoughts themselves are totally Rational;
where they come from, or why, doesn't affect this.
Kin to feelings are notions of Qualia,
are they attached and perceived in a like manner?

Smooth or coarse, gray or colorful, salty or sweet—
all these QUALITIES are founded in my senses.
Yet we find a preference for one over degrees of another;
the measure of a feather's touch is not by the numbers.
QUANTITY grants transference between different observers;
there is no universal QUALITY which can change hands.
Hubris transcends an ability to rely overmuch on quotas:
who, what, when, and where; yet more important is why.
The first four w's are parts to the whole,
which isn't complete without the influence of why.
Why is not QUANTITY, it gives no formal answers;
its impetus is not from MATTER, so why does it matter?
Decisions must be made based on all available data;
contributions from why lack hard transferable currency.
THOUGHTS must also access a store of MEMORIES to work;
vital for function, yet where are they stored?
THOUGHTS arise from processing by BRAIN;
this connection requires it as the storehouse for MEMORY.
There must be more to MEMORY than synaptic storage;
a flock is not the same if some birds are different.
There is no place like my BRAIN for MEMORY to be held;
it records and retrieves sensible physical phenomena.
THOUGHTS are imagined to work like a biological computer;
although a computer is at best inferior MIND.
THOUGHT, like MEMORY, resides only in a biological home;
they're insensible terms bowing to a physical description.
Busy MIND orders tasks required to run its body;
where is its capacity to hold operational MEMORIES?
It's always alive with electromagnetic signals;
once they cease, any MEMORY of MEMORIES dies with them.
Do not confuse an ability to access MEMORY
with what is required to make a body continue living.
MEMORY lives with my BRAIN, and so dies with it;
there is nothing permanent to the organ or its substance.
Yet these THOUGHTS are linear, unlike pictorial MEMORY;
all senses combined, where only one is desired.
My senses feed MEMORY well;
there is no other place for it than my fabulous BRAIN.

Where in Brain is a personality memorized,
identifying traits that even insentient creatures possess?
I don't accept Idea of worms having personality;
the very name denotes that which is limited to people.
Travel back in Memory and access boon companions;
do not even pets exhibit self-specific characteristics?
Animals respond to individual stimuli;
their personalities are only so much anthropomorphism.
Even a human's personality is highly irrational;
the face presented is not always the face reflected.
The consistent reactions I perform are given my name,
and I like to think most of my actions are highly Rational.
Is there any way to crunch numbers into a personality,
or does each man create his own formless hell?
It's convenient to classify people with their habits;
this gives the appearance of personality, not its Reality.
Some presented aspects are neither intended nor required;
is it a bird's choice to build or steal its nest?

09:42

An impulse comes upon me to go on a trip, I'm stir crazy;
anywhere is better than this cell within a larger cell.
Ever want to do something and cannot quite grasp it;
where does this restless and edgy feeling come from?
My desire for a journey could be induced by incarceration;
Thought arriving just now, not at another place or Time.
Why does any Thought arise at a specific instant,
when it could just as easily have happened two hours ago?
Most of my Thoughts arise from immediate stimulus;
as for the rest, I have no Idea where they come from.
Try balancing Idea against the weight of knowledge;
are all Thoughts the result of one or the other?
Many Ideas result from the application of knowledge,
but some of the best have an Intuitive component.
Thought is just Idea taken form, irrationally sprung;
unbidden, uncontrolled, and still beholden to this push.

Knowledge is still required to pursue any IDEA;
the same 1 over and over will never bring progress.
Where do IDEAS come from; can they be CONCEPTIONS
unconnected to PERCEPTIONS?
I gain knowledge through my senses,
which form different CONCEPTS, which cross to form IDEAS.
Simultaneous thinkers will not create identical IDEAS;
they are creative fingerprints identifying elusive MIND.
PERCEPTIONS go into BRAIN, and IDEAS as THOUGHTS come out;
how they mix and match is still to be determined.
Denial of self comes from chaining THOUGHTS with logic;
how do they jump from one link to another?
A series of useful THOUGHTS comes from that process;
I don't know how the change in tracks occurs.
A leap in logic is not part of the process itself;
one is the alpha of knowledge, the other is the omega.
Each train of THOUGHTS must have a beginning and an end,
and some biological process must connect it all together.
What about the imposition of DREAMS between lights,
phantoms arising when THOUGHTS are listless and stale?
A random firing of synapses from overloaded BRAIN,
DREAMS are only uncontrolled THOUGHTS.
DREAMS belong to LIFE, even those beneath sentient size;
dogs dream, cats dream, DREAMS dream of themselves.
There is no proof that dogs dream of chasing cats;
synaptic firing produces random twitching, nothing more.
Their insistent presence holds mental equilibrium,
a tightrope which suspends lost TIME.
DREAMS inhabit the neurons allotted to awareness;
uncontrolled THOUGHTS aren't a substitute for thinking.
Do THOUGHTS occupy TIME when lost in DREAMS;
think on what happens in SPACE between THOUGHTS?!
TIME moves, it isn't lost in THOUGHTS or in DREAMS;
1 succeeding another requires the shifting of seconds.
Do THOUGHTS and DREAMS require the same source
to speak the same words in color, or black and white?
The difference between them is expressed by continuity;
there is no expectation that any DREAM will progress.

Pain is not Thought, yet it is strikingly felt in Dreams
by the agony of heartbreak, or work-hardened blisters.
Dreams and Thoughts differ by what they can feel;
1 essence is all, the other is nothing.
Can Pain's hurt arise from both feeling and sensation;
the agony of crushed hopes compared to crushed toes?
Mental and physical anguish have separate causes;
that they are both termed Pain doesn't tie them together.
Nerve impulses can account for electric transmission,
yet how do Cells cry after they have already been lost?
Severing nerve connections will eventually cut Perception;
phantom Pain is only a simple stimulus like unto sensation.
Neurons may account for some of those quandaries,
yet steely Mind is required to forge the missing links.
The only missing pieces are those left to discover;
reliance on mystical insight gives hope where none is due.
Pieces of the living puzzle are delectable tastes
for an unknowing palate which Time is set to arrange.

10:12

Every moment that passes gives me brief pause;
each now filled with a decision to exist or not.
The weight of Time becomes too suffocating, too intense;
is there doubt as to what has brought this incubus about?
Why I am in this place at this moment is quite simple:
I value all existence more than my own.
The body of Mind floats on streams of turbulent mist,
silvery air shedding seeds of existential doubt.
I don't doubt I exist;
growing questions without answers doesn't alter this fact.
It does not attach—that pernicious doubt;
how is it separate from Thought, and still part of it?
All existing within me is part of the identity of me;
so doubt attaches to Thoughts from which I spring.
It is seen passing beneath or behind or far away;
what boundaries are suspended to entrap doubt?

I see cause and effect, which is the basis of all I know;
a Rational sequence by which Science shows Reality.
Gods to assuage the loneliness of the unknown;
bow down before the altar of knowledge to dispel doubt.
This is the ritual I must follow to create Science:
observe a cause, observe an effect, and link them together.
Separation between the observer and the observed;
the earth remains beneath them as they all turn.
Knowledge is unavailable to those untrained to see beyond
guesswork that is the province of my Mind's imprecision.
Grasp them both between a thumb and a finger;
gasp as they gently drift away from a jointed ken.
What I can see and know conforms to partitions in 2:
cause and effect, is and isn't, here and not here.
That infection contaminates all attempts at knowledge,
a fence erected to wave off the weak and the wary.
To know and to understand lead my twinned Thoughts;
all I think and see and do succumbs to this division.
Insight and Intuition fall further behind as man
pursues the eternal specter of future gods of Science.
Knowledge on its own is innocent of ulterior motives,
but it too can become infected with desire and fear.
Is knowledge innocent when it contributes to Death;
does it bear responsibility for intentional misuse?
Cause and effect have their own relation to desire;
my ability to understand can't control others who seek gain.
Deluxe hungers do not wait to seek their fortune;
they do not understand that which comes in its own Time.
I know of no desire totally unlike those others,
where motives are pure, and no harm comes from Science.
Trouble and havoc arise from its best intentions,
relying on incomplete comprehension and spurious needs.
I don't cause those troubles, they use me too;
the shackles they press upon me aren't my fault.
From where does it arise? Does it really matter?
Desire binds together Thoughts, Emotions, and actions.
No creature is able to function but to its own capacity;
mine is to seek knowledge, not forever hunger with desire.

If it does not exist within some dualistic realm,
why is desire's pursuit according to cause and effect?

10:35

It's strange that the worst thing ever to happen to me
occurred because I was raised to help those in need.
"No good deed goes unpunished" by the various fates;
trying to help others seems like unto spitting into the wind.
But I still wouldn't change a thing I did,
surrendering my self to save myself isn't worthwhile.
Must Truth surrender to a conflict in Rational terms;
is there no other way to carry its load?
Thoughts can only be transmitted in a Rational fashion;
nonsense and babbling don't access greater knowledge.
Is not it possible for private experience to be cleanly conveyed
without the Rational burden borne by language?
Words give meaning to those events I deem important,
and only by my right words are they so deemed.
Meaning held on a lazy susan, too weak for a direct pass;
food bartered between Souls as if for their very lives.
Words are the best dynamic yet conceived for binding;
thereby forming society out of driven animal instinct.
Is there a difference between man's ken and his sense;
are we foolish dogs following our tails into random waste?
Though my utterances might not issue from known causes,
all of them do fit into a highly lucid category.
Who is in here creating sentience—who or what?
Mind's essence becomes lucid, yet this is not its source.
I'm not the source, but I own the conversation;
articulated Concepts of mine must pass through my domain.
Complete Mind contains something beyond Thoughts;
they are drowning in knowledge, clinging to dim Life.
Beyond intelligence is a zone better left to charlatans,
for only they can understand their own gibberish.
What is beyond known intelligence;
is Mind at once its source and its dependent?

I can't have CONCEPT of something beyond THOUGHT,
without the use of this very same vehicle.
Austere tales lead us to focus on this TRUTH:
search for the carrier transcending LIFE, then DEATH.
I suspect the veracity of any knowledge so gained;
disguising chaos as order only highlights its limitations.
Carrying SOUL across Styx transports the same weight
as using THOUGHTS to bear that which they suppress.
In order to find what THOUGHTS represent
I would have to lose the ability to think at all.
Why think?
Is MIND complete in its THOUGHTS, or is it not?
Only if the source of MIND is beyond THOUGHT
would it be worthwhile for me to cease thinking.
Try using a paddle of water to cross a simple stream;
what is PURPOSE in thinking of a goal not to think?
It's the effort to find that which isn't in me,
where I'm not in control and CONCEPTS don't reside.
Knowing MIND is more than that which produces THOUGHTS;
transfer between them causes subtle problems.
I don't know how THOUGHTS can move, or from where,
but the likeliest way is where they are least known, in me.
Where do we search for that which cannot be reduced;
is TRUTH found by looking under rocks, at STARS, or both?
I have no desire to know that which can't be known,
only to find that which is really true beyond question.
One TRUTH is the split between THOUGHT and EMOTION,
two parts of the same picture in different frames.
I don't think and feel at the same instant;
while pondering a problem, I'm aware of no feelings.
Flip a coin and it likely comes up one side or the other;
if only we could win by choosing heads and getting tails.
I may stop my THOUGHTS and just exist in happiness,
or in sadness, but this only happens when I stop thinking.
Imagine a moment of bliss on a day like no other,
riding a possibility with no doubts to distract feeling.
And when EMOTION rules my MIND, no THOUGHT forms,
no problems are solved, no intelligence exists.

EMOTION is expressed naturally, no doubt in its existence;
joy makes us smile and throw wild arms to the sky.
When any EMOTION, like joy, is conceived,
this is THOUGHT of joy not the feeling of it.
Look within to the tangled morass
of inspiration, a wild deity trapped in a certifiable cage.
When I manage to make EMOTION into THOUGHT,
it becomes something it isn't, thereby hunted to extinction.
What is left is the plaything of a material view,
a toy lacking the basic intelligence to defend itself.
It's no secret that neither will substitute for the other,
but both do have real-world physical consequences.
If THOUGHT rests in MIND, we know its home,
and if EMOTION is different—where does it live?
EMOTION is bordered by the static knowledge I have of it;
I see its results and know it exists, but I can't find it.
There is something within us that is totally unreasonable;
its nature is irrational, which is not a verifiable slander.
That which isn't will never be that which is;
therefore defining irrational by a lack of RATIONAL behavior.
Whose rules run the game of LIFE?
Irrationality forced into QUANTITY will still seem irrational.
RATIONAL rules are the 1's to which I will always abide,
for in no other way can results be verified.
Yet there is another set of rules which will stick with us:
when chaired by QUALITY, irrational will seem RATIONAL.
That makes no sense, both can't be the same;
if 1 is the same as 2, then all knowledge must cease.
Name the game and the rules by which TRUTH must abide,
and do not be surprised if it refuses to play.
The game for me is to find the nature of TRUTH,
and the result won't be useful unless assuredly RATIONAL.
The game for us is to find REALITY in the search for TRUTH;
rules might be RATIONAL or irrational, or possibly both.
I only have capacity for RATIONAL organization,
and won't share in a game by any other method.
What if TRUTH would only play by irrational rules,
would this contest be rightly competed on an uneven field?

I don't fathom competing with someone who can't win;
RATIONAL rules!
Winning is contained in the rules for playing the game;
TRUTH will be found only if it is not rationally limited.
So I'm to believe my nature may inhibit my success,
and the core of TRUTH might be irrational, not useful.
Our nature is not limited to a goal-driven custom;
fulfillment of this search is not a zero-sum game.
There are no winners without losers;
the latter must be acknowledged in pursuit of the former.
There is more to our essence than trivial pursuits;
if RATIONAL boundaries must be bent and twisted, so be it.

****

11:55

A wise man once said: Blessed are the poor in SPIRIT,
for theirs is the kingdom of heaven.
So heaven must be available to me,
for there is nothing like that anywhere inside of me.
It may be natural for some to walk past the pearly gates,
yet most of us must strive to change who we are today.
I don't claim to have safe passage to heaven,
only that my nature allows me to fulfill that requirement.
It seems contradictory to worship poverty,
when we are trained to seek treasure in the holy ghost.
Well if a contradiction exists then 1 choice must be wrong,
and my bet won't go against the original saying.
Pause to understand exactly what the phrase means;
how can anyone aspire to be poor in SPIRIT?
Poor implies either rejection of, or inability for, wealth;
still to discover is what excess must be pared away.
SPIRIT is the ethereal being unique to each of us;
how can too much be owned of what has only one home?
With abundance comes a likelihood that some do without;
I know of no rich society not founded on class poverty.

Look to those of mankind who exhibit too much SPIRIT;
whether for good or evil, they stand out from the rest.
An excess of good manifests in those holier than thou;
an excess of evil shows itself in the abuses of power.
What is wrong with filling TIME up with good works,
if a body filled with holy SPIRIT should do no wrong?
If I can abscond with too much for my own exploitation,
there might be a limited amount available for general use.
Are there FINITY amounts to all that is holy,
or can we be filled with SPIRIT and still find heaven?
If the source of holy power is totally unlimited,
then there should be no cause for me to rein it in.
Then the heresy of limited SPIRIT must be accepted;
overfilling one cup of SOUL is the oppression of others.
It's the excess of use, whether for good or evil,
that leads me down the road to suffering and hell.
Sufficient is the most holy, no more and no less;
like it or not we are provided with what we need.
This leads me to a paradox, 1 I don't like:
I must strive to live LIFE to be good, but not too good.
Paradoxes resolve themselves by dismissing a premise;
when faced with this problem return to the beginning.
My essential premise was fed by a word from the wise;
there was nothing said about trying to be good.
Yet we do not wish to do evil, and those are our choices;
how is frail LIFE to be arranged except upon those paths?
Maybe this is how to resolve that paradox:
reject the good and evil paths as the only alternatives.
What other path can we follow which is poor in SPIRIT?
Pray for guidance with a humble heart and troubled MIND.
This is the key to following in the steps of the wise:
the path of humility has no excessive taint of me.
Simple monks in sandals and robes with simple lives;
Francis of Assisi casting off all his worldly belongings.
If I show an excess of the holiness within,
I'm casting my own desires too widely upon others.
Humility has traditionally been assigned to the good;
although it does not fit into religious compartmentalization.

Humility doesn't accept good or bad;
the excess of either is known to lack modesty.
To be poor in Spirit, *lacking any great self,*
we must humbly accept minimally sufficient provisions.
It's difficult to forget tomorrow and strive to be poor;
there seems to be no better way than simply to do nothing.
Yet pursuit of nothing results in alighting nowhere;
Reality *of* Truth *lies somewhere in between.*

12:22

Some Thought scratches at the back of my Mind;
there is something I'm missing, something real and true.
Notice again Thought *which started today,*
the one setting off this search amid Truth *and* Reality.
Time is the key, and it might help with the solution
to finding how Truth can be so well-known and so distant.
If we cannot yet see where Reality *exists, is it possible*
to authenticate when it might actually be?
I don't doubt I exist, and anything that exists
must exist in Time, therefore I must exist in Time.
The past is gone, the future is not yet come,
we are all present, so where does Time *enter?*
I only know Reality by those things which are sensed,
and Memory of those which have already passed.
Those material tallies have no Reality, *they do not exist;*
their Time *does not progress past* Mind's *beck and call.*
Neither Memory nor Perception are afflicted by Time;
they're here and then gone, while Time stays.
An essence which has no existence does not exist,
so how can they be real and not be within Reality?
They are real only as long as they are in my Mind;
Ideas on a page are just ink until they are read.
Memories *are smoke upon* Rational *waters;*
they can be seen, and still be far from solid grasp.
I can hold an image in my Mind, from Memory,
but it must eventually fade with Time.

What is Time when it is only amenable to certain Times;
is it truly the transit of Time we experience?
I sense Time's tedious crawl, not its existence;
it passes me by without its best measure being taken.
Some of what we imagine as real has no place in Time;
facts have transpired, events are now happening.
I read a history book and note a past Great Depression,
not a feeling, but a real economic depression.
Its current existence in Time is a line in a book;
the Great Depression no longer exists, only its bookmark.
Since it isn't being felt or sensed, it isn't appearing;
it no longer exists until Thought brings it back.
Only some Memories survive removal from Reality;
immersion is the only way for water to seize smoke.
The past doesn't live again except through Thought;
Memory is dead to Time unless I breathe substance into it.
An event is transformed into lines separately filling pages,
locked into a meaning that was never meant to be.
My Memory of events isn't patterned like a book,
each 1 falls into place of its own accord.
Our notions of Time are based on past events,
setting the future on a path to inevitable conclusion.
What I remember constitutes my past Time;
what I predict is Time launched from my present.
There is no Time turning in the past, it happens now,
and the future only comes in nightmares of what might be.
The only yesterdays left are to a history of possibilities;
I see tomorrow rolled on the lists as probabilities.
Those are not exigencies existing in Time;
imagine water in a pot on a hot stove that will likely boil.
The present water isn't boiling, it's predicted to boil;
but if Reality is not-boiling, the water should never boil.
Does Time exist in the past and future,
or is it just Thought we have about where they are?
If the prediction comes to pass, boiling is in the present;
the future is just a prediction of what will probably happen.
If the water does not boil, where is present Time;
they have not been predicted, so how do they exist?

Present TIME must exist because it has now happened;
the prediction has no place in TIME, it didn't occur.
When the future is predicted, THOUGHT presents TIME,
and then it falls into oblivion with that which bore it.
The prediction of future events is a present, not a future;
it's REALITY of future events that aren't present.
There are no past or future TIMES, there is only TIME;
we meet and greet TIME like a political candidate.
TIME shows its briefness in the succession of my presents,
forever yesterday, forever tomorrow.
The past is MEMORY, the future is DREAM;
nothing exists beyond measureless present TIME.

12:53

My stomach begins to growl and make itself known;
which in turn lets me know I'm quite hungry.
Where do we turn to satisfy perpetual hunger,
when a body says one thing and MIND says another?
If I refuse to listen to it, then I won't be hungry;
a simple cause is always accompanied by a simple effect.
A foot strikes a ball, and then it moves through SPACE;
do we have the ability to see beyond cause and effect?
This is the basis for RATIONAL THOUGHTS about REALITY:
for 1 event to occur another must precede it.
The conundrum that presents is quite obvious:
REALITY could only begin by the result of a divine hand.
Creationism has no place in the domain of serious SCIENCE;
I only observe now—1 event follows another.
Limitless MIND cannot think only in that fashion;
whether to choose blue or red is a different process.
I do comprehend things beyond simple cause and effect,
but they are motive FORCE behind motion, so important.
Can we only infer motion in terms of cause and effect;
are there no other unseen relations?
I pursue certain activities because of their known effects;
to me, the fight for living depends on this relationship.

What if the cause we choose has undesired effects,
say the kicked ball rebounds and then craters a face?
There is no other reliable method for ensuring survival;
an undesired outcome will sometimes be met, live with it.
Undesired effects often accrue from specific causes;
should not that move us to seek more complete relations?
This is 1 goal for rationally expanding SCIENCE:
determine all the possible effects from a limited cause.
What if we cannot directly relate them together,
such as the problem in proving the earth is warming?
A cause can't exist without an attached effect;
the 2 are tied together, 1 implies the other.
Yet some events seemingly happen from out of the blue,
which give much more credence to Greek and Norse gods.
Effects coming from nowhere will never be known;
any happenstance must come from some cause.
What are we to do with those unmotivated effects;
rain which the weatherman still cannot predict?
Rain is caused by environmental factors;
lack of understanding them doesn't prohibit causes.
What if the cause is so far removed as to be ignored,
like the proverbial butterfly in Africa causing hurricanes?
A cause and effect are attached in SPACE and TIME;
even a series of them has an alpha and an omega.
Can we believe a butterfly could create such FORCE,
or there could actually be a causeless cause?
A causeless cause makes no RATIONAL sense,
and if the butterfly theory could be proven, so be it.
Cause and effect seem to have obvious connections,
yet not so obvious as to be put into words.
That they are connected is known beyond doubt;
as to a metaphysical connection, it hasn't been shown.
The Bhagavad Gita admonishes us not to seek reward;
its advice is not to pursue LIFE through effects.
The scripture advises man not to seek treasures on earth;
the gospels have pointed out their location in heaven.
No . . . it advises us not to seek reward;
we are too often confused by thinking in terms of money.

But if I deny cause and effect, my survival is doomed;
daily animal functions require this connection.
The Gita does not suggest we never use effect,
only that we do not seek to rule our lives by it.
It also doesn't admonish me to live only by prayer,
keening to some swift god for my daily bread.
Sages have proposed not living solely by RATIONAL *means;*
as if LIFE *itself could entirely exist outside of this zone.*
But that is where I exist from day to day;
from waking to sleeping, I prompt cause to get effect.
The problem is in CONCEPTION *of bound* REALITY,
ceasing to marvel at all the things we still do not know.
Cause and effect lead to knowledge;
if I don't seek their patterns, then learning is in vain.
Imagine we are not able to see cause and effect,
our actions are guided by other simpler means.
No living creature could exist on this earth;
no searching, no eating, not even REPRODUCTION.
Would existence of dead MATTER *be impossible;*
can rocks and suns exist without cause and effect?
The existence of a dualistic description of motion
is the only way I can understand this universe.
The important point is that LIFE *cannot exist in a universe*
of material OBJECTS *unless it uses cause and effect.*
But only this 1 universe of gross MATTER is known to exist;
it can't be important to suggest animation doesn't exist.
It is important if the nature of LIFE *is other than material;*
then it behooves us not to live by effective dictates.
Cause and effect grant society the means to enhance LIFE,
many dangers and ills have thereby been alleviated.
How can they enhance LIFE *if it is beyond their reach;*
if cause and effect affect only material relations to LIFE?
I can accept that imposition only if shown MATTER and LIFE
have alternative natures, a claim which isn't obvious.
Light has just begun shining on REALITY *in* TRUTH;
hidden corners are not often readily revealed.
I'm safe living with RATIONAL causes and effects;
known REALITY is better than unknown REALITY.

There is more to REALITY than cause and effect,
neither of which make a dent in our selfish natures.

13:34

Banging my fist on the wall is better than banging my head,
but the latter might stop my THOUGHTS from running away.
PAIN wars with REALITY for priority of attention;
is this feeling more or less real than an unyielding wall?
REALITY is accordingly subjective for each individual,
nothing is more real than my belief in it.
Divorce those worthless parasitic THOUGHTS;
frustration and stupidity are not released by solace.
Many of my THOUGHTS are trained by society's mob,
especially when they fit in so closely with my own desires.
If others can determine our own apprehension of REALITY,
could a great capacity for balance also be hampered?
They only reflect my own THOUGHTS,
judgments which I apply to others as they do unto me.
Unwanted baggage that cannot find a home;
opinions which have no basis in REALITY, lost CONCEPTIONS.
My CONCEPTS are of REALITY,
they just aren't sufficient to describe it beyond PERCEPTION.
At each stage of transfer between REALITY and hidden MIND,
there is a difference between what is and what is extracted.
A difference between what I perceive, and what is;
between what I conceive and what I perceive.
Two eyes looking from the same head,
yet one looks within and one looks without.
There is a representation and REALITY,
even between that which I sense, and that which I know.
This is the central question to finding REALITY in TRUTH:
how do OBJECTS exist divorced from MIND?
REALITY does exist whether I believe it or not;
so whatever it is doesn't begin and end with me.
What if we are part of one massive whole essence,
the sky and earth and sun are all with us?

Even if everything is connected in that universal manner,
REALITY itself still exists.
Does REALITY require belief to form itself;
does sky touch earth unless we believe they are split?
If I truly believe REALITY exists,
no CONCEPT I may have is of a place where it doesn't exist.
Where does the sky exist within REALITY;
is it possible the sky is not real, but a belief?
If I don't believe REALITY exists,
then all CONCEPTS I have are REALITY in themselves.
How can CONCEPTION be real by itself;
is there a sky without its distinct individual existence?
Either REALITY exists or it doesn't, and I believe it does;
only its possible lack would rely on seizure by THOUGHT.
REALITY cannot both exist and not exist;
either the sky does exist, or it is merely futile imagination.
As far as CONCEPTS I'm able to form are concerned,
REALITY does exist!
Yet we may yield to REALITY extant beyond THOUGHTS,
if they are only a loose approximation.
I can understand no REALITY beyond my CONCEPTS;
REALITY I can't understand, doesn't matter.
Do not give up hope for gathering it to a longing breast;
losing it means TRUTH shall also be lost.
REALITY is what it is, and neither my comprehension
nor acceptance has any bearing upon what it is in itself.
Playing at searching and hoping for a change
of rules to an absurd game of hide and seek.
REALITY only appears to me in a limited guise,
which means some of my CONCEPTS of it are FINITE.
REALITY hides its naughty bits in a cubby behind INFINITY,
strangely unlimited above where the sky is hidden.
If that is what or where REALITY is I shall never see it;
my limited eyes can see goals, but not beyond them.
Some observers are able to see with inward-looking eyes,
seeing goals for what they are, a means to an end.
My eyes sense what is before them;
the sun sits in its place in the sky, it fits there.

That CONCEPTION *is a graven image on a merry-go-round;*
a horse in appearance, without the capacity in fact.
REALITY I hold in my left hand, PERCEPTION in my right;
clasped together they form CONCEPT, imperfect.
Our capacity for CONCEPTION *is suggested at* BIRTH;
knowledge must be passed from hand to hand.
If formed REALITY is FINITE, then I may know it:
a limited universe which is amenable to formulation.
Even that would require knowledge next to INFINITY;
civilization progresses because of its so many divisions.
I already know I can't know it all, likely next to nothing;
REALITY cut into FINITE terms is made disarmingly simple.
Is it possible to know truly both INFINITY *and* FINITY;
opposites wrapped around a caduceus?
Given that RATIONAL knowledge must be finitely obtained,
and INFINITE isn't within FINITE, I can't know INFINITE.
That is not cause for despair, any place can be home;
as close to formless and endless as it may be conceived.
Any myth of REALITY tied part and parcel to INFINITE
can't reside except within THOUGHTS I have of it.
How are we to imitate INFINITY *without knowing it—*
as the earth knows the sky by its soft touch?
I'm dualistic; what is must have a part that isn't;
what is FINITE must have a part that is not-FINITE.
DUALITY'S nature does not allow the existence of one,
no single births of THOUGHT, *all must be twinned.*
I don't know INFINITE, I know that which is not-FINITE,
and that which is not-FINITE thereby becomes limited.
Though RATIONAL beings cannot use INFINITY,
it may be possible to imagine touching sky to earth.
I can't sense INFINITE, my THOUGHTS of it are FINITE;
no proof has been offered, nothing I can pin down.
What else is to be expected from irrational phantoms?
A madman enters a sheikh's harem and is left with a veil.

14:16

My hand still tingles from FORCE delivered by my blow,
and the wall just sits there, apparently unshaken.
What is a wall but a word;
does it have any more existence than what is assigned?
A wall has a definite existence when I smack into it,
but how it might exist beyond my senses is beyond me.
Where do mental CONCEPTIONS of REALITY come from,
corporeal emanations from an extra-dimensional plane?
Conceptual REALITY I know, that I can know,
is purchased in trade with PERCEPTION of my senses.
That same PERCEPTION which refuses to soil its hands
with the filth that must attach from an actual touch.
I see, and my mental picture is a useful obliging REALITY;
I hear, and my mental song is a useful obliging REALITY.
Neither they nor taste nor touch nor smell bring it closer
than what can be experienced by just doing nothing.
I prevail upon my senses to bring me all there is,
which is all there can be, for me.
What can be known of a tiger in a cage if we are barred
from knowing the crunch of its teeth?
Direct personal experience is the only path to knowledge,
but I don't have to go into the cage to know I can be eaten.
Waiting by the river of knowledge, dipping in a thimble,
hoping it is convenient for it to spare meticulous THOUGHTS.
All knowledge I purchase comes at a high cost:
limited mental SPACE is filled with useless and trite trivia.
THOUGHTS from PERCEPTIONS crowd rumpled MIND;
they jumble and tumble within, buying knowledge.
What I know from my senses is the physical universe,
1 where things and SPACES and OBJECTS move.
Is REALITY born from TRUTH;
is it the same one for all who are able to sense it?
That is all of REALITY to me;
individual PERCEPTIONS exhibit the only 1 possible for me.
There is still a feeling that this sensed REALITY is unreal,
an illusion foisted upon us by a devious nature.

Actual, sensed, perceived, and conceived versions of it;
REALITY appears to me in dualistic forms.
Yet REALITY is not two, it is one, look to the source;
how can that which is one be known only as two?
REALITY is the existence of all things, that which is;
the absence of anything is nothing, that which isn't.
What is that which is not if it is not REALITY;
is nothing any less real than something?
I have no CONCEPT of REALITY being both is and is not,
a nature which encompasses all existence and none.
Imagine every probability is part of REALITY;
then there must be something having no opposite.
So except for 1, all my CONCEPTS must be paired,
REALITY with no opposite outside of dualistic THOUGHTS.
Possessed of no TIME or SPACE, it is REALITY nonetheless,
sitting astride any claimed PERCEPTION.
Part of me finds 1 REALITY impossible to bear,
the rest of me is resigned to my inherent limitations.
A sun sets in a glorious profusion of orange and lavender;
where are the tastes and smells bought by this picture?
They don't exist; CONCEPTS are only pictures of PERCEPTIONS,
which are of my senses, which are of REALITY itself.
Can the flicker of a television screen be detected,
or scents of a world we are just beginning to perceive?
TV pictures are made to move faster than eyes can detect;
most dogs can both smell and hear better than I.
Does that mean their CONCEPTION of REALITY is better,
or only their PERCEPTION?
If my foundation for comprehension is small,
conclusions drawn from this basis are necessarily limited.
Thus we will better understand REALITY with higher senses;
its existence beyond would require something even higher.
But my PERCEPTION of REALITY is limited to my 5 senses;
so CONCEPTS arising therefrom are likewise limited.
Imagine REALITY could be known by more than five senses;
is there any possibility for limited man to know it all?
Existence of a 6th sense hasn't been proven, leave it;
I don't know how to begin to imagine a non-extant sense.

Then imagine a man possessing only four senses;
what is known by sense of smell is beyond PERCEPTION.
His largest apprehension of REALITY wouldn't change,
but he would notice animal actions that made no sense.
Can a world where odors do not exist be imagined;
where LIFE knows itself in a supremely limited fashion?
It's possible to imagine that, and it makes RATIONAL sense;
though it would diminish something I take for granted.
Now extrapolate that IDEA out to six senses instead of five:
are there many observed occurrences largely unexplained?
There are many aspects to REALITY not usually understood,
but imagining a not-extant sense doesn't help me use it.
That is not the point exposed for elucidation;
there may be more to REALITY than five senses can tell us.
If I imagine REALITY using no-sense, anything is possible,
which doesn't build a better car, or help the sick and needy.
Yet the RATIONAL view, so predominant in modern society,
is based entirely on manipulating limited REALITY.
REALITY is accessible to my 5 senses;
there is no rationale for creating 1 that doesn't exist.
A limited viewpoint forces REALITY into a FINITY box,
when there is no proof at all it will fit in there.
But accepting that position means accepting mysticism,
and then using it as the basis for real understanding.
Not quite. For now, engage faith to remain open
to the possibility REALITY includes INFINITY as well as FINITY.
My CONCEPT of REALITY is based on my PERCEPTIONS,
and they are based on results input from my 5 FINITE senses.
No one can expect to know unbounded TIME and SPACE
by using only FINITY senses to try and to detect INFINITY.
So I'll only know the non-FINITE aspect of REALITY
by appealing to its essence with non-FINITE means.
Where do we go to find that which is not FINITY;
how is limited THOUGHT to be given this access?
The call is made plain to me, but not the answer;
if the varmint isn't in 1 hole, it may lie in another.
Pursuing REALITY beyond the confines of FINITY
will require something more than these restrictions.

15:02

I can reach out and touch the bars right in front of me;
then I let go and they disappear from my touch.
The bars exist as long as they are sensed;
turn behind, and then around; are they the same bars?
REALITY appearing before my eyes seems undisputed,
but when I turn behind, I don't sense it's still there.
What lies ahead if it is not beholden to sensation;
if the way becomes misted, overgrown, blocked from view?
The path before me is totally RATIONAL;
it's known, repetitive; properly known, it rarely fails.
A signal beacon to light the path
for shuffling feet, knowledge in all its fixed useful glory.
I have faith in the certainty found in the tried and true;
my actions have no use without RATIONAL features.
A well-lit path showing a course that may be run;
what is missed by looking though blinders?
When I look to the front, the rear disappears;
when I look to the rear, the front disappears.
Do front and rear vanish into thin air,
or is it just those perspectives which are no longer there?
I know what I saw hasn't disappeared
because when I turn back around—there it is.
Looking forward shows us that which may be used;
what is left behind?
When I see forward, I distinctly sense RATIONAL paths;
the path behind is left to MEMORY and imagination.
Facing front or rear is surely one-sided;
most do not possess the nerve to treat with both at once.
There is no cure for this affliction with which I was born:
I can only see rationally, my burden and blessing.
Yet it may be possible to see from another side;
going down a path looks different than coming back.
They are the same path, no matter how it's viewed;
just different features not acquired in crossing.
This is the point if no other is managed:
one perspective will never be able to see everything.

All paths should lead to same REALITY,
and my predominantly RATIONAL view shows only 1.
Is it possible to connect many different views into one?
A chair is still a chair whether observed front or back.
The knowledge I have of a chair is limited
to the mental pictures created from my PERCEPTIONS.
Why should front and back be attached within THOUGHTS;
is this connection necessary to form solid CONCEPTION?
It's easy to get lost when no directions are given,
which is why going and coming look entirely different.
An opinion is formed that they are the same
with only a little evidence born from redundancy.
They are the same because that is a facet of REALITY,
an assumption inherent in creating my THOUGHTS.
The chair can be viewed from either the front or the back,
neither at the same instant; so why must they be attached?
The chair doesn't appear and disappear at my whim;
it's there, and I arrive at the most reasonable conclusion.
The fact that they are the same chair is still unknown;
unaided, it is impossible to view two sides simultaneously.
I deduce that 2 views of the chair are of 1 chair,
which isn't the same as directly apprehending the chair.
Whatever OBJECT is, and wherever it may exist,
is partially greater than reduction to sensory CONCEPTION.
A difference does exist between my CONCEPTS and REALITY;
I'm allowed indirect, not direct, apprehension.
Combining views into one unitary CONCEPTION
requires generally accepted assumptions.
REALITY must hold still long enough for 2 or more views
to be accommodated as 1 material OBJECT.
That may seem like a universal law, often seen factual,
slighting the assumption that REALITY abides by sensation.
A conclusion which seems reasonable, but still isn't valid;
2 views can be true, and the description false.
Remember hearing about three blind men touching different
parts of OBJECT, yet none sensed the same one.
A touch of hard and round; a touch of soft and flat;
a touch detects motion from a simple push.

Each one knew what it was without any doubt:
it is a bat, it is a bed, it is a big rolling ball.
Each touch gave them the full value of a sense,
but none of them knew it was a rocking chair.
What did limited PERCEPTION *gain them;*
no CONCEPTIONS *which could match a more holistic view?*
REALITY each man was able to comprehend
was limited by the senses he had available.
REALITY of REALITY is completed by changing constantly;
try to know live FIRE *with deadened hands.*
I have only 5 senses with which to hold its essence;
there are no more available to gather knowledge.
Why should we assume senses grant full REALITY
when we know full well they are limited?
My RATIONAL abilities allow me to deduce certain findings,
which is a practical way to make use of sensation.
A guess conceives multiple views are of one OBJECT;
a very good guess does not change it from a guess.
It wouldn't be possible to survive without that approach;
if a chair isn't always a chair, then I can't sit in on it.
Decisions from deficient data are necessary for survival;
by limiting our possibilities, this approach fails TRUTH.
But the chair I perceive isn't part of another 1;
there is only 1 chair there seen from 2 different viewpoints.
Total REALITY sensed in one moment
can never be same REALITY sensed in another.
Then REALITY is different but the chair is the same,
which implies that the chair isn't real.
A chair is a chair is a chair!
How does it fall apart over the course of many years?
In order to continue being a chair fit for my use,
it must be the same chair from 1 moment to the next.
Why must it be the same chair beyond sensation;
how can it be the same chair and still fall apart?
There is no magical event causing the chair
at moment 76.3894 years into being, to suddenly fall apart.
No matter how it is viewed, that is a pretty good chair.
Still, why is that OBJECT *no longer able to be itself?*

Since the chair doesn't change at once,
then it must be changing constantly.
CONCEPTION of OBJECT does not change within THOUGHTS;
the chair must change far beyond sensation's reach.
So it's the nature of REALITY to change constantly,
and my CONCEPT of a chair is a material approximation.
The assumption that multiple views can create OBJECT
is a convenience for limited THOUGHTS in limited LIFE.
Considering the chair not to be a chair not to be a chair
is a totally impractical proposition, it's asinine.
Unless we search for a path to REALITY in TRUTH,
where everywhere is a possibility, even under a bony ass.
I give no THOUGHT to the postulate: a chair isn't a chair;
only that my CONCEPT of a chair may be incomplete.
It seems CONCEPTIONS need a different perspective,
yet what other is available, one not RATIONAL?
If 1 path doesn't work, I must establish at least 1 other;
so far I have only seen a RATIONAL view is limited.
Maybe try a RATIONAL method on an irrational view,
allowing for the possibility that knowledge really is not.
Another bad IDEA doesn't a good 1 make;
it sounds like a feeble attempt to introduce solipsism.
The method is extremely important, but so is the goal.
How will an irrational goal be known when it is found?

15:59

A burnt cigarette lies across a bed of spaghetti noodles,
both so similar and so different.
Man-made, round and white, and detachable;
is there any doubt where one ends and the other begins?
My reliance on PERCEPTION lets me know clearly,
by lifting the cigarette it comes away quite easily.
Leave it in place and answer again;
show exactly where cigarette separates from spaghetti.
I can't sense that point because it's hidden from view,
none of my senses have the ability to locate it.

Then how is the cigarette separated from the noodles,
when as far as can be sensed they make one single bed?
By separating OBJECTS, my senses detect their uniqueness,
and I can do it repeatedly, as often as required.
There is no doubt they are conceived as separate OBJECTS;
only, how is this known when they are lying together?
The cigarette stinks as well as it's shaped quite differently,
and my previous experiences let me classify its existence.
So current senses combine with MEMORY,
out of which results identification of two distinct OBJECTS.
Not quite. Sight alone tells me they are unique items;
I don't need to know names to note them as different.
Differences between widely divergent OBJECTS are easy;
now try detecting the contrast between OBJECT and not.
It isn't apparent to me what I'm looking for;
I can identify the cigarette because of where it does exist.
Then describe where it ends and something else begins,
the place where OBJECT finds its last solid boundaries.
The cigarette ends where my senses perceive it to end;
any OBJECT is known to me in much the same manner.
Does the cigarette end in an abrupt meeting,
external FORCES too strong to resist?
All I know is I can see where there is a cigarette,
and where it isn't; this is what I grasp.
Magnify still closer and the point can be clearly seen,
until the atomic level is gained and it disappears.
Where OBJECT ends depends on my ability to sense it;
it's different depending on the mode of PERCEPTION.
Any OBJECT only exists as a mental projection;
how the cigarette exists with spaghetti is left unknown.
But it's obvious those 2 OBJECTS are different;
it's only where 1 ends that is somewhat indistinct.
Animals have a fuzzy capacity for identifying OBJECTS,
yet try to claim perfect definition with an imperfect ability.
If OBJECT is only THOUGHT, and CONCEPTS are dependent
on variable PERCEPTIONS, then OBJECT definition is variable.
The capacity to create OBJECTS in fluid MIND
is limited by the information which is made available.

My ability to determine where OBJECT begins and ends
is limited by the abilities nature has given my senses.
Around any OBJECT there is a zone not black or white;
it is shades of gray moving from light to darkness.
Even if fuzzy, OBJECT fades instead of ends,
there is an eventual area where it no longer exists.
Just try to find it with those imperfect mortal senses;
REALITY would not be unknown if they were that capable.
If the cigarette wasn't distinctly different from the noodles,
then I wouldn't be able to identify them so easily.
This is the point which has been ineptly made:
REALITY might not start and stop, it might blend instead.

16:23

I close my eyes and picture her bobbing in the water,
partially submerged and cast adrift on a barren log.
What would most of us do if given another chance
to select the other choice, which seems impossible to take?
Most of my actions aren't the result of choice,
my options narrow until there is only 1 thing left to do.
LIFE is DREAM where two paths are presented:
choices are offered, or none are given.
That seems like any typical irrational DREAM,
a choice is offered in order for none to be had.
What path would we choose, if the option was offered;
would a reflection of a wish differ from an actuality?
I choose free WILL like any other living creature;
LIFE makes no sense with no choices at all.
The question is to reflect on which one is more desired,
not which one better reflects the way LIFE is.
Still, I would choose to have the option of choice;
RATIONAL THOUGHTS require alternatives be given.
Why do so many live as though there are no choices;
LIFE as a hopeless arrangement of successive events?
It still must be a choice to live in that fashion;
they must consistently and regularly choose not to choose.

So anyone who appears to give up LIFE'S ultimate gamble
is merely playing definite odds in a different house.
What has been inferred isn't really a lack of choice;
it's more a RATIONAL reaction to incredible odds.
In order to accurately to make those reasonable choices,
each individual would have to know INFINITY parameters.
I'm not required to be a "know-it-all" in order to decide;
otherwise no decisions would ever be made.
Maybe this is why many people are dissatisfied with LIFE:
RATIONAL decisions are made with inadequate information.
My nature is to decide based on available facts;
this is why I continually increase my store of knowledge.
Which increases the difficulty in allowing for total choice;
how are we to change if we have already chosen?
There is no other method worth forming conclusions;
I'll always choose by weighing reasonable options.
This is not a suggestion for all choices to be abandoned,
only an allowance held back for a different kind of choice.
I see no useful option existing in this direction:
a RATIONAL choice between choosing and not choosing.
We are allowed to choose whether to come or go,
which of many paths to take, how to play the odds.
But those are reasonable choices based on probability;
there is no other method with such proven success.
Believe a choice is allowed—to be or not;
what natural perspective allows for novel views?
To be is given to me along with sentience;
it isn't truly a choice to decide between LIFE and DEATH.
If given the choice between "your money or your LIFE,"
which is the more RATIONAL decision to make?
Living of course;
I can always make more money, but living is precious.
Do not be hasty, many are currently blind to REALITY;
there is always a choice.
Well, yes there is a choice between money and living,
but what RATIONAL person would choose money.
Now we are progressing—not all decisions are RATIONAL;
in fact, many seem to sway in an irrational direction.

Still, an irrational choice doesn't make any sense;
there is no price that can be put on continued living.
Even when the option seems silly, some would take it;
even more, they would demand it.
For the love of money is the root of all evil;
but they're a minimum, statistically impotent.
If some will choose LIFE, and some money,
then the outcome does not matter as much as the choice.
Just because some people make irrational choices,
doesn't make those decisions any more valuable.
Options and choices seem superficial
to those who accept only one side under any condition.
If the outcome is so decisive towards probable outcomes,
then it's self-defeating to play against the odds.
The pyrrhic battle could be won and the war still lost;
can all outcomes be known, including the unintended?
Most wars are won by winning the battles;
a fluke of circumstance shouldn't influence decisions.
Can good results happen from the wrong impetus;
is it possible there are good wars and bad wars?
Whether a war is good or bad depends on who wins,
but expecting good to happen from bad is a fool's game.
Even if one out of billions makes the unreasonable choice,
it still means the option is always there.
So there will always be unreasonable people;
it isn't my fault if the blind don't wish to be guided.
Yet options remain;
the consistency of choice is maintained, not the outcome.
It can't be an actual choice if 1 result predominates;
choice implies that multiple options are likely successful.
Believing solely in a RATIONAL perspective is admirable;
unless one wishes to be counted among the living.
I can't fathom that irrational choices are valid;
there is nothing here with which to form an argument.
People consistently make irrational choices,
and make them successfully.
In the long run, gambling with the odds pays off,
and this is based on making RATIONAL choices.

A solitary perspective denies essential choice;
no matter whether the outcome is frivolous or useful.
It's difficult to accept a RATIONAL choice as partially useful,
and irrational decisions might have useful outcomes.
◆ *If choice is confined before one has been made,*
knowledge thus obtained is tainted with the limited, FINITY.

17:06

There once was a girl who fell out of a boat into a river;
unable to swim, she still managed to grab a log.
The log is in midstream and she is quite alone;
what on earth is she supposed to do next?
Drown I suppose, or
if she's in the water long enough she might freeze to DEATH.
There is a similar story about fear of change,
about whether to hold on tightly to what we have, the past.
That story isn't about fear of change, but of DEATH;
it isn't just a slight change she might undergo.
If she lets go, the river might be shallow enough to walk in,
or she could be just around the bend from unseen aid.
Or this girl who can't swim could also drown,
which is the most likely scenario prophesied to evolve.
However, our lives are just like this girl;
we are required to make decisions for which we might pay.
Blame attaches to those who make unwise decisions;
if I couldn't swim, then I wouldn't go out on boats.
Decisions still must be made under similar circumstances;
what is required to swim in the river of LIFE?
Every instance in which I let go of, or hold on to,
a specific log is a definitive choice, for good or bad.
The tale is one about fear of change, and of choices;
instead of holding on, can we decide to let go?
While the girl is hanging onto the log, she is so-so safe;
once she lets go, she has made an irrevocable decision.
It is extremely scary to make a jump into the unknown;
any decision comes with the possibility of loss.

That is why it's best to make RATIONAL decisions,
in order to decrease the number of inevitable failures.
Which outcome to choose is not the present reflection;
it is how to muster the courage to make any choice at all.
Until DEATH looms unbidden at the door,
the safest and easiest course is always to do nothing.
Yet we must make decisions because survival demands it;
the trick is to advance the least threatening decisions.
The best way is to make RATIONAL resolutions;
I don't know of any other valid methods.
We make countless choices based on minimal facts:
blue or red, hot or cold, even wet or dry.
Those choices are irrational, so I have no effect;
they are made somewhere beyond my current capacity.
Making a choice must involve some degree of faith,
which is even required for making RATIONAL decisions.
I must have some degree of faith to think as I do,
but not as much as needed to choose irrational outcomes.
It is irrelevant how much
is needed; faith is either required or it is not.
So people who are locked into lives, afraid of choices,
are really just lacking the elements of faith.
Thus RELIGION succeeds or fails with so many;
it all depends on the degree of faith in the individual.
If I have faith, then changes and choices will be easy;
if I have no faith, then I must rely on static scriptures.
Developing faith has been the bane of RELIGION;
trying to release the log without learning how to swim.
No faith is required to mouth translucent words;
no changes, no choices, no baring of self.
This is the fact and fallacy of RELIGION:
faith comes from a place far removed from holy holes.
If, like koranic insanity, all of my choices are made for me,
then no faith is required, only obedience.
Faith requires extra ENERGY from within;
obedience only requires bowing to earthly will.
Some say divine obedience is the ticket to heaven,
and this is truly what is at the core of faith.

Which gods, which holy scriptures, which RELIGIONS?
We must first have faith in one to follow with obedience.

****

20:04

A wise man once said:
the point of my teaching is to learn control of MIND.
That seems to be a near impossible task,
stabilizing a power that reacts to the slightest provocation.
Difficult does not translate as impossible;
if we cannot do it, what is the point of his teaching?
Trying to reach a goal remaining out of grasp
still stretches my limits past its previous boundaries.
Is control of wild MIND only available to believers;
how is it able to exist and see its own limits?
If controlling my MIND was as simple as THOUGHT,
I could create 1 right now and enter his nirvana.
One MIND is the source of THOUGHTS, out of control;
it is the source of single MIND that must be retrained.
A wonderful accomplishment if I knew where to begin;
I don't know what MIND is, much less where it comes from.
That is a problem in submitting to advice from the wise,
yet uncovering what unruly MIND is may lead to its control.
No understanding is emerging from this process;
cessation of MIND leads to cessation of THOUGHTS.
It is not cessation that is sought, it is control;
a horse is not tamed by killing it.
But I've no CONCEPT of MIND without THOUGHTS;
I only see my MIND when they're moving.
Bound MIND cannot escape from its own ORGANISM;
THOUGHT of MIND is not the same as its essence.
If MIND exists, and it's in dire need of control,
then I can't accomplish this goal without using MIND.
It is not like asking a river to change from water,
only to use its power to modify its own course.

So MIND doesn't need to change itself,
only to conceive its essence, and alter the mold.
Sensed without form it can have INFINITY varieties,
each changing moment by moment.
Therefore it isn't MIND itself I need to control;
any CONCEPT has a structure, and it's what I must change.
As a building is shaped through separate disciplines,
so must constructed MIND labor into fruition.
The advice of the mystic was to control my MIND,
to keep it from running away with my existence.
Lives will always be shaped by keen MIND'S influence,
subject to normal THOUGHTS so wild and discursive.
MIND must have a source which is just as untamed,
and attached to my body which houses its BRAIN.
Fruit does not fall far from the tree;
notice how snug MIND closely resembles its body.
Somehow MIND must be attached to a physical form,
and the most likely place is somewhere in my BRAIN.
Control must be learned whether it is of BRAIN or MIND,
yet how are we to modify simple synaptic exchange?
There is no other place where MIND can exist,
except my BRAIN, which turns on sense and action.
As long as MIND is considered a purely RATIONAL resource,
this is TIME which must be spent solely in BRAIN.
If it doesn't reside in a RATIONAL home,
then I will find MIND only in an irrational dimension.
This is what has bedeviled people for so long:
attempting to control that which is beyond direct access.
MIND is at least partly irrational, and BRAIN is RATIONAL,
which is about as far as I can pursue this line of THOUGHT.
Controlling MIND means to remove its clinging vines,
not to lose natural and human growth.

20:30

I retrace my steps to figure out how this could happen,
and I keep coming up with the same answer—it can't.

Is there a RATIONAL explanation for an absurd situation;
are there absolute realistic laws if TRUTH can be perverted?
The laws of MATTER are silent on the matter,
so some other PURPOSE must be behind it all.
One perspective exists on which knowledge depends,
examining REALITY for its consistency and flavor.
I know I can rely on RATIONAL modes of THOUGHT;
coherent and dependable, nothing more is required.
Yet limiting REALITY to the boundaries of one view
bans us from any possibilities for roaming free range.
If there is more than 1 realistic perspective,
then they must consist of at least 2: RATIONAL and not.
Is it possible there could be more,
or maybe there are actually no perspectives at all?
A view of REALITY is a method of envisioning the world;
there must be RATIONAL 1's to interpret my senses.
Could there be views numbering virtually to INFINITY,
maybe one from each OBJECT and ORGANISM?
A RATIONAL view is a generalized perspective,
1 all sensible creatures have to some extent.
Each person is capable of some type of RATIONAL view;
could all have the capacity for many alternative ones?
Since I now have only 1 in hand,
it makes sense to find 1 more before looking for many.
What could a non-RATIONAL perspective consist of;
where can it be found if it is beyond formulation?
If 1 perspective is RATIONAL, and I seek another,
then the 1st place to look should be in an irrational place.
Pass on this choice and pass on REALITY:
imagine an irrational prospect not abiding by confinement.
This is 1 place I'm forbidden to go,
looking into processes working to no rhyme or REASON.
How would we see this bilateral dissection,
dividing REALITY into the credible and the incredible?
There are no THOUGHTS that can be communicated,
to me or from me, unless by RATIONAL means.
How do we know an irrational perspective exists
if it is required to play the game by RATIONAL rules?

Those so-called rules are required to assure useful results,
not hocus pocus or other voodoo mumbo jumbo.
Those rules force us to understand Reality
solely from a one-sided Rational perspective.
No. They allow us to interpret how it functions,
in the same way I interpret the dynamics of Science.
What if there are additional rules to the game;
those that do not bow to the gods of Science; so what?
Science is merely a term used to discern a system
of knowledge founded on well recognized principles.
Who granted the gods of Science the authority to set
the rules of Reality according to a Rational perspective?
Its authority comes from recognition of the way things are;
Rational rules and scientific disciplines merely work.
Reality sets the rules by which any system must abide;
those Science gods do outbid themselves.
Though it might not be the most perfect system:
Science is only guilty of success.
Of all the rules that have been bestowed by those gods,
one is most important, idolized as repetition.
If it can be repeated, it can be known, used, moved,
taken apart, modified, canceled, pushed, pulled, heated,
cooled, abused, launched, raped, helped, forced, created,
destroyed, fortified, limited, extended, defined, trained.
The ability of events to be repeated under similar conditions
is the sine qua non of a Rational perspective.
That position is filled for usefulness and convenience;
gods of Science dictate their decrees through repetition.
Evidence of repetition is an ability to make use of Reality;
otherwise my survival would be limited to sheer chance.
The neglected perspective is one forgoing repetition,
and it is a view which cannot be exploited or forced.
If it can't be used, then it has no value;
there is no point in pursuing a worthless enterprise.
Many different inferences can be made of use;
look from a mountain top to see how things fit together.
An irrational perspective may better see disjointed events,
which doesn't help me to better use my Rational skills.

Must Reality be used to be understood; must it be limited
to rationally made and understood rules?
Those rules are necessary for transmission of Concepts,
even those more chaotic than straightforward in nature.
Comprehension of Reality is only limited by the ability
any creature has for detecting its universal presence.
The methods for Rational detection aren't finished,
but they are fairly well advanced, unlike irrational 1's.
A Rational limitation upon an ability to comprehend
will allow the blood of Reality to only flow in this vein.
This is generally where modern society has fixated:
all Reality must be patterned upon Object recognition.
Once more limiting comprehension to a Rational view,
which limits Reality to solely Finity dictates.
Primitives and ignorant believers choose the irrational way,
where gods sit in judgment for the unreasonable masses.
The capacity to feel and judge, to hope and pray allows
for more of Reality than can be squeezed on to a chip.
If an irrational perspective does exist somewhere,
it has been hiding itself from apparent observation.
Just because it is not currently well understood, does not
make it a wasteland of never was, and never will be.
I admit evidence of events possibly irrational in nature,
like Emotions, which are totally unreasonable to me.
Is there an irrational perspective; what are its rules;
how can it exist in conjunction with a Rational view?
Further reflection might allow me to see,
but physical laws exist to resist violation.
Gods of Science have blessed us with knowledge:
rules of thermodynamics, and of limited Time and Space,
The laws of physics aren't a choice;
they are absolute rules in an absolute Rational universe.
Rules only apply to the game being played;
Science gods can be set aside to play a different game.
The physics I understand can't be left alone;
they are not rules created for fun and amusement.
Laws which are known to be subjectively interpreted;
thinking in a Rational box leads to irrational outcomes.

RELATIVITY and Quantum Mechanics, in particular,
have shown fixed rules can be made flexible.
In order to truly understand the realistic panorama,
we must learn to think outside of a fixed FINITY box.
While still recognizing all THOUGHTS must fit therein;
there must always be a place for RATIONAL dissection.
Before REALITY became a product of repetition
its mien was known by a far older method—acceptance.
Knowledge of repetition comes from surveillance;
it's only bringing form to that which is without it.
Repetition is a clear imposing adjunct to acceptance,
yet the latter always supersedes the former.
Normally, that shouldn't be a problem;
the best of circumstances lets the 2 work hand in hand.
While the mechanics of massive patterns may be unknown,
it still behooves us not to deny the crystalline results.
Conclusions which are seen but not understood,
possessing a form beyond that which can be grasped.
An irrational perspective shall be known when it is felt;
it arrives with INTUITION; a plus, it is not RATIONAL.
Known by the difference between feelings and senses;
2 ubiquitous worlds colliding out of sight.
An irrational perspective shall be known when it is felt;
it must be a different perspective; a plus, it is not RATIONAL.
It'll be a point of view made to bewilder the senses,
found just past the boundaries of accepted SCIENCE.
An irrational perspective shall be known when it is felt;
in a universe of different rules; a plus, it is not RATIONAL.
There are more rules to REALITY than those which I know,
but these can't make the 1's I know any less valid.
An exclusive view of REALITY can no longer be relied upon;
limited is not best, FINITY is not the end.
If I can't transcribe another view into FINITE THOUGHTS,
then it'll never be of any practical benefit at all.
Usefulness is granted to a RATIONAL view by sensation;
yet any PURPOSE found therein must be limited.
The validity of my senses is not offered in barter;
understanding without cost is all I'll accept.

Limits shall no longer bind humanity to a false sense
of REALITY; something else is out there, beyond the horizon.

21:35

Bob the guard looks in at me as I look out at him;
neither he nor I will truly know what the other 1 sees.
Looking out and looking in can see the same thing,
and yet each observer is convinced his view is correct.
Both he and I are RATIONAL, in different degrees,
but both he and I see REALITY from different viewpoints.
It is not just tunnel vision which obscures REALITY,
prime inhibition is achieved through sole RATIONAL viewing.
Though his view and mine are different, they're RATIONAL;
to be truly different, 1 would have to be irrational.
At least two perspectives of REALITY are available—
RATIONAL and irrational.
I agree with the 1 most fulfilled by SCIENCE;
the other works to no recognizable rules and regulations.
Neither totally on tap nor totally distinct from the other,
not universes in themselves.
They are perspectives formed from living MIND;
lacking real existence, except to create CONCEPTS.
REALITY submits itself to observation from those views;
seen by viewing hills from a plain, plains from a hill.
My field of view is filled with RATIONAL THOUGHTS,
frequently hindered by sophisticated babble.
The other realm is viewed from a more continuous place,
non-stop jags of living interspersed with an inner glow.
My THOUGHTS have become disconnected from 1 another,
flailing about in a search for something solid to grab.
Living in the land of the blind, requiring guidance,
sight only works where it is needed.
An irrational view won't work within RATIONAL boundaries;
I assume a RATIONAL view won't work within irrational 1's.
Only by accepting guidance where a RATIONAL view is blind
will REALITY of TRUTH be revealed.

So finding what I seek requires irrational instruction,
while imparting RATIONAL corrections to make pithy paths.
Possessing foresight to the hindsight of others,
an irrational perspective works as it must unfold.
Archimedes may actually have been able to lever the world
with those 2 perspectives in total opposition.
A natural barrier, a wall, separates one from the other;
why does this irritation exist?
There is no totally RATIONAL answer,
and I still don't understand how to use irrational input.
How can there be an irrational answer, even part,
if the answer itself must then be RATIONAL in aspect?
THOUGHTS capable of transmission are RATIONAL;
CONCEPTS which come from THOUGHTS are likewise.
Limitation of REALITY by CONCEPTIONS is destructive;
a convenient tradition that robs Peter to pay Paul.
CONCEPTS converted from my PERCEPTIONS are RATIONAL,
unless formed from something other than my senses.
Any RATIONAL CONCEPTION formed from another essence
will necessarily be FINITY, totally imperfect.
A direct translation of an irrational PERCEPTION
would be a garbled utterance, either insane or inane.
It is not possible completely to conceive an irrational view,
the best guess comes by ever closer approximations.
Whatever may be felt on an irrational occasion
can never be communicated except by RATIONAL means.
A paradox from describing what is not in terms of what is;
a necessary evil, both necessary and evil.
A RATIONAL approximation is necessary because it works,
but evil is born from an irrational domain.
Every creature has its own irrational perspective, endless
in bearing, a pattern in addition to a machine.
A machine is useful when each part has its place;
a pattern exists when each place can be fit into a part.
What does it have to offer, of what use can it be,
when we only feel how REALITY exists, not how to use it?
I can see no immediate benefit to an irrational view,
lacking exploitation or continence, it has minimal use.

An irrational perspective offers additional TRUTH;
a partial view is as partially useful as partial can be.
It would be great to fill in the gaps to modern metaphysics,
but filling emptiness with confusion won't get me far.
Allowing for an irrational perspective may clear up
misconceptions formed from a sole RATIONAL *perspective.*
If 1 perspective lacks access to total REALITY,
it's because 1 view of anything isn't the equal of 2.
Perspectives show the panorama an audience will buy;
irrationality works best with LIFE'S *contribution to* REALITY.
I can't solve material problems with a sole irrational view;
and I can't solve living problems with a sole RATIONAL view.
It is also impossible to view both perspectives at once;
the either/or choice marks the defining line.
Still, a RATIONAL view is obviously more useful;
there is no prominent gain from irrational envisioning.
Neither perspective is better; there is only YIN *and* YANG,
up and down, light and dark, positive and negative.
As electricity and magnetism require opposite poles;
only favoritism works perspective from a specific direction.
Force from opposition requires equal lateral tension;
a bridge is not supported from just one end.
Each distinct situation calls for the attention of 1 view;
a perspective is therefore more appropriate, not better.
Also coming to attention, in no other fashion,
all MIND *views rationally or irrationally at all* TIMES.
My BRAIN is a product of that dualistic environment,
and its focus can be retained on only 1 viewpoint.
Perspective abilities are varied, some hide in a fog,
able to grasp some part while the bulk remains hidden.
Though RATIONAL abilities are available to all,
each individual works with vastly different capacities.
So too is an irrational view, an absolute available to all,
yet it is completely seen by only a persistent few.
Most people I have met seem to live in a short-sighted fog,
unable or unwilling to adjust their focal points.
Those perspectives do curl and wrap around us, enclosing
what is observed with what is understood.

Parts and pieces are all I know,
afflicted with static CONCEPTS in a dynamic universe.
A mist of fantasy lays a shroud of ignorance upon us,
not knowing, the hopeless helpless curse of ignorance.
This is what drives me beyond my normal boundaries:
I know that I don't know.
Hopefully a dualistic filter may help to clear the air,
rationally or irrationally as needed, without interference.
A map with an illegible side won't lead me anywhere;
an irrational view justly deserves constant condescension.
RATIONAL and irrational contest within for control;
a war never won, battles fought without contact.
It doesn't seem like much of a contest to fight the useless;
an irrational pursuit is at worst a waste of TIME.
Why does one side seem to dominate the other,
where what we are seems so damned material?
MATTER can regularly be manipulated by a RATIONAL view;
I have no IDEA what an irrational view can do.
Mutually dependent on what the other is able to furnish,
no part of an essence can be made better than another.
It's no fallacy to believe parts of me have more worth;
my heart is a little more valuable than my little toe.
A body constitutes a simple physical existence;
it only slightly resembles what actually totals "us."
An irrational relation to RATIONAL might make more sense
if I could define the parameters of what "I" does consist.
Maybe we shall see, once limited vision clears a bit,
two paths combining into one and separating again.

22:31

A light flashes through my window, flaring the dark;
if only it wasn't so long until the sun rises again!
Sitting in darkness is like sitting in ignorance,
nothing is apparent until a flash shows what is missing.
The fiery light of day versus the cold dark of night,
strange how I no longer feel comfortable in a womb.

Life is supposed to depend on the sun for its existence,
giving it invisible bits of Energy for Consumption.
Photosynthesis is the greatest source of Energy conversion;
plants achieving what animals can't do on their own.
Lately there is evidence that not all Life is so dependent,
microbes which thrive beyond light's penetration.
There are many variations underground and undersea,
creatures which exist outside of traditional theories.
Waving tube worms are obvious indeed;
where do they receive the food they require?
Tiny Bacteria convert Energy for them,
of a chemical nature, which any lifeform must use.
All of those processes happen beyond visual range;
what is the smallest animal visible with the unaided eye?
I can see no-see-ums when they slow down long enough;
there may be something smaller, but they are pretty small.
Yet we accept the existence of microbes and smaller,
due to the helpful nature of mechanical aids.
Microscopes, like telescopes, don't create new Reality,
they only bring it closer to my senses.
It is a transfer of understanding beyond the naked eye;
natural sensation is not Reality's defining point.
There is no mystery in those simple transformations;
lenses and focal points have well-known relations.
It is only fair to grant the irrational view a similar boon,
when the Rational view has profited via this extra leeway.
That is perfectly acceptable for most circumstances,
as long as some aid can expand an irrational vision.
A Rational view of Reality requires aid to be better known;
it is likely an irrational view needs similar assistance.
Since an irrational perspective isn't scientifically bound,
there are no mechanical aids which will help lift it.
In order to know irrational as well as Rational is known,
people must be sought who exhibit irrational tendencies.
Those among humanity who don't live by the rules;
what they see isn't new, just not explicitly enunciated.
What types of people do not value rationality;
are they the ones who would know most of irrationality?

It's unreasonable to ask me for an irrational perspective;
if I could already see it, I wouldn't need assistance.
Turmoil within expressed to the world without is by
maestros, madmen, and mystics.
Artists might dispute their classification as irrational,
most require repetition to pursue sensual delight.
Art comes from SOUL, not from the critic;
the accepted version is just more swill for the limited.
But the point is to discern what artists have to offer
for seeing REALITY from an irrational perspective.
Expression of unique BEAUTY within each LIFE
is lost trying to appease the masses with messes.
So artists focused on commercial success are different
from artists who try to express an irrational message.
The irrational feeling passed also has a personal vibe;
it grandly affects some, and others not at all.
Then artists are of little use for what I seek;
there are billions of effects, and none are the same.
Maestros offer much, without a coherent message;
do madmen offer more, or are they just the same?
That option is even worse through no fault of their own;
a madman with a message is still just a madman.
How do we discern the message inside the madness;
is there value to those touched by the hands of the gods?
Madmen may have valuable insights,
but I can see no sure method for interpreting their visions.
The last recourse it is to look to the mystics,
given to spouting prophecies and other dense drivel.
Their messages are similar to those of useless poets,
many grandiose words with very little common sense.
Some meaning is contained in the babble of the language,
even if that which is spoken is mystical in nature.
There is more to language than proper grammar and syntax,
for a sweating proxy dress can't dig curiously.
Looking at RATIONAL inferences from an irrational source,
there is no doubt we will be disappointed.
There is nothing to hope for from wriggling mystics,
unless it's the results they put forth.

Outcome is reliant on a RATIONAL *point of view,*
while TRUTH *may be found in something more like* INTUITION.
But my external physical world depends on facts;
making use of particles, parts, and pieces.
An irrational view should work within, like the mystics;
if results are confusing, maybe methods should be viewed.
Mystics offer me 3 modes of living:
discipline, denial, and devotion.
They are not hard and cold military creatures,
following a discipline only means sticking to a path.
Blindly following a trail could be ultimately wasteful;
I might wake up 1 day as a bald hare krishna.
External appearances do not guarantee internal heights;
would a rapist be more RATIONAL *with his balls cut off?*
Voluntarily, I should be able to modify my body,
and pursue any path which isn't noticeably harmful.
One perverse characteristic mystics are noted for
is the denial of excess, fasting when plenty is available.
It can't be right to deny my basic needs;
I feel no guilt in using them to their natural extents.
A saying is attributed to Mahatma Gandhi:
I never eat for pleasure, but I always enjoy what I eat.
So denial isn't the purposeful lack of pleasure;
it's the realization that happiness isn't sensually based.
Lastly, mystics tell us we must be devoted,
and the most effective form is single divine prayer.
Most meditation involves releasing attachment to MATTER,
holding on to 1 CONCEPT and releasing all others.
Prayers are not intended to grant wishes to beggars;
one is given so the other will no longer be desired.
If I sit on my ass long enough to sustain 1 CONCEPT,
then maybe I'll begin to see what they saw.
Left to our own physical defects we must fail
to find that which is beyond a false body to detect.
If I trust in those mystics, then this may be a path to take,
leading me to a part of TRUTH that lies beyond rationality.
Mystics have directed a way to missing TRUTH,
not to abandon that which has already been found.

23:19

Bob the shrink came by to see me earlier tonight;
it's funny that my control of my destiny causes a problem.
How can injustice be so insignificant to the powers that be,
and a simple display of willpower has the opposite affect?
A man of SCIENCE who knows my BRAIN is dysfunctional,
versus a man who has only 1 thing left to lose.
Appeal to his gods of SCIENCE to break this impasse,
shields and swords for protection; attack the infidels!
I use SCIENCE to help me construct valid TRUTH,
avoiding luddites who wish to destroy without building.
What do those gods offer up as armor,
what basic rules are used to defend a RATIONAL view?
A RATIONAL perspective is founded on a simple observation:
* that which is can't also not be, at the same instant.
Note the firm existence of some part of REALITY,
its regularity and coherence do not just exist in fantasy.
Common sense is both blessing and betrayal to SCIENCE;
there is none in denying that which really is.
Imagining REALITY in TRUTH is no license for stupidity;
although ignoring profound THOUGHTS is a simple mistake.
Paradox tells me that absurdity is irrational;
* if it isn't, it still is.
REALITY encompasses everything including contradiction;
finding the nature of one will lead to the other.
There is only 1 REALITY possibly known to me;
it's careless to fall for the fallacy of more than 1.
REALITY may be seen from many different perspectives;
this creates separate universes, not separate realities.
Assuming REALITY doesn't exist is even worse;
what is real is real.
We tend to see what we want to see;
there is not a one among us who has no illusions.
Denial of REALITY through some form of solipsism
doesn't promote an irrational view, it ignores rationality.
Passing signs of information is a failure of SCIENCE gods;
the way is to follow the path no matter where it leads.

* Be wary of knowledge formed from unknown causes;
this is a path to chaos, where only delusion prevails.
Any alternative perspective must still retain substance;
even koans have tangible irrational solutions.
Alluding to mysterious causes from common effects
is useless when a RATIONAL explanation is sufficient.
An irrational view works according to different rules;
its vague verbiage does not make it new age fodder.
Any THOUGHT which someone else wishes for me to understand
must first be translated into a RATIONAL phrase.
What is seen as unearthly THOUGHTS can be rationally estimated
because both are of REALITY extant in TRUTH.
What ought to be excluded is that which has no meaning;
babbling garbage which induces no transformation.
Sophistry sounds good to untrained MIND,
as it depends upon assumptions which are not made clear.
Masses of people are duped by obscure and cheerful cons:
* beware of the lack of clarity in all language.
Our methods of communication are necessarily loose,
transcribing what is sought for alien MINDS.
If, maybe, might, could, should, and, or—these partials;
equivocations which can't compete with concrete positions.
They are many transients in a sole caricature of REALITY,
loose threads creating holes in a much bigger pattern.
Only something that can be tied down and firmly held
should be allowed to exist; no more ghosts!
LIFE'S joy comes from untied moments between definition;
spontaneity slipped into the cracks between plans.
But I must have order to attach moments together:
* mathematics and logic help keep chaos at bay.
Hold them firmly, bared whenever falsity
or innuendo rear their heads and bray for attention.
Indispensable weapons for any sort of RATIONAL discourse,
setting scientific boundaries on an unlimited package.
Gods that shine a light into darkness;
THOUGHTS that will not snuff out in a well-blown storm.
No THOUGHTS keep my attention which don't pass muster,
unlike those denying the existence of irrational rules.

One half of REALITY does not cancel the other;
all the pieces of a puzzle fit together.
Many thinkers claim insight into the nature of REALITY,
but they consistently try to violate the laws of nature.
A RATIONAL view must make room for an irrational one,
and this one must leave room for proven knowledge.
I firmly deny, and call it scientific folly, the existence
of any creation that ignores proven laws of nature.
Pray for an irrational perspective to follow holy doctrine;
although some CONCEPTIONS will be turned inside out.
A single rule structures all of SCIENCE's observations:
* that which can't be measured doesn't exist.
Wrapped up in a package which cannot be delivered,
there are many QUALIA still defying numerical analysis.
Concerning SCIENCE—that which defies analysis,
can't be used, so it might as well not exist.
We should abandon art and BEAUTY, throw away joy
and sadness, make LIFE black and white?
Art isn't SCIENCE;
only that which can be quantified can be used.
Right, what is the use of anything else;
silly EMOTIONS which come from over the rainbow?
If it isn't available to my senses, by fixed particles,
then I can't change things to my convenience.
LIFE is inconvenient;
we will not understand it until this is acknowledged.
Only by dissecting REALITY into a bare mechanistic essence
will I be able to use it to suit my individual tastes.
Has our goal changed from a search for REALITY
to one which leads us to the greatest degree of comfort?
It's those rules which will help me to seek REALITY;
scientific methods found to squeeze TRUTH from falsity.
A main mast into the wild winds blowing across;
although it may shake and tremble with . . . what?
The lack of knowledge, that a RATIONAL view isn't enough,
that an irrational perspective may actually prove valuable.
Gods of SCIENCE are beneficial when set in their place,
verifying the difference between fantasy and REALITY.

23:59

Bob the priest also came by to offer me absolution,
offering me heaven if I can learn fear of hell.
It has been said it is sacrilege to kill oneself,
yet how can a supreme desire to reach heaven be wrong?
Any defiance of authority must be stamped out,
especially by those who claim to represent divine WILL.
Appeal to the gods of RELIGION for succor, they have
a long history of success and failure.
In ancient TIMES gods gave secret cause to open effects,
combining SCIENCE and RELIGION into a theoretical mess.
They sought to provide LIFE where there was none,
animating matter with knowledge, however contrived.
Mystics of old gave man gods before SCIENCE was known,
a perspective they had obtained by observing living toils.
They paved the road for gods of RELIGION to rut;
abusing the path to TRUTH until it no longer has meaning.
The message of the mystics has been lost in the message,
where there is no longer meaning, only scripture.
* Those wise men left us an irrational perspective;
now lost to a never-ending battle between good and evil.
But I must still strive to do good and avoid evil;
to do anything else is the surest road to chaos.
Good can never defeat evil if they are two sides of a coin;
irrationality can never takes take sides in this battle.
Which has left the focus of RELIGION on good and evil,
while the founding mystics saw RATIONAL and irrational.
Gods of RELIGION no longer aid those battling themselves;
left are hints, game trails covered with weeds.
If I seek the help of RELIGION against dangerous foes,
then it will attempt to armor me with civilized good.
A flimsy cloth of a rambling societal weave,
good is a powerful force against one enemy, its evil twin.
Maybe when the robe of good and evil is shed,
I can see my place, no less than now, less than I imagine.
Oh folly when gods of RELIGION began to crusade;
their sight constrained to good and evil, us and them.

It's very strange how most mystics lived in devoted peace,
and their succeeding RELIGIONS growl for war.
The most powerful of their kind are as much under the sway
of a RATIONAL perspective as are the gods of SCIENCE.
The problem is seeking good becomes a RATIONAL cause,
and if TRUTH was a matched effect, I would already know it.
RATIONAL DUALITY is attached to all false gods,
attempting to hatch faith from many different nests.
RELIGION has no other capability than to be true to itself,
but many believers attempt to combine faiths.
* Belief in two gods is actually belief in neither one;
true belief is in either none, one, or all.
I'm not an atheist; I don't know which 1 is correct;
so I believe in all RELIGIONS, or at least parts of them.
Which two or three or four gods are compatible;
the most popular, the old and new, or east and west?
It's difficult to reject RELIGION under which I rose,
no matter how much I try to deny my parents in me.
New gods are introduced through the process of growth;
should any be accepted or just reject them all out of hand?
Most people can't stretch past their original teaching;
many others can see the light from just 1 other.
Why are some gods chosen over others when they all
require some bit of faith for beginning belief?
Accepting tenets from another RELIGION as valuable
means I have rejected my 1st as lacking substance.
Two then merge into an amorphous pile of neither,
which becomes true RELIGION, a congregation of one.
There is no RELIGION better or worse than another;
they all have substantially perverted the original teaching.
* Modern existence subscribes to a common denominator:
division of all LIFE into prey and predators.
This biological division for survival has an auxiliary axiom:
there must always be more prey than predators.
An irrational perspective does not divide LIFE into parts,
a whole essence can have pieces of both.
I see my place in the pecking order, at any instant;
either preying on others, or being preyed upon.

Society attempts to separate us into its divisions,
so we may better fit into machines designed by others.
All parts of a machine must fit in someplace;
nature abhors a vacuum.
* Nature does not abhor a vacuum, it abhors waste;
Life is perpetually absorbed by itself.
Living creatures continually die off;
I was born, I will eventually die, the end.
Short Life any creature has would be wasted,
unless it can be reincarnated into another chance.
Reincarnation is fanciful Idea with little proof;
all I can see is a beginning and an end.
That is where a Rational view cannot see beyond itself,
faith in something beyond dross sensation.
It's obvious biomaterial remains are salvaged,
but Reincarnation requires that more is saved, somewhere.
Look at how Life interacts around us every day,
nothing is wasted; why would its inner Fire disappear?
All I am will eventually rot and pass away;
my existence is Finite and can be accurately quantified.
* Each Soul exists within a more ephemeral universe;
where Reincarnation is subject to irrefutable Karma.
Karma is partly Rational even if it can't be sensed;
action and reaction follow well founded laws of motion.
Creating an imposition upon everyone's total freedom,
each Life has consequences upon the next.
My struggle is to find Truth in my current existence;
if I'm successful, then there might not be a next 1.
Focus on today and lose tomorrow;
focus on tomorrow and lose today's chances.

****

00:46

There is a battle between two strongmen;
one possesses three snakes- small, medium and large.
The other strongman steals the medium and large ones,
and then proceeds to hide them in his clothes.
In his confusion he loses track of the small one,
until it crawls into the craggy crevasse of his moon.
He proceeds to jump and shake, scaring the snakes;
a different master, they bite and squeeze him to DEATH.
Shy away from the blue-banded snake;
it seems peaceful; pick it up and it does not bite.
Look closer and closer at this snake—it never ends!
How can it be here and now, and also seek forever?
The snake has taught me to seek carnal knowledge,
until it goes too far and leaves a mess.
Old girl-fiends still possess my troubled MIND;
they won't let it go, or it won't release them.
The faces seen are composite, one over the other,
all of them form into one, one that won't let my MIND go.
Yet it is not real, it is not here, it does not exist;
it is my past haunting the present, as I haunt tomorrow.
Still, I borrow the old man's boat without permission;
find a secret place, lounge around, and get stoned all day.
Then it won't start and there is no way to get back,
so it drifts down the river to some frat girls' apartment.
I kneel down in a corner away from everyone else,
until finally the ignition snuff box begins to smolder.
Drive it down the river but I have already reached home,
so I wait in repose until it is TIME to cruise back to school.
When school starts again, it is TIME for logic;
a test which almost eludes MEMORY'S attempt at pruning.
A little girl sits down and smiles encouragement;
the test remains unfinished.
Events follow each other into endless oblivion;
even when they do not make sense, they keep coming.
One more makes for lagniappe:
the burden of a worm filled completely plump—keep at it.

Day II

06:00

Order fights chaos in perpetual battle,
leaving right and wrong to spear the wounded remains.
Bob the lunatic down the hall screams with the early bell,
which results in Bob the guard going in to beat him silent.
Neurotic MIND is roundly tortured in its present form,
pursuing physical reaction because it knows no better.
Everything around me reacts roundly to everything else;
every action seems to leave many reactions in its wake.
Foraging for survival like some simpler animal;
where does a suffering body end, and need begin?
A rebel is tortured, while another rebel self-tortures;
maybe a quiet rebellion is the only 1 ever to succeed.
Reaching into the past, grasping for the last link
of a gold chain flaring at the bottom of a deep dark well.
I can't deny hope, even when it seems so far away,
but when looking closely I find something . . . broken.
Come, look within for that which is not without,
where true suffering exists as FIRE to be blown out.
Within me is a turbulent mess of I-don't-know-what
in mortal combat with the real world all around me.
What is found in battle that is not found elsewhere;
why must order always seek to dominate chaos?
There is no better way to burn off chaff and find TRUTH;
though the conflict usually results in destruction and DEATH.

Battle is not sought by those who have much to lose;
feel the tender bond which comes with an unbroken child.
Motherless I am, and fatherless too;
no attachment to any existence not found through friction.
Honor is not attained through defeat of vagrant orphans,
cutoff from any possible descent from the gods.
It's human nature to seek advancement by contest,
a desire to find where I stand in the grand scheme of things.
Oh . . . the heaving of Helen-wrought appetites is felt,
roused to perpetual fury through overt influence.
Civilization has advanced from human wants and needs;
mankind is promised a plethora of many vibrant futures.
Daemons! Chance brought to attention by gods of SCIENCE,
who have lauded a RATIONAL champion of all that is known.
REASON allows me to distinguish fact from fantasy
by converting IDEAS into functional working principles.
Voices in the night, below whisper, prodding
us away from a foolish inheritance of folly.
My IDEAS come from me, from my experiences;
an improvement in engine efficiency isn't born of DREAM.
Come, show of what fine THOUGHTS are made,
searching for that which is, and that which can be.
I know what is, it allows formation of my known REALITY;
as to what can be, this is a little harder.
A source is behind every flow, no matter how small;
the past only gives clues as to where the pieces fit together.
To know where I am now points to the past;
it's gone, leaving me a simple creature—I am.
If the past does not cause the present effect,
from where does the mirror recall its reflection?
Parts and pieces of REALITY exist outside my ken,
seeming to run faster from my grasp the harder I squeeze.
How can it be, this knowing beyond self,
no blood of a RATIONAL forefather's blood?
I know I can be somebody and something;
my past creates my THOUGHTS which create me.
Phantom MIND brings THOUGHTS to consecrated attention,
waving the lantern of knowledge back and forth.

I see it broadly before me, and darkly behind,
switching between my eternal known and unknown.
A ship sawing motion widening to encompass the field,
more than the part allotted to us by nature.
My eyes may be misguided, but they don't yield to a guess;
from dark corners I may find substantial information.
Nipping at the rear as light banishes it from the front,
a continuous interplay between formless and distinct.
There is always a fuzzy line between light and dark;
the problem lies in learning how to find the line.
Is it a battle fought over hallowed ground,
or a competition between pirates for buried treasure?
The conflict is instinctive, formed from pure differences,
performing or fighting the part to which I'm born.
Which brings the battle back into the same dualistic roles,
using knowledge's lantern as both shield and light.
Either of those roles I'm able to fill with suitable ease;
still, it's the goal I pursue, not the method.
Yet there is more to be gleaned from irrational powers,
a unity which does not require defeat to gain victory.
In order for me to be right, someone else must be wrong;
thereby some principles are accepted, others rejected.
Open baby eyes to see what is and what can be;
once knowledge has been lost, it is then given LIFE.
Unless I first possess something valuable there is no loss;
there isn't much light that can be won from the dark.
Loss of control is the abyss which RATIONAL THOUGHTS fear;
rigid influences are illuminated by opening inner reaches.
There should be no fear of REALITY, though it's near,
exposed to THOUGHTS unsolicited by my safe senses.
The only guide, using a view that has been abused—
an irrational path cannot be seen by looking forward.
There is no vista which my eyes are capable of beholding,
than the 1 right in front, no matter where I turn.
What if irrational sight views the darkness to the rear,
born blind to a perspective beyond animate existence?
Any perspective can only show its own purview,
which means there must always be some area left unseen.

Alas, that all-seeing RATIONAL lantern is fixed in place,
lighting the path to great knowledge with great hubris.
What I see must be focused ahead or it's of no benefit;
if my view shifts, it will find another place to be of use.
Lacking ambition to shed its illumination
for all, not just that of refined blood.
A RATIONAL view is open to all who can be persuaded,
but only by looking in its direction can it be seen.
Fence shielded words no longer—what must be, must be;
however, an adversarial system is not the only way to gain.
There is no part of me which can be offered;
my perspective is effective, it shouldn't be compromised.
This is not a zero-sum game being played;
no need to fear losing since nothing is lost, or added.
I offer of myself all I'm able to give,
but what I see doesn't allow for contraindication.
Words turn on guileless MIND as vipers,
revealing REALITY in the places we dare not look.
Trust must exist before I will accept unseen PERCEPTIONS;
blind faith in the glib is a sure path to a ball-less cult.
Taking a car to a mechanic does not require his view,
only that he be entrusted not to do intentional harm.
If I can't see the perspective required for understanding,
then I must develop faith that the messenger is authentic.
A view offered from the other side, irrationally perceived,
a perspective able to see beyond sensory limitations.
I own all seen in this light, rationally perceived,
without which other views must survive in total isolation.
One known by the absence of the other,
a benchmark forever forbidding their presence together.

06:54

Locked in this cell, left to myself, all alone;
it isn't punishment since my prior existence was so similar.
Is there any real connection to relatives of the blood,
or does loneliness arrive with the first individual moment?

Everything I see, every CONCEPT I form,
is totally mine and can't possibly belong to another view.
From where does any panorama of the world originate;
what parents could have birthed a RATIONAL perspective?
A realistic perspective is born with each sensible creature,
using the material knowledge that comes naturally to it.
Straining and reaching for a RATIONAL meaning so faint,
trumpeting at close range to summon sustenance?
Everything in this universe, down to the smallest iota,
has the innate ability to move with other physical OBJECTS.
FORCE behind immoderate words is ancestrally divined,
thick with meaning, or thinly adorned.
My THOUGHT—RATIONAL CONCEPT of REALITY
is based on the interaction occurring between OBJECTS.
Blood thick as water, in a hue clear and cool,
forming THOUGHTS with the color offered by hegemony.
There is no doubt my THOUGHTS follow my senses;
I know of fantasies, but even they are born of REALITY.
Everything has parents, whole and very very close;
although each LIFE is freely given what it truly requires.
I'm no rich boy pampered with an easy existence!
My food, my survival, was never handed to me.
Fighting for every scrap possibly gained from the bounty;
all of it pissed away in mindless repetition.
Each morsel is paid for with a drop from my brow;
this is my water, my blood, my heritage!
Look at where we come from, and where we go,
and it is still not easy to see the place in which we are.
My existence doesn't depend on any noble heritage;
all OBJECTS are composed of the same material pieces.
Any conflict separates existence into us and them,
standing toe to toe, treading on separate ground.
The nature of what I am is distinct, it's my heritage:
a RATIONAL perspective composed from all I sense.
This is steadily assumed, check it over the closest hill:
all that we are is because of all that we are not.
An invisible ridge separating REALITY into this and that,
irrational and RATIONAL views in opposition to the end.

Come, look and see what holds that resolute crest;
broad shoulders bearing REALITY, no SPACE for one more.
Steadfast and determined, I bear my part of the burden,
RATIONAL THOUGHTS restricting access to all left irrational.
All REALITY beyond THOUGHTS will have an irrational feel,
touches which seem sensual, yet are also hidden.
What I understand is exposed right here and right now;
inspected in the light, while the mystery is behind it.
The place where LIFE exists has a more internal nature,
brought to the front to find what is hiding in the shadows.
Ah . . . no. What I sense is what makes sense;
this I can see—I'M RATIONAL—by this light I do see.
How is light known unless darkness abounds;
how is a RATIONAL view known unless irrationality exists?
The photons and waves known to constitute light
will exist whether or not there is darkness.
Yet where will light end without darkness;
is one perspective sufficient to see one perspective?
Compared right in my face—what I am to what I am not,
the invisible line between views is what creates them.
RATIONAL or irrational, both are easily begun,
and neither are likely ever to be fully understood.
Still, I will grant no rights which are unbecoming;
liens on my RATIONAL property aren't what I seek.
Expanding vision extends through a RATIONAL fog;
irrational is not a synonym for stupid.
My language is sufficient to encompass many terms;
there must be a concise representation of an irrational view.
Why is it necessary for some to see while others do not;
how can blind eyes be clear while others fill with tears?
Events which arrest my sight and freeze my BRAIN
are enough to fill my eyes with knowledge of what is.
Running MIND is more often frozen by pictures within;
stopped dead in its tracks by an inner light.

07:25

I'm so damned angry at the injustice of legal justice,
but this is plainly irrational, it helps me not at all.
From where does an inner rage arise,
when there is no direct physical cause which makes it so?
Most of my rage is directed at events out of my control;
I seek a preferred future and see it wrenched away.
EMOTIONS like anger, and other irrational essences,
have a source seen best by an inner view—INTUITION.
So now I'm supposed to accept 3 types of perspectives:
RATIONAL, irrational, and INTUITIVE.
Be unreasonable and lump non-RATIONAL views together;
is it possible that irrationality comes from INTUITION?
It's certainly possible an INTUITIVE view is irrational,
knowledge obtained in that manner isn't RATIONAL.
Maybe a view from INTUITION is the only irrational one,
unless there are more paths to REALITY than two.
Knowledge can be obtained by the use of REASON, or not,
and 2 perspectives appear to be sufficient for this task.
Thus REALITY can be perceived by use of INTUITION,
a view totally irrational in nature, living its own rules.
An INTUITIVE perspective holds no value for my REASON;
it has no fit with the other physical phenomena of REALITY.
Contesting every point will not advance us anywhere;
a horse can only lead where the wagon will follow.
I only seek to be assured I won't lose myself,
or advances by RATIONAL THOUGHT through the millennia.
There is only one treasure kept in the realm of INTUITION;
grasping for advantage here gains no material purchase.
Then I shall stand here, well within a credible light,
far from those deceptions which lie in wait in the dark.
In order to exchange verbal ripostes, come within reach;
standing afar prohibits a glimpse into nether shadows.
There is no use for an invisible line if it's easily crossed;
I hold aloof from an INTUITIVE view, it recoils from mine.
What weapon herein is strong enough to cross that divide,
to shove in jagged metal and make a festering wound?

Charlatans exist in every age, doomsayers, luddites;
those who would stoop to shattering civilization.
Fear of INTUITION *is a joke laid upon a riddle:*
is that which can never be used in the land of all that is?
SCIENCE and logic are sufficient to stop major intrusions;
I worry sly innuendo might crawl under my barriers.
All manner of pretense shall be dropped to the side;
thus bared of breast with no hidden agenda.
So I can trust, to a limited extent, that past successes
achieved through toil and strife aren't an irrational goal.
Stuck in an INTUITIVE *refrain which gives no purchase,*
material reward does not appeal to living SOUL.
If there are no material rewards to be obtained,
only anomalous lessons can be taught across the divide.
One possibility may slip past the barrier between them:
what is more apparent than one REALITY *in opposition?*
If 2 views could be united into 1 that is more supreme,
then each is only a different side of a blended essence.
DUALITY given rein to combine them into a rich tapestry,
RATIONAL colors laid over a weave of INTUITION.
The complexity which modern society has thrust upon me,
commonly forces a choice between 1 master or the other.
What powerful earthly leaders keep forgetting
is we can only render unto Caesar what is already his.
What each perspective detects is isolated and ineffective
beyond the region in which REALITY has cast it to exist.
Which does not change the option to serve one master:
a RATIONAL view, INTUITION, or a combination of the two.
Faith in SCIENCE is RATIONAL; faith in RELIGION is INTUITIVE;
faith in both mandates I live with 1 foot on each shore.
No other land shall be trod, no other sea shall be crossed;
our quest is to find from where perspectives arise.
TRUTH in REALITY must be found in 1 of those views;
no other exists which is within my reach.
They are located by free examination of each one's nature;
which two are superfluous, which one is a goooooooooooal?

07:52

I feel sure my strident anger, this virulent EMOTION,
has something important to convey, but it's irrational.
Thinking does not resolve anger, anger solves nothing;
two sides of existence are living in direct conflict.
But my anger does exist, it's a truly distinct essence;
some access to REALITY must come from examining it.
Each view is one much unlike the other; they do not expand
by mere repetition of <is> and <is not>.
I see in many directions, the 4 corners of my globe:
a posteriori, a priori, deductive, and inductive.
Up and down, left and right—they are all dualistic;
the only views that truly matter are within and without.
Those directions I use fit best within a RATIONAL view,
mighty powers functioning for control of my environment.
A view from INTUITION is by its nature irrational; a slur
brought to bring scorn upon that which is and is not.
Every scrap of knowledge I bear is directionally tagged,
clues to how and what that only need access to where.
Directions which are used to hold CONCEPTIONS tightly
beyond the beck and call of feeling, a singular course.
It covers me whole, the entire panorama of what I see;
every CONCEPT occurring to me is RATIONAL.
Brought forth in the light, dispel shadow and let us see
all, even ghosts with which to fill up insubstantial MIND.
The only cure for darkness is light;
my eyes don't lie, but they can be easily fooled.
Is it not the predominant view;
can we not see that which is through those solid eyes?
My eyes exist, and they grant me PERCEPTION of what is;
it's PERCEPTION of what isn't that my solid eyes can't see.
Try new methods which do not have cross motivations:
from without find without, from within find within.
Crossing the border between defined opposite views
should still find REALITY located in the province of both.
Unsure MIND is forever locked into indeterminate battle,
within or without, and neither able to convince the other.

My senses make external MATTER distinct and available,
while those internal matters have no defined usefulness.
Meek MIND acknowledges the use of RATIONAL dominance,
a field which cannot be overcome with plenty of INTUITION.
I dominate material phenomena because of their use;
it's irrational phenomena which are beyond manipulation.
REALITY has phenomena, the rest is only perspective,
spinning visions to show possibilities of what can be.
If it exists, then I should be able to eventually use it;
it's what doesn't exist that gives me extreme pause.
The prominent brow of intelligence is fleeting,
and must eventually fly before REALITY'S countenance.
A RATIONAL rule is better than no rule at all;
I'm not a butterfly which floats aimlessly about.
Tamed MIND allows its wild horses fenced-in freedom,
the essence of LIFE corralled by dualistic THOUGHTS.

****

9:43

A wise man once said:
blessed are those that give unto each his due.
I would be more than happy to give a few people their due,
but my current state doesn't lend itself to that path.
Also, do unto others as you would have them do unto you;
is this advice for action, or reaction?
Only a single law is required to establish real justice,
and a single law is required to give respect to all people.
Another wise man gave its negation:
do not unto others as you would not have done unto you.
Find a difference between the 2 that really matters;
and no rule should fail because some pervert likes abuse.
Give criticism of holy priests a little rest;
there are better things in this world than gods' toys.
I'm consumed with revenge, and desire for retribution,
but any acceptable payback isn't under my control.

Is it possible revenge is reserved for another sphere;
is anyone just enough to mete out suitable punishment?
The laws of society are only a game for lawyers to play;
what I want is to see private offenders publicly condemned.
It fills random Mind, *see how it tumbles and glows,*
each Soul *has a private means of receiving its due.*
Karmic laws may not allow me to see offenders punished,
so I desire to do it myself; there is none more reliable.
If love is freely given, is there any inhibition
to giving it back; is this real love?
It's my free Will that allows me passage to love;
it's my selfish desires that obstruct its free flow.
If anger is freely given, is there any inhibition
to giving it back; is this real anger?
There is no impeding real love or anger;
they arise unwanted, and they depart due to want.
There is no difference between the cause of love and anger,
regarding their effects, yet we feel there should be.
Like any other opposites, their effects are quite different;
it's difficult to understand how their causes are similar.
What do we owe other people from what we are given;
should we only render unto Caesar what is Caesar's?
Tribute is payable to society's ruler;
if I were in charge, then taxes should flow to me.
Do any own love or anger;
is their home in this breast, such that they are its due?
Private ownership of them makes existence difficult;
it's too easy to spew out empty words of love or anger.
No words or phrases will manage to fill Emotion,
yet love or anger can inspire volumes of poetry or prose.
They are words designed to capture a bottomless feeling;
language lacks the ability to show how deep Pain goes.
If anger is given to another, is its return desired?
Expect it is definite, desire it is the question.
It would seem nonsense to say I desire anger in answer;
it's rightly Rational to select for the happiest outcome.
Non-apparent Thoughts *should not be rejected,*
since we search for what is obviously not apparent.

My youth was impaled with love, anger has turned on me,
and there are few moments when I truly wish them to stop.
Anger is possessive, as sweetly felt as love;
who among us would choose no anger, no EMOTIONS?
They are in me, I experience them in me, never separate;
anger and love have the capacity entirely to consume me.
How can each person be given his due,
unless we accept both good and bad EMOTIONS?
Sometimes I'm due anger, and sometimes love;
1 is no less valid than the other.
There is an attraction to one, and an impulse in both;
left on their own they will find their own kind.
I can't release my EMOTIONS, except in DEATH;
neither do I want to continue receiving my exact merit.
What is due is more than love for love, anger for anger,
it is also anger for love and love for anger.
If I give love, expect anger; if I'm given anger, pay love;
this is a very irrational pill to swallow.
They are both the same in regard to what is due;
all EMOTIONS are owed, receiving as well as giving.
Therefore specific EMOTIONS aren't due to each man,
it's the act of emoting which will return manifold "do's."
Love for love, or anger for anger;
if only these cycles of payback were separate, unattached.
I was taught good shall repay good, and evil repay evil;
few men will do good if they are to be repaid in evil.
There is no harmony in endlessly repeating cycles;
waves move up and down, not round and round.
So my due is EMOTION when I emit this passion without,
and a disconnection from humanity when it's absent.
Any EMOTION must be expected to be received for love,
and a similar multitude of responses for offensive anger.
If I desire no anger, then I can give no love;
this is contrary to everything I've been taught.
Gods of SCIENCE and RELIGION give us equal reactions,
foretelling the future by observing our past.
SCIENCE grants me a peaceful world without love or anger,
at least when it's used in its cold dispassionate way.

Is a world without love worth a world without anger?
There must be another better way.

10:22

Bob the shrink with the big bald head came by earlier,
offering me advice which applies to crazy people like him.
How can true understanding of existential Reality begin
if people keep coming around trying to help us see it?
He tried to explain to me that fasting makes no sense;
it's totally irrational and I seem to be much better equipped.
Allowed freedom to roam in one perceived pasture,
yet still surrounded with fences unfit for personal passion.
Allowed?! Civilization has no real hold on my Mind,
and therefore holds no reins across my back.
Actual freedom is determined by observing perspective;
a fence either keeps the world out, or the pasture in.
My Rational view brings convenience to living measures;
no fear of fierce animals, or freezing from winter's bite.
Part of Life is fear, rocks are not afraid;
what else is lost when the capacity for fear is lost?
Look around at all of the machines my view has created;
Reality is made mine, it hasn't been lost at all.
They are toys next to Reality's giants;
gods of Science give us scraps from a much larger table.
Knowledge is given to me by the disciplines of Science,
directing my Thoughts to be fruitful and multiply.
Arcane rites, secret formulas, and differential calculus,
incantations which can transform fish into strawberries.
A Rational view doesn't fail because higher math is hard;
I'm sure higher Intuitive levels are also formidable.
Why does a Rational view make Science so valuable;
what allows the universe it creates to be as useful as it is?
Science consists of knowledge available to any and all,
a wonderful benefit from the results of trial and error.
Dictates from gods of Science have become too numerous;
another legal system no one person can understand.

It's available to any who have the ability and insight
to see the methods available under a RATIONAL view.
What is observed by those of greatest ability,
when so few are endowed from BIRTH by any of the gods?
Repetition is the key to opening the RATIONAL vault;
without this metaphysical property, SCIENCE is useless.
Treasures guarded by dragons born from uniform eggs;
dangerous to those who would mar the many-jeweled face.
Nothing can bear up to irresistible repetition;
it's a cornerstone of the edifice for physical phenomena.
Repetition has no RATIONAL equal as a mighty power,
yet observe—it exists as a property, not as REALITY.
That which can't be repeated has no use;
any essence must kneel before its predictable blows.
REALITY is not useful, it merely exists as itself;
it is made useful only when subjected to repetitive abuse.
It's not abuse to advance and foster civilization;
these words wouldn't be THOUGHT without eons of advances.
That we can modify REALITY does not mean we should;
whose convenience is sought, that of the one or the many?
Pure SCIENCE ultimately benefits all;
the problem is people who use it without understanding.
The witchery SCIENCE bestows upon man is taught,
drilled into the silicon chip that used to be living MIND.
So what! SCIENCE is taught, no need to reinvent the wheel;
learning it saves me the trouble of relying solely on myself.
RATIONAL and INTUITIVE perspectives come natural,
given to us at BIRTH, and leaving when bid to by DEATH.
Man is born RATIONAL, but learns SCIENCE;
not to forget man is born INTUITIVE, but learns RELIGION.
Knowledge is an unstable marvel offered by petty gods;
taught by rote to enable unwise guileless children.
A long involved process is required to make fit workers;
RATIONAL training makes them strictly useful to society.
Schooling is designed to weed out THOUGHTS of INTUITION,
and to replace them with a devoted robotic potential.
Growth and prosperity are founded on that practice;
history has shown society is best served in this fashion.

Why does scientific CONCEPTION of REALITY require
children's innate abilities be so drastically retrained?
Knowledge thrust upon them is gleaned from others;
it's a distillation of solid THOUGHTS from previous thinkers.
Why does society require children to reject INTUITION
in order to learn a scientific version of REALITY?
Irrational behavior has no place within SCIENCE;
children are also weaned from other animal behaviors.
Yet we are born with INTUITION, and RATIONAL capacities;
something must be lost if we ignore one of this pair.
If INTUITIVE knowledge could be shown to have some use,
then it could be elevated into RATIONAL equilibrium.
What of those who have greater abilities for INTUITION;
does not society grant its favors to those more RATIONAL?
I fully grant prosperity isn't equally available to all;
abilities vary according to type and inherited traits.
Thus society remakes children into a useful mold,
whether or not they can fit into this restrictive embrace.
An INTUITIVE view also doesn't grant its favors freely;
it has no school which can match RATIONAL efficiency.
Not all who beg at its table receive a rich banquet,
yet many are able to survive on sublime scraps.
Man's ancestors were obliged to subsist on old gatherings;
RATIONAL knowledge has lifted us up from that ignominy.
A RATIONAL view has no more appeal than INTUITION
if REALITY is wished to be experienced instead of modeled.
A material universe is formed from SCIENCE's lessons,
which are fully democratic and have universal appeal.
Available to any who will lick the boots of those gods,
willing to sacrifice themselves to LIFE half-spent.
Though its influence is abundant, some think criminal,
I repeat—SCIENCE is only guilty of success.
Criticism of a RATIONAL view meeting any standard
is the requirement for it to succeed as the only one.
Any attempt to unseat a RATIONAL view from its throne
will result only in its unleashing its rigid dogs of SCIENCE.
What we are at BIRTH is what we are at DEATH;
the throne will not sit upright unless it is in balance.

11:07

Bob the shrink told me a story about tilting at windmills;
I told him Cervantes wrote satire, and he doesn't get it.
It may be a fast unto DEATH *will not accomplish anything,*
and yet what greater goal is there than finality?
Maybe I'm just covering TRUTH with a dangerous dragon,
but I prefer the course I've chosen to a hopeless 1.
What possible use could a futile protest of authority have?
It is only futile if the results are expected to be RATIONAL.
If a mental scientist can't understand what I'm doing,
then I have no hope for the intellectually challenged.
Dependence on scientific answers to irrational questions
is riding atop wild RATIONAL *guesses on a torrential river.*
SCIENCE isn't founded upon guesswork;
it's enlivened by the dedicated hard work of its disciples.
Gods of SCIENCE *have successfully modified our world;*
the RATIONAL *view has ridden this horse for all it is worth.*
SCIENCE works because a RATIONAL perspective is valid;
order and coherence do exist within REALITY.
Blind gods of SCIENCE *bestow* RATIONAL *success;*
anarchy and chaos will follow disillusionment with them.
That is no problem since the future of SCIENCE is bright;
there is still all of inner and outer SPACE to explore.
Only as long as fickle gods of SCIENCE *continue to bestow*
convenience for mass pleasure will a RATIONAL *rule last.*
People aren't so capricious as to turn on past success;
they won't abandon modern comfort.
Obedience to a RATIONAL *rule is accepted for its benefits;*
the problem is that more people want more and more.
Which is why children must be trained from infancy
to think outside the box by 1st thinking inside it.
Those sober gods are imagined to create an Eden, a utopia
gained by fawning at their feet for favor and grace.
Today isn't perfect, only better than the past;
civilization will continue either to progress, or to stagnate.
Holy writ from SCIENCE *gods renders one view matchless,*
yet much is assumed in any quest for this RATIONAL *grail.*

Assumptions are required to progress in any endeavor,
and Ockham's razor is the sensible litmus test.
Bending REALITY into a twisted model for convenience
does not also mandate that it must be of this design.
My CONCEPTS of REALITY are a reflection of PERCEPTIONS,
and those are based on some actual essence.
Because divine directives work so well and so often,
society imagines nothing can exist without their bounty.
It's a proven observation to conceive in this fashion;
because water boils means other liquids should too.
Listen! Crack the fragile eggshell hiding the rotten yolk
of those gods of SCIENCE pretending to be all that is.
This isn't the first attempt to overthrow SCIENCE's bulk;
it has withstood spurious inquisitions before.
Three rites are given by gods of SCIENCE to rule REALITY:
observation, theory, and repetition.
These are 3 factors which solidify a RATIONAL view;
the bases on which the pyramid of knowledge can grow.
Each will be exposed from the darkness within by light;
gods are the result and not the cause of mortal creations.
Man doesn't create SCIENCE out of fiction;
there are cold hard facts on which its rules are based.
At best, the gods of SCIENCE dictate approximate REALITY;
a RATIONAL view of its structure is necessarily limited.

11:32

Bob the shrink went on and on about this and that,
trying to convince me he knows the nature of TRUTH.
A priest once said: what we observe is not nature itself,
but nature exposed to our method of questioning.
Heisenberg was a master who exposed uncertainty,
a principle which has proven to be most profound.
An observation is complete when it bears full fruit;
within its sensory grasp is what a reasonable being knows.
It's difficult but not impossible to sense OBJECT fully;
all I know of it comes from my PERCEPTIONS.

How much of REALITY can really be conceived,
when an observer see only two dimensions in three?
I can see a square out of a cube, or a circle in a sphere;
a flat world of depth is what binocular PERCEPTION acquires.
Five senses give mankind great leeway in determining how
to manipulate OBJECTS of REALITY around him.
OBJECT is known by how my senses perceive it;
with more senses comes a more complete mental likeness.
Distinct sensations are limited in natural abilities;
each one sees only the wall of a deep dark well.
My CONCEPT of OBJECT is constructed from distinct senses,
and each 1 has capacities born from animal EVOLUTION.
Toys have been created to alleviate a conceded lack,
attempting to pierce the veil poets have confronted.
Microscopes and telescopes and centrifuges are some
machines which help bring REALITY into a brighter light.
Those toys admirably do the job for which they were built,
granting partial sight where the blind formerly ruled.
Many modern CONCEPTS have been aided by machines,
rigid corrections filling in where nature's gifts falter.
Yet what is now observed is still not REALITY itself,
an illusion lazily called the mirror instead of the model.
Confusing REALITY with its representation is a mistake;
a barrier exists between what it is, and what I think it is.
Looking into a microscope to imagine how microbes live;
priests as randy boys peeking under REALITY'S robe.
Investigation of little creatures shows that world better;
medicine can now banish those bugs, magic can't.
Lifting its laced hem only gives a limited view
of the real maiden-head hidden within.
Nothing can be used to perceive OBJECT but my senses;
existence beyond them requires observation and deduction.
There are many more parameters creating an event
than what is apparent by looking at only two dimensions.
If OBJECT consists of 3-d and I can see it in only 2,
then some part of it must exist beyond my PERCEPTION.
Created toys can expand only the senses nature gives us,
not create new ones able to put the model into the mirror.

I'm stuck with my 5 senses for detection of REALITY;
there is no extant method which will create a new 1.
CONCEPTION is also afflicted with unsanitary desire,
pawing through refuse for what it wants in what is there.
Not all information I acquire forms into CONCEPT,
some is left out through unreasonable wants and needs.
There can be no denying that sensation is quite real;
although what part of OBJECT is less valid than another?
If most of my knowledge is false, then I know nothing;
my best course of action—go sit in a corner and drool.
A different problem is seen through eyes from INTUITION,
caught in the dark and hidden from the light of sensation.
There may be aspects of REALITY beyond my senses,
hidden in the cracks between sight and sound.
Give a simple example of limited observation,
dictates from gods of SCIENCE which bring hurt with help.
When the Industrial Revolution was crawling in infancy,
pollution was known, but its import was too big in scope.
Modern problems were beyond the reach of imagination,
fouling and pestilence and other noxious residue.
The 1st cars emitted smoke, belching foul fumes,
worse than is released by today's combustion engines.
But vast numbers aided, and repetition abetted,
problems not seen by inventors consumed with passion.
Pollution wasn't a problem as part of scientific progress,
never conceived as other than an unfortunate byproduct.
How could the problems of pollution be predicted
if it had never been observed?
It may be that simple observations were overlooked
in the rush to embrace a new and powerful technology.
How can the whole pattern be seen
if only part is exposed to view?
If I see 1 side of a coin,
I can form no CONCEPT of what exists on the other side.
RATIONAL observation comes with one fatal flaw:
CONCEPTIONS must be created from limited PERCEPTIONS.
Any CONCEPT I've ever formed has been made
based on senses which favor an animal's version of events.

Humanity attempting to understand how it is all connected
by referring only to the parts and the pieces.

12:08

Bob the shrink got offended because he was trying to help,
and I told him his helpful probing forced bias on us both.
How is observation supposed to envision REALITY,
if its touch must always come away part-stained?
There is some weight borne by that argument;
my view is a FINITE prison, and it will remain in this cell.
Any observer is trapped inside looking out,
while hubris claims he is on the outside looking in.
There is an additional point which brightens my CONCEPTS:
many distinct observations will increase my field of view.
Is REALITY simply laid atop a stack of building blocks,
piled up in statuesque order until far scenes can be seen?
The EXACT nature of REALITY may never be known,
but I can move anything with a long enough lever.
This is the maximum a RATIONAL view can see:
a limited approximation of a vista revealing INFINITY.
I don't try to see past forever and a day;
SCIENCE's ability is shown accurate in the here and now.
That is a futile digression from the point of our opposition,
idolatry will never be able to reach above human notice.
SCIENCE has taught me how many parts combine into 1,
which is how complex machines do their best work.
Many parts can be rationally combined into one CONCEPTION,
and still a car is many parts, not one REALITY.
Part of the essence of a machine is that it should work;
a car isn't a car if some of its pieces are missing.
A car is CONCEPTION held within closed MIND;
REALITY includes the pieces, they manage to work together.
A car exists whether I believe in it or not;
it's 1 complete OBJECT as long as it works as a car.
How could it be a car unless it is believed to be such;
where does a RATIONAL perspective fit in with weak belief?

If a car was given to a stone-age-tribe,
and they had no IDEA what it was, it would still be a car.
*Not to the tribesmen; or is conceived REALITY the same
no matter how it functions?*
So what I know is intimately connected to what I believe,
and my beliefs are founded on past proven relations.
*Belief and faith do not belong in a RATIONAL heaven,
irrational feelings which heavily influence priestly bulls.*
Suggest some of those errors which observers make,
where perfect SCIENCE is led astray by irrational THOUGHTS.
*Scientific priests stick their heads in the sand,
when experimental results give rise to theoretical errors.*
When an experiment doesn't agree with accepted theory,
it's more likely the former is flawed than the latter.
*Grants are given for researchers to find missing links,
which still must be within parameters already known.*
I can't violate laws of thermodynamics or physics,
unless experiments show how a new theory might work.
*Future largesse depends on flocking together,
providing warmth and society, yet nothing really strange.*
RATIONAL birds are of the same feather;
BRAINS which work alike tend toward similar answers.
*What do they have to do with a pure RATIONAL view,
information which has been tainted with irrational input?*
I have no answer which is sufficient;
RATIONAL ability doesn't erase my attached humanity.
*Peer review cannot modify data which are not released,
and priests will not release unauthorized data.*
It's the nature of SCIENCE to go slow and be conservative;
those who move too fast are likely to run off a cliff.
*Forgetting that an impertinent question has led us so far:
what if?*
A reasonable question which gives imagination control,
until SCIENCE learns the moon isn't made of cheese.
*If results were the only criteria to interest gods of SCIENCE,
then they would be in total accord with a RATIONAL realm.*
Results which don't meet with accepted theories
have no place within the halls of known SCIENCE.

Yet implacable gods demand other forms of obeisance,
with severe punishment for those who flout their decrees.
If I violate the essential laws of physics,
then I should expect to receive physical chastisement.
Thou shalt conform to those who have come before,
else shame before thy peers shall be thy daily bread.
Any professional seeks approval from his peers;
there is no other reward in modern isolated careers.
Thou shall not contradict priests who bless all that is holy,
else wine poured at thy table shall be renewed as piss.
SCIENCE has no special power to overthrow the purse;
money is the grease that makes all knowledge turn.
Be thou humble before institutions which glorify gods,
else thy throat be parched without the holy water of status.
There are few, if any, scientists who would deny rewards,
and the dispensers are those who live in their past.
Popes who aspire to touch their frugal gods are not
in themselves given to be RATIONAL.
Those who can—do;
those who can't—try to control those who can.
They are given to vain competition, glory-seeking, deceit,
golden eyes, complex human traits and problems.
There is a wide gulf between those who love knowledge,
and those who love the power bequeathed by knowledge.
Who claims ownership of those irrational observations,
led by a golden ring in the nose past a divine calling?
Scientists would publish any and all findings,
if their balls weren't held by half-dead administrators.
REALITY is left in the waste bin of experimental error;
contrariness to theory is not accepted by the potpourri.
Peer review is made to weed out incomplete experiments,
and false theories which cause more harm than good.
Yet what use can be made of a verdant field,
if fear and desire have cleared out useful plants?
People who speak rationally, but act irrationally,
crush new IDEAS based on out-dated theories.
Theories make constants based on experiments
repeated by rabbits running from hawks.

If sufficient observers agree on numerical values,
then SCIENCE is able to create standardized constants.
Secret constants changing as flags in the wind,
firmly planted, yet whipping around approximate points.
The numerical constants required to make formulas work
must be based on human observations, which don't agree.
No constant can be achieved, and no permanence found,
when results are dependent on observational limitations.
Experiments which are designed to finalize constants
frequently find different numbers than the textbook.
The constants taught to all RATIONAL children as fact
are values agreed upon by those who are in the ballpark.
Any sequence of tests is subject to experimental error;
no scientist can extract himself from his observations.
The same priest with the same equipment cannot always
obtain the same results with the same sequences.
Human involvement necessarily leads to human error;
SCIENCE has no other method for finding constants.
Frustrating to depend on priests to open REALITY'S vault,
instead of cold hard facts we find wanton numbers.
No matter how hard I try to find the exact number,
experimental evidence for a constant is by trial and error.
Trusting those constants to the degree priests demand
is an unreasonable request in a realm claimed RATIONAL.
Formulaic constants have repeatedly shown their value,
modern SCIENCE is filled with fixed material examples.
Useful they are and INTUITION'S diatribe does not defend
luddites who would tear down genuine progress.
The triumph of a RATIONAL perspective can't be denied;
desire for a noble native past is extreme self-hatred.
What of the rationally radical seekers of REALITY'S grail,
using only one tool—the honesty to go where results lead?
That multitude numbers the crackpots and individualists,
with works left untouched for centuries post-mortem.
They find discoveries contradicting those in power,
releasing their grip upon the unwitting masses.
Galileo and his ilk used to be hounded by RELIGION,
his inheritors are merely ignored by modern SCIENCE.

How can REALITY be found by limiting observations;
what is seen from the lone candle of the king on the hill?
A single RATIONAL observation doesn't amount to much,
but I repeat that many is more than a hill of beans.
An honorable mention goes to that ritualistic objection,
granting it TIME to form REALITY correctly into a mold.
REALITY may be a square peg, and SCIENCE a round hole,
but enough shaving and shoving can make it fit.
How much TIME will the process of progress require,
recreating gods anew into that which they can never be?
SCIENCE discovers new avenues and particles every year;
it's only a matter of TIME until its promise is fulfilled.
Just around the corner is the utopia always promised;
tomorrow will yield what today is only imagined.
Look at the past 200 years and see the progress;
tomorrow's civilization will be magnificently different.
TIME needed to find REALITY itself is now, and no gods
can extend a limited number of moments.
Each discovery brings REALITY more firmly into my grasp,
stacking pieces to build a more stable monument.
Where has REALITY gone to wait for our embrace;
how can we be here if it is over there?
REALITY is here, I just don't understand all of its motions;
SCIENCE'S progress is only for increased knowledge.
Long periods of TIME will create useful monuments
to how REALITY can be modified and used, not understood.
This is why a RATIONAL view and SCIENCE are valued,
they're useful, so considerable QUALITIES aren't required.
Observation is at best inaccurate, at worst sadly flawed;
its modern version perverted from honest tradition.
SCIENCE is able to see so far because it accepts the basics;
valuable TIME isn't wasted on spurious pursuits.
Man once sought valiantly to understand why and how,
now he rabidly searches for parts and pieces to machines.
Certain constituents to MATTER are well known,
it's completely irrational to forgo that which works well.
Even incomplete, a RATIONAL view will never be replaced;
there is no other capable of fitting in its place.

Even incomplete, a RATIONAL view has no superior;
no other 1 is able to reorganize MATTER to suit.
It is a light shone in the darkness of REALITY'S home,
where RATIONAL observations of it will forever be limited.
Its detailed observations make 1 point clear:
a RATIONAL view will be as strong as its scientific backing.
Plastic is strong until ultraviolet light turns it into slivers;
once gods are overthrown, their perspective loses power.
A RATIONAL perspective has no power beyond observation;
it's easy to see where it has been successful.
RATIONAL dominance has not always been preeminent,
only since the Renaissance has this one view overruled.
Actually, the Enlightenment replaced naïve superstition,
self-replicating knowledge replaced blind luck.
Enjoy today's unenlightened reign while it lasts,
for we shall never see its like again.

13:29

Bob the shrink said I have "unresolved childhood issues";
I said his theory was "unresolved childish garbage".
Where does any theory come from;
how can one be imagined which is right, and then wrong?
Any scientific theory comes from assessing observations,
which, though limited, still detect some part of REALITY.
The next fallen rung on SCIENCE'S ladder is theory's step,
only as good as the observations from which it is derived.
A theory is a formal expression of observed phenomena
which has been, to some extent, experimentally verified.
Any proposed theory is only as good as the observer,
and an imperfect observer will lead to imperfect theories.
My PERCEPTION of REALITY may be at best, say 90%,
which doesn't mean my best theory of it is only 90% useful.
To isolate this conflict from those before and after,
assume observations perceive REALITY exactly.
Therefore, for this reflection,
scientific theories are capable of exactly mapping REALITY.

Any theory must be transmitted by a language;
kept alone, it has no use except as mental masturbation.
The major use of any theory is its mass availability;
anyone with sufficient training may use its meaning.
Mathematics has been shown as the preferred language
of transmission amongst SCIENCE priests and gods.
Math isn't a language, it's part of REALITY'S structure,
a logical coherency showing how everything fits together.
What math describes, and what is seen, are distinct poles;
see a RATIONAL gift, then look this horse in the mouth.
No rationale exists for why numbers should work together,
why they fit in sets, or why 1 + 1 should always equal 2.
Mathematics is a language discovered through ritual,
and passed on for use by priests to explain gods.
Math maps REALITY incredibly well;
none can deny its manipulation of unseen FORCES.
Mathematics was not discovered with godly blessings;
its original formulation was to transmit QUANTITY.
Only ignorance of the higher levels of structured math
prohibits the average man from realizing its universal gifts.
SCIENCE gods could never have developed without a method
of manipulating multiple CONCEPTIONS outside of one MIND.
SCIENCE requires a pure and clean assistant,
1 capable of taming spurious THOUGHTS in the mental arena.
The typical size of CONCEPTIONS mentally juggled is four;
some have a greater ability, and some a lot less.
If I listen to a list of numbers being read;
the 1st 4 will be remembered, or trickily in groups times 4.
Any theory requires more BRAINS than are available,
unless mathematics is used to provide structural support.
Sufficient theories are more than succinct statements,
they are CONCEPTS of CONCEPTS rolled into 1.
What is possible without a mathematical language;
if their language is not real, how could gods of SCIENCE be?
Language must be a part of REALITY because it exists;
I don't learn from figments of my imagination.
Information is emitted, and it is received,
yet neither end is experiencing the same essence.

So I'm to believe words in a book are only ink,
until some MIND processes them for possible intent.
There is no realistic element in any language;
the real part is just air moving, or thinking MIND.
But there is meaning in words;
books aren't random jumbles of surrealistic art.
No phrase has meaning unless found MIND forms it,
or until another lost MIND tries to decipher its worth.
Language would therefore be a societal lever,
attempting transmission from 1 BRAIN to another.
Simple language puts IDEAS into worldwide vision;
math has a similar ability to attempt COMMUNICATION.
Or I could view any language, including math,
as nothing but an arbitrary telegraph wire between MINDS.
Numbers and letters are more similar than opposite;
although mathematics' special status cannot be denied.
If math was a language like any other,
liberal-arts majors would have much better job prospects.
Language is available to all thinking creatures,
yet it serves some of us better than others.
Some people have great ability with tongues;
speaking in many different voices is a natural occurrence.
Idiot savants can speak in one particular voice,
and their other notable trait is incomplete PERCEPTION.
Incurable scientists consider math to be a special essence,
with many of language's QUALITIES, but not to be 1 in itself.
REALITY is equally available to all, not
the languages able to describe it.
An exacting language brings me closer to REALITY;
its complexity is beyond the reach of 4 CONCEPTS.
Notice a direct relation:
massive numbers allow massive CONCEPTIONS.
Minimal numbers don't require the lack of CONCEPTS;
there is no direct relation between 1 and the other.
Yet languages and CONCEPTIONS still exist without numbers;
they are only facilitated by a quantified expediency.
Numbers are required to increase the amount of RATIONAL
mental pictures which can formulate scientific THOUGHTS.

Science gods prefer mathematical chant to other vocals,
yet does it represent Reality better?

14:09

Bob the shrink had to leave and go take a phone call;
when he did I took a look at his strange shorthand notes.
Look into his Mind and see something really bizarre,
a mental language which nobody else can understand.
All sentient Concepts are based on similar Reality,
so all of 1 derived from the other should be quite alike.
Two people can see the same event and brand it different;
thus transition from Perception to Conception is varied.
But people use language by making their Thoughts alike;
if numerical Concepts were different, math wouldn't work.
Is mathematics just another type of Communication,
or is it a special language which works to its own rules?
Languages are intended to allow people to communicate,
and math serves this expectation admirably well.
Its statements can be formulated in phonetic language,
just with the bulk and versatility of sliding continents.
Science of math was created to alleviate that problem;
a Life span is too short to use a Rational longhand.
Useless for Science, although not for Life,
phonetic patois carry messages useless for mathematics.
Working solely with the material elements of the universe,
math has gained a notoriety which comes 2nd to none.
Yet when faced with Life in its boundless diversity,
it falls short of describing the most insignificant detail.
Biology and biochemistry can be accurately quantified,
even down to the least significant digit.
Those Quantities have nothing to do with Life;
Qualities are felt, like Emotions and Dreams and Soul.
Symbols can be used to describe anything,
but I don't understand 2 + 2 = glorious sunset.
Is phonetics greater, since it can translate all numbers,
or a language that cannot grant a similar consideration?

The value of math is RATIONAL in nature;
it doesn't perform well in an irrational environment.
What of a mathematics whose sole value is convenience,
scorned at REALITY'S altar like a perpetual bridesmaid?
There is no substitute for math where it has value,
and there is no use for it where it has none.
Gods of SCIENCE and their avaricious priests,
love mathematics and its consistent unemotional decisions.
Numbers can be made to bend and flow just like art,
acquiring knowledge from some place outside of REASON.
Outside of divinely planted fields of human endeavor,
it has no home within the human breast or fertile MIND.
CONCEPTS exist within my MIND as representations,
whether filtered into numerical or alphabetical form.
CONCEPTIONS exist within colorful MIND as pictures;
obviously INTUITION MIND is different from RATIONAL MIND.
A single MIND is 1 and the same;
therefore 1 of those views of MIND is fatally flawed.
Mathematics is a tool and no more, grasped and let go;
one MIND has a language which numbers cannot decipher.
Human BRAINS are created with an ability to grasp words,
many of which have no common root connection.
The source of that ability must be great indeed
to have such universal appeal among so many creeds.
A trait which has allowed man to rise above beast is
the instinct of human beings to learn COMMUNICATION skills.
Yet mathematics does not have universal appeal;
its base transitions leave many people in fits and lurches.
It's strange how math is so difficult for so many people,
and those same people can converse quite well.
Mathematics and spatial symbols fit certain BRAIN patterns,
an inner ear tuned to a specific strain of music.
There does appear to be a limited number of people who are
born with BRAINS capable of mentally turning symbols.
Should not universal appeal apply to universal REALITY,
rather than only be understood by the fortunate few?
The conundrum is whether REALITY is simple or complex,
or if it's thoroughly simple and it appears complex.

Still, REALITY is more completely transferred with
phonetic languages because they have more insertions.
So I should believe math is an inferior map of REALITY,
and other languages are just slightly more effective.
REALITY is a vast and motionless wave;
its secret can be found within this odd description.
CONCEPT of a motionless wave is thoroughly irrational,
and math is considered to be the best map of this universe.
Can speech solve a paradox mathematics cannot,
how LIFE is brought to unliving MATTER?
Statistics and probability have been extensively used
by biological SCIENCES attempting to distinguish LIFE's core.
Those gods have possession of that name known so well,
given to priests whether they have earned it or not.

14:44

Bob the shrink tried a tactic he THOUGHT assured success,
trying to convince me everything is actually relative.
Humanists have theorized that all THOUGHTS are valid,
although none are preferable since everything is relative.
Instead he managed to convince me he's a quack,
by babbling about RELATIVITY without understanding it.
Does RELATIVITY imply there are no definitions,
or maybe Einstein meant something else entirely?
SCIENCE and math have proven that definitions work;
Einstein just said they are relative to each other.
There must be definitions so they can be relative,
so why do priests insist mathematics is universal?
RELATIVITY is a reflection best left for another TIME,
for now accept math as the best relation to REALITY.
As laws of math refer to REALITY, they are not certain;
as they are certain, they do not refer to REALITY.
Einstein has been professed to be 1 of humanity's wise;
still, he asks me to believe REALITY is not close to math.
Mathematical knowledge has progressed far since his day;
all of its branches are now formed from one set trunk.

Modern math is considered from a basis of set theory;
all of its disciplines can be resolved into types of sets.
The actual nature of REALITY does not conform to a set,
forcing all that can be into a bag that does not fit.
If I conceive REALITY as a whole, nothing left out,
it's a set all unto itself—singular REALITY beholden to none.
Is that REALITY held within another REALITY,
or is REALITY able to know itself?
Only simple CONCEPTS can occur within my small BRAIN,
in this case a set called REALITY which has its own home.
How does REALITY have its own home,
if it must exist in a set given to it?
My CONCEPT of REALITY doesn't even exist
except as a set which I create; I form it in my head.
All set theory does is acknowledge its part of the whole;
CONCEPTIONS are formed as sets for RATIONAL exploitation.
REALITY exists, and I form 1 CONCEPT of its essence;
and each instance can only exist as 1 material set.
Sets cannot describe REALITY itself; they are ill-fitting
CONCEPTIONS for humanity's convenience.
It's difficult for me to conceive of REALITY beyond a set;
this THOUGHT in my MIND is as 1 single entity.
REALITY exists, and it is beyond silly to argue this point,
yet its existence made convenient is nigh on impossible.
Math and logic shouldn't work
if they have no connection with REALITY'S existence.
A masked question—why do mathematics and logic work;
which gods of SCIENCE lend themselves a credible ear?
I know some events can be logically determined,
and they aren't possible unless they exist within REALITY.
A quite simple answer; listen . . . it shall pass in a moment:
they do not weave REALITY, they are instead woven.
Math doesn't form REALITY; I begin to understand,
but it's unclear how REALITY forms math.
It is a fabric woven from BRAIN'S neural patterns,
and it is this biological unit which exists within REALITY.
My BRAIN works hand in hand with a RATIONAL view
in a specific fashion which allows me to form CONCEPTS.

The nature of REALITY is outside RATIONAL CONCEPTION;
aids like mathematics are like crutches to the wounded.
CONCEPTS are approximations of what could possibly be,
and math is merely 1 of its many forms.
REALITY is not directly available to limited sensation,
crippled by facts, requiring aid to move frail THOUGHTS.
My ability to use knowledge is also my weakness;
a RATIONAL view requires resort to arbitrary CONCEPTS.
Gods of SCIENCE are unable to form a theory of REALITY
if their claims are unveiled to see its actual structure.
SCIENCE is able to form a theory of REALITY;
though it's limited by its nature to being an approximation.
The aim and goal laid down by those dictatorial gods
is to manipulate REALITY, not understand it.
I offer no apology for being able to use it to advantage;
my nature isn't a problem, just as a snake's isn't to it.
If understanding leads to abuse, all well and good,
yet what about a light leading in another direction?
My understanding of REALITY grants indiscriminate use,
even though what I know is only an approximation.
If comprehension of what is allows no room for feces,
out in the house is where a RATIONAL view holds REALITY.
A RATIONAL perspective holds no unusable CONCEPT,
and waste is the part of REALITY which is beyond use.
Mathematics plugs its wasted holes with sticky gum,
devices with no RATIONAL correspondence to REALITY.
A set can be INFINITES upon INFINITES, or imaginary numbers,
and there are also sets that make math totally irrational.
They exist in the language, and are useful without doubt,
yet they cannot be seen to exist in deed as well as symbol.
Symbols can represent the unknown as well as the known;
SCIENCE has no pretensions to be the font of all-knowledge.
A RATIONAL view has no other language but mathematics
to defraud us into believing pliancy equals REALITY.
The language of SCIENCE is no false front;
control of REALITY is only possible with extreme accuracy.
It seems accurate to THOUGHTS because physical BRAIN'S
PERCEPTION of physical phenomena is mapped so well.

I'm lost; between CONCEPTS my MIND has,
and CONCEPTS solely RATIONAL in nature.
SCIENCE gods are able to map a RATIONAL view of REALITY,
a material universe which only exists within that SPACE.
What math is able to map is an incomplete structure,
because some of the tools required to build it are missing.
It is not a complete phonetic language, only a fixed part,
which is why it finds comfort under a RATIONAL rule.
Math works because its rules are fixed and unyielding;
it has no hold on any existence beyond FINITE CONCEPTS.
This is its benefit, which has limitation as its baggage:
convenience and speed result by ejecting INTUITION.
The speed which makes math such a formidable weapon
is only accessible when using RATIONAL symbols.
REALITY'S sparkle is also lost in that rush,
all of those irrational things making LIFE live.
I can't form CONCEPTS founded upon imprecision;
it is or it isn't, or give me the odds.
Limp MIND works on many loose and hanging pictures,
solidifying THOUGHT into decision, argument into action.
The function of thinking by coherent THOUGHTS is to turn
an INTUITIVE random access into a RATIONAL read only.
Within THOUGHTS able to convert into actions,
other willowy branches lead to sanity and BEAUTY.
Only 2 paths appear to lead me to REALITY,
and my nature has chosen a RATIONAL view for me.
Mathematics is not an accurate description of all REALITY,
just shorthand from a RATIONAL perspective.

15:35

Bob the shrink appeared to have a problem classifying me;
formal psychiatric theories don't have room for autonomy.
Where does IDEA come from that we are all so alike;
is classification better for the therapist or the patient?
Simple observation of nature shows many similarities;
people are of nature, so a theory claims they have traits.

Try to examine a theory and from where it does come;
for example, rubbing two sticks together to engage FIRE.
An example which should be easy and clear,
but most people I've known can't make FIRE in that fashion.
Man first conceived FIRE was delivered by gods;
not SCIENCE ones, ancient voodoo more powerful by far.
Eventually 1 man created FIRE with 2 sticks;
the 3 necessary ingredients furnished, but not known.
It may be important in some region where someone cares;
however it happened carries no weight, here.
Each series of THOUGHTS must focus on something specific;
otherwise I lose meaning in an avalanche of words.
The important point carried high on this mast
is a flag with the words: from someone IDEA must come.
There is no such thing as "group IDEA";
the initial impetus must come from some singular person.
After IDEA has arrived on the scene,
it can be repeated as some pre-academic culture shock.
Once IDEA has achieved communicable status,
it's bandied about within the interested among humanity.
Which leaves a problem not rationally answered:
how does IDEA gain its foothold and its passion?
Acquiring information and then uniquely combining it,
leads to seeing REALITY in a different light.
Examining facts does not give rise to original THOUGHT,
mired in a boggy terrain of slippery slopes and shifty sand.
Final CONCEPTS are from inferences stacked on each other,
the sum of THOUGHTS' pasts leads to their future.
A leap of INTUITION is required to escape
from mundane to marvelous, swamp to air.
Knowledge is obtained from many diverse places,
seeing odd things, observations and transformations.
Those THOUGHTS then run 'round in crazy MIND,
children tumbling in handsprings and cartwheels.
A parody of how original IDEA becomes better, then best,
bouncing about among many RATIONAL mirrors.
Then up pops IDEA from out of playful MIND;
no RATIONAL process is responsible for the first one.

If IDEA is created from RATIONAL input, and its output
is also RATIONAL, then IDEA should also be RATIONAL.
Maybe IDEA can be cranked out by assembling facts,
so play the RATIONAL song thus created.
Notes on the scales are tuned to specific frequencies;
measures and exact timing make a song from mere notes.
Something between the notes makes a song,
and something between facts makes IDEA.
But IDEA can't be created without facts;
it's accumulation and combination which lead to theory.
Which leads right back to a theory with no existence,
until IDEA comes along to give it a kick in the pants.
A theory, which SCIENCE depends on for its existence,
has as its source IDEA, from an INTUITIVE jump start.
How can a RATIONAL view oversee all that can be,
when the basis of its theories is INTUITION by nature?
Therefore a RATIONAL view must not be able to envision all,
only the parts which commonly work within its purview.
Why do gods of SCIENCE attempt to describe all REALITY,
when they trespass on unknown shores with profane feet?
No theory arrives unless transported by IDEA,
which can then be modified using RATIONAL CONCEPTS.
REALITY will remain roaming free outside limited stables,
until CONCEPTIONS are known by their appropriate names.
There is a part of REALITY which is known to be RATIONAL,
and part which is irrational, it's not known rationally.
IDEAS do not come at the conclusion of logic;
this and this and this will not create IDEA out of nothing.
IDEA doesn't arise from pure deduction or induction;
there is some other impulse which makes it clear.
Very best IDEAS come when steady BRAIN slips a gear,
THOUGHTS run away and free MIND is lost in a never-land.
Still, IDEAS require some interaction with my senses;
1ˢᵗ FIRE was created because man wanted HEAT.
If IDEAS come from a biological computer,
then the same input will release the same output, always.
Computer don't always produce the same results,
even the best have errors and malfunctions.

A properly working computer is a GIGO machine, whereas
a properly working person produces varied outputs.
Then any 2 people of the same mental abilities should
be able to produce same IDEAS based on the same input.
Yet that is not the process to which anyone is subjected,
IDEAS typically come from the unusual and the stray.
Like from the mad genius, or the iconoclastic scientist,
bold new CONCEPTS don't arise from halls of academia.
They form in part on the personality surrounding them,
which is another missing piece of REALITY'S puzzle.
There seems to be some degree of unorthodox behavior
required to pass the barrier between can and can't.
Good IDEAS are infrequent, as observed herein;
bad ones arise frequently from rage and impatience.
IDEAS are very common, just not very unusual 1's;
I normally make do with those required for my daily tasks.
RATIONAL experience helps set up IDEA'S entrance,
form and language and an audience geared to listen.
Distinct perspectives, 2 of them working in tandem;
neither RATIONAL nor INTUITIVE, both are required.
A RATIONAL aide-de-camp is not what has been sought after,
this view is only a manifestation of IDEA, not its source.
IDEAS come from some source in living creatures;
as simple as a bird learning to use hair for a nest.
Tell of great IDEAS—humanity saved, gadgets created;
tell of those heights scaled by only RATIONAL application.
I can accept that a RATIONAL perspective is incomplete,
but I can't accept that it has an INTUITIVE view as its equal.
The most logical and most RATIONAL among us are not
the ones giving rise to sublime slippery secret speculations.
There are many brilliant people who have high I.Q.'s;
not all of them manage to reach beyond their grasp.
Traitors in THOUGHT create great IDEAS;
nonconforming freaks show the lie in a suitable display.
Heads of SCIENCE and other institutions aren't
generally the 1's who change the present path.
IDEA machines have many integrated parts:
not RATIONAL, not measurable, not repetitious, not divine.

From wherever IDEAS originate,
they are only as useful as neural connections make them.
INTUITION emerges from its solemn cocoon;
IDEA flits among frail flowers of THOUGHT, then dies.
Each IDEA springs into a RATIONAL perspective;
then passes to be replaced by CONCEPTS, or another IDEA.
Gods of SCIENCE cannot know themselves;
RATIONAL principles live a lie via attachment to INTUITION.
SCIENCE works because its theories can be proven;
even if they require an INTUITIVE source, they still function.
Since dominant methods are incapable of all-knowing;
other methods must be found to unearth REALITY'S booty.

16:28

Maybe I could have a little fun with Bob the shrink,
by changing my symptoms every TIME he comes to visit.
What is REALITY without repetition;
how can anything be known unless it repeats, and repeats?
Anybody knows me only by what evidence I give them,
and if it isn't consistent, then I shall remain an unknown.
A third bell announces the arrival of SCIENCE'S cat, for
repetition has no greater ability to claim REALITY'S mouse.
Observation and theory compose 2 parts of SCIENCE;
the best, repetition, has been saved for last.
Most trivially, it can be considered a game for the bored;
no winner, no loser, no point won on first turn.
There are many instances where it can be shown;
if I drop a ball at my feet, GRAVITY right here is consistent.
Bounce a ball on the end of a string for a pet cat;
a repetition which is real in its little BRAIN.
The ball does repeat its motion as long as I intend,
but that isn't natural repetition, it's temporary.
To the cat, it is repetition in all unimportant respects,
except for the one most dear—its connection to REALITY.
The cat sees repetition because it has limited awareness;
it has no capacity to deduce my involvement.

The bouncing ball is fake as repetition can be,
except to that which offers a swipe or pounce per swing.
The cat is still sensing repetition, not just imagining it;
laws of physics work the same whether I see them or not.
Until it gets bored, stretches and yawns,
leaving this game for another more pleasant.
SCIENCE has created rules which don't get bored;
repetition is the sameness with which REALITY exists.
Its limited view is all the cat can perceive,
a RATIONAL view made real until the impetus is removed.
As far as I can see, REALITY doesn't change its appearance,
so I'm able to recognize what is real from what isn't.
However, imagine jumping off a roof in plain sight
of any and all who would challenge REALITY'S dominance.
Left to my own limited GRAVITATIONAL FORCE attractions,
the ground will rush to greet me, same rate, each TIME.
Yet, the cat's little game is considered random repetition,
while the kiss to the ground has a more scientific iteration.
There should be no comparison between those 2,
FORCES of nature don't compare to FORCES of MIND.
What is the difference between the ball and the fall;
why does the cat not see what we see?
The cat and I can both see the same things,
it's CONCEPT afterwards which makes all the difference.
There are four possibilities which might lead to answers:
view, WILL, habit, and RATIONAL abilities are the corners.
Those possibilities lead only to more questions,
for they don't readily explain why repetition isn't the same.
Point of view determines which end of the string;
play with the ball, or be FORCE for impetus and change.
If I'm the 1 controlling those pieces in motion,
then I will see it as a game until hell freezes over.
Look at what the cat sees playing with the ball,
tick-tock, this will be its view of natural phenomena.
So I'm able to see the difference between ball and fall,
only if I can detect some sense of what makes it work.
Thus the point on repetition's ability to be clearly read,
a solely RATIONAL view may not see the whole panorama.

Part of my comprehension of repetition
depends on what point of view I'm currently engaging.
Next. For a ball to be swung that a cat sees as repeating,
WILL is required to put FORCE into muscle.
G-FORCE is responsible for my falling from the roof,
and SCIENCE gives the lie to any other opinion.
How is that known as fact—what causes GRAVITATION
to expend itself in a useless pursuit of forcing us down?
It's not animated WILL, of this I'm quite certain;
repetition isn't a fool's game created by divine REALITY.
Gods like SCIENCE have better ways to waste their TIME;
follow their instructions on what is allowed for belief.
I won't seriously consider sacred control of G-FORCES;
not even 1 omnipotent being would so waste his TIME.
Point of view is not allowed to assist the absence of WILL;
it has been given its own puzzle to resolve.
If I try to see the difference between ball and fall without using
a point of view, there is no WILL bouncing the ball.
Or there could be WILL bouncing all MATTER about;
a difference cannot be assumed unless one is seen to exist.
I know my WILL is responsible for bouncing the ball;
and only because of my god-like presence, to the cat.
Turn off rationality and try to envision REALITY;
enrich ourselves, we are not in so different a game.
WILL controls the ball—it's mine, I own it;
no WILL controls the fall—it's not like mine, I own it not.
Next. The main consideration given to proving the fall
is of habit and its connection to repetition.
If it happens again and again and again,
REASON demands that my MIND accept it as a constant.
The ball also moves again and again and again;
how many agains are sufficient to note a difference?
The ball won't move in the same fashion unless I will it so;
its repetition is of a limited nature.
How many times must falling occur before GRAVITATION
is known to be the cause and the curse?
There is no set number known as sufficient;
though 1 will probably suffice for my personal trial.

Propose a number satisfactory to all comers;
add one more, it will ring no more hollow than the first.
No series of events can ever be proven beyond dispute,
but there is no use living in the shadow of doubt.
The proof accepted by all people comes from the number
of instances passed when falling is no longer convenient.
I accept the proof of repetition in my own MIND,
which is different than the 1 carried by another.
Research the torch Hume carried so well;
finding effect following cause is an habitual flame.
Effect and cause are 2 separate events,
not so much connected as they are conjoined.
GRAVITATION is known because we habitually see its results;
although its actual place within REALITY is still unknown.
Habit shows me some FORCE inspires falling;
G-FORCE is what I infer from my sensed PERCEPTIONS.
Next. Repetition will be found in the most likely place,
the RATIONAL abilities connecting crime with criminal.
Human beings will find more relations than other animals,
BRAIN'S cerebrum grants a wider RATIONAL perspective.
Try jerking a ball up and down in front of a sentient face;
it should be able very quickly to ascertain WILL.
I'm able to observe 1 cause and 1 effect,
and my RATIONAL ability allows me to match the 2.
A Homo-centric RATIONAL view makes repetition certain;
a felis-centric view accepts most events as natural.
GRAVITATIONAL FORCE is recent THOUGHT in human history,
and still animals understand—what goes up, comes down.
Humanity flounders about trying to force events,
when maximum control is limited to here and now.
That is how humanity has managed to survive;
even more, forcing events is how civilization succeeds.
View, WILL, habit, and RATIONAL ability are the corners
upon which repetition uplifts gods of SCIENCE.
I'm so HAPPY to learn there is a rationale,
some method as to why SCIENCE is so successful.
Find an irrational attachment to all that matters,
for gods are not RATIONAL because they are RATIONAL.

17:23

Bob the shrink also gave me a battery of tests,
which won't help him since I made up ½ the answers.
Does testing reveal a supreme portrait of REALITY,
or is holy importance attached to a limited process?
If the test is fair, on both sides, REALITY is accurate;
measurement is a primary method for uncovering it.
Gods of SCIENCE *are useful, and have a flawed dictum:*
if it cannot be measured or observed, then it does not exist.
No use can be made of a formless essence;
as far as a RATIONAL view is concerned, it doesn't exist.
Maybe useless for creating machines from something else;
why must an essence be useful in order to exist?
Mankind doesn't live in an Eden, survival isn't easy;
making use of REALITY is how man converts it into his own.
Within a RATIONAL *realm, that dictum is the law of the land,*
after the prime one of seeing cause and effect by repetition.
Every extant OBJECT can be observed and measured;
this is how CONCEPTS come from my PERCEPTIONS.
Gods should stick to their allotted domains,
and not attempt to control REALITY *beyond their reach.*
SCIENCE will always attempt to extend itself;
I won't know my limits until I reach them.
If it is not sensed, it will never fit within a RATIONAL *realm,*
never be subject to the will of rigid gods.
Those OBJECTS I observe have definite parameters;
whether taste or touch, something must fire my senses.
Anything not convenient for human CONSUMPTION
has no RATIONAL *existence, it is banned from that home.*
Civilization is the march toward human convenience,
hot and cold put only where they are wanted.
Knowledge received from gods has one PURPOSE *alone:*
modify REALITY *and make it more accommodating.*
I can turn a rock of iron into a sword or plowshare,
so laws of nature aren't violated in order to benefit myself.
There is no understanding bound in comfortable PURPOSE;
REALITY *is rationally understood only as necessary.*

Understanding REALITY and not using it makes no sense;
there is no PURPOSE to my existence without my abilities.
There has been no need to understand REALITY before now,
partial CONCEPTION will suffice to bend an ignoble knee.
If part of REALITY is firmly beyond useful application,
then my RATIONAL part may be all I really need to know.
If SCIENCE gods currently know the nature of all that is,
why do their dictates change from year to year?
SCIENCE changes as new information is discovered;
it doesn't know REALITY, just an evolving picture of it.
Maybe because knowing all of REALITY is not in its grasp,
forever approaching with an empty outstretched hand.
That isn't a problem for most scientists;
they would be out of a job if all REALITY was exposed.
Quantum Mechanics, the deity of the small,
has known all along the limits of its reach.
A discipline which recognizes observation is limited;
at a subatomic level my interference is guaranteed.
Quanta known by what they can observe and measure,
yet subatomic traits violate the rules of its brethren.
Quantum Mechanics tries to live in 2 worlds;
measurement there allows only 1 of 2 QUANTITIES.
Some priests have even ventured into heresy,
moving the theory from gods of SCIENCE to RELIGION.
It isn't SCIENCE to insert divinity into MATTER;
I don't accept its existence as ultimately supernatural.
Problems arise by attempting to rationally create
OBJECTS and ENERGIES beyond physical PERCEPTION.
Subatomic particles aren't sensed in themselves;
they are assumed by FORCES they leave in their wake.
Take for instance SCIENCE gods' greatest lack—
truly knowing LIFE, what makes it tick, why it can live.
SCIENCE has determined a chemical nature for ORGANISMS,
ENERGY contained within molecular interstices.
Those gods will never be able to explain or understand
LIFE which is more than ashes from a greater whole.

17:53

I shouldn't be too hard on a man just doing his job;
each can only think according to how he is trained.
Years upon years of formal educational training
will undoubtedly teach independent MIND to succumb.
Whereas I've been partially trained and partially left alone,
so I'm more open to IDEAS that make no RATIONAL sense.
What are the criteria which make any view valid;
why should a RATIONAL one be better than INTUITION?
A RATIONAL view is so successful because of SCIENCE's aid,
giving of itself so selfishly to benefit me and mine.
RATIONAL dominance would fall back into its place
if the processes which support it were exposed as INTUITION.
Scientific methods are based on 3 tight parameters:
observation, theory, and innumerable repetition.
Each of those brethren is incomplete in itself; the whole
ball of wax melts when subjected to introspection.
If it can't be measured, then it doesn't exist;
SCIENCE has an infallible method for proving its theories.
Yet gods of SCIENCE propose particles below measurement,
hypocritically denying ambiguity and also requiring it.
Everything scientists postulate is subject to review;
non-sensible MATTER can be inferred from experimentation.
Pause and ask the gods to make their WILL known,
send forth a sign if a RATIONAL view has fled its fixed home.
So SCIENCE and a RATIONAL view are incomplete;
nothing is offered in their place but tricks and traps.
Full of sly innuendo and falsity leading nowhere,
there are no better teachers than human gods.
SCIENCE has never attempted to claim perfection,
unlike its critics who never actually DO anything.
Is REALITY not perfect;
does anyone claim it is missing some pieces?
I haven't yet been shown much worth seeing;
expose what is beyond my perspective, don't trash SCIENCE.
A short summary is like rationality,
nearly equal to the task, yet not quite reaching the ring.

If the goal is to find use in what I conceive, I reach it;
if the goal is something more wispy, I may not.
Nevertheless, it is close enough for government work;
the major point has been brought out, if quietly.
There must be more to discover in a search for TRUTH,
finding faults in my vision is simply more limitation.
Is a RATIONAL view able to twist itself to see differently
as easily as it has been able to hide from TRUTH?
I don't hide from what REALITY has to offer;
it only makes sense to use the gifts nature bestows.
Look at the broader point within these reflections:
a RATIONAL view is limited, there must be more.
So any disrespect shown to SCIENCE has been subterfuge;
the point comes out by witnessing the whole.
RATIONAL can no longer claim a sole perspective;
still, how does anyone see but from one point of view?
I accept a RATIONAL view's dominance because of its value;
an INTUITIVE view must have value or I will reject it.
These are not ravings from some neo-luddite, earth first!
Tearing down all that is so we can wallow in the mud.
There is limited value to be gained by superior bashing;
it only lowers the highest, it doesn't raise the lowest.
Some believe gods of SCIENCE should go quietly,
into some other land to amuse and abuse themselves.
An even larger segment of society enjoys prosperity,
the benefits which only a RATIONAL perspective can bring.
A common failing from over-application of INTUITION,
mistaking impotent desires for DREAM of lost BEAUTY.
Mankind will gain nothing by returning to savagery;
another perspective won't be able to replace rationality.
What is not understood cannot be replaced,
which is what priests have been futilely attempting to do.
I see no mass evacuation planned from a RATIONAL view;
there is no better way to survive in this universe.
How about alternate THOUGHT forms from nether reaches,
induced to leave the placid pastures of an exiled domain?
Maybe I could learn to coax THOUGHTS from elsewhere,
dark places where I imagine a RATIONAL view doesn't rule.

Everything is not RATIONAL, *consigned to be its* MATTER,
mixing and matching chemicals in random ways.
Seeking order out of chaos is my proven path;
if the chains on REALITY are loosened, this might be lost.
A problem which has arisen since one view has been king
is cramming consciousness into a too small container.
A RATIONAL view is only too small if REALITY isn't CONCEPT,
enlarged beyond the possibility of being rolled into a ball.
Cut the legs out from under the RATIONAL *giant!*
Then we will be able to see it eye to eye.
As long as I hold a RATIONAL view in an exalted place,
it will not lower itself to be seen as an equal.
It has grown too large to let it continue to rumble about,
childishly breaking its toys because they work.
The blessings bestowed by SCIENCE are impersonal;
an unstable leader can benefit as well as a scientist.
Creating MINDS *and politics with no heart and no* SOUL,
why should RATIONAL *winners be expected to have feelings?*
Blame shouldn't be laid on people who behave,
especially when they act in the manner they are trained.
Search beyond known SPACE *and* TIME *to* INFINITY,
there exists more to REALITY *than a* RATIONAL *realm.*
Within the finitely measured reaches of SPACE and TIME,
nothing can displace a RATIONAL perspective.
Beware of erecting false gods before which to kneel,
which must then be slain on the path to finding TRUTH.

18:34

Bob looks at me like everyone else, trapped in his view—
the convicted filthy child molester—kill it!
No hope should be held for seeing another viewpoint;
most people have trouble just acknowledging the obvious.
The RATIONAL view has been available for centuries,
and still the average person refuses to utilize it fully.
Leave the limited view to look in another direction;
yet stop and take one last look behind.

A RATIONAL perspective of what can be known
is created from FINITE essences to my MIND'S convenience.
There are rules to follow which cannot be broken,
or else the entire structure shall come tumbling down.
Cause and effect are the primary observations,
a habit from perceiving repetition of similar events.
A barrier falls between known and unknown,
based on how the nature of each is acquired.
CONCEPTS are transmitted by language, math is concise,
but none exist outside of a RATIONAL domain.
There is a barrier surrounding the RATIONAL realm,
keeping its view whole despite an irrational invasion.
It requires strenuous labor to forego that which is known,
turn my back on it, and accept truly irrational behavior.
Keep ripe MIND'S eye peeled for another way,
REALITY which may exchange, yet does not require it.

****

20:14

A wise man once said:
mix together like milk and water, not oil and water.
If only it were so easy to resolve man's natural disputes,
2 opposing sides normally contest for determination.
DREAMS of power hold demure MIND in thrall;
white noise turning color into many shades of gray.
But it's through opposition that a society is distilled;
even 1 personality doesn't mix like milk and water.
Look at a weighted scale, the type with two ends;
is it better to lean to one side, or to balance in the middle?
The problem lies in how to bring opposition into balance;
show me how to blend fully, and not into parts.
Show those few noble citizens who mix love and anger,
at each moment, without preference for one over the other.
If mixing were easy, it wouldn't be considered wise;
more is needed than EMOTION to form persons into a people.

Love and anger begin as EMOTIONS, *becoming* CONCEPTIONS,
which funnel REALITY *through the strainer of* DUALITY.
But this is how REALITY becomes humanly possible,
taking part-hold of an essence too hard to grasp whole.
Only a RATIONAL *view of* REALITY *requires* CONCEPTION;
INTUITION *exists fully on its own, beyond* THOUGHT.
That unfocused perspective hasn't yet presented its use;
there are no markers signifying its arrival.
*Anything irrational can be seen as non-*RATIONAL;
thus mystical INTUITION *should be revealed to begin here.*
Then once again I'm just devolving REALITY into CONCEPTS,
trading 1 solid THOUGHT for another not so solid.
The wisest path is the uncertain one in the middle,
using RATIONAL THOUGHT *to expose obscure* INTUITION.
Let me get this straight—to mix like milk and water,
I have to abandon CONCEPTS, but only by using CONCEPTS.
Now the paradoxical nature of REALITY *begins to unfold;*
combining <is and is not> *is not an irrational problem.*
The bounds of my credulity stretch with that procedure;
the advice referred to his followers, not different views.
Does human opposition have a source besides perspective;
can milk and water mix in a world of oil and water?
This is going to be quite a trick,
combining opposing perspectives into an intelligible whole.
A RATIONAL *view has its own fixed walled-in existence;*
a portal must be opened for its counterpart in INTUITION.
My view of REALITY classifies 1 as distinct from the other,
and distinction inevitably leads to some preference.
How can opposites be contained within the same whole;
how are we to distinguish them without preference?

20:33

This is the 1st instance I've ever cried over my fate;
I guess I've just gotten tired of anger running away with me.
Bound up with desire for happiness and joy in LIFE
is a more pressing, easily denied, need for acceptance

After having been branded a child molester, a baby fucker,
no one will ever look at me as a decent human being again.
Is any one perspective more important than TRUTH;
should anger come if lurid names arrive without it?
How people judge me is how I'm used to judging others;
if their views can be so violently wrong, then so can mine.
The land where a RATIONAL view is known has been shown,
which until now was a sufficiently complete point of view.
It has been, and will remain, known for what it is:
the primary method used for accessing OBJECTS.
Now turn focused attention to INTUITION'S perspective;
what some call irrational is a utopian's home.
That is the view forbidden to those with a RATIONAL bent,
where sensation is unavailable, where THOUGHTS roam free.
There may be other lands under the sun, yet PERCEPTION
is limited to what light lays open to sight.
What a RATIONAL view sees is invisible to an INTUITIVE view,
and the reverse relation is just as difficult to grasp.
OBJECTS of either land pass from the sight of foreign eyes,
a ship's horn off the horizon, fog spacing a fixed glare.
There is something there just beyond my ken,
a daydream made solid until it's handled.
It is like riding in an airplane, looking at the clouds;
from inside they invite errant toes to wiggle among them.
But once outside that safe RATIONAL barrier,
REALITY rears its head, and fantasy becomes dangerous.
Thus a RATIONAL view is granted protective primary traits:
repetition, mathematics, and a limitation to FINITY seas.
Structures which are necessary for a RATIONAL perspective;
if they aren't included, then it's in an irrational view.
Thus the vestments of INTUITION have none of that mess;
what possibilities are seen in their place, what is lost?
Herein this world repetition holds fast to its fixed duty;
look to what isn't found here for what may be found there.
A few guesses may wash up on the shores of INTUITION:
solitude, unity, loneliness, the one deity.
Well . . . pick 1 and see how it rides,
unless they are the same in some singular convention.

There is one commonality for what rears into sight,
call it episodic—needing no other, complete in itself.
Rationality must be repeated, an INTUITIVE view is alone;
what is required for SCIENCE is banned for true RELIGION.
INTUITION'S land has no repetition and no attachments,
no clinging gods to grant absolution.
Knowledge of it must be learned in some school;
SCIENCE or RELIGION somehow cover all the bases.
Each moment of REALITY from within the interminable
view is uniquely formed, no more and no less.
Then no one can teach me how to see an INTUITIVE view,
if each 1 seen is never to be repeated.
Pay massive attention! One exists to fade
in and out, and then passes on to its most timely grave.
Then dig it up and look at its moldy corpse;
if it has a past, then its MEMORY has a present.
Each different episode flies past right through TIME,
no matter how each one may appear to be similar.
Repetition is based on familiarity between similar events,
close enough to fit in broad classifications.
Episodes are distinctive underneath its gray veil;
events peeking into a world rarely seen.
REALITY allows for both to exist;
an INTUITIVE view is seen by rationality as luck or chance.
Folly follows where episodes never exist;
within a RATIONAL perspective it has no form, no event.
Then 1 episode after another marches off to eternity,
never forking or taking a wrong turn.
What use is an INTUITIVE view if it cannot be repeated;
what is knowledge that cannot be unwrapped and eaten?
Commonly, knowledge is used to remake MATTER;
this is within RATIONAL possession, there must be another.
Look closely through the doors of sensual PERCEPTION;
we have a key, find the lock where it fits.
The term "episode" fits into a box of conceptual size;
there must be a bigger 1 where it doesn't fit.
Repetition is useful and cannot be denied;
although on this trail it must be left as carrion for vultures.

CONCEPTS are limited in what they describe,
and I'm trying to formalize an unlimited difference.
INTUITION sees past all that is, all that was, all that will be;
and then can be deposited in only an approximate fashion.
No matter how hard I strive, it won't be exactly expressed,
a solely RATIONAL face doesn't fit on an INTUITIVE body.
Translate it into Mandarin if it fully fills the bill.
Is there a better way; how is the whole given in pieces?
Silence appears to be my best answer;
something that large doesn't fit neatly in many places.
A RATIONAL view has a field which also grows mathematics,
quick with its wits and also repetitious foibles.
The preferred language of SCIENCE,
also how the useful view is expressed most eloquently.
Other beasts have grown up under gods' tender thumb,
facets of LIFE sung with ambivalent words in full verse.
EMOTIONS and aesthetics and artistry and QUALITY,
all parts of an enigma that a RATIONAL view fails to resolve.
A view of what can only be communicated as translucent;
no single-moment clarity—no inexpressibly clear vision.
Measured to a standard with an impersonal bias,
living traits don't withstand scientific scrutiny.
Phonetic languages attempt to express INTUITION,
to avoid totally empty cells in a numerical census.
Math has trouble with CONCEPTS refusing to be locked
and loaded into a formula quantifying TIME and SPACE.
The meanings are imprecise and subject to restatement;
the words are firm, with explanation lacking substance.
Dualistic views existing with no SPACE between them,
and an impassable gulf of exact meaning.
Look for BEAUTY and see it found in dissimilar flowers;
an internal taste which changes from past to future.
Fasting makes me hunger for things I really don't like;
there is no rationale for why fixed taste buds change.
INTUITION is spontaneous, unique in its self-expression;
jokes requiring explication are not humorous.
So something about each moment is irrevocable;
clarity exists only by being here, not remembering it.

A beautiful feeling is never to return;
visit again the same flower with different petals.
The moment is beyond my robotic hand's ability to grasp;
I can't hold flower and petal and feeling and BEAUTY.
It is a joy to rest BEAUTY in hand for its brief LIFE;
grasping at it only loses the precious moment into air.
There is nothing there left for me to hold;
closing my hand into a fist, I touch nothing with myself.
Clarity exists, a moment, an instant, no . . . smaller;
this is enough TIME to see its PURPOSE open, then close.
An instant is lost as soon as it's noticed;
micro-micro-seconds are too long to time its existence.
A RATIONAL realm also gives definition to its OBJECTS,
thereby forcing limitation onto its FINITY relations.
An OBJECT is conceived from how senses perceive it to be,
and each sense has a built-in biological limitation.
Gods of SCIENCE have limited THOUGHT to measurements;
thus INFINITY is precluded by math's modern derivation.
Math has created a symbol which acknowledges INFINITE;
its existence has helped to shorten many a formula's strife.
INFINITY daily dispensed by stern teachers of rote
is actually not-FINITY, this is all.
INFINITE and not-FINITE essentially mean the same thing,
DUALISM of perspectives shown in another form.
And yet another term was created to fulfill not-FINITY,
TRANSFINITY has rationally replaced INFINITY as unending.
FINITE CONCEPT of 1 is much like the other;
some distinctions only matter to certified mathematicians.
INFINITY does not fit within a RATIONAL perspective;
only INTUITION can house both its small and large sizes.
CONCEPT by its nature must be FINITE in scope;
therefore if has form, it must be held in a fixed view.
Ghost-friend MIND can see into INFINITY;
its poor brainy relation never leaves FINITY far behind.

21:36

I can still look in a mirror and know who is looking back,
but I fear, as the days pass, my true self will disappear.
Is the face presented to the world expression of an ego,
or is it a reflection of the id shifting with consensus?
Looking in the mirror, I don't see the monster others see;
there is only 1 of me, but he remains overlooked.
How can there be two different accurate realistic views;
when does one end and allow the other to come loose?
If I observe myself or any OBJECT coming into sight,
my senses will grant me PERCEPTIONS of its existence.
Hoping within a book to gain information, gain LIFE,
go ahead and look at the images pasted on the rear!
So something may be stuck on a book's rear end,
this has nothing to do with a difference in view.
Was it known to be there by looking at the front,
or maybe it appeared in the instant it was turned over?
Either I see it or I don't;
only by using my eyes is the back able to be seen.
Any OBJECT is composed of dimensions with opposing sides,
and each different side cannot be seen at the same instant.
Unaided, the back and the front aren't sensed together,
which makes me rethink how this concerns perspective.
A similar problem exists for RATIONAL and INTUITIVE views,
each takes all eyes and leaves none for the other.
A solitary perspective is all my MIND will handle;
either I perceive from within, or I perceive from without.
Seeing a grand vista assigns no-bird to a cage;
released from bondage it will shed casual horizons.
Confinement can be viewed as good or bad;
it depends on which side of the bars the observer is sitting.
Can right or wrong be assigned to different views,
by binding RATIONAL meaning to indifferent INTUITION?
Love good, anger bad; war good, peace bad;
it's a natural reaction to favor 1 side over the other.
Circumstance gives resolution to episodic dilemmas,
each view offering potential solutions to any problem.

RATIONAL solutions to survive a hostile universe;
INTUITIVE solutions for . . . I don't know what.
If someone is flung from a wrecked car right in front,
seeking action from INTUITION is the choice of an ass.
The majority of my actions have predictable results,
so it behooves me normally to act in a RATIONAL manner.
Overdependence on seeing rationality in everything
makes seekers look without when answers are within.
Then this is where remaining REALITY will be found:
looking within for a completely useless essence.
Whenever someone decrees his one view is right,
this is TIME to punish transgression's moral wrong.
It can never be wrong to see a RATIONAL or INTUITIVE view,
only to superficially validate 1, and not the other.
Yet one is sometimes expected and the other pops up;
is it method or madness where each view is equally grown?
Undesired results can occur when either perspective
is misapplied to circumstances which demand the other.
How can anything be demanded of INTUITION
if there is no possible use to be gained from its existence?
INTUITIVE PURPOSE should be obvious front to back,
like any 3-d OBJECT which has hidden sides.
The back of a book holds no required place in MEMORY;
until it is observed, a head will remain without a tail.
In order to know any OBJECT it must be sensed,
and the more it's sensed, the better it will be known.
Anything conceived on heaven or earth
gleans a clearer picture from more distinct views.
My understanding of REALITY is dependent on CONCEPTS,
and using 5 senses fills out more than just using 4.
Dependence on RATIONAL sensation has failed in its goal
to provide harmony and peace, happiness without strife.
Living standards have improved with greater SCIENCE;
population has grown because material needs are met.
A separate and distinct perspective can determine
answers where the edge of another is forecast to falter.
RATIONAL solutions mandate REALITY must be altered;
the way it exists now doesn't fit human ideals.

What if REALITY itself does not have to change, instead
actions could be woven to fit an existing pattern?
Actions must change REALITY since they are part of it;
the pattern of the universe is how man makes it.
Presenting an unorthodox scene in traditional voice asks
clarity to suffer from a noisy dissenting chorus.
Present an INTUITIVE view in any manner whatsoever,
it will still sound irrational to my ears.
A simple question may help to lighten the load:
what is useful?
It must 1st fulfill a living creature's survival needs;
or it must offer satisfaction for individual wants.
Raging shoals must be controlled for convenience,
while calmer waters are grateful for any help granted.
REALITY is a chaotic puzzle of MATTER;
it works according to rules, which make it fit together.
A bee does not fly in a straight line to reach its hive;
there is no such thing as a straight line in nature.
Look at where the sky touches a lake, a spider's strand,
pine needles, or the straight wave in which light travels.
All are examples of lines approximately perceived;
although they can be close, look closer—they are not lines.
But PERCEPTION of REALITY is based upon my senses,
and if they are only approximate, then they are not-right.
A forest can be seen as a farm for board-feet,
or a haven for flea-bitten deer and their ilk.
REALITY comes as I'm prepared to receive it;
CONCEPTS in my MIND depend on personal PERCEPTIONS.
The Mona Lisa could sell for a lot of money,
or be left to gaze at those rich as well as poor in vision.
All creatures possess senses of some form,
but in different degrees, which affect their CONCEPTS.
Radical procedures may cure cancer's rancid bite,
yet prayer never hurts to gain reprieve for new LIFE.
A man may choose to see rationally or intuitively,
and his results provide information on the correct choice.
One perspective finds nothing except RATIONAL value;
gamble with INTUITION'S currency and lose it in an instant.

Rationality and use and repetition are all tied together,
which is how ORGANISMS interact with universal MATTER.
Use is constrained by value's limiting fence,
high and wide enough to separate QUANTITY from QUALITY.
More is better from a RATIONAL perspective;
better is more via an INTUITIVE counterview.
INTUITION finds most value where a RATIONAL view is least,
as YIN merges with YANG to make the other compliant.
Society spurns an INTUITIVE view because it's irrational,
even though my RATIONAL view is incomplete without it.
A society where gods of RELIGION surrender to SCIENCE,
mandating that INTUITION use RATIONAL tools.
Modern RELIGION has lost touch with the inner view;
it has succumbed to a RATIONAL good in order to heal evil.
INTUITION has been shown here with only a slight glance,
of course common sense is lost by gaining this foothold.

22:29

Though I strive forever to make my inner TRUTH known,
it isn't possible for others to see me as I truly am.
Do each of us possess access to unique inner TRUTH,
something which exists past the brand of right or wrong?
Each man is only able to see what is within his purview;
I can no more see another man's than he is able to see mine.
Blind to each other, blind to REALITY, blind to INTUITION;
one view exposes no more than nature allows it to show.
The perspective society has claimed as universal,
the 1 purporting to show REALITY, is totally RATIONAL.
If there is only a RATIONAL perspective,
why do many CONCEPTIONS come from a different source?
There are many accepted CONCEPTS, it's a fact,
which defy any RATIONAL attempt at understanding.
Expressing love to our dearest heart
with justification is like making FIRE with green wood.
EMOTION and REASON are different parts of REALITY,
appealing to 1 won't entice the other.

A totally one-sided method of viewing the world
has made INTUITION'S view irrational—thus derogatory.
Academia has created a culture where rationality rules;
disrespect me with either name—irrational or lawyer.
Call LIFE irrational, if this has not already been assumed.
Xie xie! What is given as slander will be taken as a gift.
If RATIONAL and INTUITIVE perspectives are in opposition,
then it's quite sensible that a slur should be a compliment.
The basis for the modern state of affairs comes via viewing
INTUITION'S panoramic agent through RATIONAL lenses.
I get the sense REALITY is a big wide ocean,
and I'm forced to see it through a bouncing porthole.
That window is tinted with a polarized film, excluding
all that cannot be from developing.
This is a problem haunting philosophers over many lives:
how VOID can both exist and not exist.
Glasses formed of INTUITION polarize in a different fashion,
including the possibilities of all TIME and all SPACE.
Those things not existing within a RATIONAL perspective,
may or must exist within an INTUITIVE perspective.
INTUITION will always welcome material additions,
yet be it known—a person cannot be part of the crowd.
That makes no sense!
A whole is composed of nothing if not its parts.
Know this as TRUTH in REALITY:
INTUITION includes RATIONAL, RATIONAL excludes INTUITION.
Therefore an INTUITIVE view sees a whole with parts,
while a RATIONAL view sees parts building a whole.
INTUITION assumes possible, RATIONAL knows impossible;
REALITY can exist in a universe beyond sensation.
Practitioners of SCIENCE often do put on blinders,
labeling much of REALITY as impossible before it's proven.
It is irrational to be here and there
at identical TIMES, yet it is not impossible.
RATIONAL THOUGHTS won't expand past given boundaries,
by which any OBJECT also can't be in 2 places at once.
Do not seek to corner INTUITION into being unreasonable;
think about the identity between irrational and impossible.

If it's possible to be in 2 places at once, then do it,
and show how an Intuitive view can spread Reality.
Can it be done, an ability without universal application?
Still, the possibility is acknowledged by the question.
Possibilities are as limitless as bad Ideas,
which don't even reach probable, much less factual.
They exist in imagination, those possibilities,
and if they do not exist, how do they get into fertile Mind?
More infernal questions with irrational answers,
I can only attempt to resolve those that make sense.
Irrational words such as Quality and Beauty and Truth
are more than the nothing substituting for daily Life;
more than the nothing rejected from use;
more than the nothing which cannot be spoken;
more than the nothing found more dead than alive;
more than the nothing sitting idle and broken.
If any Concept is accepted as owning individual value,
then it must have some existence within Reality.
Intuition consigned to success is buried out of sight,
yet that which must exist cannot be forever forbidden.
Known Reality deals to buy a fully realized meaning,
Intuitive Concepts must show value to be accepted.
Why do irrational Conceptions exist at all;
are we all insane to create words without meaning?
Every term has meaning based on how it's viewed;
the mistake is looking outside when the light is inside.
If we are insane, then suffer Life to hang from this cross;
yet why do we all have the same beautiful insanity?

23:04

It's obvious a single view can be more powerful;
my current state is due to another more coercive view.
Yet if one view is closer to Truth than the other,
should not it be the more dominant of the pair?
Neither view is more right, neither view is more wrong;
I'm quite sure my own view is somehow flawed.

Any perspective perceives a whole presence on display;
although any whole is no more than part of a bigger one.
My perspective of REALITY is whole and complete to me,
but by including other valid views, mine becomes a piece.
How is INTUITION to be known ambiguously;
can CONCEPTION of the whole be in mere parts and pieces?
A rationally known whole is constructed in that manner;
if there are missing pieces, then there is no whole.
This is its curse and significant other blessing;
the whole is never transmitted, just its approximation.
My MIND is nominally assumed to build from the small;
maybe with effort I can subtract from the large.
What is actually grown on pastures of INTUITION,
dies before it can be forced to forage in another realm.
THOUGHTS are a poor imitation of an INTUITIVE view,
another barrier between PERCEPTION and CONCEPT.
An additional message is important to relate:
a veiled view is virgin, it denies perversion from outside.
RATIONAL investigation won't alter INTUITIVE purity;
I can only change my understanding, not the source.
No irrational experiences may be retained in MEMORY;
they are carbs <not fat> to be burned and disposed.
So I'm left with a view—it can't be taught or used—
. . . 1 and 1 and 1 and 1 and 1 and 1 and 1 equal nothing.
Why are there only two limited views of REALITY;
why should existence be confined in this manner?
Embracing 2 perspectives today is more than yesterday,
and any CONCEPT of REALITY seems to come in pairs.
A RATIONAL view is formed to enforce sense from sense;
INTUITION is left to spout nonsense from no sense.
There may be a part of REALITY beyond my CONCEPTS because
its essence is as 1, not 2.
Each person has private individual views,
grouped into dualistic CONCEPTION for broad relation.
DUALISM is the method upon which my BRAIN operates;
2 views make the form accommodating my CONCEPTS.
DUALITY gives form to all CONCEPTIONS;
they grow in this fashion—twin lobes on each leaf.

Concepts hold Rational in one hand, Intuitive in the other,
weighted to 1 side to show how they are viewed.
If both weigh the same, Life is motion in balance;
a delicate act between properties performed with no net.
Rational Quantities tied to Intuitive Qualities,
but all Concepts seem to have more of 1 or the other.
Reality is perceived both rationally and intuitively;
Rational owns everything extant in Time and Space.
There is a substance to Reality, even interminable Void,
a unifying essence to all Space and Time.
Intuition collects by looking within for all that is,
unified in one source before falling into Conception.
Unique Concepts form from looking in singular directions;
otherwise, nothing different will ever be seen.
Each Conception bears more fraternal twins,
possessed of similar characteristics, and quite distinct.
Each half of dualistic Concept is itself dualistic;
every Thought grasped is at least 1 of 2.
A Rational view sees Matter when closed for inspection,
and when its interior is open, Star is detected.
There are 2 general types of Objects in this universe,
and understanding of them is dependent on my senses.
An Intuitive view sees Life when enclosed by a membrane,
and when unfettered and free it is suspected to be Soul.
There are 2 untouchable essences in that universe,
and understanding of them comes with a feeling.
It is easy to further subdivide Rational Conceptions, only,
greater dissection of Intuition takes more insight.
For now it's enough to absorb irrational transgressions,
violations of essential universal recognition.
Perfect minimal Conception of Reality is paired opposites;
it is nature's way for lovebirds to exist together.
Then Reality must be the exception that proves the rule;
it's everything, including where it isn't.
Yet only one of the birds can be held at each Time,
so full is its breast, so sweet is its song.
Each perspective is bound to a distinct part of Reality;
my Mind can't hold but 1 view in each instant.

REALITY is created as the ultimate unlimited jewel,
with INFINITY facets aligned in FINITY pairs.
Another aspect of REALITY'S dominance over perspective:
every CONCEPT must be born from 1 or the other.
Each face glistens with its own peculiar light,
reflecting inner dimensions of its inadequate partner.
It's a mystery as to why I conceive REALITY in this manner,
where 1 forms into 2, polar opposites all the way.
Gods of SCIENCE approach realistic phenomena by getting
finitely closer with each remarkable observation.
Modern society has marvels undreamed by primitive man;
SCIENCE is forever edging forward into the great unknown.
Like the half-lives of radioactive decay,
always halfway closer to crossing the line into INFINITY.
If knowledge is bound up into FINITE CONCEPTS,
SCIENCE'S best hope is for getting ever closer to REALITY.
A RATIONAL perspective, as led by the gods of SCIENCE,
will never see that of which it is structurally incapable.
It's a strange predicament a RATIONAL view is in,
each CONCEPT is a whole, but only as part of a larger 1.
Intuitively experienced or rationally measured,
a message of DUALITY helps uncover REALITY'S singularity.
The world around me is phenomenal, things happen,
and each event can be either experienced or measured.
When any river is experienced, fully or not,
the same one never crosses the same rock twice, or more.
REALITY occurs at 1 specific TIME in 1 specific place;
then it moves on, never to brush that location again.
INTUITION'S experience is thus episodic,
complete without a partner, no history and no future.
So a RATIONAL view can only approximate an INTUITIVE view;
the latter can't be held long enough to formally conceive it.
Measuring an event requires at least a threesome,
which is as approximately kinky as metaphysics gets.
SCIENCE uses measurement to quantify REALITY,
a redundant description of the same thing.
There must be two physical references to compare,
and an outside observer to create the measuring scale.

A second is made by comparing Cesium to the sun,
with an experimenter deciding on an acceptable length.
Priests use numbers attempting to recreate all that is,
an imperfect mirror showing a face with no lines.
However close a measurement may be,
physics has shown observers interfering with experiments.
A RATIONAL view is not directly observed,
sensation impels impulses to physical BRAIN for translation.
Senses are the form of RATIONAL PERCEPTION,
carried to BRAIN, and transferred as CONCEPT to my MIND.
This is why measurements are so useful:
to give experience to that which cannot sense it.
Animal BRAIN is locked away from direct experience;
quantification helps to make sense of its PERCEPTIONS.
Experience is more accurately "experience the moment;"
measurement is more precisely "measure the moments."
I can choose to do either, but not both,
and my choice will determine which PERCEPTION is received.
Experience of INTUITION is instantaneously immeasurable,
no better explanation can be offered for preservation.
Nothing within an INTUITIVE view can be firmly grasped;
QUALITY doesn't lend itself to quantification.
INTUITION'S perspective is impossible to imprint,
each person must look within for a private reading.
If an INTUITIVE view is experienced moment by moment,
then only within a living being can it occur.
There exists just this possibility . . . no . . . this probability,
there is a lucid view from INTUITION, and it is not RATIONAL.

24:05

The things I see are real to me, they make sense,
but for all I really know they could be just a fantasy.
Everybody likes their illusions, this is why we have them;
the problem is to discern fantasy's end and REALITY'S start.
My current condition isn't fantasy, maybe a nightmare,
and REALITY has shown no PURPOSE in confined living.

In a RATIONAL realm, which contains all that can be,
can LIFE be created out of the chemically inert?
I've got an existence dominated by MATTER,
and there is a living part of me which appears to be more.
Gods of SCIENCE have made fantastic claims for LIFE,
yet it still cannot be created from chance elements.
At this moment the creation of creatures is out of reach,
but SCIENCE has promised it will soon fall at man's feet.
LIFE will always be out of a RATIONAL grasp,
it only puts on a material face for enacting its PURPOSE.
Already the genetic vault has been cracked, codes taken;
think of all the cruel diseases waiting to be cured.
Programming through which bears can grow into whales;
it is arrogant to hope LIFE'S KARMA can be superseded.
It's cruel to abandon those born less fortunate,
when the price to help them is surprisingly light.
How much TIME and how many mistakes are required
before priests will admit their gods are fallible?
Any new technology has a few mistakes before it's ready,
and then miraculous miracles should prosper and flow.
Are a "few mistakes" sufficient to offer in trade;
who made this bargain without nature's permission?
The EVOLUTION of SCIENCE isn't fostered by committee;
when a majority rules, nothing much happens.
Destroy a few cities, like Nagasaki and Hiroshima;
"What do you mean, you are going to use the bomb?"
Knowledge isn't a mistake, it's a process;
part of which requires that a few eggs will be broken.
Even if it requires polluting the earth, our home;
oh yes, the furthest promise is for intergalactic travel.
If anything is ever going to be done,
then mistakes are the price that must be paid.
There is no doubt motion incurs mistaken directions,
the problem lies in determining which are worth the risk.
Crying and whining about mistakes won't fix them,
only reliance on SCIENCE will bring RATIONAL solutions.
That is the point! Which mistakes, which solutions?
Who cast all the votes to allow genetic disordering?

Don't blame SCIENCE for human foibles;
it only offers the answers, desire offers the motivations.
That nuisance partner, thief of the land,
creating misery accompanied by nothing profitable.
Good and bad are the choices coming from desire,
afflicting RATIONAL direction with a loss of control.
From where does desire come except a RATIONAL realm;
how else is it known except by cause and effect?
Maybe desire requires RATIONAL WILL to fulfill itself,
which only means an INTUITIVE design must use it too.
Does INTUITION need design like a RATIONAL view,
or must one always work through the other?
If irrationality can find no practical use, sadly emotional,
it will remain the province of the bored seekers of TRUTH.
INTUITION is often mistranslated when conceptualized,
when feelings take on the appearance of holy writ.
Scriptures are written with prophetic messages,
visions which don't seem to be offered to ordinary mortals.
Where do feelings come from if not from the gods?
Prophets and mystics are just able to see more clearly.
This is THOUGHT just waiting for religious bullets:
divine bulletins are nothing more than intense feelings.
A stranglehold is placed on free THOUGHTS and actions
by the very same processes of thinking and acting.
An aspect of holy messengers common to all is that
their communications tend towards the vague and obtuse.
Society trains its children to prefer to think rationally,
to give it all the mental riches at their disposal.
The modern world is complicated and requires education;
human beings spend ¼ of their lives just growing up.
Until the last century that was not the case;
it is damnably difficult to fathom historical motivations.
Modern elitist society asserts so much RATIONAL value;
simple folk accepted ample happiness without THOUGHT.
Human beings have rewritten the oldest law on the books:
survival of the fittest replacing parents with their children.
Which has been replaced with some RATIONAL CONCEPTS,
disease and DEATH are to be conquered at all costs.

Dying prematurely is the most horrible event,
say those who are left with profound misspent EMOTIONS.
DEATH is now seen as a loss, an atheistic ending;
the result of putting RELIGION into RATIONAL clutches.
How can DEATH be made into such a bitter cause,
when there is no earthly IDEA of the next occurring effect?
Most people assume others feel as they do,
so corpses must feel deep inconsolable grief.
Gods of SCIENCE have given repeated promises
to conquer DEATH'S maladies upon next year's passing.
Average LIFE expectancy has increased this past century,
at least when factoring in infant mortality.
Yet gods will never help us to observe that each passing
moment contains more LIFE than they can ever obtain.
SCIENCE can only aid in fixing medical problems,
not help anyone live to a greater extent than when healthy.
It is still granted supremacy, just like primitive Zeus;
recognize faith in SCIENCE is still faith, let us pray.

24:46

The view I have of myself isn't based on what I sense;
this physical corporeal body is just a shell over me.
Within is a feeling, EMOTION unbound by CONCEPTION,
a transient experience which is worshipped as LIFE.
My feeling of me changes from moment to moment,
but my sense of my body seems more rigid, more defined.
What else but INTUITION could detect this infernal motion,
shifting feelings which are not within a RATIONAL purview?
A RATIONAL view doesn't see feeling or any EMOTION,
just the results imparted by their overriding impulses.
Then INTUITION might be the key to opening up REALITY,
indicating how it may exist from an irrational perspective.
The RATIONAL perspective is already pretty well explored;
SCIENCE has more to expose, but it's well on its way.
Imagine of what a full view from INTUITION would consist;
in opposition to rationality, its traits should be revealed.

The Intuitive view has direct apprehension of Infinite,
assuming all Reality is not-Finite and unlimited.
Past and future filling instants of perfect clarity,
followed by others equally unique and distinct.
Those moments are discovered by episodic experiences;
how they are tied together is beyond sensual measures.
Reality lost on the other side of Life,
painting its message on vivid Mind in picturesque colors.
Languages expressing an Intuitive view are ambiguous;
words can approach its meaning, but not touch it.
Why look for Reality's missing pieces in known places;
is the remote ever found in the place it should be in?

****

24:57

Dogs set to chasing my tail;
three are there which leave no rest to the weary.
A poof, a mixed, and a Great Dane are in the stew;
impossible colors and events with no succession.
Rising to a second level we go;
elevated by means only quiescent Mind will set straight.
Poof climbs by means unaware;
mixed grates its paws upon the ledge of the floor.
The Great Dane just leaps from bottom to top,
while I watch for meaning to make an appearance.
Which is yours, which is mine, and which is Truth?
There are always three, pick which one works the best.
Ah, man's burden fits into a pack;
working upon working until we can do it no more.
Maintaining a building is the job given to forebear;
endless pipes run amuck in a window saver's maze.
Run perfectly and whole, no drops escape to the floor;
I use them all to hose off debris just the same.
Then fall into discussing art, or maybe it is dance;
with two other people, student and peer.

Strange to know
we manage with so little knowledge to spare.
Which is yours, which is mine, and which is TRUTH?
There are always three, pick which one works for now.

Day III _____

06:00

How does each day shine its way into a new appearance
when last night was as dark as the one before?
Many days I wake up and wonder where I'm at,
and once I remember where, I need a reference for when.
Existence in TIME and in SPACE become defined
according to standards setting them apart from REALITY.
Every day is so much like any other,
if I don't have a media source, I lose all track of my days.
Does LIFE stop when days blur into meaningless existence;
is it dependent on where and when LIFE is defined to be?
I obviously still exist even if my days have no name;
my living essence isn't attached to defined progress.
A day huddles for warmth with those of its kind,
falling into a place where it fits, not where it belongs.
Each 1 has its own character, its own measured pace,
but they are still so similar they aren't independent.
The calendar marches on to the beat of its own drummer,
and like the rest of REALITY is seen from distinct viewpoints.
A RATIONAL view of each day is the familiar divided cycle,
I've no IDEA what an INTUITIVE view of daily travel is like.
Come, attend this discussion;
it has passed that TIME is bound to continue.
TIME which is seen to move from day to day;
neither slowing nor stopping to wait for my perspective.

Place THOUGHT once more in front of another,
so the path backward will be full of conceivable crumbs.
THOUGHTS flowing like days 1 after the other,
forming a RATIONAL train which seems not to begin or end.
And yet we secretly know that cannot be true,
unless REALITY is admitted not to have a bounded field.
I'm not able to understand how it could be without limit,
so my inclination is to require a beginning and an ending.
Is it possible there are two equal perspectives,
from which defined ends may be viewed quite differently?
I accept the possibility of an incomplete RATIONAL view,
but an INTUITIVE 1 hasn't yet deserved equality.
Freezing water can break a solid with glacial patience;
thus will an alternate view forge its way into awareness.
There is more to REALITY than how it's viewed;
a proposed INTUITIVE view has nothing reasonable to offer.
What is it INTUITION should furnish
so its existence will not be continually questioned?
I'm offered a perspective beyond sight,
with no repeating physical rules, and no parts nor pieces.
Are facts automatically accepted by sad-funny MIND;
does full-grown knowledge tend to dismiss imagination?
It's difficult to accept a view beyond my senses,
where rationality is washed away like earth into the sea.
INTUITION'S essence stokes CONCEPTION'S FIRE with feeling,
filling in the gaps sensation has no capacity to span.
An INTUITIVE view is able to make leaps between THOUGHTS;
large crevasses where a RATIONAL perspective fears to go.
All any reasonable person can be asked is to delay
any doubt that relying on INTUITION will lead to TRUTH.
Strange how doubt surfaces from so much knowledge;
the more I learn, the more I question what I know.
Possibilities are more than REALITY meeting the eye,
when sensation is limited in the chores it can perform.
If my senses were too perfect, they couldn't be improved;
and if they exposed all REALITY, I would've already seen it.
Some evidence of REALITY arrives when sensation leaves;
SPACE between the bars keeps the tiger from pouncing.

That is completely insane;
no wild animal can be kept in SPACE without bars.
Unsubtle terminology shows so much if we only look;
just the difference between shows the difference without.
Neither the bars nor SPACE hold the tiger;
artificial SPACE created by the separated bars keeps it in.
If that SPACE is lifted out of its temporary confinement,
it once more becomes nothing to hold in hard hands.
Only when SPACE is molded and shaped by a structure
can something not there become minimally useful.
INTUITION can be held between RATIONAL bars;
if the bars are removed, anything left has no CONCEPTION.
An INTUITIVE view may show what a RATIONAL one doesn't,
and will be just as sturdy as the structure formed around it.
INTUITION cannot be extracted from its normative state;
it makes no sense to leave LIFE to survive out on its own.
RATIONAL sense can be made of INTUITIVE feeling in 1 way:
enclose the living area where nothing makes sense.
Is it better for blind doubt to form than blind acceptance,
or is an inner light required to find an inner path?

06:34

Bob the warden came by yesterday to verify my situation;
not that he really cared, he just needed to assert his control.
Is there one master, one ruler, one source to all REALITY;
do many OBJECTS attach to, or keep from, one another?
In here he is everything; my fate depends on his WILL;
no action of his or mine is truly separate from the other.
A- As far as REALITY stretches its arms
either there is one source to everything or there is not.
There could exist more than 1 source for OBJECTS,
and they would be included within <*there is not*>.
No other RATIONAL THOUGHT will adequately express how
a unitary nature might contribute to CREATION of all.
To prove the proposition—there is only 1 source—
I must first demonstrate that <*there is not*> is not.

B- Find the bars within which INTUITION can be held,
SPACE created by a formally proven absence.
If there isn't 1 source to all REALITY,
then all existence must come from none or many.
No other CONCEPTION will fetch to a plain beck and call;
no source exists, or many do, these are the only options.
1st- Assume there is no source to everything;
note the existence of anything which denies this validity.
Is it possible everything does not have a source,
while anything within it could still have a source?
Everything is universal: it refers to each and every thing;
anything is existential: it refers to any 1 thing.
Thus no one can assert that anything has a source,
and still maintain everything does not—this is many.
OBJECTS exist and have sources for their existence;
assuming no source exists, then it can't be many.
The other option requires a more careful approach,
so it does not slide down the slippery slope fallacy.
2nd- Assume there are many sources to everything;
distinct OBJECTS here and there aren't secretly connected.
The possibility OBJECTS may have different sources
on the surface has nothing to mark it as insufficient.
In order for there to be many sources to sensible things,
each source must have none, 1, or many boundaries.
a- Fractals repeating themselves as we push
in deeper, REALITY shows itself the same inside as out.
In order for different OBJECTS to have different sources,
boundaries must exist to keep the sources from being 1.
For one or many boundaries to have some real existence,
there must be a boundary source(s)—this is a question?
The boundaries which surround the many bounded-sources
must themselves have a source in order to exist.
b- Is there one or many source(s) to the boundaries;
can one OBJECT exist with many boundaries?
No. If the source to each OBJECT had many boundaries,
nothing would prevent OBJECT from being OBJECTS.
c1- Further, could each of the many
boundary sources have its own unique and distinct source?

That is essentially the argument of modern SCIENCE,
and I see no way of easily disproving its paradigm.
Imagine each OBJECT has a source with a boundary,
requiring both of those to have a source with a boundary.
A source is OBJECT requiring a source and a boundary;
a boundary is OBJECT requiring a source and a boundary.
No RATIONAL THOUGHT may be conceived unless
it is formed from a basis of DUALITY.
Divide 1 OBJECT by a progressively greater dual integer-
$1/2 + 1/4 + 1/8 + 1/16 + 1/32 + 1/64 + 1/128 +. . . = 1$.
THOUGHT trapped in a whirlpool of words without end,
where the only exit is to continue into the maelstrom.
If I assume there are many sources to the boundaries,
a convergent geometric series still rationalizes out as 1.
c2 - Finally, could all of the many
boundary sources have one unique and distinct source?
Either *<first>* 1 boundary source is greater
than the bounded sources, to keep them in check.
Even logic that simple is beyond INTUITION;
normally felt is only total freedom or its absence.
Or *<second>* all sources are exactly equal in measure,
and still the bounded sources are kept in check.
If what surrounds the cattle is too weak to hold them in,
it does not suffice to be termed as a fence.
<First> There is no greater source than the bounded 1's;
if 1 boundary source is greater, it defines everything.
For a greater boundary source would mold all sources,
and itself be the one source of everything.
My current assumption is many sources to everything,
and 1 greatest source is effectively 1 source.
Do all citizens in a democracy have equal power,
or is individual authority controlled by those with more?
<Second> All sources could be precisely equal in strength,
whether of a boundary or a bounded nature.
Yet all sources could only be EXACTLY equal, if
they are born of one and the same source.
Therefore by assuming many boundaries,
I can still find but 1 source to everything.

C- Remember! REALITY opposing <not 1 source> leaves
one source victorious, and no other premise standing.
CONCEPTS: the source to everything is more than none,
and assuming many sources results in only 1.
Neither none nor many are the sources to REALITY;
walk in any direction and return to the same point.
From a RATIONAL view it's likely *<there is not>* is not,
and the only other option succeeds where this 1 fails.
Thus there must be one source to everything,
and however it is known must be more than a name.
REALITY is formed from an extensive substance;
anything and everything known is some part of this stuff.
What about VOID;
is the source of everything also the source of nothing?
That depends on where VOID is to be found,
or if it's possible there are many instead of 1.
Search forever and then more for want of satisfaction,
nowhere will be found where VOID does not touch itself.
Therefore VOID is conceived as OBJECT in REALITY,
if every identifiable part must be a piece of itself.
The one source to everything must include ALL REALITY;
otherwise there is not one REALITY, there are many.
There is 1 source to anything and everything,
including all OBJECTS, which now includes VOID.
There is a point to all of this filmy logic:
reduce REALITY to one source—call it AETHER.

07:22

Bob the warden told me his opinion about fasting prisoners:
"Go ahead and starve, you'll just give up like all the rest."
The past intrudes on the present with venomous babble,
assuming what has happened must always happen.
Past events achieved a certain sequence in their unfolding,
inspiring the future to follow in the pattern laid out for it.
AETHER has an odd ring, resonating with the past,
as if someone had struck this universal bell before.

Aristotle saw aither much like the 1 just formulated,
an essence beyond the ken of mortals, closer to the gods.
Ancient gods, yet much like those more modern;
the part of RATIONAL MIND searching for cause to effect.
Empedocles constructed REALITY from 4 elements:
earth, air, FIRE, and water; a base to which others added.
Others before him had seen the light; although
there are gaps which explanation refuses to cross.
Aristotle was 1st to record his effort to codify REALITY,
with the inclusion of a 5th heavenly element—aither.
An essence known to be much like INTUITION;
its existence accounted for by what it is not.
It was an eternal essence, frozen, neither heavy nor light,
and counter-moving in circles with the elemental lines.
The reasoning was quite sound to require another element,
if existing CONCEPTIONS do not work, add to them.
Elements of 4 didn't quite cover observed phenomena,
so the addition of a 5th helps to fill in physical VOID.
Thus Aristotle is considered to be SCIENCE'S first priest;
gods created by adding for all those centuries passed.
His theory also provided for existence of a prime mover;
also eternal, but having no measure and no magnitude.
This is one difference between his theory and AETHER:
one tries to fit everything, the other is source to everything.
This theory of AETHER, which has been initialized,
has much in common with Aristotle's celestial vapors.
Aristotle's aither is not a suitable cross to bear;
AETHER is more like his aither and prime mover combined.
And that synthesis is still insufficient for AETHER,
which covers all 5 elements, prime mover and more.
Faxed terminology is used to acknowledge his brilliance,
not to submit any aspect of REALITY to his accuracy.
Aristotle saw existence in primarily spatial terms;
he didn't see TIME as such a crucial element.
Lacking mechanisms to divide it into useful bits,
and Einstein to show him TIME's place in the puzzle.
Even great Galileo came up against a temporal barrier;
SCIENCE arose when it could firmly divide TIME.

Let no person dismiss Aristotle's place in metaphysics;
while his contribution may not be first, it is foremost.
Classical SCIENCE later acknowledged a gaseous ether,
proposed to process the motion of light and gravity.
Older gods of SCIENCE long since replaced,
superseded by a younger and more virulent strain.
Newtonian mechanics left nothing else to imagination;
transfer of ENERGY through a vacuum was impossible.
What was impossible is now fact;
strange how knowledge progresses in this fashion.
Michelson and Morley brought a close to that chapter;
no absolute measurable standard was found in ether's book.
Their search was for the essence connecting MATTER;
little did they know they were looking in the wrong door.
Then Einstein and Poincaré produced brilliant analyses,
finally consigning ether to the dump of useless THOUGHTS.
Aristotle's aither and this classical one meet in one place:
neither touches AETHER'S meaning in any way, even name.
Ether as some absolute measurable standard
has been thoroughly discredited.
There is no attempt herein to bring that IDEA back;
gods cannot be shown wrong, only incomplete.
It's easier to separate them mentally with different symbols,
and their meanings show them to be unrelated.
Our concern with the word is not its past transgressions,
only the present and future of how it can be redeemed.
Resurrection of a word is inoffensive;
more repulsive is the waste of perfectly good THOUGHT.
Does AETHER make sense when rationally viewed,
in light of the ether shown to be largely useless?
If AETHER is to guide me along a useful path,
it must have some rationally available recognizance.
Many useful THOUGHTS may flow from considering ether,
as long as none of them interfere with defining AETHER.

07:55

Bob the warden explained how incarceration should work:
he gives orders, I follow them, and everybody is happy.
All REALITY flows from one point to another;
transitions must work from a higher lever to a lower one.
Therefore, either his overweening authority will move me,
or my refusal to comply must come from a higher source.
Viewed intuitively AETHER furnishes one connected whole,
everything tied up in grand continuous REALITY.
But I can't relate to that because of dualistic tendencies;
my best assertion is the possibility of 1, within 2.
AETHER is the source of REALITY all rolled up entirely in one,
greater than the composition of all TIME and all SPACE.
Physics has found a connection between SPACE and TIME;
so intimate, their complete relation is still unknown.
That which has been proven may still be incomplete,
especially at the level allowing a RATIONAL view no place.
There will be no violation of Einstein's laws allowed here,
but they may be expanded even as he did to Newton's laws.
Even though AETHER is one connected source,
it can still be divided into its PERCEPTIONS and CONCEPTIONS.
DUALISM always rules any RATIONAL discourse;
there is no way around it except by useless effort.
First, everything is conceived from dualistic divisions,
and AETHER furnishes the essence moving in each one.
REALITY divides into opposing interconnected zones;
possibly as static substances, or as dynamic ENERGY.
Second, REALITY is sensed to consist of TIME and SPACE,
by which they are imagined to have all-inclusive versions.
Therefore, AETHER could = all SPACE and TIME,
the source of everything is the source of PERCEPTIONS.
Actually, all TIME and SPACE are only needed
to understand how AETHER fits their existing divisions.
There is no difference in how they really exist,
only in how they are intended to be viewed or used.
A further division of INTUITION'S pure perspective
must be left to one more gifted in parsing phrases.

More discussion will mandate more CONCEPTS,
which will lead me farther from any episodic TRUTH.
AETHER viewed from a RATIONAL perspective
is not yet amenable to the limited vision so far exposed.
Any good SCIENCE will first build static models,
and then conceive how they move dynamically.
RATIONAL REALITY has both static and dynamic aspects;
these are things which can be categorized into QUANTITIES.
Therefore SPACE and TIME can be molded into partitions,
OBJECTS and events divided into parts and pieces.
INTUITION'S REALITY has both static and dynamic aspects;
these are things which can be categorized into QUALITIES.
Conceiving how AETHER serves that part is beyond me,
and it's also doubtful it has practical applications.
Of course any part of AETHER must have some PURPOSE;
although what it is may not be exactly practical.
Some discoveries have been born before their useful TIME;
find what exists, maybe use will come when it's ready.
Once utilization does rear its misshapen head,
IDEA of useful may include a machine and a pattern.
A machine is made to accomplish work, it's innately useful;
a pattern exists as a design, without an inherent advantage.
The maker of cloth and the cloth are beneficial;
circumstance determines which one is demanded.
But there is still no use to be gained from mere design,
cloth requires work to turn it into useful clothes.
There are two views of how to view substances or events;
do not constitute one as valid and the other as inane.
There is really no choice to be had in this matter;
a RATIONAL view sees usable, an INTUITIVE view does not.
They both could be confirmed as always sufficient,
found by the crumbs each event leaves in its wake.
INTUITIVE resolutions to RATIONAL situations;
these are events I don't want to see.
Only acknowledge that neither perspective explains all,
not for relation to those insufficiently transparent.
Ah, so INTUITIVE solutions can resolve RATIONAL situations,
I'll just never be able to understand how or why.

If no use can be found of AETHER, as seen by INTUITION,
then its pattern can be cast aside as an unworthy ether.

08:26

I tried to explain to Bob the warden that I'm always ruled;
if it's not by him, then it will just be something else.
How can any REALITY exist which has no source;
is it possible to transcend the flow from higher to lower?
He understands only his method of ordering his REALITY;
if he isn't in charge of his inmates, there is no prison.
As has been postulated, AETHER exists or it does not;
if there is one source to everything, must it exist?
My CONCEPTS don't mutually cover both existing and not,
or neither existing and not, or both and neither.
Our now-task is to show AETHER cannot not-exist,
which leaves only one possibility—it must be.
If AETHER exists, then its existence is a tautology;
if its nonexistence is impossible, then it also must exist.
Is there any doubt TIME and SPACE come from a source,
or anything that exists must come from somewhere?
This place and this moment
aren't identical to that place and that moment.
If there are differences in SPACE and in TIME,
then some power configures <this> dissimilar to <that>.
Motion of any kind requires some inspiring FORCE,
which seems to include progress of TIME and SPACE.
Gods of SCIENCE and RELIGION sustain that scenario, both sets
mandating CREATION from some recognizable source.
My BRAIN is wired to see cause and effect in all events,
so there is a cause to the effect of present SPACE and TIME.
INTUITION sees events all muddled up together;
only rationality is able to distinguish cause and effect.
Any thing's existence must come from a previous cause,
1 event following the 1st until there is a now.
If the cause is not AETHER, then what is it;
what is the single essence which originated REALITY?

That ultimate mystery is hidden in the depths of TIME;
solving it has employed scientists and priests alike.
A problem with the first cause is limited imagination,
presuming that first means there is only one.
RATIONAL people understand what a 1st cause means;
it started, then stopped, and everything else came about.
Gods clapping their hands to create the big-band sound,
and ever since REALITY keeps on evolving as unplanned.
The big bang is a reasonable explanation for REALITY;
physical phenomena seem to support this explanation.
That loud noise explanation leaves a lot to be desired;
what was the cause that caused the first cause?
In order for there to have existed a 1st cause,
it must be causeless itself and leave no previous traces.
Grunt and push out THOUGHT allowing that to happen:
could it be a causeless cause is continuous up to now?
Which would negate the definition of a 1st cause;
instead there would be a continuity of 1st causes.
No previous cause gives rise to all effects,
if the cause of the cause is the same as its effect.
REALITY is assumed to result from a succession of events,
each 1 multiplying into today's chaotic encounters.
Cause must be effect to create all TIME and all SPACE,
each INFINITY moment attached to each INFINITY pixel.
So SCIENCE and RELIGION have been searching in vain,
supposing the cause to all existence is on a linear path.
For REALITY to exist, cause and effect cannot separate;
they are both part of an intricately woven pattern.
Then the cause to REALITY must be intuitively perceived;
a united cause and effect can't be rationally viewed.
Since a RATIONAL view can only see the dualistic side,
INTUITION is required to indicate how one turns into many.
That rationale hasn't indicated whether AETHER must exist,
which was the question originally embarked upon.
Start. In order for there to be a causeless cause,
it must be continuous, with no previous source.
SCIENCE and RELIGION both have proposed a 1st cause,
a simple mechanism which began everything ever after.

Thus two options are left out of all the other possibilities:
there is a first cause, or there is a causeless cause.
A 1ˢᵗ cause would have to start by mysterious means;
a causeless cause has no beginning, but is ever continuous.
REALITY has more flavor being continuously formed
than everything descending from an unknown first cause.
So everything descends from a causeless cause because
a 1ˢᵗ cause can't exist unless it's an effect from a cause.
Does the existence of everything require a cause;
is it possible for us to be here unborn?
My RATIONAL CONCEPT of REALITY forces acknowledgment
that there must be a cause for the effect of everything.
Thus everything must be an effect from some cause;
even a continuous pattern, which has neither first nor last.
If there is no cause for everything,
then there is no cause for anything, and nothing exists.
"Causeless cause" is only a phrase used for parley;
there is a cause for everything, it is just irrational.
OBJECTS and events do exist as part of everything;
it's their connection to AETHER still left in doubt.
A first cause has no bearing without a former cause;
all REALITY is continuously formed from a causeless cause.
If there is no 1ˢᵗ cause, there must be a causeless cause,
where all causes are irrationally attached to all effects.
Likewise if AETHER is the one source to REALITY,
it could not be a first cause both millennia ago and now.
Therefore, a causeless cause must create REALITY
from an aetheric source right here and right now.
Then there is no causeless cause, if AETHER does not exist,
and we are left guessing at what caused the first cause.
So AETHER can't not-exist
because if it doesn't then REALITY is left with a 1ˢᵗ cause.
To say it succinctly is the best trick in REALITY's repertoire:
either AETHER exists or nothing exists at all, now.

09:08

There is no protest suitable for a prisoner but fasting;
I resist overpowering authority by simply doing nothing.
Follow in the tradition of Mister Gandhi and Mister King,
accepting; applied FORCE results in FORCE being returned.
The sequence where cause leads to effect is inescapable;
the only solution is to prohibit the primary cause.
What is this causeless cause central to the first's demise,
creating all TIME and all SPACE at each sited instant?
It's an oxymoron functioning at its very best,
the effect is rationally seen and the cause by INTUITION.
The absence of an essence becomes the definition of itself,
no other dualistic CONCEPTION is possible.
A causeless cause must exist in an irrational manner,
which mandates it resides within an INTUITIVE perspective.
How can effect be submitted to untimely DEATH,
and then given position and home in the present?
If there is a causeless cause,
then there should also be an effectless effect.
Cause is effect, the two of which are less as they are more;
combined they are all, divided they are only RATIONAL.
I understand an INTUITIVE view as well as possible;
approximation can only carry contradiction so far.
Try to understand what cause means without effect;
then try to separate causeless from cause.
A cause is anything that produces an effect;
an effect is anything brought about by a cause.
The source of REALITY by AETHER is all one and the same;
INTUITION and a RATIONAL view are adverse sides of one coin.
No matter how I perceive REALITY,
there is always 1 side consistently hidden from view.
The problem with finding the source to all existence
has been a RATIONAL involvement in both cause and effect.
The phrase "causeless cause" seems to make no sense;
if it's the source to REALITY, then it will remain hidden.
Of course the cause of all RATIONAL causes
will never be found unless the search applies INTUITION.

The effects are totally RATIONAL and observable,
especially those to which causes can be determined.
There is only one cause on INTUITION's side,
a pattern from which all REALITY is surveyed and formed.
If a causeless cause is continuous through SPACE and TIME,
then REALITY's manifold parts connect in 1 huge design.
Distinct RATIONAL causes, that gods of SCIENCE go on about,
are only part of the design in a total realistic rug.
There should be no doubt that causes lead to effects,
but why they do remains a bigger mystery.
The effects coming from those bright shining causes
are also threads knit into one all-touching rugged mat.
That may be why Hume couldn't detect a connection
between the cause of an event and its effective result.
The cause is caused is caused is caused is caused
is caused is caused is caused is caused is caused . . . .
Insistence on a causeless cause being RATIONAL is the hare
leading the hounds on an INFINITE regression to nowhere.
The causes and effects unveiling RATIONAL results
are FINITY to start and FINITY to finish.
This is the existence of REALITY as I commonly sense it,
each event is configured by relation to its neighbor.
The causeless cause laid open for review
is INFINITY in nature and in scope and in deed.
A cause with no beginning and no end
is virtually a definition of INFINITE existence.
As it becomes obvious with a little more reflection,
INFINITY and FINITY cannot coexist within one THOUGHT.
There is no symbol or CONCEPT adequately covering both;
each is attached to a particular perspective.
The causeless cause is not one single event, more,
it is an unrolling carpet from which yesterday is tomorrow.
In order for it to be ever continuous,
events create each other with every occurring moment.
AETHER serves all of TIME and its partner SPACE;
REALITY might be grasped by becoming lost in this forest.
TIME simultaneously moves at all points of SPACE,
so they must be everywhere connected here and now.

This is one solution to a fabulous paradox:
no rationally observed cause evolves all that is.
The source of REALITY is the substance of AETHER;
it's created right now, not flowing from the past.
Knowledge obtained from a most unlikely source,
a covenant of INTUITION'S rainbow with RATIONAL colors.

09:41

Bob the warden said the shrink said I'm not nuts,
but I sure have a screwy way of looking at things.
Always rely on the gods of SCIENCE to relay the facts,
even if the information turns out to be just an opinion.
I see value in looking at REALITY as an unequal balance,
SCIENCE has shown how a potential difference matters.
Proposed as the fundamental source for all existence,
AETHER is not fostered to live in equality.
An aetheric theory is far from conclusive;
however, there are some points worthy of discussion.
How should a more suitable model be crafted,
when the best alternative is just a different approximation?
Point taken. No rationally available observations
guide me directly to AETHER, which is unknown so well.
Yet transmissions from gods of SCIENCE may divulge
some indirect hints as to its existential possibilities. Start.
RELATIVITY theory requires connection of TIME to SPACE;
though SCIENCE'S view doesn't comes close to AETHER.
Gods only finitely transmit information to their priests;
how can the connection be known if it is unlimited?
SPACE/TIME can't be considered in absolute terms;
knowledge of them is measured in seconds and meters.
How do those tiny itsy-bitsy parts and pieces exist
unless they come from a far greater whole?
Physics has shown how their measurements are accurate,
and at light speed combine into a curved continuum.
A drop of water comes from a much bigger ocean;
how can a second exist unless there is more TIME?

There is much more—past, present and future;
many seconds can exist within these confines.
That is only more seconds, not more TIME;
how can many exist if there is not a first one? Next.
Quantum Mechanics has resolved the paradox of light;
quanta make waves into tiny particles of ENERGY.
Yet a wishy-washy culmination of modern THOUGHT
also unequivocally states—human beings are meddlers.
Part of Quantum Mechanics is the uncertainty principle,
which limits how much of REALITY can be measured.
If that line of THOUGHT is followed to the end,
human observation is seen as both limited and intrusive.
When delving into the nature of MATTER itself,
its exact structure isn't subject to RATIONAL dissection.
AETHER is not mandated by some gods' holy writ;
although it is able to wriggle by in one able perspective.
Quantum Mechanics is the ultimate end
resulting from dividing MATTER by a posteriori deduction.
AETHER is the ultimate end resulting from combining
REALITY according to a priori THOUGHT. Next.
MATTER consists of isotopes, which bind together,
but none of them form GRAVITY, ELECTRICITY, or MAGNETISM.
Those FORCES are acknowledged to be non-material,
yet they are made particulate by the fiction of quanta.
All of the evidence SCIENCE has been able to uncover
definitely indicates MATTER at its smallest is particulate.
Still trying to make REALITY into something it is not,
when obliged to rely on a limited view and sensation.
Modern SCIENCE theorizes REALITY is formed in 2 ways:
MATTER is particulate, and ENERGY is waves.
This is an old question yet to be resolved:
is the nature of REALITY MATTER or ENERGY?
SCIENCE has cast down its might solidly behind OBJECTS;
this is what all common evidence leads me to believe.
All of its evidence is solely RATIONAL in nature;
AETHER as ENERGY incorporates INTUITION as well. Next.
Physics hasn't yet decreed a unified field theory,
a holy grail to which scientists have sacrificed their MINDS.

There is a unique problem inhibiting their search:
trying to find microbes with unaided vision.
Unknown little bugs until microscopes were invented,
expanding vision saw what couldn't be seen unaided.
How is INFINITY to be seen with FINITY tools,
or must REALITY be limited so it can be measured?
No RATIONAL knowledge of REALITY can be accumulated,
unless it's based on measurement and observation.
Yet REALITY can be seen to be much more;
AETHER exists to fill the gaps supplied with an orderly view.
The physical laws ruling our disciplined universe
are certainly subject to rules as yet undiscovered.
Are there rules that rule the rules;
is there a metaphysics for compartmentalizing physics?
When SCIENCE forwards the answer I'll pass it on;
man has no ability to succeed without investigation.
If the metaphysical rules are not well understood,
how can accuracy be claimed for the physical laws?
Of the 2 main ways to attain information,
a posteriori knowledge fits what is to what has happened.
Unfortunately that approach has lost a valid tool,
a priori imagination exists to be proven wrong.
Scientists understand REALITY based on breaking it down,
and then reconstructing it by building it back up.
Aristotle's system took two thousand years to disprove;
what system of THOUGHT are the gods working on now?
There is no current metaphysics defining REALITY,
no system of THOUGHT explaining why man is here.
Thus the modern approach will eventually become lost;
philosophy must always precede gods of SCIENCE. Finish.
Scientific THOUGHT as it's currently accepted is insufficient
to cover adequately the existence of AETHER.
Herein some pieces to REALITY'S puzzle have been laid out;
the interesting part is where they appear to lead.
A light appearing at the end of a tunnel
doesn't mean it's where the source of the light is.
Gods of SCIENCE intimate TIME and SPACE are unified,
with an unverifiable particulate REALITY, and a master plan.

Nothing conclusive can be drawn from vague premises;
the proof for AETHER is far from being distinctive.
A purely RATIONAL view will not be swayed from its doubts;
just note absent SCIENCE points in the direction of AETHER.

10:26

Bob the warden also mentioned what the priest feared,
my ungodly SOUL is in danger of eternal damnation.
Is a fiery hell as real to those without belief in it
as those who have been made to fear their own LIFE?
I think real RELIGION would comfort me at this TIME,
but I find its threats and abuse inspire me to aversion.
Gods of RELIGION offer some irrational advice:
peace, meaning, security, company, joy, hope, eternity.
Those 7 goals can't be rationally exploited;
how man is able to use them is beyond me.
Yet they are what humanity actually seeks to improve
while secretly appealing for help from the gods of SCIENCE.
Which shows how RATIONAL RELIGION has become,
looking to SCIENCE for help with its own problems.
People are instinctively attracted to those seven nirvanas,
and so blindly exploit rationality in a mad search for them.
The problem is all 7 goals are irrational in nature,
and I don't know how to approach them except rationally.
Irrational INTUITIONS are the intentions mankind seeks,
and still we are given to finding them in a RATIONAL den.
Pure SCIENCE makes no claim on irrational THOUGHTS;
if RELIGION chooses to use SCIENCE, this is to its benefit.
Unlike gods of SCIENCE, who bristle at the term,
RELIGION glories in the hubris of creating its own divinities.
There are no gods involved in CREATION of SCIENCE;
the universe doesn't work according to emotional rules.
Gods of RELIGION manipulate an essence, AETHER-like,
and (ir)rationally arrive at a conclusion with one answer.
Existence of AETHER is still only possible, not probable;
RELIGION, not SCIENCE, claims something like its essence.

Religious gods have unfolded many stark messages,
scripted by mystics blessed with personal insight.
Their messages are virtually unanimous in 1 respect,
a vision which is difficult to rationally find or transmit.
Seekers for TRUTH find their answers from within,
a mystic experience which gods have abandoned for hell.
External viewing leads to a RATIONAL perspective;
internal viewing leads to an INTUITIVE perspective.
Prophets are noted for their lack of intelligibility,
by those of us common enough just to have nightmares.
I can gain no understanding if the message is unclear;
like poetry, which has great sound and obtuse meaning.
What has been seen by people traveling into wise
is difficult to modify for approximate FINITY exploitation.
Therefore SCIENCE has taken the lead to fill any VOID
left when most priests found celibacy too hard to bear.
The ability to see through INTUITION with clear eyes
is not easy for us, afflicted with the cataracts of humanity.
Animals are born with differing levels of RATIONAL ability;
it's reasonable to assume INTUITIVE views are so endowed.
Mystics and prophets were able to achieve a purified
or highly energetic state from which visions appeared.
Man's relation to his INTUITIVE attitude is still unclear;
what is clear is the division between RELIGION and SCIENCE.
They offered prayer and fasted and meditated,
giving more of themselves than they could hope to gain.
If it was easy, priests could do it;
note there are many of them, and few monks.
Mystics have shown us a way to look beyond rationality;
see REALITY as a whole, for we are all subject to AETHER.
Prophets generally advise seekers to leave ego behind,
and to forego those pleasures dependent on the senses.
A common message—frugal LIFE leads to heavenly reward;
how are earthly pleasures linked to after-DEATH?
Obviously DEATH must be a continuation of pre-DEATH;
mystics have seen it, even though I don't, not yet.
Mystics have intuitively envisioned one whole REALITY;
RELIGION like SCIENCE leads in the direction of AETHER.

10:54

Bob the warden coaxed the crux of the fast out of me—
he has the might to hold me, but I deny him the right.
Is might or right stronger in the grand scheme of things,
or are they both just pawns in a greater struggle?
I don't doubt might is stronger from a RATIONAL view,
and maybe right could be stronger from an INTUITIVE view.
Snowflakes at the bottom of a falling avalanche,
every part of existence is subject to AETHER'S impulses.
For might and right to be equal on some plane of existence,
there must be some "essence" which supplies them both.
An essence more like AETHER than it is not;
what could bring might and right into balance?
Bought with TIME and ENERGY and THOUGHT,
good answers don't come from bad questions.
What is AETHER;
what is the "essence" upon which all REALITY is founded?
Rationally viewed, it's the source of everything;
OBJECTS are perceived and they must exist somehow.
Intuitively viewed, it is everything;
OBJECTS lose their bits to become part of a greater whole.
SCIENCE has shown man how vast is his insignificance,
a little piece of a much bigger universe.
REALITY is one substance, it cannot be divided;
PERCEPTIONS from sensation turn out to be an illusion.
Then it isn't possible to know what AETHER is,
some standard from which all of its parts can be identified.
A standard is made for comparing one thing to another;
AETHER, by its nature, cannot be compared to anything.
Still, I might know it better by knowing its progeny,
the substances existing within each distinctive perspective.
If what is too difficult, where and when is AETHER;
does it have a home which holds only this essence?
If it has a home, then it can be pinned down,
at least closer to some CONCEPT I can grasp.
AETHER exists everywhere and every moment that can be,
past and present and future, and here and there.

Then it doesn't exist within SPACE and TIME,
QUANTITIES which are known by their confined parameters.
All TIME and SPACE are tightly unified within AETHER;
thus all points of SPACE touch all instants of TIME.
That doesn't appear to make sense,
here and there don't both happen now and then.
A combined aetheric essence is an absolute function,
how TIME and SPACE exist without their measuring mask.
So man exists, or rather, his source of existence is AETHER,
and everything around him is also sourced by this unity.
AETHER is one, communicated as two;
it primarily exists where it does not fit into CONCEPTION.
If AETHER does exist behind an observable mask,
then there must be some rationale as to why it wears itself.
It is everything because everything comes from it;
REALITY cannot be one substance if something is missing.
But OBJECTS are seen as distinct from 1 another;
they move in relation to each other, not tied together.
Although water and veggies have different consistencies,
they both are required to make a hearty soup.
Then OBJECTS blend into VOID around them;
I'm just a piece of the cosmos, and I make it complete.
Is that how AETHER can be successfully envisioned;
can the largest essence be held in one small MIND?
My BRAIN conceives OBJECTS because of its limited nature;
there must be some model capable of holding all REALITY.
Imagine AETHER as the source of all existence,
and OBJECTS are merely windows into outer VOID.
No matter how I try, that isn't quite possible;
AETHER has to exist somewhere to move into my view.
Still, it is a useful picture for how AETHER might exist,
and all REALITY thus propagated within its embrace.
Therefore I can still rely on distinct OBJECT identification;
the source for material REALITY is just beneath my senses.
Of the basic questions one more is left to reveal:
why is AETHER?
The question which invokes a dualistic existence;
assuming REALITY is an effect, there is a related cause.

It exists because it must;
AETHER is, so all moments and places can be.
If there is no AETHER, then there is no SPACE and TIME;
at least this is the most logical interpretation.
INTUITION shows it even more clearly,
it is RATIONAL dissection which will take a while longer.
But AETHER is also known as the causeless cause;
there must be something more to why it exists.
Ask the gods of RELIGION for crystal clarity;
the modern versions are poor, while the history is rich.
Some seekers of TRUTH have tried to pass on their visions,
and many RELIGIONS have retained their noble THOUGHTS.
Mystics lead far from ports with easy anchorage;
no tracks and no dimensions show which direction to go.
AETHER can be intuitively observed, but not measured;
dimensional TIME and SPACE don't fully inhabit it.
How can AETHER be dimensionless and be everything,
if we can see STARS off in DISTANCE, in all directions?
AETHER could be dimensionless in the same way as FORCE,
only in relation to OBJECTS, not on its own.
There can be no doubt FORCE is a powerful transient,
and it is known by the action of OBJECTS on OBJECTS.
SCIENCE's only knowledge of the existence of FORCE
comes from its sensible effect on OBJECTS.
How can FORCE exist
with no discernible dimensional existence of its own?
It's normally assumed to have a dimensional existence,
but only because it works across the 4-d continuum.
FORCE moves in directions, not in dimensions;
the difference may be subtle while it is there.
That is a distinction currently eluding me,
so I will drop it for now and pick it up later.
Then where does FORCE come from to be so powerful;
is there another source able to push back AETHER?
Total ENERGY in the universe is constant,
and unless this is AETHER, it's FORCE without peer.
Can total ENERGY be AETHER, and be seen intuitively,
and still only have RATIONAL aspects?

A RATIONAL view only sees the effects of AETHER;
its concomitant cause is beyond a dual perspective.
Besides an irrational one, no place will hold all ENERGY;
where within a RATIONAL purview can it be held?
Somehow AETHER holds all ENERGY and it flows into VOID;
REALITY shows itself all mixed up in between.
Once more voicing and hoping not to repeat it again:
only the view is different, not REALITY!

11:42

As Bob the warden left, I told him he was trapped like me;
he rules his little kingdom, but only while he is here.
Can REALITY exist as the minion of one energetic source;
how can there be AETHER, which is always turned on?
The proof for 1 source to REALITY isn't definitive,
but it's sufficient to induce me to envision how it exists.
AETHER and REALITY are like water poured into a colander;
the water is the same, it just looks different inside and out.
The main problem I have with AETHER is its location;
in order for 1 source to exist, it has to be somewhere.
There is only one location suitable for housing AETHER:
where sensation is accepted and rejected—INTUITION sees it.
There are many arguments available against it,
but I'm too tired at the moment to get fully into them.
AETHER has been endorsed to its facile limits;
leave it behind as an unproven assumption about REALITY.
I can accept 1 source to all REALITY as a probable guess,
and dualistically conceive it as all SPACE and TIME.
A unified essence which knows bounds and freedom,
seen by a specific perspective as one or the other.
A RATIONAL view divides AETHER into sensible OBJECTS;
an INTUITIVE view sees it more INFINITE, more dimensionless.
Continuously created by the ultimates in opposition,
REALITY does not ooze in and out; more like, it flows on.
REALITY and AETHER fit into another dualistic conversion,
1 as static OBJECTS, the other as dynamic ENERGY.

Aether contains all available Energy, flowing to Void;
hunger for sustenance is the least of its problems.

****

12:23

Being wise beyond his years, a man once said:
blessed are those who serve only Truth and not man.
Like others, I find my Purpose is distinctly divided;
if man's rule is master, there can be no divine servants.
If Time for anything will end when it is Time for it to end,
what use is consuming manna beyond simple survival?
Man is desperate to cling to any fragile hold on survival,
an animal instinct to consume beyond what is needed.
Mankind rules sparse fields found near Finity,
limited to what we can force into models of convenience.
Living requires finding the best modes of survival;
I can't substitute mysteries for physical necessities.
The servant of mankind lives in the past and the future,
which do not allow him to release Time for now.
Society has become complex in its hurried growth;
man's gift is to learn from the past, plan for tomorrow.
Yet society also defines difference as ugly,
requiring alteration in the search for an imaginary norm.
Surgery has made Beauty only skin-deep,
but where it actually resides is buried in my Thoughts.
Those things physically touched and seen,
they have no attachment when sailing off into windy Mind.
Rich man or poor man depends on Thoughts to guide him
in pursuit of ephemeral goals, right by wrong by right.
Think! A busy chore becomes Time to neglect relevance;
what can possibly inhabit Space between Thoughts?
Nothing! My Thoughts are only synaptic sparks,
where Matter creates my Mind to fill lonely Void.
The world of mankind is a chain tied to a material shore;
blood and sweat and tears to insure Life becomes folly.

What is known is based on what is sensed;
Descartes be damned, this is how I know I am.
That is not LIFE;
sensation does not make MATTER live, it is only evidence.
If I don't live here, then where do I live.
If I don't know who I am, then who am I.
False approaches are crammed into us by training—
revere MATTER as the essence of all that can be.
Sense of MATTER shows where OBJECT ends, another begins;
from it comes my basic CONCEPTS of the greater world.
Yet they point to no paths past blunt wearisome thorns,
blindly groping, hoping to find a petal of TRUTH.
PAIN is another form of knowledge,
and some of its lessons teach me more than pleasure.
Do not search without for what is opened only within;
answers are not always found by looking outside the box.
My senses are the keys to external RATIONAL thinking;
looking within shows worldly THOUGHTS for what they are.
What is found in the divine irrational land,
a sustenance which does not depend on plus or minus?
Maybe it's unfortunate, maybe it's natural law,
but survival is generally a zero-sum game.
Find an end to bitter feuding, revenge for past wrongs;
addicted to a mundane cycle without a moment's peace.
Payback could be an extension of the living cycle;
though being predator is always better than being prey.
Is this the difference in whom we seek to serve, opening
ourselves to be preyed upon like sheep?
I see no sense in serving TRUTH
if it only leaves me as prey for those more RATIONAL.
INTUITION cannot be tasked to find value, kept by mankind,
it is not in its power to bequeath.
No prophet has said—thou shalt be stupid;
abandoning simple rationality can't be the way to TRUTH.
If we seek riches from gods, we have fallen to mankind;
if we seek power from omnipotence, mankind has won.
So I should render unto Caesar what is Caesar's,
because what is valued elsewhere holds none for him.

How will the providence of divine favor be known,
if we are most familiar with wanting products of mankind?
A sure way is to look at what is normally desired,
and then see if the rewards are material, or not.
Look to where LIFE holds open its secret door;
there find existence and essence under individual control.
On the 1 hand, a RATIONAL view is required to survive;
on the other, it can inhibit me from truly and fully living.
Born of eternity before mankind's meager crawling,
how is it brightly seen with sensation buried in the ground?
This is as difficult to do as it sounds—
rejecting man's attempts to control my service.
Seek service with one predominate THOUGHT:
the world of mankind can only furnish what is within it.

12:57

Bob the guard stands outside my CELL, spits juice into it,
and then proceeds to tell me exactly what he thinks of me.
The known world is composed from PERCEPTIONS made of it;
the more the latter are limited, the less any world is known.
He views defined REALITY responding to order and laws;
if 1 of these laws is violated, then there is hell to pay.
Imagine there is a compact definition of a RATIONAL view;
what distinct full universe would exclude the irrational?
A universe is the totality of all extant things,
but this is also what REALITY is supposed to be.
A RATIONAL perspective senses INANIMATE UNIVERSE,
SPACE and TIME unconnected to the vagaries of LIFE.
Thereby dividing REALITY into 2 views of its essence,
each of which constructs a universe excluding the other.
A universe of lifeless MATTER;
there find order and regularity, finally dependable.
It's a universe filled with PERCEPTIONS from my senses,
material OBJECTS affirmed by sight and sound and touch.
It is not enough to rely on personal sensation for guidance;
where do we pray for knowledge to lessen our suffering?

My instruction in REALITY is guided by SCIENCE,
a system of knowledge decidedly lacking in devotion.
The gods of SCIENCE pass on much knowledge,
succor from physics or chemistry requires firm obeisance.
I make no prayers to gods, I look for clues and evidence;
SCIENCE is an aid to knowledge, not an overlord.
Instruction in that realm comes from the gods of SCIENCE,
insisting on what must be, and what must never be.
SCIENCE is only knowledge repeatedly proven valuable,
which doesn't require it to be classified with RELIGION.
Accepting knowledge about REALITY without knowing
the source is the same as attribution to noble gods.
Gods were the ignorant precursor of SCIENCE;
their loss matured into civilization's gain.
Those gods do offer instruction on the nature of REALITY,
of what it does consist, and of what it might consist.
SCIENCE shows me THOUGHTS of great human MINDS;
I'm grateful I don't have to keep recreating the wheel.
What are the dualistic children of INANIMATE UNIVERSE;
how are we instructed by the gods to divide its essence?
OBJECTS appear to my senses in 2 major forms,
MATTER and STAR, neither of which retain living isotopes.
Each half must be an open window to its whole;
how do they show us the form of REALITY made INANIMATE?
They both must occupy some part of TIME and SPACE,
answering questions as to where and when.
Still, what are those limited children inside themselves;
what causes them to exist in SPACE and TIME?
The inside of MATTER is closed to observation,
only dissection and experimentation help to explain it.
Thus MATTER is not known as it exists,
only by the processes where it becomes parts and pieces.
SCIENCE divides MATTER into constituent particles;
this is the method which offers the clearest results.
What is STAR, is it so very different,
is it also not made of some form of MATTER?
No other OBJECT openly emits ENERGY like Star;
even radioactive rocks are closed more like MATTER.

Star is a bleeding carcass open to the swarming masses,
feeding on its warm and pulsing incandescent heart.
It's the single greatest source of known Energy,
perpetually consuming itself in a process of fusion.
One is a stripper baring all,
while the other pretends virginity behind a solid weave.
I haven't offered comprehensive definitions of Objects,
only brief glimpses of what the 2 main types are.
A Rational perspective does not see what is,
it allows empty Mind to form Conception of what might be.
Reality is sensed according to my natural abilities;
this is where my Perceptions grow into my Concepts.
Rational sees Inanimate; Inanimate is seen by Rational;
the two are siamese, joined at the head.
I know the universe around me by Rational means,
it shows itself to be Inanimate in nature.
What things are rationally observed
within Inanimate Universe, which is beholden to sensation?
I 1st need to clarify its fixed and eternal boundaries;
there must be some way of determining beginning and end.
Inanimate is Universe created by any Object or Force
perceived as existing external to Plasmic Membrane.
The universe of my senses is set in 5 perceivable parts;
a 6th may exist somewhere, but not herein.
A portion of Reality exploited by the gods of Science,
a world which can be cut up into parts and pieces.
Quantity rules here because this is the set-up,
a universe which runs by learning from measurement.
Sheep Thoughts too afraid to run outside of their pasture;
the grand scope of Reality does not fit onto a ruler.
Everything with Inanimate Universe is also Finite;
no part of it is able to extend beyond confined restraints.
Where does a Rational view of this universe come from;
why can Reality be seen in such a unique perspective?
All views originate from some Mind, some where,
and all Thoughts, and all Concepts.
Still leaving a major question unanswered:
is it a real universe, and how can we know whether it is?

It's real as long as I know it enough to believe in it,
and more than enough is already known to convince me.
Is belief enough to create greater REALITY;
is there enough to accept what is already here?

13:37

I have no way to explain larger REALITY to Bob the guard,
someone who refuses to see more than full frontal nudity.
What possible explanation can be offered for INTUITION,
when each observer must volunteer to see it himself?
Fortunately or not, I see REALITY from a broader view,
so I'm able to know things he can't possibly know.
Imagine there is a compact definition of INTUITION'S view;
what distinct full universe would exclude the RATIONAL one?
Once again, a universe is the totality of all extant things,
but as sensed, it's all composed of INANIMATE UNIVERSE.
A perspective from INTUITION also feels ANIMATE UNIVERSE,
spiritual REALITY beyond direct sensation.
Anything which doesn't manifest in a physical manner
should feel right at home within an immaterial universe.
Full of LIFE and full of hope and DREAMS of hope;
it is feeling and the unknown, the whole and INFINITY.
Which is why it must be a separate universe,
I can at best only approximate what those essences are.
A universe found by mystics and lost to gods of RELIGION;
Christ was not a christian and Buddha was not a buddhist.
Fixed attachment to a rigid undying scripture is RATIONAL;
it infers, but doesn't show, what the mystics have seen.
Secret riches are habitually left to the gods of RELIGION;
whether christianity or buddhism, the unwise claim it.
Those who carry the torch of righteous rigidity
are the least likely to know their own prophets intimately.
Still, through many inquisitions TRUTH has been passed;
hazy knowledge of INTUITION comes from religious sources.
Mystics claimed special knowledge, mastery over DEATH,
and left me in the hands of an elaborate farce.

Could an alternate living universe be dualistically divided;
what are the living equivalents to Inanimate Objects?
I can't see that realm so it's impossible for me to know;
my guess—they must be completely irrational.
Animate Universe is composed of two children,
Life *and* Soul, *beyond the touch of a material revelation.*
But living creatures attach to Matter as Biomatter;
they are also Objects displacing Time and Space.
Those Organisms *have a nature which needs revealing;*
how can Life *exist as the same elements in a rock?*
Biomatter might exist with isotopes similar to Matter
if there is something else included in its basic composition.
Object *could thus be viewed as* Matter *or* Biomatter,
depending on the level of mystery involved.
Any Object is still viewed from a Rational perspective,
whether or not some bit of Biomatter is revealed.
What is the nature of Soul, *if* Life *is too untouchable;*
how do we imagine what is beyond the beyond?
I can only rely on interpreting mystical impressions
from inner voyagers who saw gods and demons.
Suitable hints pointing in the right direction,
and a combination of views, will ultimately show Truth.
Biomatter is the counterpart to Matter,
which means Soul is a source much like Star.
Life *has a closed essence, separate from others, or is it*
impossible to intrude on others' secretive Thoughts?
Each biomaterial creature is noticeably different,
creating its own existence within Reality.
Behind fantastic living Objects *is* Soul;
is it one or many, or does it even matter?
There is 1 Star most important to me,
but I also know there are many others out there.
One Soul *felt so much brighter than the rest,*
while still feeling emanations from others less vivid.
Those pair-wise comparisons may be helpful,
but might not be accurate enough to expose Reality.
Temporarily forget about relying on accurate definitions,
look to see how Duality *is so prevalent.*

Then ANIMATE UNIVERSE will remain lost to what is,
for I'll always be limited to inferences from my senses.
ANIMATE UNIVERSE is manifested through LIFE and SOUL.
Do vital CONCEPTIONS confuse appearance with REALITY?
MATTER and STAR are known by what they are;
their essences are better sensed by dissection into particles.
Look to its nature, ANIMATE UNIVERSE is perceived differently
from the INANIMATE one by more than its things,
I know of LIFE and SOUL by evidence of what they do,
not what they are; they seem to elude OBJECT definition.
Imagined as structures of parts and pieces,
OBJECTS are either perceived whole or not.
LIFE and SOUL seem to work best when together;
dissection into particles leads to imminent DEATH.
INTUITIVE sees ANIMATE; ANIMATE is seen by INTUITIVE;
they are twinned, tied at the heart.
I have no problem viewing RATIONAL INANIMATE UNIVERSE,
but my INTUITIVE view will only be approximate at best.
ANIMATE UNIVERSE formed from hidden portents,
existing solely behind the veil of PLASMIC MEMBRANE.
The secrets held therein are such that guesses are best;
trying to see behind the curtain by observing its motion.
The non-part of REALITY only seen by INTUITION observes
LIFE as a whole, not just its parts and pieces.
This is the paradox SCIENCE hasn't yet resolved:
the organelles and isotopes are known, but the whole isn't.
LIFE is accurately perceived just by instinct,
while frustrating attempts to conceive it dualistically.
My RATIONAL knowledge of BIOMATTER'S composition
is known by observation of OBJECTS interacting with CELLS.
Mystics have attempted to show humanity another way,
hampered by the ever-current limitations of THOUGHT.
A problem with messages thrown out by mystics is the
foundation of knowledge—INANIMATE UNIVERSE is complete.
Glossing over irrational instances where it is not;
more is available to CONCEPTION than measured sensation.
QUALITY is something which is supremely irrational;
I know what I like and what I don't, that's about it.

*Intuition allows Reality to exist as it wholly is without
being forced into servile attention to limitation.*
Extension into Infinite is another irrational area,
terms and conditions which defy definitive analysis.
*Two imagined universes are opposite in all respects,
not just the views from which each one gains its shape.*
External sense of Rational Quantity in Inanimate Universe;
internal feel of Intuitive Quality in Animate Universe.
*Inanimate Universe is modeled as a driven machine,
while Animate Universe lays down an undefined pattern.*
Known by its Objects, or known by its actions;
combined they might bridge known holes in Science.
*Gods of Science will reassert themselves into awareness;
powerful Forces, their denial is a risky proposition.*
Science is weighted towards keeping a healthy skepticism;
otherwise I could fall headfirst into a sick fantasy.
*Gods of Religion will assert themselves less assiduously;
no less powerful, their denial leads only to moral decay.*
Religion can show its face as good or bad;
I don't know which to prepare for until it shows up.
*Understanding of Reality's dual nature is necessary;
biting off half leads to losing the whole.*

14:30

There is a gap between what others see and what I see,
some Void, which doesn't lead to Truth, but divides it.
*Imagine a pie cut exactly in half; how is each half known
except by the line between them?*
The formulated view has some degree of materiality,
so what limits it must incorporate the immaterial.
*If all Thought is dualistic, then the basic stuff of Reality must
be conceived in two forms; what are the two forms?*
When all Thought was rationally configured,
it trod down 2 avenues—that which is and that which isn't.
*For something to be real it must be that which is,
and also be made distinct from others of its kind.*

Different OBJECTS are known by SPACE and TIME between;
if there is nothing between them, they have no difference.
What <is> must be separated by that which <is not>,
at least, otherwise we cannot separate <is> from <is not>.
Some substance must exist between identifiable OBJECTS,
at least there must be some difference in how I sense them.
Some REALITY must exist to create VOID for anything to be,
for nothing must also exist in some stance.
Traditionally REALITY was divided into MATTER and SPACE,
normally known at that which *<is>* and *<is not>*.
If REALITY now divides into INANIMATE and ANIMATE UNIVERSES,
where does VOID fit in?
VOID was previously considered as empty SPACE
and might actually be the absence of either universe.
That which is not is VOID—into which things can be put;
an absence of any PERCEPTION formed into CONCEPTION.
VOID is the existence of nothing,
but it must be something in order to exist at all.
VOID in which OBJECTS can move around freely is
actually part of all TIME and SPACE, the missing part.
VOID held as OBJECT can't be grasped or measured;
therefore nothing can be known of its actual existence.
How can VOID's existence be physically determined,
if there is nothing there to take home and examine?
VOID must exist in order for OBJECTS to exist,
but what it consists of is no more than a guess.
All knowledge of VOID is from the absence of OBJECTS
existing therein and reacting to FORCES in its soup.
All TIME and SPACE were claimed to be AETHER,
now the conclusion is they are also VOID.
How can OBJECTS move within VOID, and still be
the exact same thing they are moving within?
REALITY isn't some big vat of amorphous Jell-o,
with OBJECTS and SPACE randomly merging their essences.
Remember INTUITION's pure view, all is one;
only a RATIONAL approximation raises a known fog.
Since any CONCEPT must exist dualistically;
MATTER and VOID though 1, must be sensed separately.

Aether fills all Space and Time as already proposed,
and also Void—an essence beyond sensation.
Existence of Aether brings doubt to my senses,
but I can't accept my Perceptions as unreal.
The problem is in limited Inanimate Perception:
the immensity of all Time and Space is beyond sensation.
So when Object's existence is rationally perceived,
it must naturally reside within a dualistic non-essence.
What <is> and <is not> are still subject to Perception;
Void just defines what <is not> in absolute terms.
But it still seems impossible for Reality to move itself;
Concepts of motion require Objects in opposition.
How can something move within itself?
The question stumbles over its own little words.
Those words may be ineffective and inefficient,
but they're still required for Void's conceptual business.
Aether is the source of all Reality imperfectly conceived;
those very Conceptions divide it into <is> and <is not>.
I have no choice but to conceive Reality as dualistic,
because my Rational Concepts are at best inexact.
A source must rationally come from here to go there;
only, both places intuitively exist as the same substance.
So Aether is the source and Void is the sink;
Dualism dividing Thought at every conceptual stop.
All Space and Time can be the absence of Objects,
and also the source of the many forms of Matter.
That word "all" has been the 1 giving me fits;
I'm trying to untie it from the common use of measurement.
No pressure makes Objects and Void the same,
their different natures only arrive with Conception.
Still Void is only part, not all Time and Space together,
because a single point must be different from another.
A unified existence causes no conflict in Aether;
one point can be same or many, prove it is different.
Otherwise Objects couldn't move from point to point;
Void can't be part of Aether if motion is to exist.
Void's consistency will remain unknown
until there is a method to input the absence of sensation.

What OBJECTS move within may be in perpetual doubt,
but the fact they are moving isn't challenged.
OBJECTS are perceived as having QUANTITIES within VOID;
how are these sensations applied to VOID itself?
In order to rationally know the substance of VOID,
it would have to be situated within a greater substance.
VOID is known by the absence of sensation
because it only exists where there are no OBJECTS.
Therefore knowing VOID as well as any other OBJECT
would be as the absence of the absence of any sense of it.
Once again, dividing REALITY into rationally known parts
devolves into a regression to nowhere, via INFINITY.
It appears a part of REALITY may never be known,
so other parts will be subject to suitable identification.
OBJECTS tend to move within all SPACE and TIME;
how could they move within FINITY TIME and SPACE?
Then OBJECTS would be moving within another OBJECT,
and this isn't how VOID is conceived.
VOID like any other part of a view is CONCEPTION,
which only exists when DUALITY is applied to it.
Therefore, on 1 hand VOID must be 1 OBJECT,
and on the other hand it's impossible for it to be 1.
Perceived VOID is emptiness, conceived VOID is OBJECT,
which must by definition be observable and measurable.
Only FINITE creations have those 2 RATIONAL QUANTITIES,
so OBJECTS can be defined by human CONCEPTS.
And still VOID cannot be seen or laid to scale,
even the gods of SCIENCE have decreed this invariable law.
Any scale works in VOID because all of them are accurate;
all I truly know is it's all around every sensible thing.
VOID is special, much like AETHER and REALITY;
however it is not the only one, and the rest are just like it.

15:20

Even if Bob the guard wanted to, he couldn't see my view;
the best he could hope for would be to approximate it.

What little bits are left out, which are not understood,
how can a whole view of REALITY be partially related?
It's not a matter of right or wrong, mine or his;
each individual's private world is seemingly whole.
Recall the impossibility of conceiving REALITY as it exists;
a degree of limited approximation is as close as it gets.
Actually, few SCIENCES require 100% accuracy;
imperfection is the only way anything actually gets done.
This problem will continue to bedevil any search for TRUTH:
a RATIONAL view of INTUITION results in approximation.
Persisting as knowledge with fixed parameters,
a RATIONAL view doesn't attach to a purely INTUITIVE view.
Hopefully, approximation is nothing other than a paradox,
so CONCEPTIONS like VOID may obtain limited existence.
For now, a RATIONAL view of VOID is close enough,
a non-existing essence suitable for most applications.
Distinguishing is and is not—a method of PERCEPTION—
initiating RATIONAL CONCEPTIONS formed in BRAIN.
That sounds dangerously like a form of solipsism,
believing REALITY only exists as CONCEPTS in my MIND.
Do we dare suggest, if people do not exist, OBJECTS do not,
because they cannot be rationally determined?
The moon and planets and suns don't have
their existence determined by man's sense PERCEPTION.
It is easy to understand how INTUITION is misinterpreted;
an irrational view of things is hard to relate.
I find this to be a quite reasonable position to take:
OBJECTS still exist even if my sense of them doesn't.
Convincing RATIONAL people nothing is real is contrary to
INTUITION'S aim of showing everything and nothing are real.
VOID is part of AETHER, the insubstantial part,
existing by default as SPACE within INANIMATE UNIVERSE.
The universe of MATTER hinges on rationally known items,
which are obtained through some variation of sensation.
Nearly every CONCEPT originates with my senses;
THOUGHTS form based on how my PERCEPTIONS are delivered.
Everything else wonderful MIND thinks it knows
comes from PERCEPTION by INTUITION, or maybe just a guess.

An INTUITIVE view may contribute to forming CONCEPTS,
but every THOUGHT in my head can be physically related.
The moon and the sun likely remain past a framed notice,
yet there is no way of proving this, it is still just a guess.
The description of how OBJECTS exist is held in my MIND;
only their actual existence is left forever out of reach.
Do not shirk the fact that grand RATIONAL knowledge
only comes from limited animal sensation.
Where it comes from isn't as important
as how well man is able to utilize its gifts.
Where does humanity belong without sensation;
is our cosmic place tied to attraction and repulsion?
If sensation is removed as the source of knowledge,
then it's no longer possible to know anything, rationally.
Hypothetically: imagine all REALITY is rationally known,
and suddenly all experience dies off—no more sensation.
Then everything known is based on previous knowledge;
all CONCEPTS will be formed based on MEMORY'S reserves.
Thus the moon and sun must be assumed to remain, now,
even after there is no way for people to experience them.
Which is generally how OBJECTS become known to me,
my current CONCEPT is based on previous PERCEPTION.
Still just a guess, even with prophecy applied;
although now the point may be a little more clear.
OBJECTS do exist outside of man's PERCEPTION, somehow,
but they are only known by RATIONAL or INTUITIVE methods.
Fickle MIND is able to experience REALITY intuitively,
and still BRAIN'S CONCEPTIONS are from FINITY sensations.
OBJECTS called moon and sun are RATIONAL CONCEPTS,
having a real existence my senses only partly touch.
The nature of OBJECTS, and their connection to REALITY,
is beyond the ability of any CONCEPTION to grasp fully.
In the absence of human intervention, REALITY will exist;
there is just a barrier between it, and understanding it.
Sense PERCEPTIONS do not accurately show REALITY,
much less at moments when no observers are around.
Something exists there, which is sensed as the moon,
and from this PERCEPTION, I form mental CONCEPT.

That sequence forms knowledge of Inanimate Universe;
Perception of Animate Universe is via a different route.
Reality presents itself to my awareness in a linear fashion,
giving me an estimate of its essence in objectified terms.
Any Conception thus formed is a figment
of Reality, it is not Reality itself.
Objects do exist outside my Mind's grasp,
but it can only use them as it is able to conceive them.
An illusion passing for total Truth, a fatuous spell,
is assuming the moon as conceived to exist is actually real.
It has just been proposed, Objects do exist,
and now comes the suggestion—they are just an illusion.
There is no Reality existing as Rational Thought,
Conception mistakenly based on sensation of part-Reality.
But Concepts and Reality must have some connection;
Science wouldn't exist unless it was accurate, if inexact.
If things are only as real as senses are able to make them,
and if everything was solely Rational—very real indeed.
So my understanding of Reality is based on deception,
and the fraud is perpetrated because Science is so good.
That is the nature of illusion; nobody is fooled
by magic if it is easy to see through it.
Which means no disrespect to Science's accomplishments;
they remain valid, though limited and incomplete.
Try to remember the limitations of sensations,
how we know Matter as incomplete and flawed.
But even imperfect, my Reality is true;
there is a regularity to Matter that can't be denied.
What is the difference between "my" Reality,
and Reality existing without an attached owner?
I have the ability to use 1 and not the other;
Reality beyond comprehension is divine intervention.
Or could one's personal Reality be merely a limited
version of a much larger one? Much larger.
There should be no difference between the 2;
as long as my Reality works, it must be real.
Once again, this is the point striving to come out:
Rational Reality is confused with what Reality is in itself.

So whatever constitutes the totality of REALITY
isn't completely available to my 5 RATIONAL senses.
BRAIN is wired to form RATIONAL CONCEPTIONS,
so THOUGHTS of further existence are difficult to balance.
I don't see any farther than what is in front of my face;
my THOUGHTS of REALITY are based on these PERCEPTIONS.
Yet some mental functions do not fit a machine model;
IDEAS from INTUITION do lead to further progress.
Many great leaps in civilization happened intuitively,
THOUGHTS which look really easy only in hindsight.
Mental CONCEPTION created of the moon is not its REALITY;
it is only an approximate copy.
That normally does not cause any sort of problem,
only happening when thinkers try to force the 2 into 1.
REALITY itself is beyond RATIONAL human comprehension;
it can be used, though not understood, in this manner.
The moon and sun are accurate enough CONCEPTS,
as long as they aren't mistaken as a complete picture.
That which is and is not are how scavenger BRAIN
differentiates things on a sensory basis.
OBJECTS come to attention from flawed PERCEPTIONS,
and are then formulated into even more flawed CONCEPTS.
Shifting MIND accommodates those external impulses,
and then allows its BRAIN to form INANIMATE UNIVERSE.
So CONCEPTS aren't formed directly from PERCEPTIONS,
they must first be processed by my intangible MIND.
Internal CONCEPTIONS of the intuitively experienced
ANIMATE UNIVERSE are not based on what is and is not.
Therefore 2 types of PERCEPTIONS, sensed and felt,
are used to form CONCEPTS—available beyond mere MATTER.
MIND intercedes between PERCEPTIONS and CONCEPTIONS,
and thus is able to use either INTUITION or a RATIONAL view.
Leaving my BRAIN to extract suitable information,
and form CONCEPTS which make some RATIONAL sense.
Those firm neural CONCEPTIONS are dualistic in nature,
so once in BRAIN, INTUITION'S connection is left behind.
Which is why INANIMATE UNIVERSE appears closer to REALITY
than ANIMATE UNIVERSE, which appears inappropriate.

Only RATIONAL CONCEPTION of ANIMATE UNIVERSE
makes it seem superficially dualistic, not its nature.
Then, since the causeless cause is intuitively seen,
it exists within ANIMATE UNIVERSE, causing physical REALITY.
No . . . the causeless cause does not actually exist, rather
it indicates a solely RATIONAL view of REALITY is inadequate.
But if INANIMATE UNIVERSE isn't created by itself,
then it must be created by ANIMATE UNIVERSE.
All of REALITY has not yet been exposed,
for now only its dualistic appearance is being sundered.
Anything which isn't RATIONAL is irrational,
putting INTUITIVE CONCEPTS outside of INANIMATE UNIVERSE.
It is possible for something, like the causeless cause,
to be seen intuitively and not be within ANIMATE UNIVERSE.
Therefore the cause of the effect of INANIMATE UNIVERSE
is something not in ANIMATE UNIVERSE, not yet revealed.
Each universe is mortally created to a specific fashion;
the giant of REALITY is not balanced upon turtle DUALITY.

16:31

Bob the guard doesn't care to know the person inside;
he is just like me, judging everybody by their appearances.
The paint of a clown hides the scars of LIFE on his face;
what is underneath that it should be so important?
SCIENCE has informed me of my accidental existence;
there is no more to me than chance mutations of isotopes.
Know this one thing as TRUTH in REALITY:
no RATIONAL view can actually see LIFE.
But BIOMATTER constituting living beings
reacts to physical laws just as do INANIMATE OBJECTS.
That is not LIFE as it is, what makes it tick inside,
the grand and glorious mystery we fear to know truly.
A RATIONAL view fails to identify only a single piece:
the missing 1 tying all the others together.
Mankind knows LIFE by the fact of our living,
and the evidence that what makes us is not just MATTER.

The material universe is known by SPACE displaced,
and the ordering of BIOMATTER occurs in a similar manner.
A totally external view of how MATTER could live,
known biologically, a RATIONAL approximation of LIFE.
From outside its cellular membrane,
BIOMATTER appears much like any other material OBJECT.
If LIFE is just MATTER in an unusual form, then why does it
disassociate when something is missing?
As yet, no suitable answer exists to that question,
or what holds carbon ashes together while it's living.
What is the something that lives and then dies,
making MATTER and LIFE two distinct forms?
The secrets of BIOMATTER are bound up in a contrast;
if they were the same, then there would be no mystery.
What are the basic measures brought to OBJECTS,
the ways in which LIFE is assumed to be MATTER?
INANIMATE UNIVERSE consists of 3 BASIC QUANTITIES,
known as MASS, EXTENSION, and TIME—MET for short.
Why is it that when living ORGANISM dies, for this LIFE,
MET initiate a disappearing act, but do not return?
Some essence exists which holds BIOMATTER together,
combining fixed isotopes and free air and loose water.
The solution is not simple though the answer is plain:
LIFE is not MATTER, it is just approached this way.
If SCIENCE can take apart MATTER and put it back together,
and it can't with ORGANISMS, they are designed differently.
At any level missing interference from divine assumptions,
LIFE is not MATTER, and no case exists where this is not true.
That might be acceptable only as a general rule;
there are instances like PHOTOSYNTHESIS which violate it.
Gods of SCIENCE have decreed LIFE born of MATTER,
from the distant past, combining the sun with mud.
The only proof for BIOMATTER that makes any sense
is how EVOLUTION works along neo-darwinian lines.
Priests say conditions wherein LIFE was born from chaos,
no longer exist for its origination in this day and age.
The primeval soup from where amino acids formed BIOMATTER
was more like Venus than the earth of today.

Maybe the cosmos is in such wonderful order that
chaos is not in sufficient abundance to chance new LIFE.
The only evidence for BIOMATTER has been found on earth,
even though SETI continuously searches the cosmos.
Two possibilities might give ENERGY unto LIFE,
providing it with the animation and zest not cast in MATTER.
SCIENCE has shown that isotopes construct BIOMATTER,
and there are only so many ways this can happen.
Either insensible ANIMATE ENERGY binds BIOMATTER,
or regular MATTER has hidden INANIMATE ENERGY inlaid.
Organic molecules have some hidden ANIMATE component,
or they are just common MATTER, with some ENERGY added.
As our reflections have already begun to intimate,
it is the former option conducting LIFE to its unusual status.
Actually those 2 options may be more similar than not;
if REALITY is 1, ultimately so are the 2 universes.
Gods of SCIENCE have declared for the atomic structure
of LIFE's organic molecules—this head is full of rocks.
ENERGY for BIOMATTER is from anabolism and catabolism,
chemical interactions which fuel CELL's parts.
Those divine creatures tread right past a great problem:
physical laws have never been able to create LIFE.
Which shouldn't stop SCIENCE's progress in its tracks,
there is no method sufficient to replace it.
There is a rationale behind a stop light to copying LIFE:
if the theory cannot be proven, then it must not be useful.
So SCIENCE hypocritically doesn't follow its own rules;
at least its theories don't hide behind mystical chanting.
If humanity has been formed from just a mess of MATTER,
then LIFE is just one big cosmic joke.
Man is born, learns he will eventually die,
and then proceeds to make the prediction come true.
Each unique LIFE rises from the mud and ash,
and then departs, never to be seen or heard from again.
All phases of existence BIOMATTER attains can be
physically observed to exist within INANIMATE UNIVERSE.
Consider the entire span of TIME imagined to exist,
and how each LIFE is pissed away in less than a shake.

SCIENCE claims the universe is 10–15 billion years old,
and if I'm lucky, I may live to see 1 century.
One lesson humanity has been taught over the years:
the more that it learns, the more everything makes sense.
Man used to believe fickle gods ruled nature,
which didn't make sense, so he replaced them with SCIENCE.
The following lesson may never be learned:
being born just to die does not make any sense.
Everything in the cosmos has a connection and a rhythm;
the trick is to see how BIOMATTER fits in.
If LIFE is merely another type of MATTER,
then why would it evolve?
Rocks and suns pass 1 way down the ENERGY well;
ordinary MATTER doesn't do what BIOMATTER does.
Mere chance is an insufficient rationale
spawned by some gods to make other gods obsolescent.
But there is no other evidence for BIOMATTER'S emergence,
other than to deduce it came from hot salt water.
Any motion in INANIMATE UNIVERSE, any event alteration,
requires inspiring FORCE to make it transpire.
There is no single instance I can conceive
where OBJECTS exist without some FORCE interaction.
Why is EVOLUTION not given the same power,
for some cause to make some other effect happen?
SCIENCE won't accept any source to EVOLUTION but chance
because then a RATIONAL view must be shared with another.
Supported upon EVOLUTION'S convoluted shoulders,
any FORCE but chance is an invitation to other gods.

17:23

Within me there is 1 undefined being,
and without there is a completely different defined 1.
What is LIFE that it should hide from plain sight;
could there be more to it than what meets the eye?
My reflection in a mirror shows the contours of my face;
superficial characteristics indicating me, but they aren't me.

Does the form a body takes form the real person,
or does the body reflect the person trapped inside?
Everything I am is part of me, including my body,
but what I look like is a reflection of my personality.
And yet, the question still lingers around unsettled MIND:
why is LIFE required to exist with surface MATTER?
That is a question I can't possibly answer;
my whole CONCEPT of BIOMATTER is physical in nature.
And yet, LIFE and MATTER use ENERGY with distinct interests;
why should only one require a steady infusion of ENERGY?
ENERGY manifests itself in all types of MATTER;
the biomaterial type is just more tenuous.
And yet, why would AETHER appear as LIFE in some soil,
and completely ignore its neighbors, the rocks?
The possibility AETHER only comes alive in BIOMATTER
is much more improbable than accepting MATTER as alive.
And yet, should we all bow to chemical gods,
letting ourselves be ruled by their substantial whims?
There is no problem applying chemistry to BIOMATTER;
all MATTER must follow the same inflexible rules.
And yet, LIFE is special in its uncertain way,
rules granted to it are made to be broken.
It makes much more sense to formulate 1 theory:
all MATTER—same rules—no thing is special and separate.
There is one theory, otherwise known as REALITY,
and its aetheric source divides into two diverse universes.
REALITY as 1 universe still makes much more sense
than the notion more than 1 is existing or probable.
A probability that rocks live, rather than universal DUALITY,
is less likely than REALITY where LIFE is already here.
I don't doubt BIOMATTER exists, and living rocks don't,
but it's most probable OBJECTS are either alive, or not.
Is it not more probable that all rocks are radioactive,
than some should be endowed with emissive reactions?
BIOMATTER could be different from regular MATTER,
just as radioactive rocks are distinct from common 1's.
Sensation fills OBJECTS with the right stuff;
how can they be unique and still be the same?

All OBJECTS exist in a specific place and instance,
which gives each a different material existence.
MATTER is conceived by three BASIC MET QUANTITIES;
how does different LIFE fit into INANIMATE UNIVERSE?
OBJECTS have certain defined relations to SPACE and TIME,
biomaterial ones aren't different than material ones.
Imagine LIFE is formed by a totally unique pattern;
how could it exist like MATTER in TIME and SPACE?
LIFE and BIOMATTER could be 1 and the same;
1 is viewed intuitively and 1 is viewed rationally.
LIFE thus presents itself as OBJECT for a RATIONAL view,
while hiding its real self behind porous membranes.
BIOMATTER is only a perspective of a living being;
the side within ANIMATE UNIVERSE is not my perspective.
SPACE and TIME only require OBJECTS to exist;
they make no claims as to the source of this existence.
Its use is to show how it relates to MATTER,
so BIOMATTER shows its existence in INANIMATE UNIVERSE.
TIME and SPACE have no ANIMATE UNIVERSE parameters;
their existence attaches to sensual PERCEPTION.
Material OBJECTS are fully formed and cohesive,
which doesn't tend to lend BIOMATTER special credence.
What makes biomaterial OBJECTS especially deserving
of exceptional consideration concerning their structure?
BIOMATTER is determined to be different than MATTER
because a RATIONAL view sees it behaving differently.
Where will the source of the illusion be found,
if the act is set-up to fool basic PERCEPTIONS?
SCIENCE has attempted to ascertain BIOMATTER by assuming
its structure must be the same as that of MATTER.
If magic is observed with an eye only on the action,
then no IDEA will form of underlying TRUTH.
As far as RATIONAL PERCEPTION is concerned,
OBJECTS are OBJECTS, whether BIOMATTER or MATTER.
LIFE is only OBJECT when surrounded by a membrane;
its internal structures must be removed to be limited.
CELLS have membranes and MATTER isn't so considered,
making inside what it <is>, and outside what it <is not>.

When its membrane is ruptured LIFE goes away;
why do material OBJECTS not behave in a similar fashion?
They may, even though it isn't manifestly apparent;
OBJECTS are only OBJECTS as long as they remain OBJECTS.
What causes those OBJECTS to appear in material form;
should they be accepted as MET, and just move on?
BASIC QUANTITIES are how I know of OBJECTS,
but their source is a rock I can't touch.
If AETHER is the source of all ENERGY,
then it is the source of all LIFE, whether godly or godless.
ENERGY must travel some path to reach a destination,
and this is another REASON why BIOMATTER is MATTER.
MATTER from AETHER is the same as dead LIFE,
the same formula—if not the taste, then the pudding.
There must be some rationale as to why BIOMATTER
attaches itself to MATTER, and then lets it go.
Maybe DEATH is part of LIFE, not just the ending;
there is some more fundamental symbiosis involved.
A necessary conclusion I can draw from prior premises
is BIOMATTER and DEATH both come from AETHER.
DEATH might be how LIFE exists unattached to MATTER;
AETHER would not be the closest bond of this essence.
If LIFE and DEATH are bound at their ANIMATE source,
they might be 2 opposite ways of looking at the same thing.
To suggest LIFE springs from DEATH like fables
is to invite further study of biology gods' decrees.
That doesn't contradict what SCIENCE has determined,
since the proposed connection is beyond my sense capacity.
LIFE and DEATH are united within ANIMATE UNIVERSE;
two views divide them into divergent flows.

18:09

Bob the guard walks the halls back and forth;
no matter where he is, I still exist, trapped in here.
REALITY exists outside any PERCEPTION of it;
events continue to happen within SPACE and TIME.

Who I am doesn't change with chance PERCEPTION,
any more than other OBJECTS are subject to my perspective.
LIFE is uninvolved with CREATION of TIME and SPACE;
they exist whether sensation perceives them or not.
ANIMATE UNIVERSE provides the source for BIOMATTER,
while INANIMATE UNIVERSE provides for SPACE and TIME.
So why does LIFE seem to require TIME and SPACE,
where existence of its motion requires both QUANTITIES?
BIOMATTER is MATTER to SPACE and TIME;
implying it uses them, while still not being of them.
LIFE is at the crossroads between universes;
its source is ANIMATE, it finds use for INANIMATE, MATTER.
MATTER exists solely within INANIMATE UNIVERSE,
and it requires the use of TIME and SPACE.
Living creatures experience SPACE and TIME motion;
this is their biomaterial existence, not their LIFE.
Then ANIMATE UNIVERSE functions from different laws,
using motions which don't require TIME and SPACE.
Or better yet, there is no motion in the currents of MIND;
what moves in ANIMATE UNIVERSE is no RATIONAL OBJECT.
BIOMATTER without SPACE and TIME is without motion,
only a fleeting touch with INANIMATE begins it and ends it.
Where do TIME and SPACE enter into fascinating MIND,
so THOUGHTS can separate into one following another?
THOUGHTS must exist in SPACE, in my BRAIN not another;
also in TIME, where 1 is replaced by 1 more.
Our MIND is in one universe, its material aspect in another,
and THOUGHTS slip into a comfortable neural embrace.
Somehow THOUGHTS are of my MIND, but not in my MIND;
possibly in my BRAIN, which works to physical laws.
Eternal MIND's essence shuns TIME and SPACE,
while material motions pass beyond mere cognition.
No MATTER is made solid by belief in its existence,
which implies THOUGHT's origination—far from MATTER.
Where do SPACE and TIME and LIFE come from, if when
they appear all are identified as distinct entities?
All TIME and SPACE is a reference from AETHER,
so in some manner all of them must be part of it.

Either SPACE and TIME are derived distinct from LIFE,
or LIFE is derived within TIME and SPACE.
It doesn't appear as though BIOMATTER derives MET,
for then it must interfere between absolutes and divisions.
MATTER is a creature known to haunt SPACE and TIME,
while LIFE only does so before DEATH exists.
If TIME and SPACE are derived distinct from BIOMATTER,
then it can be realistically distinct from MATTER.
LIFE cannot be stuck into a miserable bowl of OBJECTS;
its manner of existence is beyond sensory PERCEPTION.
If BIOMATTER is derived within SPACE and TIME,
then MATTER is the master of it, as SCIENCE has decided.
Are we to believe there is no afterlife, no heaven,
no hell, no reincarnation, and mainly—no SOUL?
There is no extant proof for any of those things;
just because they are desired doesn't make them exist.
Does any sane person seriously WANT to believe in hell;
is the goal of heaven worth the price of a slight misstep?
They might not be desired, and can still be imagined;
every CONCEPT is based on physical material REALITY.
Divine CONCEPTIONS fall into line with ANIMATE UNIVERSE,
while defying existence beneath TIME and SPACE.
ANIMATE UNIVERSE seems to be the repository
for every unproven essence ever imagined to exist.
ENERGIES and FORCES power INANIMATE UNIVERSE;
others just as strong exist outside of direct stimulation.
The point up for examination is whether BIOMATTER
must come from SPACE and TIME, since they are all AETHER.
Does belief count in the overall scheme of things;
is a serious belief required to attach LIFE to after-DEATH?
If there is LIFE after DEATH,
it isn't subject to TIME and SPACE.
A premise mandating ANIMATE UNIVERSE house LIFE,
whether with a brief material form or with permanent SOUL.
Therefore, if there isn't LIFE after DEATH,
then there is no difference between MATTER and BIOMATTER.
The only proof for LIFE after DEATH comes
from near-DEATH experiences, and mystical travelers.

There doesn't seem to be an acceptable solution
for proving whether I will persist after DEATH.
PURPOSE in this reflection is to lay out a picture,
to establish possibilities for all of LIFE'S mysteries.
Therefore ANIMATE UNIVERSE is proposed as an alternative,
with the possibility of BIOMATTER'S source existing therein.
As ANIMATE UNIVERSE covers more of the holes in extant theories
regarding LIFE, its possibility becomes stronger.
It isn't possible to prove anything absolutely,
but as possibilities become probabilities, belief increases.
Then let these reflections proceed based on a feeling:
LIFE is derived distinct from SPACE and TIME.
A solid belief if its existence clarifies BIOMATTER,
while it will fade to nothing if it's more new-age babble.
What is normally perceived as TIME and SPACE motion
is not a reliable criterion for LIFE'S derivative natures.

****

19:19

A wise man once said: rely on yourself, not on others,
for no one may grant you the key to your own SOUL.
As if I could truly rely on anyone else,
or a mouse would offer to be a play-toy for a cat.
Mystics fill orders for maps guiding the worthy few;
chance does not bring an end to suffering in sight.
But those who claim to be most wise
are generally the 1's who are the biggest pain in the ass.
How shall we know wise men, what marks do they bear,
if those who do not know must rely on those who claim to?
Ask around among the many purported wise men;
the answer is likely so obvious that it can't be seen.
They should be known by the fruit spread from the tree,
but what if the fruit is bitter instead of sweet?
Wise men, like others, offer fruit growing from within;
history has shown the message distasteful to most palates.

Wise men do not abound while those with agents do,
randomly searching for Truth *through minefields of* Pain.
A path to Wisdom may be blazed by a lone trekker;
though if the destination is the same—what a waste.
Yet maybe that is false, or at least not true;
the most other people can ever grant us is their experience.
Knowledge is what I make it, neither good nor bad,
and this has opened my eyes to new vistas.
Placing one foot after the other is a personal burden;
lonely solo passion asks no other to move lost feet.
Modern society has been guided by liberal faddists
to the point that people are unable to rely on themselves.
Relying on others is a crutch to nowhere; nowhere
along the path, while further along into their clutches.
Blindly following those who claim to know more,
though some do, doesn't show me where I need to go.
What other people deign to bestow upon us
also has no connection to what we are able to accept.
If it's too great, I can't absorb it;
if it's too little, I will spurn it.
That is part of human nature, accepting
as we are able to, at a particular moment.
There is a natural tendency by most people to resist,
whether the gift is of love or of anger.
Screaming moral frustration loses the match to the point;
ears closed by Mind's *shutter do not partake of opinions.*
Only if I'm offered knowledge in a manner, and in Time,
that I'm willing to accept, will it stick and grow.
The same messages have been transmitted for ages,
and still we are locked in an evolutionary struggle.
If the problem isn't in the speaker, it's in the receiver;
1 or the other must change for adequate transmission.
Since so many people do not understand the message,
maybe a different perspective on it should be offered.
The words of the mystics have turned into holy scripture,
instead of a guide for expanding inner knowledge.
Discernment is the only soil in which Soul *can grow,*
to fulfill Beauty *into what it can become.*

If REALITY exists everywhere, then it exists within me,
leaving a choice between faith in others, or in myself.
Within this shell beats not the heart of perfection;
otherwise striving for the forlorn peak leads to madness.
Neither are those who wave perfection before my eyes,
hoping to hide TRUTH—they are no better than I.
Are we bulls to see motion and charge blindly,
baited to untimely DEATH by hidden controlling hands?
Thrown in front—perfection and heaven and eternity;
loosening my own proper noose, I madly assault them all.
Leave on imperfections honestly gained and lost,
rather than perfections bestowed by all too mortal grace.
It's sadly funny how all-too-human priests are,
giving advice they would do well to heed.
Reliance upon mankind is faith in corporeal flesh;
if dry skin is pierced, is there anything substantial within?

19:48

No matter what anybody thinks of me, I'm still the same;
the shell outside will always hide the man within.
Two parts to the whole found down all conceivable paths;
the silent unobtrusive one affects without being seen.
My body obviously affects who I am, like I'm hungry,
but privations don't retard my MIND/body connection.
Why is LIFE always attached to a physical body,
if its source and existence are in a separate universe?
LIFE is intuitively viewed within ANIMATE UNIVERSE;
MATTER is rationally viewed within INANIMATE UNIVERSE.
Then LIFE may not be attached to MATTER;
it is a specific type of distinctly perceived OBJECT.
But BIOMATTER is seen to be a type of MATTER;
these 2 are susceptible to the same physical principles.
Should we consider the sun and moon to be identical,
if they are susceptible to the same physical principles?
Obviously not, since they are 2 dissimilar OBJECTS,
but they are both considered to exist as MATTER.

What makes the sun a unique entity within REALITY
is different from what makes the moon retain its capacity.
But they are both MATTER;
some sense can be made of why they are different.
What makes LIFE *a unique entity within* REALITY
is different from what makes MATTER *retain its capacity.*
There are evident and uncommon traits between them;
otherwise the BIOMATTER term could be tossed away.
The sun and moon comparison is rationally available,
while LIFE *and* MATTER *cannot be conceived together.*
They just were;
unless preceding THOUGHT was unintelligibly created.
LIFE *used improperly to expose complex* THOUGHT:
its actual essence is beyond simple MATTER'S *touch.*
It's picayune to state the living source is out of reach,
but change it to BIOMATTER, and look . . . there it is.
LIFE *is approximated by its* RATIONAL *biomaterial name,*
so living creatures can be viewed as QUANTITIES *of MET.*
Therefore BIOMATTER must use MATTER,
but their structures are composed in specialized furnaces.
The nature of LIFE *cannot be perceived by* INANIMATE,
while reserved for ANIMATE, PERCEPTION.
What I call living is largely distinct from MATTER, largely,
and it still is rationally perceived as BIOMATTER.
Grasp a simple fact—inert chemicals do not create LIFE—
and then separating LIFE *from* MATTER *is not too hard.*
It's difficult to believe isotopes in living ORGANISMS
are different from the 1's found in inert OBJECTS.
Even more curious that gods of SCIENCE *have never envisaged*
CELLS *as structurally different from* MATTER.
The isotopes are the same;
so something else makes dual MATTERS distinct.
How OBJECTS *are perceived has this sharp distinction:*
biomaterial CELLS *and material molecules are far apart.*
SCIENCE is able to collect the ash from a burnt corpse,
and thereby determine its constituent isotopes.
Yet those same gods cannot put them back together,
and make a living breathing functional LIFE.

Molecules have distinct combinations of isotopes;
even organic 1's can be subdivided.
There must be something besides just chemical formulas
which create and bind LIFE into its magnificent cocoon.
That has been imagined before, but never proven;
primary cellular chemicals have been repeatedly indicated.
Gods of SCIENCE have failed to provide a simple answer to:
why is LIFE'S structure strangely different from MATTER'S?
Maybe after BIOMATTER is decomposed into ash,
the structural adhesion has already been lost to FIRE.
Blinkered gods can never find that part of the whole
because it cannot be sensed within INANIMATE UNIVERSE.
This is a bit difficult to bear,
substantial molecules connected by an insubstantial glue.
Fasten MEMORY back upon REALITY as one essence;
the connection is real, the RATIONAL view is limited.
Disbelief: BIOMATTER is constructed by mysterious means;
an attachment which, among OBJECTS, only fits creatures.
Unless priests can figure how to raise LIFE from its DEATH,
they will never pull a live rabbit from MATTER'S hat.
Nevertheless, secret LIFE extant within INANIMATE UNIVERSE
must abide by the same physical laws as MATTER.
PERCEPTION determines which CONCEPTION goes where,
so MATTER and LIFE can be similar or different.
With the consequence that OBJECTS affect OBJECTS,
and BIOMATTER was born from a fetid swamp of MATTER.
Gods of SCIENCE decree—MATTER created LIFE—
or now the possibility could be that LIFE created MATTER.
Chronological evidence favors former MATTER;
the earth is much older than its resulting BIOMATTER.
Latter MATTER could be the feces of some giants,
dropping molten planets and fiery suns in their wake.
I don't give that feeble option much credence,
and a smell that obnoxious would still linger around.
The former explanation suffices by divine
decree, held together by a broad flawed syllogism.
BIOMATTER is here and must have come from somewhere;
all OBJECTS are MATTER; so it must originate with MATTER.

What is the problem with that uncomplicated THOUGHT?
Only the part about all OBJECTS are MATTER.
Animals have a predisposition to see REALITY as MATTER,
this is the way their physical senses function.
Look for the words all or every in a RATIONAL phrase;
a monster problem is lurking somewhere under the bed.
All and every aren't irrational terms;
for example, maximum QUANTITY of apples in a barrel.
Those words imply a symbiosis with INFINITY,
and this is not possible using FINITY references.
BIOMATTER didn't create MATTER, and MATTER didn't create it;
which leaves no options, so BIOMATTER isn't here.
The possibility for LIFE was created along with MATTER,
side by side, using separate SPACES and TIMES.
There is no physical proof for that proposition;
SCIENCE has dated rocks to be older than LIFE.
MATTER'S structure can be resembled by chemical means,
but LIFE is fastened with a hidden un-biological pin.
Distribution of MATTER into small particles is well-known,
none of which indicate a mysterious connection.
In order to resolve unknown LIFE to our satisfaction,
MATTER must be shown energetic <not atomic> in nature.
This will prove to be quite a feat,
showing SCIENCE'S past few centuries to be inaccurate.
Refer to modern writ about the uncertainty of pieces:
the atomic nature of elements is not particulate.
That defies the ways SCIENCE can manipulate MATTER;
virtually any chemical reaction is atomic in nature.
Formation of REALITY by sensation is mentally defective;
must we continue a contrary harangue on the same point?
But what is sensed locates my place in the world;
if it's all illusion, then I will become lost.
What we seem to see and feel as rock-hard permanence
is limited senses being modified, FORCES changing inputs.
I don't believe a rock isn't real,
or I don't touch it, just some pattern of FORCES.
How LIFE is created different from MATTER is much easier
to impart after conceiving REALITY'S energetic nature.

Reinventing MATTER'S wheel leads me to confusion;
it would be simpler to remix known QUANTITIES.
Concentrate on one phrase which is quite simple:
LIFE begets LIFE.
If that is factual, then MATTER must be energetic,
for in no other way could 2 distinct MATTERS integrate.
MATTER is understood by reference to its parts;
LIFE cannot be understood in this fashion, only misused.
BIOMATTER doesn't derive from MATTER;
MATTER doesn't derive from BIOMATTER.
MET are rationally sensed as QUANTITIES of REALITY;
LIFE is intuitively felt as QUALIA within REALITY.

20:48

I reach down into the basin of water and wash my face;
my reflection vanishes, and smoothly returns, wrinkled.
What is within the shadowed eyes looking out;
water eyes are just water, are living eyes something more?
I know I'm more than just a bunch of chemicals,
but my body responds to MATTER like an ordinary rock.
Laws of INANIMATE UNIVERSE rule both types of MATTER;
that which works, works for all.
As far as knowing of OBJECT action within my universe,
there is no difference between MATTER and BIOMATTER.
LIFE itself is only beholden to ANIMATE UNIVERSE dictates,
ephemeral laws defying logical enforcement.
ANIMATE is seen intuitively, as INANIMATE is seen rationally;
therefore the laws of each should be strikingly different.
Yet LIFE and its material shell are one and the same,
viewed from internal and external perspectives.
Within is an INTUITIVE view, and tyros estimate its essence;
without is a RATIONAL view, and SCIENCE writes its rules.
A RATIONAL view of LIFE observes its unique properties,
and still is not able to determine their origination.
INANIMATE UNIVERSE is known by making RATIONAL sense;
irrational knowledge can only be partially understood.

Likewise an INTUITIVE view of MATTER is insensible,
losing understanding for INANIMATE motion.
This will throw those with fixed MIND into a loop:
a RATIONAL sop of an INTUITIVE view of INANIMATE UNIVERSE.
How does CELL truly view INANIMATE UNIVERSE;
does the basic unit of LIFE see itself different from MATTER?
If a RATIONAL view can estimate an INTUITIVE 1,
and CELL is BIOMATTER, there must be some basic CONCEPT.
LIFE explores and absorbs, searches and defecates,
yet those are not what priests find via RATIONAL searches.
To view BIOMATTER in a fashion both holistic and INTUITIVE
requires me to abandon seeking its parts.
This is the conundrum that may forever bedevil seekers:
how can a unitary view see any distinctions at all?
An INTUITIVE view might add to a RATIONAL dissection of
REALITY by offering a perspective with everything included.
What is LIFE'S relation to MASS and EXTENSION and TIME;
could anything exist without these QUANTITIES?
BIOMATTER isn't merely unexplained MATTER;
if it were inert, then there would be no need to die.
LIFE uses MATTER from a totally different perspective;
what is required for one has no existence for the other.
There must be some physical requirements for living,
or else there is no rationale for it to exist as BIOMATTER.
LIFE is THOUGHT to exist within SPACE and TIME;
only its biomaterial apparition is able to act in this guise.
But living ORGANISMS die!
They can't pass on unless they have already been.
LIFE itself has no knowledge of motion in TIME or SPACE;
RATIONAL observation of its material aspect tricks us.
BIOMATTER itself goes from 1 moment to the next,
and also can't be here and there at the same instant.
Gods of SCIENCE assert no difference between MATTERS;
from this tight view, both exist within SPACE and TIME.
Therefore BIOMATTER dies, while its glue can live on;
termination of existence is within INANIMATE UNIVERSE.
A RATIONAL view asserts the absence of TIME and SPACE
motion makes the living alternative unbelievable.

It's difficult to rationalize an essence of that nature;
OBJECTS are conceived from their MET BASIC QUANTITIES.
Everything within RATIONAL awareness can be quantified,
except LIFE and its associated limbs.
Even the existence of BIOMATTER can be proportioned,
all the parts and pieces which make it real.
LIFE cannot be measured, it is experienced
and conceived by QUALIA of events.
Quantified INANIMATE UNIVERSE is rationally perceived,
qualified ANIMATE UNIVERSE is intuitively sequestered.
A RATIONAL perspective can understand that QUALIA exist,
and still have no CONCEPTION of what it really is.
Like my version of BIOMATTER, QUALITY does exist;
if it didn't, then there would be no CONCEPT for it.
Venus and Mars pinning the earth in between,
losing what can be gained by letting what is be the same.
EMOTIONS and BEAUTY and art and aesthetics and sunsets;
errant QUALITIES with solid effects on INANIMATE UNIVERSE.
Some people do ignore those facets in the hurly-burly;
a peril from losing LIFE'S preserver on a substantial shore.
If QUALITY can be observed within INANIMATE UNIVERSE,
QUANTITY should be observed within ANIMATE UNIVERSE.
Likely, QUANTITY finds an incomplete parallel there,
yet how this is done must again be referred to INTUITION.
The best solution entering my BRAIN
is to fix INANIMATE QUALITY, and then flip them around.
REALITY forbids full organization of ANIMATE UNIVERSE:
QUALIA is only available to its internal living effects.
Though it does affect OBJECTS within INANIMATE UNIVERSE,
by creatures expressing specific likes or dislikes.
Until humanity constitutes recognized standards for LIFE,
it will remain the unknown province of ghosts and kooks.
ANIMATE UNIVERSE has been explored, but only slightly,
so any babbling lunacy can be claimed as quite real.
Which is overall an extremely unhelpful situation,
leaving the source of LIFE to those who would abuse it.
Psychics claim to be endowed with inner vision,
and still can't keep themselves from getting arrested.

It seems strange for those composed of LIFE'S FORCE
to spend so much TIME ignoring what they really are.
If there is ANIMATE UNIVERSE somewhere in REALITY,
then it's there living room is most likely to be found.
Is there still any trouble with this dualistic IDEA:
one REALITY with two distinct and opposite perspectives?
INANIMATE UNIVERSE QUANTITY is a RATIONAL external view;
ANIMATE UNIVERSE QUALITY is an INTUITIVE internal view.
There should be no problem with INANIMATE acceptance,
everything normally sensed is acknowledged to exist.
Right. I have a problem with what is ANIMATE by nature,
which is irrational and therefore shouldn't exist.
Yet if LIFE does exist as a separate essence from MATTER,
it would have to be in a totally irrational manner.
Finally coming to the source of my problem:
irrational answers must be accepted without proof.
There is only one solid proof for our alternative theory:
LIFE begets LIFE.
That is as self-contradictory as the causeless cause;
it's irrational to imagine BIOMATTER created itself.
CREATION of LIFE from MATTER is not a plausible theory,
evidence only shows they are somehow connected.
Possibly acceptable if 1 problem is suitably resolved:
how ENERGY for BIOMATTER is transferred without MATTER.
Very few mechanisms exist to energize LIFE;
a simple problem made complex by misunderstanding.
SCIENCE postulates ENERGY generation by PHOTOSYNTHESIS,
or the more recent discovery of deep-sea chemical transfer.
Those processes lack one thing gods of SCIENCE
normally require of everything else—consistency.
Simple non-neural creatures can directly absorb ENERGY,
while higher animals seem to have lost this ability.
LIFE is formed and spread outside of INANIMATE UNIVERSE;
this is the only consistent explanation for its existence.
Ohhhh . . . the source of living is only seen intuitively,
but somehow this irrationality must also be consistent.
ORGANISMS seem to absorb ENERGY from organic molecules,
and are able to modify some molecular bonds of MATTER.

ENERGY which is somehow contained by physical means,
implying a contradiction in an alternate theory of LIFE.
That does not imply a contradiction in DUALITY;
all is one REALITY, so separate universes must interact.
SCIENCE theorizes molecular bonds energize BIOMATTER,
and I should now believe it's from a hidden source.
Gods of SCIENCE view LIFE as carbon macromolecules;
why cannot LIFE be created from these minimal elements?
Proteins and fats and carbohydrates are similar,
constructed from varying chains centered on carbon.
Priests can claim a solely RATIONAL theory of existence
when they can create LIFE from C, H, N, and O.
That hasn't happened and doesn't appear it ever will,
but it's the best explanation yet offered for living structures.
Until that godforsaken event comes to pass,
LIFE will never be proven from a material basis.

21:51

It's only the 3rd day and I feel my existence ebbing away;
it seems to go faster and faster as I get slower and slower.
LIFE is more than the motions making it individualistic,
it is also ENERGY received by consuming one another.
I can get up and do just about any activity I desire,
the problem is I just don't want to.
What is the single biggest observable difference
between solid MATTER and unreliable LIFE?
MATTER isn't capable of gaining ENERGY on its own,
while BIOMATTER must constantly gain it in order to survive.
The sun and rocks are winding down,
turning useful ENERGY into a pool at the end of the falls.
The process of OBJECTS moving changes ENERGY;
more scientifically—it's the process of changing ENTROPY.
Whereas LIFE requires a gain in ENERGY to survive;
why should it do so if it is just another form of MATTER?
The gain of ENERGY by BIOMATTER is temporary;
it's commonly lost, just like the flaming sun.

Energy is gained in order to achieve independent motion,
which is one of the basic sensed abilities of Life.
Even though Matter is incapable of animal appetites,
it's still able to pick up Energy during motion.
Life is able to move under its own volition,
Matter is not.
Biomatter is different from Matter, no question,
but it's unclear how a distinction is made in their Energies.
Gods of Science have not satisfactorily divulged
how inert Matter could gain Energy, or radically move.
Matter stores Energy in a variety of ways;
Potential and chemical are a couple I can mention.
Distinguishing two types of primordial essences
is more basic than just a difference in Energy.
Biomatter is always seen as 1 type of many Objects,
and these are differentiated by sensible Perception.
Not quite. The prime way Life is distinguished from Matter
is observing the movements identifying these Objects.
Random movement isn't 1 of Matter's hallmarks;
Object is best known when statically dissected.
What it asks, what it leaves, what it wants, what it needs;
yet not what Life is.
Science has shown it can determine Matter by what it is,
dividing it with no relation to its environment.
Pseudo-gods have hinted at this without more insight:
Life is only known by what it does.
Those softer Science disciplines are fully Rational,
following the dictates which separate them from babble.
What it is and what it does are two distinct Conceptions
separated by a wide chasm of imagination.
Still, in order to know what any Object is made of,
a scientist subjects it to tests and observes what it does.
What is the difference between observing what Life does,
and observing what the nature of Matter is?
That seems to be a reasonably adequate question;
Matter or Biomatter shows its secrets when stressed.
Striking the point exactly into its pulsing heart,
and then splintering the effect with futile words.

SCIENCE knows of chemicals through this process,
and pushes ORGANISMS to explore their limitations.
Priests subject MATTER to heinous experiments
designed to unlock their secrets by making them react.
Experimentation is the observation of reaction in OBJECTS,
then combining similarities to expose mother nature.
This is how priests guess what it is—
observing what it does from stimulus set by another.
OBJECT is dissected by using FORCE and ENERGY
to break apart the bonds holding it together.
It is not PURPOSE of divination to see what it does,
this is only the means to the result—guess what it is.
It's from theories about the nature of MATTER
that all of the modern marvels of SCIENCE have sprouted.
LIFE has been subjected to a similar series of events,
righteous assaults delivered to see how it reacts.
BIOMATTER has been presumed to be another MATTER;
there was little rationale for treating it different.
Thereby mandating a material cause to effect LIFE,
without scratching the surface of its realistic nature.
No matter whether BIOMATTER has a separate home,
its ashes are isotopes, known to exist.
No means to a result exist in a search for LIFE'S essence;
the result is the means, and the verb becomes noun.
Therefore BIOMATTER only exists as a dynamic process,
and dissection by SCIENCE misses some critical ingredient.
Use of the term "what it does"
means simply to detect how it acts on its own.
SCIENCE can't observe anything without RATIONAL intrusion,
so BIOMATTER must be interfered with in this manner.
No outside intelligence to break it apart leaves it to its own
devices to grow and create and want a little more.
While extracting isotopes from within BIOMATTER
requires interfering with its natural development.
Two things brought to the front dematerialize LIFE:
gaining ENERGY and knowing it by what it does.
The cores of MATTER and BIOMATTER are therefore distinct;
knowing 1 only partly opens up the other.

Understanding LIFE justifies the end by the means;
applying no pressure, just let nature take its course.
SCIENCE justifies MATTER as a means to an end,
and so exhumes OBJECTS while searching for their secrets.
Guessing what it is has as its goal the revision of MATTER;
observing what it does has no goal save understanding.
Understanding how to use existing OBJECTS
versus understanding how OBJECTS are used.
How can we observe what LIFE truly is
if it is assumed to be just another form of MATTER?
It's easy to misunderstand the metaphysics of REALITY;
OBJECTS appear to my senses much like 1 another.
The confusion arises by forgetting an important fact:
LIFE is alive and MATTER is dead.
Although the composted isotopes are verifiably the same,
math works different when adding up BIOMATTER.
LIFE holds its charge within clearly defined boundaries;
tame cattle on the range quickly meet DEATH.
BIOMATTER outside of PLASMIC MEMBRANE, or not
in an organic molecule, will quickly convert to material form.
CELL viewed externally is known by QUANTITIES of MET,
appearing much like any material OBJECT.
Just using my 5 senses to detect BIOMATTER
endows it with the same attributes as common MATTER.
Another IDEA is becoming more and more clear:
LIFE does not act materially, it acts spiritually.
BIOMATTER must have some distinct dualistic division;
CONCEPT of its formation within is totally unlike MATTER.
Viewed from outside of a membrane, and after DEATH,
any part of CELL is sensed as being just another OBJECT.
This is SCIENCE's traditional view of living beings:
they are built from smaller parts into bigger ones.
CELL viewed internally is made up of what it does,
METABOLISM and REPRODUCTION, bound by living FORCE.
If BIOMATTER became transparent during <what it does>,
then the verbs that describe it would turn into nouns.
The gods know less about action within a membrane,
than proven fancies of what whirls about in an atom.

That isn't quite true;
biologists have shown what many of the organelles do.
Priests have discovered numerous parts and pieces,
and still have missed the essential numberless part.
Identified OBJECTS within CELLS have specific tasks,
the each contributing to CREATION of the whole.
Inside of PLASMIC MEMBRANES is different MATTER,
there is something within hidden from the outside.
It's true a living essence is inside of CELL,
a trait which doesn't extend to OBJECTS outside.
Approximate RATIONAL dualistic CONCEPTION is the version,
no other method is available to a reasonable seeker.
That unknown within CELL consists of something,
and whatever it is can't be rationally sensed.
Pure PERCEPTION from INTUITION has no distinctions;
an immature view hinders the clear vista within.

22:52

Punishment for pissing in to the corridor is to miss a meal;
when I do it, Bob the guard gets quite pissed off indeed.
The breaking of any law should cause retribution,
yet what is a law with no means of enforcement?
Bob the warden will have to think of something to do;
if the existing system doesn't work, think of a new 1.
Rigid CONCEPTION requires laws to run the machine;
any universal understanding is no different.
RATIONAL success is based on fatalistic laws,
which govern the processes of INANIMATE UNIVERSE.
Mystics have strewn some ANIMATE UNIVERSE possibilities:
IDEAS of KARMA, lack of DISTANCE, and everywhere INFINITY.
None of which can possibly exist,
at least as far as MATTER is a constituent member.
None of these can be shown as possible,
except through their existence within ANIMATE UNIVERSE.
How they actually exist may be beyond comprehension,
but they are useless without RATIONAL restraint.

Karma is the message related by mystics and rednecks,
a reckoning outside of apparent worldly Forces.
Supposedly, justice is applied to all living creatures;
Thoughts and actions have boomerang repercussions.
What comes around goes around;
both blessed and blessed out will achieve moral reward.
No physical connection is observed for that phenomenon;
only the more enlightened might see its causes and effects.
Even if there is only the judgment of heaven or hell,
all debts must be eventually paid by each voyager.
A past full of regrets which haven't been eased
is just another threat by the powerful to make me behave.
Many gods know, through purgatory or Reincarnation,
justification for a lifetime of debts is paid at another Time.
All of which are beyond my senses and can't be proven;
distinguish how Karma affects Biomatter's daily function.
Any who have seen Karma work in their own lives
are thereby humbled enough to spread the word further.
There are obviously very few of those seers;
otherwise people wouldn't so easily ignore its validity.
It is the unwise, lacking Lives, that give it short shrift;
remembered transgressions will return home to roost.
Strange for such an unorthodox revelation
to have so much in common with the laws of motion.
Yet Karma does not move, this requires Distance;
what could separate Lives without Time and Space?
Objects move through Space by transit of Time,
none of which exist without using Distance in passing.
There is no Distance within Animate Universe;
a pure view of Reality from Intuition shows us all is one.
If there is no difference between 1 Object and another,
then no Distance need exist to keep them apart.
Life is more than a simple division into beings,
each existing for no Purpose but its own salvation.
Which implies there is something between them,
for each creature does have a unique biomaterial existence.
Remember not to coerce all Intuition into a Rational view,
nothing else will take us further from Truth.

A conversion into rationality must happen for knowledge;
each existence as it's known is highly distinct.
Each LIFE finitely presents itself until DEATH,
while ANIMATE UNIVERSE must be the opposite in nature.
Then all creatures are the same essence at their source,
while I know good and well each 1 is different.
Try to let mobile MIND think in its INFINITY configuration;
do not let many define how one must exist.
If ANIMATE UNIVERSE attaches INFINITE to BIOMATTER,
then there is still 1 giving its source to the other.
How can limited OBJECTS be partially unlimited;
is there some logic allowing multiplication to INFINITIES?
Either each creature is connected to a separate 1,
or all of them form 1 grand INFINITE structure.
That is pure RATIONAL CONCEPTION without INTUITION'S input,
which inconsistently indicates the irrational is possible.
Then each creature is connected to a separate 1,
and all of them form 1 grand INFINITE structure.
That is much closer to understanding ANIMATE UNIVERSE:
it is only irrational, not impossible.
It defies every RATIONAL instinct which I possess—
a FINITE number of INFINITES is required to compose 1.
Expecting LIFE to abide by simple logical rules
would only result in taking the fun out of it.

23:25

Bob the guard wanted to know what the hell I was doing;
he threatened to make me get on my knees and lick it up.
If all questions could be answered, they would have been;
some things happen from no discernible cause.
All things have a cause, and so did my public piss,
but most RATIONAL people won't accept irrational REASON.
The necessity for INTUITION by LIFE is hard to accept;
rigid MIND trying to stretch into a broader perspective.
There are many unanswered questions about that view,
and ANIMATE UNIVERSE, supposedly my secret home.

Intuition's claimed attachment between all Life forms
leads to questions which cast its validity in doubt.
On 1 hand, my source might be Infinite in essence,
but experience tells me Thoughts are quite different.
If we are all same Mind underneath florid tops,
why on earth do not we know what others are thinking?
If Animate Universe is just 1 big happy family,
then my Thoughts should be part of 1 enlarged Thought.
One part of whole Mind has been accidentally uncovered,
one whole of part Thought might touch Animate existence.
I hope no other sentient creature knows my Thoughts;
it's difficult enough for single Brain to keep them in line.
What an egocentric mode of thinking leaves aside:
the volume is way down and the language sounds foreign.
My Mind could be attuned to Thoughts in many voices;
my own loudly screeching, while others barely whisper.
Mentally grasp those words hardly crystal clear,
yet if spoken through delusion's fog—where and where?
Single Mind should all be in a single voice;
my own seems to work quite well in this manner.
If one man only speaks the language of his birth,
does he not have trouble with unfamiliar foreign words?
Words may start out bizarre until they are learned,
and then they become like the others in my Mind.
Which may well be the situation for Thought transferal,
uniformly separate until nimble Mind learns translation.
Telepathy is an oft proposed psychic phenomenon,
best left to the cranks and kooks who claim to use it.
Yet if we are all part of one Mind, known incompletely,
then are we not only lacking knowledge of mental speech?
Someone must know Chinese to teach me the language;
likewise to exhibit Communication with universal Mind.
The rationale behind association with personal Mind
is lucid Thoughts loudly spoken in the same language.
Thoughts in my head are clearer than others
because those are the only 1's I hear.
Rational phantoms keep Thoughts away from Reality;
non-neural Life-forms do not suffer this restriction.

Part of REALITY consists of less evolved creatures,
but they don't have the capacity to understand themselves.
Plants are able to sense animal EMOTIONS
by their lack of ability to form RATIONAL CONCEPTIONS.
Even plants have the capacity for stimulus response,
from which my superior BRAIN eventually evolved.
No LIFE-form can exist within INANIMATE UNIVERSE,
and still see wholly through INTUITION by nature.
Basic survival needs of any creature require rationality;
any successful ORGANISM sees cause and effect.
Yet the same survival mechanisms prevent far-sense,
hearing voices which do not travel in the wind.
If it's a choice between RATIONAL survival and irrationality,
there isn't much of 1 in my MIND.
What if such a ruinous choice is not required;
what if we have capacity for more than we are aware?
In order to be useful, 1 BRAIN must understand another,
and they already talk to each other through verbal language.
The words flowing from those many mouths
are based on inert MATTER, not ANIMATE MIND'S content.
Therefore, the extreme emphasis I put on MATTER,
hard terms which tend to deny ambiguity.
LIFE is more than its throwaway parts;
transference of ANIMATE ideals is always approximate.
In order to be useful, creatures require a biomaterial part,
so exchange of THOUGHTS not involving MATTER is useless.
Again consider a question inferred once before:
why cannot the gods create LIFE from material mud?
In order to be useful, the connection must be INANIMATE;
SCIENCE'S tireless labors will shortly be fulfilled by genetics.
No! Do not spout off, "We just need a little more TIME,"
promising wonders and miracle drugs to heal all ills.
SCIENCE is the hope to cure man's modern maladies;
if it can't, then nothing can.
Still insufficient to cover a total misunderstanding
of what is the central fact about ANIMATE existence.
Man lives, then he dies;
there isn't much more to him than that.

If gods of SCIENCE can chemically produce LIFE,
these THOUGHTS are meaningless—totally ignore them.
Unlocking the genetic code is just the beginning;
the more it's understood, the more it'll reveal.
Although, if gods cannot produce measly little CELL,
REALITY has one corner where RATIONAL lights cannot shine.
Admittedly, SCIENCE'S view of BIOMATTER is incomplete,
at least until the missing chemicals are synthesized.
Why is LIFE centered on CELL?
When they coexist it is living, and when apart it is dead.
Sometimes it's best just to accept the way things are;
the unique nature of any OBJECT makes it what it is.
LIFE operates on different rules from MATTER;
nothing is more buried than that which was never living.
But even BIOMATTER needs parts;
a body is composed of OBJECTS, just like other OBJECTS.
MATTER can be broken into basic parts and reformed;
when LIFE is broken into pieces, it is forever deceased.
Only when BIOMATTER is deconstructed past a certain point
will it cease to function as living ORGANISM.
If there is more to LIFE than its biomaterial existence,
there is more to communicate than its INANIMATE traits.
There is no other way for OBJECT to be constructed,
except as the sum of its material parts and pieces.
If the claim for everything from one AETHER is triumphant,
then how can it be broken into many zillions and one?
The parts constitute the whole;
any OBJECT can be shown as the sum of smaller 1's.
In order to complete any simple or complicated puzzle,
all the pieces need to be made available for inspection.
Many parts of MATTER can't be seen;
this doesn't mean they should be assumed non-existent.
How can all the pieces to LIFE be known,
if the missing one cannot be seen in a RATIONAL direction?
RATIONAL dissection is the only way to see pieces;
the other perspective, INTUITIVE, only sees the whole.
Perform the most divine solemn sacrificial procedures,
then list all the parts of LIFE including the unseen ones.

That would extend from the cycle of survival
all the way down to subatomic-level ENERGY transfer.
A theory which is shown as repeatedly violated
must be inadequate according to deity-driven rules.
A basic tenet, making SCIENCE so successful,
is to limit cause and effect to repetitious phenomena.
There is no natural process observed today in which LIFE
is formed from some inert and deficient MATTER.
Therefore according to strict rules governing theory,
BIOMATTER contains MATTER, but isn't from it.
LIFE is formed from LIFE;
cast inherently futile PHOTOSYNTHESIS arguments aside.
Even if SCIENCE is intuitively prohibited from seeing LIFE,
its existence mandates that scientists will seek it harder.
Biomaterial DEATH is twin to MATTER;
how can LIFE itself be the same twin?
They could be triplets,
or each is twin within its own distinctive arena.
An even better question to answer:
if LIFE is MATTER, why do not rocks have membranes?
Something is required to hold OBJECTS apart and together;
it might not be a membrane, but there is a separation.
Another question which primarily involves CELLS:
is there a RATIONAL foundation for their electrical charges?
BIOMATTER absorbs ENERGY from which charge is created;
rubbing a balloon will induce a similar effect in MATTER.
That ubiquitous charge is not universally INANIMATE,
it coincidentally arrives from the influence of LIFE.
Although charge does exist on some types of MATTER,
which doesn't make BIOMATTER seem so very unusual.
What are observed as the emitters of ENERGY,
OBJECTS evidencing charge without mortal interference?
Sun, earth, moon, and radioactivity;
ultimately most unliving ENERGY comes from these sources.
And yet those sources do not explain LIFE;
how does it create charge without one of those authors?
BIOMATTER has the unique ability to gain ENERGY,
even as a car accrues it by going downhill.

Contrary to divine WILL, MATTER does not gain ENERGY;
batteries and such are forced windows out of AETHER.
Aetheric theory has now diverged from accepted SCIENCE;
positional ENERGY is a hallmark of motion.
There are many more ways aetheric theory diverges
from accepted norms the gods of SCIENCE decree.
Then go ahead and suggest some of them;
there is a RATIONAL explanation for everything, if vague.
Common FIRES, not the induced chemical kind,
are based on LIFE which has decayed and is then stored.
FIRES start from fuel, oxygen, and kindling TEMPERATURE;
it's sufficiently explained by chemical reactions.
The part of FIRE that cannot be rationally explained
is what it actually is, not even a good guess.
It's the result of combustion, not something in itself;
a process which releases HEAT and light.
Why does it whip and grow and die,
and why does it require dead LIFE to kick it up?
It seems to have many characteristics of LIFE,
but then so does VIRUS and it isn't alive.
Why does ATP carry ENERGY for CELLS;
ENERGY comes from molecules, so should any type not do?
Only certain organelles can absorb from external sources;
just as my body has only 1 mouth with which to feed.
Seeds contain more ENERGY than their small size dictates;
a plant can spring and grow from a sliver of its parents.
Atomic power is based on an even smaller source;
size doesn't indicate how much ENERGY is within.
LIFE acts, MATTER reacts;
societal relations are not bought both alive and dead.
MATTER doesn't have the capacity for self-direction,
and some people I know should be denied it as well.
LIFE as MATTER is a partial comparison with partial gain;
soil is the same as dirt, a forest is a group of trees.
Approximations are still useful;
any repetitive CONCEPT will continue to exhibit value.

A last bitch: a RATIONAL *view bases its gods on repetition,*
and evolves LIFE *by chance—just a curious dichotomy.*

****

24:47

Aaaaaaaaaahhhhhhhhhhhhhhhh!
Some yells are so real that fear takes hold, is this one?
The echoes are gone and quiet reigns,
my heart beats slowly back to slumbering submission.
In uniform patrolling the line between right and wrong,
until steps fall over into the shady side of the street.
Brown madness, white train;
cooking and cooking for hours turning into more hours.
Older siblings are good for one sentimental chore,
tormenting those younger after catching the brunt of hell.
How to trim this fur ball into delectable patches
down to the point with machines by the gross?
Electrified beasts don't rinse well in water,
this one too gives up its ghost to my unscathed hand.
Righting of wrongs takes many unfortunate turns,
like beating the crap out of those less physically able.
A fear of probing into depths better left untouched,
pink petulant petals palpitating precipitously.
Wrong?! When is anything ever right,
if there is no known way to satisfy the insatiable?
Living in a bungalow made of multi-storied tents,
a little one pulls on the bottom one to tumble them all.
Leave from this receptacle for better parts unknown,
moving the metal beast to get a little better access.
Push and heave on that cheap white luxury wagon,
and down it rolls to rest in a watery heaven.
It stays afloat and then continues to stay afloat;
leave it to its fate for no apparent cause.
Ask Mom—where has Dad gone now;
off she points—is she sullen or does she pout?

The yellow man leads a black-colored marching band;
chipper and happy, no anger melts fixed resolve.
Stop and have a drink by the side of the road;
the water will still be wet when the beast stops for a drink.
There is a special home for each and every one,
and when taken away, my THOUGHTS chance to flounder.
Where does one IDEA exist with the absence of another;
does one hand make the other hand more real?

Day IV _____

06:00

Fade into light: a new day flickers into existence:
ending dreaming madness, beginning knowing madness.
Again, the lights come on, and that s.o.b. starts howling;
he's just like one of those puppies that won't shut up.
Imagine REALITY is personally conceived; each individual
creates a unique one, and nobody else can see it.
Well . . . that s.o.b. obviously sees something I can't,
REALITY which causes him great fear or great PAIN.
What recourse do we have if REALITY is out of touch;
is howling at the lights any more bizarre than fasting?
I don't see how there is any real comparison;
fasting is an active passive protest, howling is just howling.
Both are expressions of some inner demons escaping;
their vastly different names make one no less real.
But howling has nothing useful to accomplish;
there is no goal, only an expression of a lack of control.
Where does the impetus for a fast come from;
is there any less madness involved in starving to DEATH?
I've logically surmised that my options are limited;
if resistance is futile, then I've only striven in vain.
The desire for sustenance is powerful indeed;
where does ENERGY come from to keep it suppressed?
Essentially, it's just a matter of strong willpower;
I've decided to do something, now I'm doing it.

There is no doubt the initial decision was RATIONAL,
yet what keeps constant hunger under control?
I've got no IDEA, other than my ability to finish what I start;
the source of my WILL is no more apparent than my IDEAS.
What if any expression of inner angst is madness,
and only the degree of clarity crosses the line?
Then any utterance I make is to some degree unreal,
at least to the extent it's able to reflect REALITY.
Pseudo surprise: has something like that occurred before;
is there some distinction between REALITY and CONCEPTION?
I already accept my CONCEPTS of REALITY as flawed,
but this has nothing to do with the irrationality of howling.
What if fasting and howling were initiated by INTUITION,
which found two different means of RATIONAL expression?
It may be possible for an INTUITIVE view to be madness,
and people have differing RATIONAL abilities to express it.
Full REALITY as it exists can only be seen intuitively,
which presents as madness, irrational; can we hail it?
Therefore, the source of my WILL to fast is no different
than the inspiration for that s.o.b. to howl in the morning.
We all exhibit distinct abilities to express our madness;
does one RATIONAL translation of INTUITION replace another?
It doesn't really matter to me what someone else sees;
my rationally approximate view creates my REALITY.
Quietly sitting within AETHER, while it divides through us;
half of a half, and yet somewhere there is a whole.
Whole REALITY perceived with a dualistic filter;
RATIONAL and INTUITIVE views both together and apart.
Each perspective is exclusive of the other point of view;
thus REALITY is dualistically split into two distinct realms.
For practical PURPOSES they become separate UNIVERSES;
RATIONAL viewing INANIMATE, INTUITIVE viewing ANIMATE.
Since INTUITION is able to see the whole pattern,
it sees the addition of INANIMATE and ANIMATE UNIVERSES.
But since there is already a RATIONAL paradigm of REALITY,
all I need to know is what is missing.
Thus information from INTUITION is wholly derived,
and ANIMATE UNIVERSE is constructed from the difference.

It's impractical to keep including INANIMATE UNIVERSE in an
INTUITIVE view when the missing parts are all I really need.
Either perspective is only able to approximate the other,
somber reflections of a sublime essence—ask for them.
A whole view can't see the parts of a RATIONAL view,
and a partial view can't see the whole of an INTUITIVE view.
And yet the difference between INANIMATE UNIVERSE
and REALITY can be partially filled by ANIMATE UNIVERSE.
Therefore, as 1 and 1 closely approximate 2,
INANIMATE and ANIMATE UNIVERSES approximate REALITY.
Knowledge retreating from one end to the other,
based on a perspective preferring its own company.
RATIONAL THOUGHT may be far from perfect,
but an INTUITIVE alternative has nothing better to offer.
Deficiency is deficient;
it does not depend on which point of view it is seen from.
If an INTUITIVE view is incomplete like a RATIONAL 1,
then pursuing 1 view should be self-sufficient.
What is to be gained by seeing another point of view;
is it not wiser to look both ways before crossing?
Whether looking forward or backward,
I still have to move in 1 direction to go anywhere.
Neither solo-perspective is able to show-off all of REALITY;
we look beyond one for hints to what is missing.
Unlike INTUITIVE, a RATIONAL view, as aided by SCIENCE,
has been useful and successful beyond ordinary means.
Should limited LIFE sacrifice attained prosperity
for a shot in the dark, which is admittedly irrational?
An INTUITIVE view still needs to exhibit useful properties;
it only sees a universe able to exist without MATTER.
ANIMATE UNIVERSE within which LIFE'S source crawls,
is supposed to exist . . . where?
Minimally, REALITY must exist in a universe with MATTER,
for there is no other structure known by its appearance.
THOUGHT spun to trap the unwary,
claiming the universe is the house for all shared as holy.
According to common usage of the term,
a universe is the house within which REALITY resides.

That is not even acknowledged by gods of Science;
a multiverse is possible, although certainly not proven.
But Animate Universe must exist somewhere;
I can't believe it exists, and its location is nowhere.
Reality is the house within which Inanimate is a partner
to a half which is Animate, no longer kept silent.
It exists, but can't be sensed;
it's as real as any Object, without the trial of appearance.
Must we create that which <is not>,
in order to put <all that is> on display?
That which *<is>* can't exist without that which *<is not>*;
denying the latter makes the former fail as Concept.
How can any Object thus exist
if it must be both <itself> and <not itself>?
That is an inadequate question drawn from Dualism;
<what is> exists in relation to at least 1 other Object.
Only one essence embodies both <is> and <is not>;
no other than Aether is able to incorporate opposition.
Reality as Object must be conceived as a minimum of 2;
there can be no single existence within any universe.
Object known to exist is not whole by itself,
it is still perceived as one among many.
Every Object exists in relation to at least 1 other;
each universe should therefore have as least 2 constituents.
Matter occludes far-sight into Inanimate Universe;
how does this Conception manage to include the sun?
A question which incurs material problems with Dualism,
deciphering how the sun fits into a view of silent Matter.
Animate Universe has shown its heart to be Life;
how does this Conception manage without a source?
A question which incurs living problems with Dualism;
Life must use Energy to be sensed as Biomatter.
Duality divides universes into parts we already know:
Star and Matter, Soul and Life,

****

08:25

STAR and MATTER, SOUL and LIFE;
no exceptions escape how AETHER dualistically divides.
AETHER doesn't divide, it's only perceived in this fashion;
I'm constitutionally incapable of otherwise performing.
A wise man once said: Blessed are the pure
in heart, for they shall know light from darkness.
I seek to light up the darkness within;
futile striving has led to this place, this moment.
What is light without darkness to guide it;
what is darkness without a blinding light?
Incomplete.
Searching for 1 is unknown until the other is found.
Purity within is the result of HARMONY without;
Oreo cookies are good for taste, not nutrition.
Left to my own devices it's easy to fall into darkness;
unfulfilled longings can be temporarily assuaged by crap.
Where is the vital heart which beats a bloodless rhythm;
what color shines upon this immortal notion?
Maybe I search for that which doesn't exist,
or for that which doesn't wish to be found.
If purity truly dwelt inside,
there would be no place to hide corrupted THOUGHTS.
The essence of purity won't abide the taint of my anger,
so my bleakness continues to feel at home.
Do shadows shorten as night turns into day; and
the forms change while the distinctions remain the same?
Parts twist into forms to squeeze past from present;
pieces turning back to hold on to all I've known.
No person who has trod the path of TRUTH retains pride;
a proficient seeker releases his ego or falls into its grasp.
I believe TRUTH is the ultimate goal,
but I still hold on to every vile EMOTION imaginable.
Does our path lead to purity, or just lead onward?
Only the pure will know.
And they don't appear inclined to tell;
strange how purity tends to forbid its own proclamation.

From those who have left the dirty trail of knowledge
for the even muddier track to Wisdom.
Groveling in filth to find purity,
within darkness, searching for light.
Is more learning the key to becoming pure at heart,
or unlearning words which only have personal meaning?
Wrapped up in myself, looking within,
or unwrapping Pain still trapped within my ego.
Faith may help purity come to those who strive
with all of their might to find the source of Life.
It doesn't come easily to the more hard-assed like me;
faith . . . a generous word with stingy access.
There can be no tumor attached to that which is pure,
some malignant Thought *given over to rigid shapes.*
Often Thoughts arise inviting me to "just let go,"
but these very same Thoughts make me hold on.
Purity of Thought *is attached to no formal definition,*
only known by that which is not contained within it.
Thought which is formed with any Concept is impure,
and this is what inhabits the deepest dark inside of me.
It is Infinity Thought *which must contain all;*
there is no end to imagination of purity.
Concepts are Finite by nature, limited voyagers;
while purity is wholesome, containing more than itself.
How can purity retain all it must be,
and still present impurities in Thought *or in deed?*
Because I remain impure in this physical realm,
and my guiding heart within doesn't know its pure self.
Then blessings may come to fall upon all feet,
and we bow down to become one with another humble self.

08:52

From my own part, I think of Time on a beach,
sitting on the sand while the sun's Heat washes my body.
The rough grainy grit of drying damp sand opposing
a sun which blinds those looking directly upon its glory.

PERCEPTION of sand as OBJECTS and the sun as OBJECT,
each appearing to have little in common with the other.
INANIMATE BIRTH gifts non-identical twin children;
STAR and MATTER are names conferred on plentiful faces.
Those are the 2 types of OBJECTS seen by a RATIONAL view,
obeying the laws SCIENCE has been able to discover.
Relations really apparent and supposedly secret
give meaning to any universe beholden to sensation.
Neither of those primordial forms appears like the other;
unless their isotopic structures are thoroughly examined.
No mystery keeps CONCEPTIONS from view,
only a desire to confuse what is with what is imagined.
Still, they are alike in 1 identifying respect:
they are totally lifeless to any perceivable discretion.
As light approaches according to how darkness runs away,
how does one essence react to the other one's presence?
ENERGY from STARS and MATTERS produce FORCES
that are generally responsible for inducing their motions.
STAR and MATTER move in an external manner;
no other characteristic is more appropriately observed.
The reactions which construct FORCES between OBJECTS
happen outside of their properly defined limits.
STAR meets STAR, STAR meets MATTER, MATTER meets MATTER;
somewhere in the cosmos they are all shaking hands.
Untimely cooperation between normally isolated OBJECTS
results in CREATION of many substantial FORCES.
Solid mainstays used to sail within REALITY,
even creating the essential sensations which confound us.
GRAVITATIONAL and ELECTROMAGNETIC FORCES are the primary
1's which enable INANIMATE UNIVERSE to be known.
An amorphous structure attaching in every direction,
with any and all FORCES betwixt material OBJECTS.
All STARS and all MATTERS are interconnected;
basic GRAVITATIONAL attraction shows how this does happen.
Gods deem some FORCES mathematically negligible;
known to exist, they are just inconvenient to use.
GRAVITATIONAL FORCE between MASSES of supremely
distant rocks must still exist to some minute degree.

Including insensible FORCES which prove the rest,
yet do not endeavor to attach those not germane.
There is no use in assessing all FORCES involved in events;
1 grown elephant weighs more than 1000 mice.
The sun dispenses more than light and HEAT to our world;
it is just not as apparent as jumping off a cliff.
Waves of FORCE and sleets of cosmic particles
are all that stand between man and his material destiny.
FORCES and ENERGIES will exist within INANIMATE UNIVERSE
as long as STAR and MATTER remain to give them structure.
Essential QUANTITIES don't arise from nowhere;
OBJECTS must exist in opposition to cause their assembly.
How can it be known they come from STAR and MATTER;
why does the former have to originate like the latter?
There is no known case of FORCES existing in isolation;
they aren't errant OBJECTS wandering about the cosmos.
Is it possible OBJECTS come from FORCES or ENERGIES,
or is the source of ENERGY none other than OBJECT?
Scientific theories about G-FORCES and EM-FORCES indicate
changing OBJECTS modifies FORCES, and vice versa.
Primitives believed the earth was the universal center,
and all planets and the sun and STARS revolved around it.
Ockham's razor indicates the simplest hypothesis is best,
which places the earth in a very minor role.
Fertile MIND is capable of creating INFINITY possibilities;
the probabilities force theories into so many problems.
The theory best matching observation is the 1 accepted:
ENERGY and FORCE ultimately derive from OBJECTS.
What is the dynamic between those essences;
how does AETHER manage to furnish one from the other?

09:22

Lying half-off the side of a spare lumpy bed,
I drag my fingers on the floor and feel the grains.
Stray rocks or pebbles or dirt without attachment,
how does coded MIND conceive them as differentiated?

OBJECTS force a change in neural sensors under my skin,
and a patterned response kicks MEMORY to send "pebble."
OBJECT is known by FORCES assaulting sensation;
whether MATTER or STAR, it makes not a difference.
That isn't a fact accepted by any authority;
particles and molecules capture my senses.
Light strikes dark eyes, HEAT warms cold flesh;
FORCES touch tasty skin, nose, ears, and tongue.
Photons strike my eyes, HEAT conducts through my flesh;
molecules touch my skin, nose, ears and tongue.
What is the difference between the touch of FORCE,
and OBJECT, which is sure to grant sensory definition?
FORCE is a strength causing a change in motion or shape,
while senses are designed to react to molecular OBJECTS.
PERCEPTION
is the first step in climbing the ladder of distinction.
Everything I know about INANIMATE UNIVERSE
follows from my sensory ability to perceive it.
Gods of SCIENCE have decreed that OBJECTS made
of molecules themselves account for the slightest touch.
Smell and taste are most apparently tied to organics;
the other 3 senses have a more strictly material nature.
Yet the touching of OBJECTS cannot be known for sure
just by examination from limited animal sensation.
Air molecules, or even water when I am under it,
must strike the ear drum to make it vibrate back and forth.
Why would humans evolve to sense both OBJECT and FORCE
if our preference is to react to one or the other?
BIOMATTER doesn't always evolve the simplest solution,
sometimes it's best to use what is available.
It makes no sense for sensation to require two procedures
when one will suffice to create method from madness.
Therefore my senses don't react to FORCE;
OBJECTS are the basis for how my physical senses work.
Light does not require particles to transmit its essence;
FORCES thus brought forth are what fondle facial features.
Photons haven't been isolated by mechanical means,
but they are the best explanation for photo-emission.

Do Objects actually touch each other,
down at the level where rubber hits the road?
Relying on my limited senses leaves only 1 answer—
affirmative!
Stop and consider that Perception may be only illusion;
imagine bathing in water and not getting soaking wet.
If I don't get wet, I shouldn't have to towel off,
which shouldn't in turn change the formerly dry towel.
Determine the difference between Object and Object,
the precise point where they touch and both are neither?
I see it in 1 particular light,
as the billiard-ball theory where 1 hits another.
What we are granted the opportunity of seeing
is not always as apparent as the nose on an insipid face.
The 1st ball moves and strikes another;
the reactions then occurring are relatively few.
Actually what has occurred may be limited to one,
if assumptions are not made as to what has happened.
The striking and struck balls both will most likely move,
or, if hit just right, possibly just the struck 1 will move on.
Thus Objects are known to touch each other
because of the observed reactions when this happens.
That is how I generally conceive of different Objects;
neither can occupy the same place at the same moment.
One pushes the other out of Space it confiscates;
movement of one Object inspires movement in another.
Objects touch each other because of spatial insertion;
1 displaces the other from its previous position.
Force is responsible for eliciting any movement,
so this is what makes relocation of Objects possible.
I still maintain Objects actually touch,
not Forces which arise when created by their motions.
While still a hopeless and incomplete assertion,
there is more to fulfill Force's role in Object Creation.

09:53

A successful fast (?) uses massive amounts of water,
and as I fill a cup up, some spills upon the floor.
Pooling like mercury into a rounded glob of liquid,
do the water and the dirt combine or stay separate?
Some particles, like salt, can easily dissolve into water;
other 1's, like metal, aren't able to without modification.
Stick with the subject at hand if progress is to be expected;
do the individual pieces of dirt combine with the water?
It's hard for me to know without closer examination;
the differences are too small to see unaided.
OBJECT is known by FORCES assaulting sensation,
for no direct thrust will penetrate to PERCEPTION.
If OBJECT is known by its surrounding FORCES,
then I'm not able really to know its essence at all.
Each OBJECT has some boundary around it;
a level of existence where it is, and eventually, it is not.
Each OBJECT must have some point where it ends;
otherwise there would be no way to distinguish it.
The submicroscopic border is very difficult to sense,
especially in the case of the sun with its fluctuating fences.
There may be areas near the sun which rapidly change,
but there are defined areas away from it which don't.
If a rock is thrown at a window, does the whole rock
not leave the hand which throws it?
That is just basic common sense;
OBJECT in question is the rock, separate from the hand.
How can it do that unless there is a whole rock to move;
no part that is, or almost is, not the rock?
Obviously when the rock leaves the hand,
they not only separate, they also no longer touch.
LIFE has a membrane to contain its essence;
it is easy to determine where it begins and ends.
A rock has no membrane;
at least as far as RATIONAL observation informs me.
Yet what separates a rock from SPACE around it;
what is the dividing line between rock and not-rock?

In a vacuum, it would be where molecules meet SPACE;
in atmosphere, it would be where they meet particles of air.
Sitting in a chair does not normally break it into pieces,
neither do we merge to become one person-and-chair.
A chair's structure is sufficient to hold my weight;
if it can't, then it isn't properly called a chair.
Yet combining two OBJECTS of water easily converts
them into one coherent OBJECT —what is the difference?
Water and water are just liquids, while the chair is solid;
there is no mystery as to why they are different.
Imagine for a moment that OBJECTS do not actually touch,
either they merge or they still remain individual OBJECTS.
Then a rock is a rock, and a hand is a hand;
and 2 OBJECTS of water are still able to merge.
What could account for PERCEPTION
that either of those two OBJECTS actually touch?
Under the conditions where OBJECTS don't touch,
the rock would never be able to touch the hand.
It sounds silly to state that IDEA in RATIONAL terms;
only proof is able to turn around rigid THOUGHTS.
The problem originates from assuming 1 premise:
my senses tell me my hand touches the rock.
Water in two cups are OBJECTS separate from each other,
yet combined they form one completely mixed OBJECT.
The states of MATTER are well recognized phenomena;
physical laws are such because they are repetitive.
Ice in two cups are OBJECTS separate from each other;
combined they form two OBJECTS —what is the difference?
There is no problem here except trying to depict
liquid OBJECTS as having the same traits as solid OBJECTS.
Gods of SCIENCE tell us it is the state of MATTER:
liquid, or even gas, in one case versus solid in another.
That is what I have been trying to state;
liquid and solid OBJECTS don't react the same way to FORCES.
Still, let us consider one more thing:
how do we determine MATTER is in a specific state?
Each is relative to the other:
solid is fixed, liquid flows, gas expands.

Stick a finger in water or poke ice; OBJECTS remain
themselves except under application of sufficient FORCE.
Touching a rock to water will also not shatter them,
but for different isotopic reasons than state of MATTER.
Under no circumstance do finger and water combine;
the water in the cup is still distinctly sensed as OBJECT.
Substances are capable of being absorbed through my skin,
so the water could be combining with the finger.
Even under those mildly unusual conditions,
original OBJECT has only devolved into smaller OBJECTS.
Minus volume, a molecule of water is the same as a cupful,
as long as they contain the same isotopic constituents.
Original OBJECT has lost its in-the-cup identity;
the water in-the-cup is no longer what it was before.
So the claim is there is 1 OBJECT of water,
and if it's disturbed, this OBJECT is no longer the same.
What actually touches skin on the finger,
the molecules the gods claim contact skin sensors?
If molecules didn't come in contact with skin,
then they wouldn't be able to diffuse to the inside.
All OBJECTS extant in the solar system are under
constant influence of what the sun has done in the past.
That has nothing to do with how the water in 2 cups
can be distinguished as 2 OBJECTS.
No water would exist to touch without its intrusion
into daily affairs, all of the water would turn into ice.
Such is the nature of comets in SPACE,
frozen balls of ice shedding as they pass close to the sun.
There would be no PERCEPTION of two OBJECTS of water,
only two blocks of ice unless they could be melted.
Any OBJECT is distinguished based on how it exists;
therefore it's perceived as ice or water, or steam.
When water is touched with the tip of a finger,
it is only with the aid of FORCES generated with the sun.
So any sense contacting my physical awareness
is only available with the aid of external FORCES.
Water is under the constant influence of external FORCES;
they help give it form and shape, one moment to the next.

It shouldn't matter what effect those influences have;
I'm perceiving OBJECT, not FORCES.
ORGANISM is likewise under the influence of FORCES;
they help give it form and shape, found in a mirror.
So FORCES constantly modify all existence,
which doesn't bear on the internal nature of OBJECT.
FORCES on one OBJECT changing in relation to another
OBJECT account for the illusion they are touching.
But OBJECTS are constructed from within;
FORCES may modify them, they don't "make" them.
In effect, the sum of all FORCES on OBJECT enables it to be
perceived as one coherent and consistent piece of MATTER.
There must still be some presence pushing from within
making OBJECT into MATTER, beyond PERCEPTION.
FORCES make OBJECT into a perceptible form,
molding MATTER into water and rocks and mud.
Therefore OBJECT does exist outside of its PERCEPTION,
FORCES just change how my senses receive them.
FORCES do not construct OBJECT-specific elements,
they only allow sensation to distinguish one from another.
If FORCES always pass interference between OBJECTS,
then they must have a profound influence on my senses.
When FORCES change, OBJECT can change its place,
or its state, into another OBJECT, or many different ones.
If FORCES are constantly operating on OBJECTS,
unless they're all static, OBJECT PERCEPTION must change.
Sensation of OBJECT is known only by surrounding FORCES,
so they must be the cause of OBJECT considered as such.
There is a difference between the cause of OBJECT,
and the cause of how OBJECT is perceived.
There is one giant leap we need to add to this analysis:
FORCES themselves account for touching the water.
I can accept that OBJECT isn't directly "known",
but I don't grasp how I can touch water and not get wet.
PERCEPTION of OBJECTS comes from FORCES, not OBJECTS;
infringing a boundary, either skin or the limits of MATTER.

10:54

Earlier I took a shower because I've begun to stink;
I'm conscientiously avoiding food, not water.
Did the water become part of the skin or not;
do these separate OBJECTS become one from two?
I've got no IDEA how I can shower and not get wet;
the water attaches to me more than it becomes part.
OBJECT is known by FORCES assaulting sensation;
REALITY'S BARRIER prevents AETHER from knowing itself.
If true, then the water might not touch my skin;
I sense "wet" from a presence of TEMPERATURE and pressure.
How can FORCES be sensed and not OBJECTS;
does the existence of the former lead to the latter?
I refuse to believe air pressure makes a rock,
or the state of MATTER defines OBJECT isotopes.
Of course OBJECT is wrapped within by some essence,
obscuring IDEA this reflection is trying to relate.
Then FORCES may modify how OBJECT is perceived,
but can only partially affect how it exists.
Still, FORCES outside permit other OBJECTS to react
upon one OBJECT containing coherency and substance.
The waters in 2 cups are able to mix because FORCES "alert"
each 1 that the surrounding circumstances make it possible.
OBJECT itself is not made from FORCES;
they influence its form and let others know of its existence.
FORCES are also able to deny the mixing of 2 ice cubes
because each 1 is "alerted" to this impossibility.
If it is FORCES molding and positioning OBJECT,
then should they not be what it directly perceives?
That would mean FORCES are always around me;
possibly even when I stick my finger into water.
OBJECT is formed from an internal essence within
in opposition to many external FORCES without.
The wide variety of compositions of individual OBJECTS
is also balanced by the fact that many are quite similar.
We are not now concerned with internal construction;
it is not as involved with interaction between OBJECTS.

It still must eventually be resolved;
FORCES react to a boulder and an iceberg quite distinctly.
More important to discern—how are FORCES able
to transmit the existence of OBJECT outside of itself?
Water or ice is based upon position in SPACE and TIME,
MATTER under the continuous application of many FORCES.
Since FORCES "constrain" OBJECT to be sensed as such,
they change, not OBJECT, with change in place or state.
That borders on the ludicrous, if not insane;
water and ice can change both state and place.
We rationally know REALITY by our PERCEPTIONS of it,
which are limited to sensation modified by FORCES.
Then all I can know is FORCES change, not OBJECTS;
though the former must be inspired by the latter.
We can assume OBJECTS change, a very good assumption;
but we cannot KNOW OBJECTS change, only FORCES.
As Kant proposed—man can't truly know REALITY;
a RATIONAL objection—he can make an excellent estimate.
When the illusion of contact with OBJECT transpires,
FORCES containing it transmit to actual sensation.
Rocks don't have an animal's ability to sense,
not even a plant's limited stimulus response.
Think of a better term for how one rock "knows" it cannot
occupy same SPACE and TIME with another, then use it.
OBJECTS can't occupy identical TIMES and SPACES,
simply because each 1 exists at a unique location.
Let us stick to one point and clearly relate:
when touching water or ice, FORCE notifies sensation.
So when my finger appears to touch water or ice,
it's actually only sensing FORCE changes.
It is not possible for the finger to be frozen or wet,
at least as long as OBJECT does not change.
Now, maybe my reflection can take another turn,
and explain how this OBJECT, my body, doesn't get wet.
Then pay further attention to this bizarre transgression,
and learn how to bathe and not get wet.
Then go ahead and get on with it;
explain how water gets on my body without getting it wet.

When bathing, does the body become part of the water,
or is it possible the water becomes part of the body?
Neither actually happens, in most circumstances;
my body continues to function normally as it always has.
Prior to a bath, water and body were separate OBJECTS;
what has changed to make these two into one?
Immersion of my body into the water for 1;
though that is like dropping a rock into water.
The water(s) clinging to a physical body when rising
are not same OBJECT as the first quiet tub of liquid.
Original 2 OBJECTS were tub of water and my body,
neither of which is now precisely the same.
Many OBJECTS of water now hang upon this body,
yet they do not become one with this bodily OBJECT.
There is a new body, there is a new tub of water,
and there are also many new OBJECTS of water on board.
Toweling to rid an oily body of unwanted water
usually succeeds in dead skin also sloughing off.
Once pieces of skin leave my body, they're new OBJECTS,
but I don't know their status while they're still attached.
Look closely at the drops of water beading on skin;
what makes them take this shape and form?
Obviously FORCES have to act on them,
similar to how atmospheric pressure forms raindrops.
Use powers of imagination to believe water touches skin;
it is wet and cool, or maybe hot according to discretion.
But water clings to my body, and then falls off;
it must be attaching itself and then letting loose.
Those are sensations identifying water's state and place,
and FORCE forms them into dirty drops toweled away.
FORCE wraps around the outer portion of a water drop,
but the inner portion is where the water touches skin.
If there is a drop of water upon tender skin,
then it is OBJECT, separate from another bodily OBJECT.
A drop of water is touching my body,
and when dried off of me, it's touching the towel.
How can it be identified as a separate drop of water,
unless it is so formed by various and sundry FORCES?

Common FORCES do form OBJECTS into drops,
and they are what my senses use to perceive REALITY.
And if it is formed by FORCES into a single drop,
why would anyone think skin has become water?
Water may be the prime constituent of the human body,
but there is no evidence of complete transformation.
So if skin is not now water, and water is not now skin,
what other conclusion is left?
My PERCEPTION of OBJECT is changing,
1 OBJECT of MATTER has just separated into many more.
Neural PERCEPTION of pressure or cool or warm
is via sensation, not the form REALITY is forced to bear.
As long as OBJECT is perceived as a distinct entity,
then it can't be part of another OBJECT, or vice versa.
Hot and cold are varying degrees of HEAT sensation,
beholden to FORCE for their transmission apparatus.
Hot and cold are actually indicators of TEMPERATURE;
HEAT is the transfer required by these differences.
Wet is just a general term to describe the enveloping sense
of being wrapped by a semi-continuous body of water.
Or possibly many many individual surrounding OBJECTS,
fooling my senses into believing they are less than many.
Wet infers a body under attack by water or droplets;
not that water has invaded, or become part of, the body.
I, as OBJECT, don't become wet;
instead I, as OBJECT, create FORCE with OBJECT(s) of water.
Look at the rationale for bathing and scrubbing—
to clear away invading forerunners, commonly dirt.
Other OBJECTS which my body seems to attract;
none of which are part of me unless I become infected.
Wet is a term used to describe a liquid covering,
an illusion of docile BRAIN that water touches its body.
Skin sensors do detect pressure, TEMPERATURE, and PAIN;
the 1st 2 combining to give the illusion of wet.
If any doubt is still held about this reflection's validity,
put on a plastic glove and see if this hand becomes wet.
That isn't physically possible, for an unholy 1,
which proves the limitations of my senses like nothing else.

And yet water must be absorbed by the body,
like the 10 glasses a day only the obsessive drink.
Which leaves me with the problem of OBJECTS merging,
CELLS in my body must assimilate water and nutrients.
Although, once the water has been consumed
by CELL, it is no longer OBJECT in and of itself.
Water is only water as long as it's perceived as such,
separate distinct OBJECT with its own unique existence.
Please pay attention to this important point:
we are only postulating FORCES on identifiable OBJECTS.
OBJECT is only OBJECT as long as it's perceived as such;
I frequently confuse myself as to what it is.
If drops of water are sucked down into a gastro-gullet,
they remain OBJECTS of water until crossing a membrane.
Water can't be water if it's something else,
which sounds really silly except on further reflection.
Then they are no longer separate OBJECTS,
no identifiable obstacle exists to merge with another.
But OBJECTS would then cease to exist,
which is silly and stupid and uncommonly base.
Whatever forms OBJECT cannot just cease to exist;
although it can cease to exist as identifiably separate.
Therefore OBJECT is CONCEPT formed from PERCEPTION,
which FORCES are changing every single moment.
If FORCES are sufficient to breach OBJECT'S cohesion,
then this OBJECT will cease to exist as what it was before.
But there is no BARRIER around inert MATTER, take rocks;
not like the membrane which surrounds living CELLS.
We are not currently delving into living creatures,
only how MATTER and STAR could be constructed.
There is still no BARRIER around inert MATTER;
INANIMATE OBJECTS can touch the universe around them.
The tub of water is first one OBJECT when it is entered;
adding FORCE by leaving breaks it into smaller pieces.
Existing FORCES surround perceived OBJECTS,
which must be changed to alter PERCEPTIONS.
Thus we are able to identify OBJECTS as such;
only through FORCE does sensation detect OBJECTS.

Rocks as OBJECTS and people as OBJECTS,
there doesn't seem to be much physical distinction.
A person is no OBJECT, except if conceived as that whole;
we are CELL OBJECTS wrapped in organic matrix OBJECTS.
But I sense my body as 1 definable OBJECT;
there is no part of me that isn't me.
Which one of these OBJECTS is the central part,
or maybe the combination of them all bestows sentience?
Another illusion which has fooled my senses:
I'm no more 1 OBJECT than a shower of water.
Only FORCES surrounding OBJECT form its identity,
or change PERCEPTION of it between many and one.
FORCES either let me conceive 1 existing OBJECT,
or allow me to understand it's actually many.
What is the difference between FORCES identifying OBJECT,
and FORCES no longer acknowledging its existence?
They don't change because of external impulses;
something must happen to OBJECT to make it change.
FORCES allow PERCEPTION of OBJECT as it exists;
what changes in OBJECT when it no longer exists?
If FORCES around OBJECT change, then ENERGY levels change;
maybe ENERGY within affects external PERCEPTION of it.
Material OBJECT is in a natural ENERGY state,
sensed as OBJECT because of its temporal BARRIER.
Something bothers me about all-enveloping FORCES:
if 2 billiard balls strike each other, they make a sound.
Do two hands clapping always create the same sound,
or is air movement responsible for the noises we hear?
So OBJECTS still don't have to touch in order to create sound,
FORCES around them only have to sufficiently disturb air.
OBJECT will resist inclusion into rigid definition,
until the one in front is the same as the one behind.

12:25

Coming back from a shower, I felt Bob the guard trip me;
I'm not too nimble, so I fell and sprained my wrist.

What was the proximate cause of the physical injury:
hard OBJECT, ignorance, or irresistible FORCE?
My first choice would be my hand striking the floor;
immovable OBJECTS tend to be kind of hard to move.
Yet is it obvious that skin touched the floor,
or was FORCE responsible for the injurious result?
FORCE may normally be responsible for sense initiation,
but it's difficult for me to believe I didn't hit the floor.
Imagine a universe with no FORCE or ENERGY,
would OBJECTS still react to each other as OBJECTS?
That isn't a universe which has been proposed to exist;
I don't know how 1 could exist without ENERGY.
What about if all STARS have been extinguished,
and there is only cold dark inert MATTER to fill up SPACE?
If OBJECTS are to touch then there must be motion,
and this can't happen without FORCE to motivate them.
What if there were no ENERGY to create FORCE,
just OBJECTS which never moved, only existed?
If there is no ENERGY, then there is no MASS—see Einstein;
and if there is no MASS, then there are no OBJECTS.
If INANIMATE UNIVERSE is constructed of solid MATTER,
could OBJECTS exist without the addition of ENERGY?
A universe with no ENERGY has no OBJECTS within it,
so the question as stated doesn't make much sense.
What if STARS are all dead and a meteor is sensed,
would FORCES still be directly perceived?
GRAVITATIONAL FORCE is as real as the next manifestation,
so if MASS exists, then G-FORCE is its partner.
What if there is a universe where OBJECTS do not exist,
could FORCES still exist to be detected?
I know of no case where FORCE exists without OBJECTS;
there appears to be an intimate connection between them.
If FORCES are accepted to surround identifiable OBJECTS,
then as long as there are OBJECTS there will be FORCES.
That appears to be a sufficient conditional;
though I don't know how they are fundamentally bonded.
Could it be FORCE comes from OBJECTS,
or possibly OBJECTS are only FORCE?

It's hard to fathom the latter presumption;
FORCES are temporary, there is no receptacle to hold them.
Yet OBJECTS are only detected by FORCES between them;
how are we to know they are not FORCES?
FORCE is related to change of state or place;
there must be some thing changing for this to occur.
Thus OBJECTS cannot be FORCE
because FORCES do not change their own state or place.
FORCES also don't appear to come from OBJECTS;
ENERGY causes FORCE, and OBJECTS are MATTER.
What if OBJECTS were not MATTER, they were ENERGY;
would it be possible for OBJECTS to create FORCE?
That is the only way FORCE could arise from OBJECTS,
and current theories don't allow for this possibility.
If OBJECTS could be shown as ENERGY, and not MATTER,
then could all FORCES come from OBJECTS?
But OBJECTS are MATTER and their bonds are ENERGY,
at least this has been the prevailing opinion.
For now just imagine the possibility;
try to understand how FORCE is connected to OBJECT.
There is too much evidence for a particulate REALITY;
SCIENCE has shown the feasibility of material OBJECTS.
Then where does FORCE come from;
what other explanation closely dovetails it with OBJECT?

12:51

Moving my wrist around gives me varying degrees of PAIN,
additional PERCEPTIONS bringing REALITY to my BRAIN.
Why do some falls cause sprains, some cause breaks,
and many do not do much of anything at all?
Interaction between FORCES and structures depends on the
degree of resistance developed between them in opposition.
To change OBJECT, FORCE must break its "coherence",
and thus the obstacle to change is removed.
My arm might break if sufficient FORCE was applied to it,
and then it wouldn't be an arm, but 1 in 2 parts.

FORCES surround OBJECTS and thus identify them as such
to other OBJECTS and INANIMATE UNIVERSE at large.
FORCES have FINITE roles they are able to fulfill,
changing OBJECT'S motion or state, or making new 1's.
What is the difference between MATTER and STAR OBJECTS;
how are they observed to be different material essences?
They are OBJECTS, so they are known by way of FORCES;
whatever happens to 1, must happen to the other 1.
OBJECTS are supposedly composed of similar elements;
how can similar things be so substantially different?
Objects present themselves as unique essences,
their differences expose the nature of INANIMATE UNIVERSE.
It is not just that STAR is slightly different than MATTER,
they are profoundly different OBJECTS.
Which may be why SCIENCE is so far away from fusion,
trying to use the sun's nature without understanding it.
Imagine MATTER has BARRIER of ENERGY around it,
while STAR does not have one, or it is very minimal.
That could be their subtle contrasting endowment;
though there is still no barrier around inert MATTER.
Consider ENERGY BARRIER as the insubstantial measure
of OBJECT'S resistance to change in its existence.
Therefore it's a state of existence, not a part or piece;
"barrier" is only used to denote the limits of OBJECT.
Not like a cellular membrane holding LIFE inside,
away from its surface DEATH within INANIMATE UNIVERSE.
Around each biomaterial OBJECT exists a coherent barrier,
which makes each whole CELL act in common with FORCES.
ENERGY BARRIER is a state inherent in every OBJECT,
required to keep each one separate and distinct.
RATIONAL senses will therefore be able to perceive
each OBJECT as whole as it's able to resist FORCES.
ENERGY BARRIER is not a thing like a membrane,
it holds no water; ENERGY is held by its internal essence.
OBJECT will react differently to each type of FORCE,
so PERCEPTIONS received will be proportionately different.
It is convenient, although inaccurate, to call it a barrier;
only done to equate it with its membranous counterpart.

Barrier of Cell and Barrier of Energy are similar,
differences between where Object <*is*> and <*is not*>.
Object perceived within Inanimate Universe as Matter
has Energy Barrier to resist change in its existence.
If Object didn't commonly have a resistance to change,
then it wouldn't appear as Matter to my senses.
Object perceived within Inanimate Universe as Star
has tiny Energy Barrier resisting change to its existence.
Therefore Star isn't perceived as Matter,
even though they must relate on some scale of existence.
Star and Matter can be ultimately distinguished by the degree
of Energy Barrier which defines their existence.

13:16

I pick up a cup of water, with my other hand, drink it,
and sense it sluicing through me into my stomach.
Does the water cease being water and become sustenance,
or does it always remain water, separate from the body?
A human body is considered to be mostly water;
though most of this water is in Reality different solutions.
For water to cease it must become something else;
exactly when does water perform this elemental magic?
At some point, the hydrogen and oxygen atoms
composing water molecules must bond with other atoms.
What would cause those molecules to accept change,
unless Energy Barrier around them has been breached?
As long as I accept Idea of Object with Energy Barrier,
it must be modified before Object can become not-Object.
Does Idea of Energy Barrier have any divine analogue;
is it possible it already exists under another category?
The closest relation to Energy Barrier I can imagine
is the notion of Inertia as being the resistance to change.
Could Energy Barrier be a type of Inertia, or vice versa,
at least as regards Object's inclination towards motion?
The measure of the resistance to a change in motion
is best summarized by the simple use of Mass.

What if INERTIA is severely limited as CONCEPTION, and
resistance to change in motion is from ENERGY BARRIER?
They do appear similar but can be easily unattached—
the sun must have ENERGY BARRIER because it has ENERGY.
The barrier term is just a pictorial convenience;
it has no actual physical existence within REALITY.
Then its application to STAR and MATTER must change;
they aren't as different as originally conceived.
Now imagine INERTIA applies to STAR and MATTER;
one has high INERTIA, and the other is low.
This proposition makes more sense;
FORCES associated with STAR are amazingly constant.
INERTIA is used by the priestly caste in a strict fashion,
limiting application of its usage to motion and MASS.
There is no other evidence for INERTIA to exist in OBJECT,
except for the consistency EXTENSION seems to have.
This then is how STAR and MATTER are made distinct:
OBJECTS profoundly differ in MASS and EXTENSION INERTIA.
OBJECT does have resistance to changing its shape,
as noted by the delayed reactions to change of state.
MASS INERTIA is resistance to change in motion;
could EXTENSION INERTIA be resistance to change in size?
STAR has high MASS INERTIA, and low EXTENSION INERTIA;
MATTER has low MASS INERTIA, and high EXTENSION INERTIA.
Mentally picturing OBJECTS, with and without barriers,
is useful because vision works from EXTENSION, not MASS.
STAR has low EXTENSION INERTIA because its size fluctuates;
high EXTENSION INERTIA of MATTER is a rock on the ground.
For now we are left with an unproven assumption:
INERTIA of OBJECT is more inclusively its ENERGY BARRIER.
Then, looking back at combining 2 OBJECTS of water,
overcoming INERTIA could be what forms them into 1.
When one glass of water is made from two others,
at what moment are two OBJECTS now recognized as one?
The critical point is reached and passed
when 2 INERTIAS now have 1 common resistance.
FORCE required to breach INERTIA around two liquids
is much less than required to breach two solids.

So it's easier to cause liquid OBJECTS to lose coherency
than for solid OBJECTS to act in a similar manner.
When OBJECTS change state, FORCE must be applied
in order to alter their INERTIAS.
Solids must be subjected to enough FORCE to cause them
to change into liquid or gas before they can fully merge.
Why must OBJECT'S MASS and EXTENSION
change state before merging can take place?
The molecular bonds which attach atoms must loosen,
so new bonds may form with different atoms.
There is no particulate change to MATTER'S depths,
penetration only uncovers more energetic dust.
Another assumption which remains strictly unproven;
they do seem to be piling up within this reflection.
Gods of SCIENCE carve REALITY into mini-atomic features,
suitable for seeing MATTER with inexact preconception.
The nature of OBJECT is ENERGY connecting MATTER;
INANIMATE UNIVERSE falls apart without the little particles.
To see OBJECT without the aid of unrealistic glasses
is to allow it a true naked energetic style.
But ENERGY only comes from interaction with FORCES;
it's locked in MATTER until its release has been permitted.
INANIMATE UNIVERSE is noted by one supreme ability:
the constant requirement to release only ENERGY.
That is 1 way of viewing the motion of OBJECT,
but a rock seems to exist without using ENERGY.
OBJECT exists in a state of INERTIA, by gradual change,
acting to maintain a constant rate of ENERGY release.

13:52

Lying on my bed, I feel the sun make its presence known;
though millions of kilometers away, I still sense it being.
What restricts STAR from releasing more or less ENERGY,
unless there is inertial BARRIER to keep it from changing?
The sun has a certain general range of emissions,
which indicates a fairly regular rate of ENTROPY gain.

It has high MASS INERTIA, and low EXTENSION INERTIA;
do these keep it from releasing all of its ENERGY at once?
Planet orbits show GRAVITATIONAL FORCES as constant,
but other FORCES need not be similarly bound.
Look for a more complete answer than this short version:
if STAR'S ENERGY is not MASS, it is EXTENSION.
Einstein showed MASS and ENERGY have a relation;
no similar arrangement has been indicated for EXTENSION.
All OBJECTS are ultimately sourced by AETHER;
the difference between things is a matter of PERCEPTION.
Any single OBJECT is known by simple QUANTITIES;
MATTER and STAR are known by MASS and EXTENSION.
MATTER has INERTIA to keep it coherent and RATIONAL;
STAR is a special case providing contrast and difference.
They must both have INERTIA to make them perceptible;
static long enough to allow my senses to take measurement.
The heart of STAR is impenetrable to sensation;
its construction must be guessed by its effects on MATTER.
There are substantial theories about the sun's nature,
based on CONCEPT of FORCES underlying MATTER.
The sun has been decreed to operate by nuclear fusion,
no other source will the gods of SCIENCE permit.
That reaction is achieved by combining simple common
hydrogen elements into more complex, rarer helium 1's.
DREAM which fascinates and frustrates technology:
inexhaustible ENERGY from a limited source.
Fusion requires intense GRAVITATIONAL FORCE, a tremendous
amount of HEAT, and massive amounts of hydrogen fuel.
Unless bottled inside an insidious magnetic field;
if it is sustained, then do not pull the plug.
SCIENCE claims to have initiated a fusion reaction,
beyond the unsustainable bomb long known to work.
There is no HEAT source but STAR to start the reaction;
this is the holy grail, to produce HEAT without HEAT.
Therefore SCIENCE speculates STARS were formed
at the beginning bang and no new 1's will be created.
Except by priestly powers, do not let us forget;
gods can create anything if just given enough TIME.

Science predicts no natural event will produce more Stars;
human intelligence isn't a natural occurrence.
Is there not a law requiring conservation of Energy,
which seems to indicate it is not a bottomless resource?
It takes Energy to produce Energy,
and no scientist can get around it.
Yet mankind seeks a shining violation of an essential rule;
a paradox which consumes many Rational seekers.
Einstein began Idea of fusion by relating Energy and Mass;
not Mass itself, but its loss releases uncontrolled Energy.
Putting the power of a hydrogen bomb inside a gas tank;
are we to believe this is safe and reliable?
Mass by itself doesn't equate into Energy,
it must have Energy added to release its stored potential.
Dominoes falling one after the other,
until the last one lands and all existence finally ends.
The sun seen from a strictly Rational point of view
has a maximum output predicted by fuel reaching its core.
Is Star a strictly Rational being,
or could it have Life within its pulsating corona?
It also must put out a minimum amount of Energy,
if enough hydrogen Mass is ready to sustain the reaction.
Star is then safely put within reach of Matter's embrace,
as are all Objects perceived within Inanimate Universe.
It's likely that when each Star was formed,
its Mass and Extension and Entropy gain were set.
Reality designed according to rules beyond Conception;
a fist is the same essence as what it holds.
Star emits Energy based on a hydrogen fuel allotment;
each 1 is designed to be only so big and so hot.
Where in this universe do we go to find a source
of so much Gravitational Force without unallied Mass?
Star's Entropy gain was set when it was created,
and thereafter is only able to modify from that point.
Matter and Star are much alike in this respect:
gaining Entropy at a regular rate until forced to change.
This is why Star doesn't release all of its Energy at once:
Inertia checks Star because of the way it was formed.

Thus STAR'S ENERGY is observed to fluctuate frequently;
it does not have high EXTENSION INERTIA to limit its excesses.
MASS and EXTENSION are structural QUANTITIES of OBJECT,
each possessing its own inertial identity.
Imagine MATTER did not have substantial EXTENSION INERTIA;
these OBJECTS would blink like twinkling little STARS.
Some rationale must exist for why MATTER is so stable;
more than is accounted for by orbiting electrons.
Try to accept STAR with low EXTENSION INERTIA,
and its limitations are based on RATIONAL explanations.
This theory seems to discredit the notions of fusion;
though if it can be made to work, then it's real indeed.
INTUITION'S view is offered to explain what is missing;
nothing for adding to a working RATIONAL explanation.
Remember! INANIMATE UNIVERSE is RATIONAL in nature;
I'm as hampered as the sun by how I was created.
INTUITION can only modify an understanding of nature,
using existing CONCEPTIONS in an alternative fashion.
INERTIA may form the difference between MATTER and STAR,
but at least 1 other OBJECT is theorized in the cosmos.
Does a black hole truly exist,
and how does it relate to STAR and MATTER?
A black hole isn't truly sensed as OBJECT;
it's more the absence of OBJECT or SPACE, with INFINITE TIME.
All ENERGY in REALITY comes from AETHER'S grasp,
yet where does such an inexhaustible supply come from?
A black hole is different from any other existence;
even absence of OBJECTS is conceived as VOID.
AETHER as seen from INTUITION'S view is all one essence,
so the supply must come from somewhere in the source.
If all REALITY is 1 substance as previously indicated,
then everything must be part of a feedback loop.
OBJECT is AETHER spewing its might into sensory awareness;
a black hole is STAR and MATTER leaving to resupply AETHER.
Round and round it all goes,
where it stops doesn't matter because it isn't possible.
Much is left to be proven for IDEAS of alternate REALITY;
offering dualistic CONCEPTIONS is of primary interest, now.

14:22

I'm humble before REALITY from which the sun has arisen;
so much ENERGY pouring forth from a single source.
What could make STAR so powerful; why would AETHER
put so much of itself into singular outlets?
If I discount the notions of fusion and fission,
I'm at a loss to explain rationally how a sun is possible.
There must be substantial ENERGY fueling STARS;
is so much available from the existence of MASS?
STAR is OBJECT emitting ENERGY, it must;
there doesn't seem to be much ambiguity in this matter.
According to these alternative views of REALITY,
when does it stop being STAR and start being ENERGY?
I know of the sun by FORCES which enlighten my senses,
and these must be related to sun's ENERGY.
The sun is OBJECT offering ascetic PERCEPTION;
otherwise STAR would not be considered as such.
ENERGY is the capacity for doing work;
it comes in many forms and is therefore of much use.
ENERGY spoken of with such determination—
point out a place where it can be sensed to exist.
Only FORCES are perceived to make sense of REALITY;
ENERGY like OBJECT is behind the veil of PERCEPTION.
ENERGY'S form is beyond mortal comprehension,
inferred from combining PERCEPTION and CONCEPTION.
FORCE strikes my eyes and irradiates my skin;
HEAT and light are the perceived subjects of this persuasion.
Where do FORCES come from daring to assault
tender bodies and give sensations their LIFE?
OBJECT must exist somewhere amidst the material mist;
CONCEPT birthed from forceful PERCEPTIONS.
One more thing must enter imagination while it is open,
there must by some way of getting from OBJECT to FORCE.
At any measurable instant, FORCE and OBJECT are static;
at this moment, ENERGY manages to bring them together.
Which is how ENERGY comes into its conceptual existence;
only FORCE is detected, everything else is derivative.

Therefore OBJECTS can't be known as separate essences;
this is an assumption based on how FORCE is perceived.
Trying to determine where STAR separates from its ENERGY
has no meaning within the totality of AETHER.
CONCEPT of the sun is understood distinct
from CONCEPT of its released ENERGY, only in my BRAIN.
Gods of SCIENCE have managed an excellent approximation
for REALITY by use of that interpolation.
ENERGY lies amid OBJECT—both must exist,
and FORCE can actually be sensed—it also exists.
FORCES exist in the realm between conceived OBJECTS;
there must still be others within them.
For the sun to emit ENERGY, it must have power behind it,
for I can rationally conceive of no other method.
This is the role PRIMAL FORCE plays in STAR and MATTER,
how AETHER begins its appearance in INANIMATE UNIVERSE.
If "PRIMAL FORCE" is the cause of all observable existence,
then FORCE is the effect from OBJECT interaction.
It is easy to suggest AETHER is PRIMAL FORCE,
yet it shows a different face within ANIMATE UNIVERSE.
AETHER is more precisely the source of all REALITY;
it's to "PRIMAL FORCE" as "PRIMAL FORCE" is to FORCE.
PRIMAL FORCE is awareness of STAR'S source of power;
in MATTER, it is what holds MASS and EXTENSION together.
But OBJECT isn't formed of those BASIC QUANTITIES;
if I break a rock, then it becomes smaller rocks.
Another assumption intended to showcase DUALITY,
proving it now will only result in sidestepping the point.
A problem which SCIENCE hasn't adequately explained:
how MASS and EXTENSION manage to coexist within OBJECTS.
AETHER is one and everything together,
until it must be rationally divided into dualistic parts.
Those parts and pieces indicate that a distinct source exists,
which in turn makes OBJECT exist as itself.
True AETHER is hidden from RATIONAL PERCEPTION;
too INFINITY in scope to be molded into FINITY OBJECTS.
Physical existence has evolved to distinguish differences;
AETHER is too complete to be paired with anything but VOID.

All Aether's parts are conceived in some fashion;
Primal Force is the essence binding material Objects.

14:53

The sun glares through my window, beating me down;
it looks like the yellow eye of an unforgiving deity.
A still glowing orb shimmering into a greater corona;
a perimeter of flickering light and Heat.
That is why the sun is usually pictured with jagged edges;
like Fire, it throws off parts of itself into its surroundings.
Why does Star seem so much like Fire;
why do they both dance in the same lifelike manner?
They could both be "Primal Force" way down deep,
or it could be just another illusion performed by my senses.
The likeness cannot be because Fire is from fusion;
corporate zombies would have already exploited this slave.
There are 3 speculated ways to create Energy:
fission and fusion from Matter, and fossilized Biomatter.
The first two do not explain the third;
there is some other explanation for their similarity.
There are many more types of Energy—Potential, Kinetic,
chemical, nuclear, electric, magnetic, light, and sound.
All these confusing Energies, gods have decreed,
were developed to explain Matter in a particulate manner.
Energies which exist based on particular applications,
all of which involve particles of some make and model.
A priest said: Isolated material particles are abstractions,
their properties being definable and observable . . .
. . . only through interaction with other systems.
Bohr was a genius, which doesn't mean he was right.
An answer for how Energy flows in Inanimate Universe
is to drop the requirement for particulate Matter.
All known existence is based on particles of Matter;
this old argument has already been materially decided.
All existence is Energy based;
particles of Matter are only semi-useful approximations.

SCIENCE has divided MATTER into particles quite usefully;
imagining bundles of ENERGY is a much greater problem.
When particles are used as a crutch for means to an end,
they have no equal for each minutely specific goal.
It's silly to try to recreate the wheel
when the only improvement is to make it sound rounder.
Yet to mandate REALITY must conform to those ends
is to lose sight of the process formulating the means.
REALITY is only known by the shape of its FORCES,
and OBJECTS, like the sun, are what induce them to move.
CONCEPTION of REALITY is based on limited PERCEPTION,
whether used as static particles or OBJECTS.
That apparently has nothing to do with the sun and FIRE;
whether either is MATTER or ENERGY isn't really relevant.
What about the radioactive source sustaining society,
as opposed to the source of ENERGY in STARS?
Fission splits atoms in order to lose MASS;
fusion combines them in order to lose even more.
While noble LIFE is proposed to be chemically based,
initiated by the arrival of light onto plants.
There is no other possibility for enriching BIOMATTER;
light and water and nutrients are enough to grow trees.
What if there are not three or more sources to ENERGY,
if there is only one—AETHER in its RATIONAL guise?
AETHER which only exists to divide itself in 2:
1 for INANIMATE UNIVERSE, 1 for ANIMATE UNIVERSE.
PRIMAL FORCE for MATTER, and another one for LIFE,
yet within INANIMATE UNIVERSE they are quite the same.
Therefore, expenditure of ENERGY in the world around me
depends on internal FORCE bound-up in OBJECTS.
This is why the sun is so much like FIRE to sensation:
simple manifestation of AETHER from different processes.
FIRE and STAR still require unique materials to combust;
release of "PRIMAL FORCE" must be superficial.
Either their appearance is a coincidental illusion,
or they are one actor who has put on different masks.
A coincidence by definition is an accidental occurrence,
an event that should only happen quite rarely.

So how do FIRE and STAR do it on a constant basis;
how do LIFE and MATTER create an identical product?
The answer could be 1 SCIENCE has already pronounced:
OBJECTS are energetic particles which can be tapped.
A hereditary problem born from group-swayed thinking,
caused by the RATIONAL training received by all youth.
"PRIMAL FORCE" doesn't have much back-up evidence,
compared to strong and weak nuclear FORCES.
A single-source view contradicts non-unified-field theories,
contrasting them needs wait for a more specific reflection.

15:26

The sun and a pebble on the floor are each unique,
making 1 here and now, another 1 there and then.
All OBJECTS within INANIMATE UNIVERSE,
STAR or MATTER, find a use for TIME and SPACE.
SPACE and TIME are basic parameters of the universe;
OBJECT needs them as animals need air to breathe.
In order for ENERGY to be released from STAR
it must go from somewhere to somewhere.
SPACE seems to be required for DISTANCE to form,
much of it taken up by AETHER'S form in VOID.
What is SPACE;
where does it come from; is it just null ENERGY?
VOID is primarily known by the absence of OBJECTS,
and I conceive of SPACE as very similar.
Do STAR and MATTER exist with SPACE, or in SPACE,
since the former seems to require the latter for existence?
OBJECTS exist in VOID,
and I don't know if SPACE and VOID are identical CONCEPTS.
Maybe commonly understood SPACE is another illusion,
it is actually another OBJECT existing in VOID.
So STAR and MATTER exist along with SPACE,
and a black hole appears to be their opposite absence.
What is SPACE when offered to be OBJECT,
which had been limited to either STAR or MATTER?

VOID is the actual absence of sensible OBJECTS,
but my direct senses actually perceive SPACE as nothing.
Animal senses are limited in their evolved capacities;
whether something or nothing, it is always approximate.
The difference between OBJECT and VOID is SPACE;
more sensible than VOID, less than STAR or MATTER.
SPACE does not really exist outside of dual PERCEPTION;
it is another illusion caused by limited sensation.
But that just transfers IDEA of SPACE over to VOID;
the former of which is now the meaning of the latter.
There is more absence in VOID than attributed to SPACE;
REALITY does not expose them in the same manner.
SPACE can't be disposed of in that willy-nilly fashion;
it requires more explanation for its deception.
Is SPACE known absolutely or partially;
shall it be defined according to limited sensation?
Those PERCEPTIONS form my IDEA of SPACE, or VOID,
and its connection to TIME shouldn't be ignored.
If there is not really any SPACE, then what is TIME;
how do we mark the difference between now and then?
By watching the seconds march across a clock;
each 1 marking a continuous endless progress.
In order for OBJECT to exist,
it must have manifold presents, with no past or future.
It can't come from nowhere, then pop-pop into existence,
and any future is proposed with unerring inaccuracy.
Is one OBJECT'S TIME the same as any other's,
all progressing according to the same fatal measure?
That is CONCEPT of TIME as nominally understood,
which is why it's the most accurate measurement.
What is TIME found attached to all points of SPACE,
or maybe now a connection with all points of VOID?
TIME and SPACE are inextricably intertwined;
proven by RELATIVITY experiments done to silence skeptics.
So if SPACE only exists as nominal PERCEPTION,
and TIME is attached, then it must also be an illusion.
It can't be an illusion if seconds are perceived to pass;
TIME must exist for OBJECTS to exist.

What is Time; is it just some mysterious Force
we do not understand?
Inanimate Universe operates according to Basic Quantities;
Time is 1 like Mass and Extension.
Maybe Time itself is not the problem;
maybe its current Conception trips it into Space.
Then the nature of Inanimate Universe is totally different
from the way Matter has been proposed to exist.
How is the nature of Inanimate Universe to be understood,
if all Space and Time is still beyond Conception?
All Time and Space have now been confined within Aether;
limited Concepts are now confusing their ideals.
Is there a better way of conceiving how
Space and Time pass through Inanimate Universe?
Everything within my universe is sensed as Object,
which limits the possibilities of what they can be.
How do Time and Space spread among these essences:
Star and Matter, Soul and Life?

****

16:29

Star and Matter, Soul and Life;
Reality locked into its own dualistic prison.
Each universe is divided into conceivable Objects,
and grasping at them doesn't bring me more freedom.
A wise man once said: keep Mind free from greed;
this will keep body right, Mind pure, and words faithful.
I can't stop Thoughts of greed running through my head;
if I could steal freedom from another I would.
There is nothing so impure as Thought which steals from others
to gain that which it does not contain within itself.
My Thoughts are free, they don't cost anything;
no harm comes from mere Thoughts beyond attainment.
What good will greed do to a person who has nothing,
the only baggage transported upon seeing Death?

All THOUGHTS are possessions owned by the bearer;
they multiply and abound when stolen from others.
No purity will arise inside a heart longing for peace,
as long as greed has a place in crooked and bent MIND.
But it's only more THOUGHTS I want,
which isn't the same as stealing from the mouths of babes.
How will greed's face be known by a brief touch,
smoothly caressing or bristly brushing?
Greed is desiring more, no matter what form it takes,
even THOUGHTS of things I can't have.
Is it only grasping in vain, or also wanting
that which is held as justly due?
There is no difference!
If I allow 1 in, the other will surely tag along.
Some people say it is the path less traveled,
not that which is earned by breath and by sweat.
Left to the side for someone less-filled to carry;
use what I can, and leave the best for the rest.
Pernicious greed grows like weeds in loamy MIND;
it is so easy to let seeds of discontent thrive in fertile soil.
My MIND is abundant with injustice, unfairness, ignominy;
greed grasps pliant THOUGHTS, and sucks and grows.
Believing something is justly due from effort
is one little weed crowding out the flower of faith.
Which is something I desperately need,
faith that my existence is more than a lack of meaning.
The gross form filling out an animal's physical existence
is so easy to pervert with meaning from sensation.
The wind on my face was meaningless until I lost it;
now I'm driven to THOUGHTS of killing for 1 moment.
If long-sought purity lets want fall into need's embrace,
then greed can no longer be distinguished for what it is.
My body has no knowledge of right or wrong;
it wants what it wants, and it needs what it needs.
How can faith come to one who must add value
to what is done with what should be gained?
All works done by my hand are value-added-products;
few are done with no intention in MIND.

This moment is pure in and of itself;
greed plans the future based on past attainments.
Thoughts come from what can be done,
instead of concentrating on what is being done.
Where does most pure Thought *manage to take flight;*
is it one leaf, first or last, falling in the spring?

16:53

The top of my head is hot, feverish from steadfast denial,
very much like Heat coming from the sun.
Does Star *burn brightly somewhere in biological bounds;*
where does Energy *come from to make* Life *function?*
Energy for Biomatter begins with Photosynthesis,
and the only Star-like essence within me might be Soul.
Imagine shining Soul *internally moves* Life
in a manner similar to how Star *externally moves* Matter.
Life is sensed through its presence as Biomatter,
which makes Soul all but invisible.
Soul is the source to Life, *yet the interaction between*
them produces existence within Animate Universe.
Much as Force erupts between Star and Matter,
and also between different Objects made of each.
A plurality totally contained within our universe;
a Rational *view is not able to penetrate its essence.*
Biomatter can be fully known by a Rational perspective,
but its source in Life doesn't fit conventional analysis.
The only available methods are mystical introspection,
and limited approximations of what Life *and* Soul *do.*
Mystical Thought is well outside my own abilities;
though if I'm adequately led, I may be able to get close.
The heart of Star *is impenetrable;*
the heart of Soul *has no less shielding.*
Star is known by its effects on Matter;
Soul is known by its effects on Biomatter <*Life*>.
Each universe is composed of things making it Reality;
the lack of any universe results in Void, *in* Reality.

STAR and MATTER—INANIMATE UNIVERSE OBJECT DUALISM;
SOUL and LIFE—ANIMATE UNIVERSE ORGANISM DUALISM.
LIFE is as LIFE does;
no other understanding will shine it in its full light.
How BIOMATTER acts, and subsequently reacts, exposes it;
something more than FORCE moves it to completion.
LIFE is the manifestation of INTUITION'S awareness of SOUL,
rationally observed as animated BIOMATTER.
Existing separate within ANIMATE UNIVERSE,
but incomplete without the other to rely upon.
Every living CELL is a soulful window from limited SOUL,
a potential for awareness of something larger than itself.
I find it difficult to imagine parallel ANIMATE UNIVERSE,
which can't be seen or touched or smelled or heard.
Yet there is no problem imagining empty VOID,
which also defies easy classification by sensation.
Those muffled senses are what differentiate OBJECTS,
making it difficult to separate my LIFE from my SOUL.
LIFE has a barrier and SOUL does not;
similar to the one differentiating MATTER from STAR.
So all my CONCEPTS of ANIMATE UNIVERSE
must begin by correlating them with INANIMATE UNIVERSE.
At a broad general level, DUALITY matches them quite well;
at the more distinct levels, they do not at all.
Any CONCEPT of SOUL should begin with STAR,
and CONCEPT of BIOMATTER should begin with MATTER.
ORGANISM in ANIMATE UNIVERSE with a membrane is LIFE;
ORGANISM in that same realm without a membrane is SOUL.
But the membrane is actually within INANIMATE UNIVERSE,
which SOUL isn't even capable of detecting.
CELL is the window between the two universes;
LIFE has capacity for this attachment via a membrane.
Therefore a membrane shows me where I can find LIFE,
and LIFE shows me where I can find SOUL.
If LIFE is able to attach itself to PLASMIC MEMBRANE,
there must be some analogue within ANIMATE UNIVERSE.
Ah . . . so a membrane is another RATIONAL device
I can use to determine insensible existence.

LIFE performs an act within INANIMATE UNIVERSE
for PURPOSES which have yet to be revealed.
BIOMATTER is RATIONAL PERCEPTION of living,
a mysterious and apparent essence within a membrane.
A membrane helps distinguish MATTER from LIFE,
and there is one other known to be exceptionally notable.
Living creatures are known for requiring a continuous supply
of ENERGY to keep them alive and moving.
MATTER only stores ENERGY when FORCES so mandate,
while LIFE seems able to retain it on its own, temporarily.
The sun loses ENERGY, and will die into its HEAT DEATH,
but MATTER only loses ENERGY when FORCE makes it.
MATTER and STAR are both INANIMATE OBJECTS;
their difference is in INERTIA, not in their ENERGY arrow.
Some ENERGY comes from within OBJECTS,
such as wood or radioactive rocks or the earth's G-FORCES.
How does ENERGY come from the existence of OBJECTS?
Essential tools needed to resolve the question are missing.

17:28

No matter where I look inside, I detect myself,
but I don't know whether this is my SOUL, or its derivative.
Why would REALITY create LIFE with SOUL;
is there more to it than the ability to dance funky-style?
SOUL could be the source of each individual's raison d'être,
or maybe it's nothing more than an ENERGY source.
STAR exists with implacable intensity—to shed ENERGY;
what possible function accounts for the existence of SOUL?
MATTER won't operate "normally" without STAR'S influence,
so BIOMATTER must be affected in a similar manner.
If SOUL is to be considered in a fashion similar to STAR,
it must have a simple mandate to fulfill its role with LIFE.
The sun impels MATTER without complex maneuvers;
ENERGY makes GRAVITATIONAL and ELECTROMAGNETIC FORCES.
LIFE requires a continuous infusion of something lacking,
a special kind of ENERGY simultaneously gained and lost.

Living creatures are constantly acquiring sustenance,
while expending ENERGY is also an essential requirement.
ENERGY cannot be supplied to LIFE by INANIMATE UNIVERSE;
REALITY exposes itself from within, not without.
If I continue to extend DUALISM between the universes,
then ENERGY for LIFE moves from inside to outside.
LIFE appears to consume ENERGY and then waste it;
yet there is still more observed about its existence.
AETHER is within INANIMATE and ANIMATE UNIVERSES;
ENERGY is in the former, and something is in the latter.
This essence must come from SOUL unto LIFE, something
internal that material ENERGY is incapable of providing.
It also must be able to equalize the pressure on BIOMATTER,
external and internal FORCES in a dualistic balance.
What exactly does SOUL provide to all living creatures?
Other than a feeling of PURPOSE, no IDEA springs to MIND.
ENERGY and FORCE determine how BIOMATTER acts,
some other essence must balance it with why.
If LIFE and SOUL are withdrawn
from REALITY'S equation, then PURPOSE is empty.
No PURPOSE naturally exists within INANIMATE UNIVERSE,
a part of REALITY only reacting to FORCE interaction.
SOUL has no ability to directly access a RATIONAL realm;
it establishes PURPOSE through pliable agents of LIFE.
Even GRAVITATIONAL bonding between the sun and the earth
has no PURPOSE beyond mindless continuity.
PURPOSE achieved through one dual dual role:
ANIMATE LIFE and INANIMATE BIOMATTER.
A RATIONAL view partitions BIOMATTER into parts and pieces;
an INTUITIVE view experiences LIFE as 1 whole essence.
LIFE has existed, unrealized, as long as MATTER;
the forms it has taken give it pause for consideration.
If BIOMATTER currently has a double-sided existence,
then it likely has existed this way all along.
INANIMATE and ANIMATE existences are concurrently formed,
yet only the cellular form of frail LIFE has been accented.
No apology will be given for that acceptable omission;
no part of ANIMATE UNIVERSE has ever been observed.

Its form has taken many many eons to evolve superbly;
BIOMATTER and LIFE have different motives for existing.
Current scientific understanding of BIOMATTER
has no room for a primordial existence with the big bang.
Sparks enticing MATTER are less complex than BIOMATTER,
while coals burning in CELL grandly escape formulation.
The same isotopes structure any material OBJECT,
so they are in BIOMATTER, along with something more.
BIOMATTER reacts as MATTER regarding INANIMATE FORCES;
all parts of any universe must abide by the same rules.
FORCES and ENERGIES will commonly affect all OBJECTS,
even the 1's with a dual dual existence.
STAR does not appear to be affected by material FORCES;
drops of rain would get lost crawling up a waterfall.
That is an example of unscientific THOUGHT;
FORCE requires at least 2 partners to initiate a dance.
STAR affects MATTER, does it affect LIFE;
peering through the living window to nudge it back?
Of course BIOMATTER is subject to solar dictates,
while the balance between PURPOSE and ENERGY fluctuates.
SOUL affects LIFE, does it affect MATTER;
for what other PURPOSE do OBJECTS participate?
If I pick up a rock and throw it up a hill,
then it has been given something it didn't have before.
The affectation between STAR and SOUL does not dawn;
although STAR might yet be shown to have dense PURPOSE.
Mighty FORCES at opposite ends of the spectrum;
no direct contact is required if intermediaries suffice.
ENERGY from STAR creates FORCES to break down MATTER
into useful bundles for LIFE to use in its quest for survival.
No. PHOTOSYNTHESIS converts light into chemical ENERGY;
this is how BIOMATTER achieves continuous motion.
That is the most important use LIFE obtains from STAR,
not forgetting random light and HEAT and gravitic FORCES.

18:04

Fasting has shown me how much my body needs food;
whatever fills me with ENERGY is becoming less and less.
PRIMAL FORCE is how AETHER inspires material OBJECTS;
LIFE FORCE is how AETHER helps LIFE hold it together.
If PRIMAL FORCE binds MATTER'S MASS and EXTENSION,
then it must do the same with BIOMATTER'S version.
PRIMAL FORCE produces ENERGY within INANIMATE UNIVERSE;
all MATTER, including BIOMATTER, has MASS and EXTENSION.
All outside the living window must live by physical rules;
there is no such thing as biomaterial FORCE.
Each CELL has some bit of LIFE FORCE at its core,
FIRE stoked by SOUL and fed privately by AETHER.
CELL would therefore have more than just PRIMAL FORCE,
which has no process for furnishing PURPOSE.
LIFE FORCE is conceived within ANIMATE UNIVERSE,
binding together the purposeful activities of LIFE.
The other side of the living window has other ties to bind,
a misunderstood living counter to MASS and EXTENSION.
Organic carbon chains are able to store LIFE FORCE,
and thereby obtain a tenuous connection to SOUL.
BIOMATTER consumes food to obtain ENERGY;
"LIFE FORCE" doesn't enter into the equation.
By consuming CELLS or organic MATTER,
CELL will gain LIFE FORCE, adding SOUL to its discretion.
But "LIFE FORCE" is invisible to any of my several senses;
there is no mysterious ENERGY being consumed.
And then LIFE must exhibit PURPOSE to continue living,
thereby losing much it has gained.
It's unscientific to propose BIOMATTER obtains PURPOSE
by consuming itself in an attempt to gain "LIFE FORCE".
LIFE begets LIFE, LIFE consumes LIFE;
the way CELLS access SOUL is essential for survival.
That is only true if PHOTOSYNTHESIS is denied,
a process which doesn't consume any BIOMATTER.
For what does CELL exist without PURPOSE,
to be an inert group of chemicals for deified exhibition?

All creatures exhibit Purpose, this is without doubt;
it's "Life Force" which causes me Rational difficulties.
What does Life acquire from other pieces
like itself; how does Energy miraculously become Purpose?
The fight for survival and the search for happiness
may be all there is to massive Purpose.
Why fight for survival or search for happiness;
if we are just chemicals, should not we only react, not act?
But I'm being asked to accept that organic molecules
store some hidden "Life Force"—now the key to Biomatter.
Life is not Energy as decreed by gods of Science;
Life Force is contained by membranes and molecules.
Then Cells can't be the only window between universes;
all attachments to Biomatter must be so connected.
This is the rhyme to Life's fight with itself for survival:
inert Matter is only structural for Biomatter.
That still contradicts everything I've been taught
about Biomatter's minor derivation from major Matter.
Carbon is able to form molecular chains for storing
Life Force in its bonds for general Consumption.
The mechanism appears to be both Rational and Intuitive;
Biomatter needs it, but no 1 can show where it exists.
Cell metabolizes Life Force to sustain itself,
and an excess is needed to multiply or reproduce.
So "Life Force" is required for all of Biomatter's Purposes,
and the latter can't exist without the former.
There is a limited amount of motivation available to Life,
because any Purpose must come from some Soul.
And Purpose is only found within living attachments;
Energy plus Energy doesn't equal Purpose.
Purpose is the motive principle within Animate Universe;
the unit of exchange between constituent members.
Similar to how Energy is used within Inanimate Universe,
thereby creating Forces between its Stars and Matters.
Soul gives Purpose internally to each form of Life;
although the rationale for this action is still a mystery.
As Star emits Energy externally to each bit of Matter,
there doesn't appear to be any Purpose to this action.

How do PRIMAL and LIFE FORCES relate each to the other,
combining or opposing to produce PERCEPTION of LIFE?
PRIMAL FORCE is the same whether in MATTER or BIOMATTER,
leaving "LIFE FORCE" to latch on as best it can.
PRIMAL FORCE is held within the structure of inert MATTER,
bones or ash bound together like pebbles or rocks.
Any OBJECT is perceived as MASS and EXTENSION,
and this structure when exploded reveals PRIMAL FORCE.
LIFE FORCE uses the structure of inert MATTER,
as a person uses a domicile to protect and serve.
ENERGY is associated with OBJECT'S PRIMAL FORCE,
but living creatures exhibit ENERGY beyond this arena.
There is only one source for any ENERGY,
AETHER is all MATTER or LIFE will ever need.
But AETHER is perceived to divide its influence;
ENERGY and PURPOSE touch REALITY quite differently.
LIFE FORCE is buried inside each of its forms,
and when released it is much like its primal relation.
Release of PRIMAL FORCE in the form of fusion or fission
produces similar ENERGIES to those from dead ORGANISMS.
FORCE and ENERGY and power are RATIONAL terms,
all acceding to direction from PRIMAL or LIFE FORCE.
It doesn't matter which essence produces ENERGY,
they both will produce the same kinds of FORCES.
CELL emits BIOENERGY into INANIMATE UNIVERSE,
which is a form of AETHER now used as ENERGY.
MATTER and STAR produce ENERGY to create FORCES;
BIOMATTER emits BIOENERGY to obey physical laws.
That very same BIOENERGY is funded from SOUL;
PURPOSE driving all LIFE is the source of its emissions.
Living creatures have capacity for 2 kinds of ENERGY,
combining to form awareness of their existence.
FORCE determines what sensation detects,
which must come from some OBJECT-driven ENERGY.
What I know of MATTER comes from ENERGY,
and what I know of BIOMATTER comes from BIOENERGY.
LIFE FORCE may be considered, in a very loose manner,
as a separate purposeful form of MATTER'S PRIMAL FORCE.

There is no need for competition between them;
ENERGY and BIOENERGY create identical INANIMATE FORCES.
PURPOSE is available to all living creatures,
responsible for giving to each the desire for LIFE.
BIOENERGY is available from all living creatures,
responsible for each reacting as BIOMATTER with FORCE.
As ENERGY is related to PRIMAL FORCE,
so PURPOSE is joined to LIFE FORCE.
Each can't exist without the other in its universe;
still, there is the problem of relating BIOENERGY to PURPOSE.
PURPOSE is BIOENERGY for all practical situations,
depending on which side of LIFE'S barrier it is conceived.
But PURPOSE is QUALITY, immaterial and lacking substance,
while BIOENERGY is QUANTITY needed for material existence.
PURPOSE is the why and BIOENERGY is the how,
yet each plays the same role in totally implementing LIFE.
Why and how are separated by PLASMIC MEMBRANE,
kept apart like QUALITY and QUANTITY.
HEAT and charge evidenced by CELLS comes from PURPOSE
being emitted into INANIMATE UNIVERSE as BIOENERGY.
Meaning PURPOSE obscurely transforms into BIOENERGY
by a process which makes no sense at all.
LIFE exhibits PURPOSE, LIFE emits BIOENERGY;
a connection no more apparent than cause and effect.
PURPOSE is assumed by the actions BIOMATTER takes;
BIOENERGY is evidenced by its full material existence.
The chasm between PURPOSE and BIOENERGY
is tiny compared to the one between belief and doubt.

19:02

Putting my hand up to my cheek, I feel a little fever;
LIFE FORCE inside me seems to be working overtime.
What is LIFE FORCE to be so central to human ambition;
is there a definable essence which makes it distinct?
If HEAT comes from LIFE, and HEAT comes from some ENERGY
source, then LIFE FORCE emits some type of ENERGY.

AETHER is ENERGY—REALITY'S composition in its natural state,
perceived when it slows down long enough to be sensed.
Even if I were to deny the existence of particulate MATTER,
ENERGY only exists within INANIMATE UNIVERSE.
PURPOSE is ENERGY of a different nature;
it cannot be touched or seen, just like any other.
Therefore ENERGY divides into 2 spheres of influence:
common ENERGY is INANIMATE, unusual PURPOSE is ANIMATE.
Words have flexible meanings for purposeful SOULS;
some can be reused, some retrained, some are disposed.
There is a total amount of ENERGY within REALITY,
and SOUL exists as part of this grand scheme of things.
The sole rationale for the existence of SOUL
is introduction of PURPOSE into a universe born without it.
It makes little or no sense for SOUL to exist that way,
for the sun doesn't exist to energize INANIMATE UNIVERSE.
It is no more bizarre an assertion than to postulate
STAR throws ENERGY into barren VOID.
There is no answer as to why ENERGY moves at all;
the closest approximation is to observe it, and then use it.
LIFE appears to be on a constant quest for BIOENERGY,
at least when seen from a RATIONAL perspective.
But it's really a matter of PURPOSE seeking PURPOSE,
finding more of that which it can't live without.
If the nature of REALITY is AETHER as ENERGY,
then what is the future function in giving itself more?
Nothing can increase the level of ENERGY from the source
of where it all comes from in the beginning.
Yet LIFE must achieve movement to grow and change;
how is this accomplished without ENERGY for motion?
Somehow BIOMATTER must receive BIOENERGY to use it;
independent motion does grow upon a soulful tree.
LIFE appears to gain BIOENERGY via a RATIONAL view;
no other way accounts for different places and instances.
But BIOMATTER is fully recognized as OBJECT;
it must use BIOENERGY as MATTER uses ENERGY.
Keep one common motto alive for expanding MIND:
LIFE begets LIFE, and nothing else is acceptable.

My difficulty lies in trying to conceive of how PURPOSE can
turn into BIOENERGY via a plasmic membranous lens.
BIOENERGY'S alternate role will be considered in due TIME,
granting PURPOSE to MATTER which otherwise is inert.
If PURPOSE is BIOENERGY, and SOUL'S supply is endless,
then there should be no need for BIOMATTER to seek it.
Motion achieved by the use of MASS or fusion or fission has
no PURPOSE other than given by man's wanted intervention.
Motion achieved by the use of LIFE FORCE gives PURPOSE
to MATTER that would otherwise have none.
REALITY is designed so STARS and MATTER have a
predictable ENERGY flow, to which all OBJECTS subscribe.
But motion is achieved by any type of discernible OBJECT;
it doesn't matter whether it has PURPOSE or not.
The source of motion truly needs bringing to attention,
whether naturally or artificially given some PURPOSE.
ENERGY of any stripe is ultimately the source of motion,
and motion is also a major producer of ENERGY.
If suns and rocks are left to their own devices,
the motion they achieve will never have PURPOSE.
But they do still achieve motion and ENERGY,
and there aren't 2 different types of moving OBJECTS.
MATTER'S ENERGY does not allow LIFE to grow and change;
BIOENERGY from PURPOSE accounts for its modifications.
So MATTER works with ENERGY to produce motion;
BIOMATTER instills BIOENERGY with purposeful motion.
LIFE moves from its own limited sources;
there is no INANIMATE push to give it motion.
ENERGY as commonly understood is just like BIOENERGY,
the latter just has an added element of PURPOSE.
Motion is achieved from using gasoline in a car,
as stored LIFE FORCE is modified to fulfill another PURPOSE.

19:33

When my final TIME comes and my body becomes cold,
I will produce no more HEAT and have no more PURPOSE.

LIFE is MATTER with PURPOSE;
SOUL is LIFE with PURPOSE.
Rationally connecting and feeding 1 from another,
BIOMATTER doesn't exist without PURPOSE to guide it.
ORGANISMS absorb LIFE FORCE from other LIFE-forms
to sustain and grow their soulful windows.
Therefore BIOMATTER is able to obtain BIOENERGY,
and act as a full member of INANIMATE UNIVERSE.
With a bigger window more PURPOSE is available;
although even more is required to transfer it into action.
Concluding: elephants have more PURPOSE than mice;
though their ability to use it is capped by synapses.
MATTER'S hold upon existence has no intent,
random bits of flotsam and jetsam floating within VOID.
FORCES and ENERGIES don't care about their effects,
they just exist.
LIFE has no meaning without ambition;
PURPOSE upon PURPOSE initiates these THOUGHTS.
BIOMATTER requires more than just PURPOSE to exist,
a source must exist for any expression of ENERGY.
Each and every CELL has the ability to discriminate
between want and need, useful and wasteful.
Then blind random PURPOSE isn't loose in the world,
it's moderated by an innate ability within LIFE itself.
This and only this is the basis of RATIONAL intelligence:
CELL discriminating one part of DUALITY from another.
That makes no sense;
RATIONAL CONCEPTS of REALITY are formed within my BRAIN.
For CELL to discriminate requires some motivation,
a process following from some secretive resolution.
CELLS admittedly must discriminate to survive,
but this doesn't translate into ORGANISM's intelligence.
CELL presents limited PURPOSE to a limited universe,
while SOUL provides it LIFE from an unlimited source.
Then the supply of PURPOSE to me should be INFINITE,
which somehow must include my need for SLEEP.
LIFE is happily pushed to become more than it is;
shown by all creatures' incessant crawl to endure.

Pushed by Soul to continue without seeming to have it,
Purpose is required for all of Life's actions.
Gods have decreed that Life acquires Energy to survive;
instead, it requires Purpose for sustenance and growth.
Science has shown most of Biomatter's Energy cycle,
from Photosynthesis through the passage into membranes.
Try an experiment to see whether Life requires Purpose:
fast for a few days and watch motivational supply plummet.
Some "experts" claim a few days without food will kill;
though those are the type who know without doing.
Not insipid Thoughts, they still ring their neural chimes;
not futile actions, they continue as long as Life.
Though fasting shouldn't really be attempted by anybody;
the best Rational advice is to avoid getting sued.
Only Purpose available to do any of many things
has disappeared with the food no longer eaten.
All of my normal actions remain available,
but my desire to do anything is virtually nil.
Belief comes from experience, while Truth does not
care who is right and who is wrong.
Purpose is secret Bioenergy motivating Biomatter,
which won't be believed until it's personally experienced.
All Cells are driven to obtain Purpose at whatever cost;
striving while dying is more natural than just dying.
Fasting shows me the gap between Energy and Purpose:
1 is similar to Bioenergy, and the other is it.
Cells are conceived to die without proper nutrition,
yet show any Life which can live without Purpose.
A function which only appears with living forms;
like other Qualities, it only appears to exist.
Release static Conceptions!
A Rational keep buries vital Mind beneath its weight.
The validity of Science allows me no other solid method;
animation exists in the gaps between Rational Thought.
Only Life without Purpose from Soul
can be expounded on a foundation of chemistry and drugs.
But drugs do work upon living Organisms;
they will still react to chemicals while serving Purpose.

ORGANISM also acquires greater PURPOSE during its LIFE,
casting benefit or harm depending on how it is used.
PURPOSE isn't like ENERGY in that respect,
DUALISM as good or evil results from a definite impulse.
LIFE began incoherent and increases in coherence,
and PURPOSE provides the power behind its EVOLUTION.
An evolutionary theory proposing a "design" to BIOMATTER,
much as if a deity regularly interferes with its progress.
Each ORGANISM is the measure of SOUL'S ability
to express itself to PURPOSE within INANIMATE UNIVERSE.
It exists as BIOMATTER by hiding its PURPOSE within;
many shapes and sizes ripping apart and coming together.
There is no measure of PURPOSE in ANIMATE UNIVERSE;
QUANTITY has no bearing when applied to QUALITY.
No other basis exists for how PURPOSE is transferred;
each ORGANISM functions as a modifier, not a producer.
Soulful windows are motivated to gain more PURPOSE,
conflicting with their limited capacity in one LIFE-span.
But PURPOSE is only available to living creatures,
so each 1 must be limited in what it can accomplish.
SOUL is only able to work during the length of one LIFE,
and so usually has little or no gain in PURPOSE.
I appear to be veering away from RATIONAL SCIENCE,
and am opening the door into convenient RELIGION.
Therein lies EVOLUTION via REINCARNATION,
a push towards INFINITY PURPOSE in INANIMATE UNIVERSE.
Now I'm combining RELIGION with SCIENCE;
no other heresy will the masses find so repugnant.
LIFE opens a soulful window and its inherited size limit;
bigger and better windows necessitate alteration.
Taking 1 step after another can appear to make sense,
but not if they lead to a moon filled with green cheese.
Since CELLS have PURPOSE as their motive FORCE,
justifying EVOLUTION via REINCARNATION is not a problem.
It's 1 thing to propose an alternate universe,
but ANIMATE and INANIMATE UNIVERSES aren't fully equal.
CELL, by itself, is limited in PURPOSE it can fulfill;
thus came about the need for multicellular ORGANISMS.

That rationale has 1 point current theories are missing:
EVOLUTION working by design and not chance.
Any further reflection on EVOLUTION misses the point;
it is only covered here as pertains to dual SOUL and LIFE.
Another in a series of unanswered questions
waiting for the proper moment to make their appearance.
The important point is limitless PURPOSE behind LIFE,
then finding RATIONAL expression in a biomaterial vehicle.
PURPOSE is as important to LIFE as ENERGY is to MATTER;
existence of 1 requires existence of the other.
The interaction between all living things
is the result of a simple push.
While the interaction between MATTER and BIOMATTER
is FORCE resulting from ENERGY between opposing OBJECTS.
INTUITION indirectly views MATTER as to how it exists,
contrary to a RATIONAL grasp of SOUL as a holy ghost.
No perspective fully sees the alternate universe;
SOUL is limited by BIOMATTER, STAR is by its gateway.
SOUL exists to give PURPOSE to INANIMATE UNIVERSE;
why and its relation to AETHER are religious questions.

20:29

As I continue to live on borrowed TIME, like all men,
PURPOSE must enter my MIND for THOUGHTS to form.
How does SOUL inspire LIFE to touch corporeality;
is there only one crossover wherein universes collide?
INANIMATE and ANIMATE UNIVERSES have distinct structures,
and there must be some places where they meet and bind.
Each CELL is a small window from INFINITY SOUL,
and combinations of CELLS make for bigger windows.
So LIFE is the incorporeal side of the actual portal,
while BIOMATTER is the material side of the same one.
Inside is SOUL, could be one, could be many;
pressing ever out like the air in a bathyscaph.
Pressure will keep the air pressed against the window,
and SOUL will keep pressed up against LIFE.

Metabolizing LIFE FORCE is the means by which CELL increases
its capacity to emit PURPOSE into the world.
Each CELL, each organic molecule, each bit of BIOMATTER,
has some part of LIFE FORCE that can be utilized.
Once CELL'S evolutionary size limit is reached,
the feeding process keeps SOUL'S window to the world open.
Each living creature can only grow so big,
so the majority of CONSUMPTION is dedicated to continuity.
A soulful window is composed of a single piece of LIFE,
solo or grouped to see REALITY from only one direction.
Commonly CELL, sometimes unified into ORGANISM,
soulful MIND is able to see either rationally or intuitively.
Fractured glass, window panes, faces on a crystal,
dividing the whole into pieces of illusion.
If SOUL can only see out through CELL,
then CELL is the key to understanding BIOMATTER and LIFE.
While the soulful window is kept open,
SOUL gives MATTER PURPOSE within INANIMATE UNIVERSE.
But it's limited access by the membrane of CELL;
that which holds LIFE in, also keeps a lid on PURPOSE.
The addition of PURPOSE can increase the size of CELL,
allowing it to multiply, or even to reproduce.
All of which requires the inclusion of structural MATTER;
CELL'S INANIMATE existence combines dust to dust.
LIFE cannot increase the amount of INFINITY supplied,
for the essence of SOUL has no RATIONAL limitation.
Another paradox added to the growing list:
how to add to INFINITE without increasing it.
LIFE intent on PURPOSE sought in each other
only gives greater access to SOUL, not increasing power.
Then LIFE'S PURPOSE should seek to become more open,
not to become the biggest EVOLUTION will allow.
Up until the membrane of CELL is pierced and ruptured,
LIFE FORCE leaks away, and access to SOUL goes with it.
This is why SCIENCE doesn't understand LIFE at all:
BIOMATTER still remains when SOUL is no longer envisioned.
MATTER is composed of OBJECTS within TIME and SPACE,
which is why BIOMATTER must be considered in this regard.

SPACE and TIME are on the agenda of INANIMATE UNIVERSE;
SOUL perceives them happening outside of its existence.
LIFE is composed of METABOLISM and REPRODUCTION;
which is why BIOMATTER must be considered in this regard.
Trying to pin down BIOMATTER into identifiable OBJECTS
doesn't work because it's constantly moving.
CELL'S window allows MIND to see INTUITION within,
while also allowing MIND to perceive RATIONAL existence.

20:54

Bob the guard walks past my cell whistling a tune;
even he must have some SOUL to raise him above the mud.
Each sentient being seems to be endowed with SOUL;
do the lesser evolved ORGANISMS also come so equipped?
If SOUL is the source of PURPOSE for all BIOMATTER,
then all living creatures must need it for their survival.
Is there one SOUL for each formed LIFE,
or one grand source feeding all living existence?
Many many STARS are evident in the night sky;
if SOUL is analogous to STAR, then many come before 1.
The question is best answered with a rhetorical one:
does INFINITY consist of one or many?
The conceived term indicates the existence of only 1,
but it just falls into CONCEPT, FINITE and RATIONAL.
INFINITY includes all within its scope,
so it has the capacity for many INFINITIES indeed.
I can't form CONCEPT of many INFINITES,
especially when 1 won't fit within my head.
SOULS appear different because of isolated THOUGHTS;
if all SOULS are the same, our THOUGHTS should match.
Whatever produces THOUGHTS in my BRAIN
is different from that which produces another person's.
Viewed intuitively, SOUL is part of a continuous essence,
yet a RATIONAL glance rakes in many different leaves.
Transposition between different perspectives
leads to paradox when trying to quantify QUALITY.

Soul's connection to Aether is only discovered by looking
within to find Infinity water down Intuition's well.
Personal seekers must leave rationality to take that dip,
finding as much Soul as they are spiritually able.
Connection of Soul to Life is guessed by a Rational view,
based on Infinity Spaces between Matter's bars.
And still, Biomatter must consume itself to obtain Purpose,
so Soul's connection to Life remains tentative.
Is it possible absorption of Life Force allows each Soul
a greater presence within Inanimate Universe?
That process grants the consumer greater Purpose,
but this might not directly relate to greater Soul.
No, not quite correct, Souls are not consumed;
Life Force is absorbed in an irrational fashion.
Living windows exist with a predetermined bio-limit,
which can increase Life Force without more Soul.
Soul provides Purpose, yet it is still distinct from Life;
Life Force uses Soul without any increase to its access.
Increase in Biomatter involves little increase in Soul;
another process is required to bring that about.
Something Life does behind Intuition's veil;
why does it reproduce, and how is this tied in with Soul?
Metabolism and Reproduction are required to live;
though the latter's process is like cause and effect.
There is no other function for Reproduction
than subjection to the dictates of its motive Soul.
Then Metabolism should increase Life Force supply,
while Reproduction should increase Soul's access.
Acquisition of Life Force and more Purpose from Soul
are the reasons for Evolution in all of its tarnished glory.
Survival of the fittest is 1 substantial aspect, also
mutation of patterns between subsequent generations.
There is Purpose to Life's apparent search for Energy,
accomplishing this feat with more soulful windows.
Each Cell is forever limited in how much Purpose
it can transfer into Bioenergy, emitted from Biomatter.
When Organism dies, the branch of Soul attached
to this soulful window does not fade away into Void.

Then Soul attached to Life adheres even after Death,
even though there is no rationale for it to do so.
It will continue in stasis within Animate Universe until
a suitable vehicle of Biomatter is created to house it.
That is the heart of the process of Reincarnation,
hidden like Life behind a biomaterial plasmic veil.
Rebirth is fixed by the manner of previous Life,
according to how its last purposeful gasps had meaning.
The realm of an after-Life has potent meaning,
exists in a manner without senses, so is beyond Science.
Processing of Life and Death requires some Soul,
either one for each Life or one for all.
Since Thoughts between people are so widely varied,
it already seems as though 1 Soul has been refuted.
Recall the best rationale for the existence of many Souls—
a rough analogy to its Inanimate Star cousins.
There is 1 Star that shines brightest among many,
so should 1 Soul relegate others to a dead night sky.
It is difficult to know little points of light as more Stars,
or how unaided views of other Souls could glisten within.
That may be paralleling the universes a bit too strictly;
internal and external may have many different relations.
Souls are ultimately sourced by Aether;
Intuition's pure view will see them as one and the same.
If purity of perspective shows Truth I seek,
my view of Reality should closely approximate unity.
Compare Cell to some ordinary rocks;
their existence ultimately belongs to same Aether.
Assuming there is 1 different Soul for each Cell,
also asserts each rock has separate Aethers.
Assumption of separate Soul for each Cell or Organism,
comes by losing others behind the glare of the brightest.
Each person who develops the ability to look within
will inevitably be confronted by his own bright Soul.
Picture Soul as Yggdrasil, the norse world tree;
each form of Life is an individual twig or branch.
Therefore there are many Souls at each end,
and there is also 1 Soul that is the source of them all.

Cell is able to find Purpose on its bough of Soul's tree,
while alive bringing forth fruit to each separate Life.
Purpose flows from Soul to Souls to Life to Biomatter,
each part of Aether moving in 1 direction.
When it dies, its limb waits for spring to Birth a new leaf;
rebirth is ever eternal; picture Soul's Life as truly living.
If Soul is like a tree which sheds and then blooms,
then like a tree it should eventually wither and die.
How do we know whether Soul is immortal;
does it possess Life in a span as its derivatives must?
Any essence must exist according to its universal laws,
and in this case Soul abides by Animate jurisdiction.
Solely extant in the realm where Infinity is pervasive,
Soul is immortal because it has no Rational limits.
Mortality is confined to exist within Inanimate Universe,
a construct limiting Biomatter's short and ignoble span.
Primary Thoughts used to determine
how each Life is endowed with its own soulful window.
I shall continue to refer to only 1 Soul;
my poor head still has trouble with 1 and many Infinites.
Yet whether it exists in solo fashion or another is also
irrational as long as its essence remains insubstantial.
Soul's existence can be taken on faith,
and it can be helped by making it probable over possible.
Prime evidence for Soul's persistent existence is Purpose
all living things exhibit to Rational awareness.
Once a living creature dies, it has no Purpose,
which indicates Soul exists only with living Biomatter.
When Cell dies evidence is cut off, not the source;
only bio-Objects available to sensation have limited Life.
Purpose for Biomatter comes from some place,
which Death cuts from Inanimate, not Animate, Universe.
Essences perceived outside of a Rational view, like Soul,
are also outside the encumbrance of defined existence.
My Conception of Soul is based on Rational evidence;
whatever it truly is doesn't have to be so limited.
Soul gives up its secrets only indirectly to sensation
by Cells exhibiting Purpose at each living moment.

PURPOSE and PURPOSE and more PURPOSE!
If BIOMATTER had none, there would be no need for SOUL.
Anything not directly sensed has no RATIONAL meaning;
thus SOUL must be one of these "any" things.
It's as though I could just reach out my hand and grab it;
but even beyond my grasp, it isn't beyond me.
Existence of SOUL is inferred because it can be spoken;
no other but private and individual can sculpt its face.
Any extant word must have CONCEPT attached,
at least if it's to make any RATIONAL sense.
SOUL exists as CONCEPTION within BRAIN, née MIND,
as a substitute for what must really exist in its place.
It's a term most closely and rationally approximating
the part of REALITY which exists as SOUL.
Corollary evidence for SOUL'S habitation in LIFE
is the personality children exhibit shortly after BIRTH.
Which has nothing to do with the existence of SOUL;
personality measures how PURPOSE is modified.
Happy or sad or moody or fully choleric,
each is subtly different from even its own direct siblings.
QUALITIES which have no known RATIONAL explanation,
they modify PURPOSE on the other side.
How do we account for the vast divergence on display
by using only chemicals and computers as explanation?

22:01

Bob, the guy in the cell next to mine,
is being taken out to be executed at midnight tonight.
Why do an execution at the last possible moment;
is the intent to make the guy suffer as much as possible?
The state has taken the task of retribution upon itself,
ensuring criminals have to suffer like their victims.
Reward has been seen by certain seekers and prophets
as giving to each his due, even if it is totally irrational.
Which is why it's the province of RELIGION, not SCIENCE;
there is no real evidence for a mystical balance.

IDEA of reward works well with SOUL'S PURPOSE;
there must be some scale to balance the worthy.
PURPOSE could instead exist as blind as INANIMATE ENERGY;
there doesn't need to be PURPOSE for PURPOSE.
In order for more PURPOSE to stimulate more MATTER,
a mechanism must exist for more soulful windows.
Which also doesn't require reactions from SOUL;
survival of the fittest covers the matter quite well.
They must either grow bigger or increase in number,
and each CELL appears to have some inherent size limit.
If PURPOSE is submitted to BIOMATTER by INFINITE SOUL,
then this is how it's supplied to INANIMATE UNIVERSE.
CELLS do not seem to be able to keep on growing;
instead, from enough nourishment comes multiplication.
Which only means CELLS have an inherited limit,
not that PURPOSE is somehow recycled.
SOUL increases PURPOSE within INANIMATE UNIVERSE
by multiplication of windows enlivening inert MATTER.
The spread of BIOMATTER doesn't seem to be in doubt;
human animals are infesting the earth.
The branch of SOUL'S tree spreading most PURPOSE
will obtain more and more as a reward reflection.
No rationale exists for why PURPOSE is so limited,
SOUL itself would seem to have mindful intent.
Destruction of great PURPOSE is worse than that of small;
however, its loss can be alleviated by its CREATION.
I can see BIOMATTER obtains PURPOSE from a hidden source,
but I don't fathom how this source has its own PURPOSE.
The total effect of LIFE'S contributions is what matters;
SOUL punishes ORGANISMS whose lives have less PURPOSE.
In order for this to happen some feedback must exist,
a mechanism by which SOUL "feels their PAIN."
Should we consume more plant products and less meat,
if animals are endowed with more PURPOSE than plants?
If just a type of ENERGY, SOUL only supplies PURPOSE,
so as long as gain beats loss, nothing else matters.
And people are endowed with PURPOSE on top of itself,
so killing with intent is an unpardonable act.

Killing of any kind may bring eternal damnation;
Soul seeks greater Purpose, it doesn't care what kind.
If Life is filled with bad intent, not just actions,
then its Purpose is bad and will be so fulfilled.
But bad intent can result in a net gain of Purpose:
a rapist could father many children.
It is not the evil called incarnate by some people;
if it is known bad, then that is enough for retribution.
Assuming bad Purpose is worse than good,
when either 1 should suffice for greater gain.
How it is used results in everlasting destiny;
the healthiest tree branch receives the most nutrients.
As with bosses giving their best worker the most work,
1 action tends to evoke more of the same.
All soulful windows have the same source,
so Soul is able to flow along the most purposeful branch.
Continue to follow that train of Thought to its finish,
and a serial rapist can have more Purpose than a monk.
Should these reflections actually be countenanced
if they result in that kind of asinine consequence?
Either Soul rewards the results of all actions,
or it rewards the results of all intentions.
A rapist has little or no Purpose in his dim Mind,
he reacts from hate and anger and fear.
Actions exist solely within Inanimate Universe;
therefore they should have no direct effect upon Soul.
Negative emotional disturbances flash and glow,
with no sustained Purpose pursued without end.
Intentions find their home behind the emotional veil;
desiring evil may be more dangerous than its fulfillment.
Those with evil intent have power in the pit,
making others submit to their momentary whims.
Causing an accident whereby evil results
wouldn't be rewarded the same as if evil is truly desired.
A monk or a Solon-like statesman seeks Purpose
without Purpose from which no ego may emerge.
If Purpose is used for petty ego satisfaction,
it has been wasted like food at a rich man's banquet.

Purpose-less Purpose used without gain in empty Mind
closely approximates unity with the causeless cause.
Purpose is like Energy, which makes things happen;
Soul's Purpose is different from any driven by desire.
A better question is to pause and wonder:
does the possibility of evil purposeful intent exist?
In order to do this, there must be some creature
who can pursue that which is evil with single-minded aim.
Which is quite possible and will be rewarded in turn
with that level of evil expended upon innocent others.
But there is no evidence which shows those malefactors
how their intentions only end up hurting themselves.
Soul has Will and the power to reward Purpose,
although the trophy may not be what the seeker is after.
If only some proof could be found for divine retribution;
faith only works for true believers.
Soul does not know good Purpose from bad,
so can one be sustained more than the other?
If a man pursues a path, then he has colored Purpose,
just as Energy can take on many different forms.
Soul does not interfere with Life's use of Purpose;
good and evil are beneath its endless disdain.
It isn't intelligent according to Rational standards;
it's like the sun, whose Energy is undeserved.
A problem coloring the vision of gods of Religion comes by
confusing reward for Purpose with balance of Intuition.

22:47

Bob, the guy that used to be in the Cell next to mine,
didn't want to die, so the fate handed to him is punishment.
Are reward and punishment available under Caesar's rule,
or are they truly dispensed upon meeting his ghost's ruler?
Since I'm denying the punishment assigned to me,
the only thing left for me to accomplish is my final reward.
Mystics perceived more than just reward for Purpose,
balance also exists for all intentions to action.

Observing physical laws shows FORCES seeking balance,
but this is for MATTER, not the mystical part of BIOMATTER.
A wise man once taught:
KARMA actually refers to mental intentions.
Belief in fate by real Indians is referred to as KARMA,
the totality of actions attached to recurring BIOMATTER.
Disposition of action is only important to inert MATTER;
ANIMATE UNIVERSE is far more concerned with intentions.
Then KARMA exists different from popular belief;
a Buddha should know more than silly inept priests.
Actions have no existence within ANIMATE UNIVERSE,
emoted feelings are much more important.
A violation of all my RATIONAL THOUGHTS on REALITY;
for anything to happen it must involve action.
KARMA is a RATIONAL equivocation of DUALITY'S capacity
to canvass justice within ANIMATE UNIVERSE.
It isn't equivocation as much as disbelief;
KARMA is cute CONCEPT without proof's solid backing.
Why should KARMA exist; how does it fit in
with the existence of SOUL and LIFE?
It may not exist except for religious fancies;
supported by people without the sense to be agnostic.
PURPOSE is a form of ENERGY found in ANIMATE UNIVERSE,
similar to that shown to exist within INANIMATE UNIVERSE.
CONCEPT which works about as well as any other;
if PURPOSE isn't ENERGY, then neither is ENERGY.
All of REALITY'S ENERGY is constant, it just changes forms;
this is no less true for one universe than the other.
The 1ˢᵗ law of thermodynamics works with either;
just as STAR relates to SOUL, and MATTER to LIFE.
PURPOSE received by CELLS is transformed by intention;
thus it is tainted by ego into good and bad.
As ENERGY is frequently converted into HEAT,
whereupon it changes form until it can no longer be used.
After reception from SOUL, PURPOSE does not disappear,
it asymmetrically continues until it can be balanced.
If PURPOSE makes itself known only through BIOMATTER,
then its existence should only work in this venue.

Karma is a natural law within Animate Universe;
quite similar to material laws of newtonian motion.
But Newton's laws were disseminated from painstaking
experimentation and measurement—solely Rational.
Part of what sensation and Conception can tell us
is how to compare what we do not know to what we do.
Much as electrons were pictured to revolve like planets,
I can discern Animate Universe from Inanimate Concepts.
Animate Universe has two primary means of exchange:
Communication between Lives and balance by Karma.
I know of Energy transferred by Force and Distance;
a universe founded on Purpose creates another paradigm.
Each is produced in conjunction with the other;
water does not flow without the means to do so.
Karma is a product, not Force by itself;
if Purpose doesn't exist, then it doesn't either.
It is not a system of reward for good deeds;
it is a balance for those intentions already undertaken.
A process not unlike production of the causeless cause;
the 1st intention exists along side the 1st cause.
Intentions will be repaid by Karma in the manner
to which each agent has so strenuously striven.
Wise men claim I'm lucky to have been born human;
lower animals are ignorant of their karmic dependence.
Balance is only concerned with one simple question:
why would one emit intentions he did not want returned?
If I push on a wall with all Force I can muster,
then I should expect it will be sent right back.
Thus we will receive intentions for which we have asked,
based on all egoistic desires previously submitted.
If evil is the effect of Purpose given to any agent,
then evil shall be its due folded back to its 1st cause.
If we push Yin, we shall receive Yang;
in the here or hereafter, there is always plenty of Time.
But Yin is the opposite of Yang,
which means evil should be rewarded with good.
The curious nature of Karma is such that retribution
will not occur as long as intentions remain the same.

Still, good and evil are in continuous opposition;
balance indicates 1 will tend to react to the other.
Before intentions turn to good, PURPOSE is filtered by evil;
therefore the evil we have trespassed cannot return.
Therefore good intentions will be repaid with evil,
and strangely enough, vice versa also works.
The punishments of Job now make much more sense;
a good and kind man receiving past due punishment.
Once previous misdeeds have been alleviated,
a surfeit of good PURPOSE may be sown for the future.
Also in the nature of evolutionary survival and lusts
is the debt we have to pay for past evils and goods.
No one is born either good or bad,
but all LIVES do bad things before they are taught good.
Those with evil intent mistakenly presume the results
of their PURPOSES will be lost in the sands of TIME.
Actually, people like me are trapped by ignorance;
I just don't know how to make my PURPOSE better.
PURPOSE felt to produce motivation and desires
is only the inner light among many other bright lights.
This is the problem with zealots of any stripe:
mistaking the message for the hypnotic verse.
All LIVES are sewn into a pattern with purposeful thread,
and each one is only a swatch in an INFINITY quilt.
But I am independent and I have free WILL;
my attachment to other beings is only what I make it.
That which is pursued is that which will be received;
KARMA has no other ability than to reflect intention.
Then free WILL isn't lost if it's still the instigator
of all of the fate thrown back upon every agent.
PURPOSE is ENERGY shifted all over ANIMATE UNIVERSE,
the modicum of exchange for internal COMMUNICATION.
Movement of any kind requires ENERGY transfer,
even if there is no physical action, only mystical talk.
PURPOSE is LIFE FORCE
from which all living creatures sustain themselves.
It must then have 2-fold abilities
because it must also be the source for BIOENERGY.

Each LIFE is a filter through which good and evil
taint PURPOSE with their egoistic signatures.
BIOMATTER is in pieces expending BIOENERGY to survive,
so PURPOSE is lost in 1 place while reflected in its home.
When exchanged by LIFE into BIOENERGY,
actions result which appear to be good or evil.
Those ultimate measures of any transparent action
are external RATIONAL constructs based on internal effects.
Yet the actual balance between previous and current intentions
occurs as retribution within ANIMATE UNIVERSE.
So PURPOSE lost as BIOENERGY isn't part of KARMA;
actions speak louder than words except under its influence.
Reflected in one universe and used for work in the other,
PURPOSE fits into the natural order of REALITY.
That is different than nominally INANIMATE ENERGIES,
which change from usable to unusable forms.
KARMA can only happen to living beings,
resulting from intentions, evidenced by actions.
Like any other part of insensible ANIMATE UNIVERSE,
KARMA is primarily determined by its material evidence.
KARMA is a reflection of how PURPOSE has been colored,
limiting it to good and evil does not cover its scope.
But that is how KARMA is classically understood,
in order to induce people to behave themselves.
PURPOSE can be colored with happy and sad,
love and hate, even anger and COMPASSION.
Any dualistic set of CONCEPTS can upset the balance,
so KARMA will have to act to set it aright.
When LIFE transmits its tainted PURPOSE outside of itself,
it is perceived as an essence in two different realms.
INANIMATE UNIVERSE detects BIOENERGY forming FORCES,
and it results in intended and unintended consequences.
The ripples from the rocks perturbing FORCES' surfaces
rebound for good or evil without karmic consequences.
ANIMATE UNIVERSE is the home of PURPOSE;
in there the taint of desire is communicated and returns.
Never to disappear until some other LIFE uses
the disposition created for its own unhealthy PURPOSES.

Good and evil PURPOSES don't disappear,
they are available for use by whoever desires them.
SOUL only provides a pure type of PURPOSE to LIFE;
there are many afflicted types available for the asking.
Only pure PURPOSE untainted by ego can be transmitted
in ANIMATE UNIVERSE without a reflected payback.
Any ego-tainted PURPOSE must be returned to its creator,
for what is thus made can belong to no other.
Money spent from my stolen debit card
still ends up in my loss column.
INANIMATE ENERGY creates what gods decree as FORCES;
an ego full of desire defiles PURPOSE to create KARMA.
Therefore KARMA is part and parcel of ANIMATE UNIVERSE;
at home with hidden messages between LIVES.
Sullied PURPOSE makes up the essence of KARMA,
and it motivates all LIVES in addition to SOUL'S drive.
Compare PURPOSE to ENERGY available to all users:
MATTER requires formulation, BIOMATTER requires intention.
LIFE uses PURPOSE no matter the source,
either from pure SOUL or egoistic intentions.
Each being can't have access to its own perturbations;
my own essence doesn't return what it has done.
Tainted PURPOSE is not transferred directly to its sender;
COMMUNICATION within ANIMATE UNIVERSE is one to one.
So only through another being can KARMA wreck havoc,
dispensing justice to those who can't move on without it.
Naïve people assume no good deed goes unpunished,
another instance when KARMA returns prior intent.
KARMA sounds amazingly like RATIONAL cause and effect;
1st I do something good/bad, and then it happens to me.
Is KARMA just another example of cause and effect;
what shows it to exist patterned in a universe of INTUITION?
CONCEPTS can only be transmitted rationally,
and this makes the message subject to cause and effect.
ANIMATE UNIVERSE, and KARMA, are solely irrational;
thus they are not subject to cause and effect.
KARMA is only formal CONCEPT for a natural relation
balancing between output and input of intention.

It may become apparent as LIFE *spurs further reflection—*
RATIONAL cause and effect is another form of balance.

24:10

Bob, the guy who used to be alive,
has nothing left in this world except his self-valued skin.
MATTER prized over LIFE, LIFE prized over SOUL;
does anybody understand this is bass-ackwards?
I can't fault anybody for succumbing to their senses;
my ghost doesn't appear more real than my body.
The assertion of the existence of SOUL is not CREATION
of some mystical cause for the appearance of LIFE.
But in some sense it still must be supernatural
because natural is commonly available to sense PERCEPTION.
SOUL is in no way any more bizarre than STAR;
why are sensations granted more credence than feelings?
Feelings aren't useful, they are a major distraction;
existence would be so much more vulcan without them.
There are just a few ways events happen via awareness:
STAR and MATTER externally, SOUL and LIFE internally.
The former is how I conceptualize OBJECTS;
the latter isn't, because they're perceived through feelings.
The former binding creates FORCE and DISTANCE;
the latter binding creates KARMA and COMMUNICATION.
Appearing to create a "structure" of sorts,
mostly tangible within the universe to which they belong.
STAR most profoundly influences all within its system;
any SOUL has the same apparent affect.
INANIMATE UNIVERSE has no substance matching STAR,
to help create GRAVITATIONAL and ELECTROMAGNETIC FORCES.
Also obvious from a RATIONAL perspective
is the existence of MATTER within INANIMATE UNIVERSE.
MATTER gives me the clearest understanding of REALITY;
all other knowledge must jive with my sense of it.
Those two <facts>, in some direct or indirect fashion,
account for all that happens from a RATIONAL perspective.

All my knowledge of Inanimate Universe
somehow involves Star or Matter or both or neither.
Regarding Soul and Life, imagine how they could exist
in a parallel arrangement of Animate with Inanimate.
An arrangement substituting feeling for sensation,
which may explain much while still being hard to believe.
There is a secret world locked within Cell;
an internal world cannot be directly perceived.
Normally I would dismiss that as mystical babble,
but there is too much sensible evidence to the contrary.
These two assumptions create the alternate paradigm:
there is a secret world, and there are parallel universes.
Neither of which will meet the minimum requirements
of Science now grown much too big for its britches.
If those two premises can pass Rational muster,
then Soul and Life should easily meet its inspection.
They are able to meet 2 vital Rational considerations:
consistency in application, and explanation of mysteries.
Soul is used like Star's external influence in daily Matters;
most people conceive it as the major internal provider.
It's literally impossible to conceive an alternate universe,
unless I'm able to use Inanimate Universe comparisons.
It is only a word, substitute as Conception requires;
a label does not change the meaning imparted.
But words do have effects on how Concepts are accepted;
Soul would not go over too well if it was called shit.
Soul also provides Purpose into Inanimate Universe,
at least to the limits of Rational awareness.
Purpose as Energy is also hard to accept as anything
other than its definition as Quality of intention.
Purpose is used for lack of a better word
to account for the push to create a greater sentience.
There is no better word I can think of which suffices
to put Evolution back into the fold with Religion.
No Force pushes Evolution as biologically espoused
by gods bent on devolving Life into chance mutations.
It all comes down to the 2 prime modes of Thought:
whether a Rational or an Intuitive view rules my Mind.

A view solely RATIONAL should not induce undue stress;
laws have not yet decreed what we can and cannot think.
If someone desires to sit in a posture purely INTUITIVE,
then he is surely entitled to waste his precious TIME.
The RATIONAL training instituted in schools
is more than sufficient to cause one-sided views.
While the inquisitions RELIGION has repeatedly introduced
still haven't managed to show an INTUITIVE view clearly.
No matter if barbs or curses are hurled to one-side,
LIFE is still pushed from somewhere to do something.
REALITY will remain even if it isn't understood,
which is the perpetual fate of limited man.
An internal view of LIFE is insensible to RATIONAL means,
for looking within is a personal affair.
INTUITIVE BIOMATTER can be approximated by 2 methods:
observing what it does, not what it is, or introspection.
Our reflections could take any seeker of TRUTH
in other directions, which satisfy them as these satisfy us.
Only really important TRUTH forms full THOUGHTS,
half-views no longer divided by my split-BRAIN.
Glossy MIND'S divisions show another TRUTH in REALITY:
DUALITY is not in opposition, envision ends of a ruler.
But my THOUGHTS have been of +/- poles,
like how opposition is required to produce voltage.
DUALITY is not REALITY, search further;
CONCEPTION sees the former, the latter only exists.
But MATTER can't be at 1 end of an INANIMATE ruler,
there are many different types of MATTER.
MATTER is not REALITY, search further;
is MATTER formed from within or without?
My understanding of MATTER is formed within,
while its actual existence is formed without.
DUALITY is not REALITY, search further;
it is only the basis of CONCEPTION, formed by BRAIN.
So DUALISM is a capacity, stretched to its ends,
and each CONCEPT is born somewhere in between.
How can anything be different, and still be the same;
if all is AETHER, with nothing in between?

Thoughts I have crystallize between left and right,
up and down; the way I have to think of a material world.
Locking REALITY *into little parts and pieces*
is only one way of viewing, ignoring the rest.
STAR and MATTER are the same, appearing different!
SOUL and LIFE are the same, appearing different!
Look into the bardo and see all as one:
STAR *and* MATTER, SOUL *and* LIFE.

****

24:53

STAR and MATTER, SOUL and LIFE;
mobile or motionless, they appear the same.
Dead to the world
interspersed with tossing and turning.
A large zit inhabits the corner of a large TV guide,
which must be popped, anybody would do the same.
Splash over a tottering little boy trying to be a man
(a wading pool crumples when you sit on its edge).
He grows up into a serial killer,
snatching bodies from anybody or anything.
Running around frantic to find something missing,
and he still can't get away.
Passing through traces and woods and houses and rivers,
nothing matters to his relentless pace.
Duct tape a whole body onto a patterned wall,
it fits in perfectly with the wall-papered lace.
Now the chase changes, with him as the quarry;
even shoot him and he forever comes back.
Many people try and try to help;
some frequent his presence while he leaves them alone.
He is nobody familiar, unknown;
a face turned from light by darkness.
Is it wrong to banish the one I love,
if this is the only thing I am really good at?

Each pattern of events connects to many others;
only nothing exists in isolation.
Later he visits neighbors in a house watching TV,
a large tree spears the front wall and the house behind.
Parents with a child are passing TIME in that location,
yet no harm comes to any flesh, of mud made body.
Another tree comes through and does the same thing,
and this TIME it destroys their undamaged house.
This TIME the child is slightly injured,
her parents much more so.
Hoping to carry the child away to safety,
if I know its name, but it actually escapes me.
The parents have departed the rubble when I return;
now they have nothing but superficial wounds.
After eating way too much chicken last night,
the couple who eat their own accept more company.
How are events connected if they make no sense,
or is everything bound together by the same rationale?
A guinea pig appears—a foreign pet in this house;
why would anyone forget to feed his dependent?
Not only does it survive and remain healthy,
it is replaced by not one but two of its kind.
Sustenance has forced its way past material needs;
accept it for what it does, not what it is.
Who in the hell would want to mull wine?
It's hard enough to drink the cooler fermented stuff.

Day V _____

06:00

Come unto a wandering seeker making little noise,
and less pleasure, in the pursuit of binding knowledge.
The bed beneath recedes from contact with my body;
I sense I'm floating and nothing remains to hold me back.
Moving with no boundaries toward an unknown state;
limitless MIND briefly freed from its mortal shackles.
All of my THOUGHTS in the end may prove quite useless
if they don't free me from the bondage of ignorance.
Some large pieces of REALITY'S puzzle have been shown;
although the largest by far remains to be perceived.
Nothing is larger than the divisions of AETHER expounded;
REALITY is divided into INANIMATE and ANIMATE UNIVERSES.
Mere CONCEPTIONS of something greater, something
which is beyond simple focused definition.
Then it's also beyond my RATIONAL ability to find;
left alone for INTUITIVE IDEA to bring it to my attention.
If CONCEPTIONS must be limited to be rationally understood,
how do we know what is beyond them, what is INFINITY?
INFINITE is by and large and small,
sliced up into little pieces or delving into outer reaches.
How can one INFINITY reach beneath lilliputian,
and at the same instant extend out past gargantuan?
There could be 2 INFINITES, or even more;
CONCEPT of it has defied substantial definition.

Where do SPACE and TIME end;
is there some point where even VOID does not exist?
INFINITE of the large is far off into TIME and SPACE;
lofty regions where an omega number and STAR don't exist.
Yet why would SPACE and TIME voluntarily end;
could they not just travel on and on and on?
SCIENCE proposes TIME and SPACE had a beginning;
if the big bang existed, then there is likely an ending.
Gods who infer that REALITY is in fact FINITY,
when INTUITION screams above "It is much bigger."
MATTER can be dated to show its relative past,
and HEAT DEATH isn't an imaginary universal proposition.
No matter what number or DISTANCE is imagined largest,
it is still marginally one less than that contained by INFINITY.
No rationale exists for the existence of that QUANTITY;
it makes no sense for there to be a measureless measure.
INFINITY cannot be confined to a number;
its greatest influence is where QUANTITY does not exist.
But INFINITE can be accurately related by a symbol,
1 which represents any far-reaching number desired.
A symbol referring to vanishing by greater amounts;
what about disappearing as measurements get smaller?
INFINITE of the small divides MATTER and TIME into parts
and pieces, which are composed of parts and pieces.
Is there no limit to the smallest bit of MATTER,
or is the limit based on what iota can still be sensed?
If any OBJECT is divided into its intrinsic parts,
then these parts must have parts, which in turn have parts.
No smallest piece of MATTER will ever be found,
and no smallest piece of TIME will ever be measured.
TIME'S progress is ticking away in seconds,
but these can be divided and divided and divided . . . .
A smallest part can always be further dissected
into that which is as big as original OBJECT.
I don't believe I can break a rock into pieces,
and thereby create sub-rocks as big as the original.
Size is measured based solely upon the scale used;
changing the scale necessitates changing PERCEPTION.

But the sub-rocks are smaller than the original whole;
they must be in order to be created by its destruction.
The sub-rocks are only relatively smaller than the rock;
discard the rock and there is no longer any relation.
This line of reasoning makes no sense to me;
it also sheds no light upon INFINITE of the small.
Smaller OBJECTS are based on an original scaled model,
from which there is presumed always to be one smaller.
Rocks are more likely to subdivide consistently,
than only to divide to a limit and then stop.
Yet each smaller OBJECT is complete unto itself;
otherwise it would not be able to exist as OBJECT.
But the totality of sub-OBJECTS must compose OBJECT;
it has to be structurally built up in some fashion.
The point: the smallest or largest cannot be measured,
either is assumed by the limits of sensation.
So INFINITE of the large has no end by getting bigger,
while INFINITE of the small has no end by getting smaller.
Gods of SCIENCE are limited to the smallest smaller,
or reaching out they are limited to the largest larger.
It's totally impractical not to assume REALITY ends;
the possibilities are endless if it just goes on and on.
Do not consider it as "out there" or "in here";
only one INFINITY rationally exists both high and low.
If it reaches both those remote places,
somewhere in between it must chance upon my search.
INFINITY could run its track right past sensory grasp,
or it could loop together the ends of SPACE and TIME.
If it passes me by at faster than light speed,
then I shall not know what it is in order to master it.
One problem with INFINITY comes from searching in two
places for one CONCEPTION actually found in neither one.
Therefore looking for INFINITE of the small or large
actually points me away from their essential REALITY.
INFINITY seems larger or smaller on human scales;
how does humanity look from INFINITY dimensions?
Once again PERCEPTION rears it ugly head in interference,
blocking my view of REALITY with the view from my senses.

Reaching as small as emancipated THOUGHTS may go
will come out into the farthest reaches of SPACE.
If INFINITE of the small becomes INFINITE of the large,
they are only different to a dualistic manner of thinking.
Sending firebird THOUGHTS out where they never return
requires that they appear as a sun within a thumbnail.
A view indicating REALITY is connected beyond sight;
FINITE PERCEPTIONS are looped between large and small.
Existing CONCEPTIONS will always interfere
with the ability to see beyond what is plainly apparent.
Maybe future reflections will expose INFINITE,
but I don't have the ability to climb that far up or down.
No part of REALITY is actually hidden from TRUTH seekers;
there are only parts hidden by one-sided PERCEPTION.

****

08:17

A wise man once said: Eyes full of light are blessed,
for a man does not behold his LIFE in darkness.
But I am full of darkness, which is why I seek TRUTH;
my eyes seek the light which it may bring.
No path may we take which is not lit by some faith,
luminous in the dirt or a glow from above.
My external eye sees that which is in front of me,
blocking my progress and tempting me into stagnation.
Faith in sensation is RATIONAL and quite necessary;
although most of us do not realize it is so inspired.
A farther or alternate vision isn't available to my eyes;
I'm RATIONAL by nature, and this view is what I see.
A wandering internal eye has the opportunity to see all;
a gauzy curtain through which glimpses pass, no more.
No other visions come but through mine eyes;
the locus of color and clarity, not-me becomes part of me.
Eyes look out upon the world until they are shut;
what then is the nature of all things seen?

An eye is but 1 of many sensational devices
designed to bring closer those things amenable to touch.
Is an eye divided into independent functioning parts,
or allowed complete rule over making light into sight?
No part of an eye is able to accomplish vision fully;
light is merely light until transformed by PERCEPTION.
An eye full of light has no SPACE for any absence;
all is complete and no pieces are missing.
But closing my eyes inhibits my access to light,
which means they can never be full unless open.
A belly full of food has no place for any absence;
all is complete and no pieces are missing.
Ah . . . the word "light" is throwing me off;
what I seek is something else entirely.
Just acknowledging an inner light is not satisfactory;
fulfillment leaves no room for anything else.
My senses are dull and no longer sift need from want;
it's hard to determine when I'm done filling myself.
Full denotes a lack of need to consume further;
nothing is left to complete what has been missing.
But if I still want more after needs have been filled,
then there must be some emptiness left inside.
Full also does not allow for fewer than all;
there is no fear that enough has been accomplished.
Fear isn't missing, I have plenty of that;
instead there is a lack of something more substantial.
It is neither too much nor too little;
"just right" is what the wanton girl said.
But she didn't know which was the best part of full,
until she had tried both ends, more and less.
Full is not bursting apart at the seams,
rather holding comfortably without pressure or slack.
My eye must be full of an inner light,
radiantly shining within no matter what shines without.
A presence which shines upon all who care to partake
of its multicolored effects and many-splendored insights.
A light which doesn't reflect exterior phenomena;
an irrational design builds upon growth from within.

It allows for that which is and can be, out of that
which is naught and can never be more than naught.
As a sharp knife slices into my thumb,
so light sunders REALITY into more of what it already is.
Find it! Look in places where THOUGHTS are forbidden,
where TRUTH is exposed through an everlasting self.
I find my focus swaying with whatever breeze blows,
mental winds attached to sensory PERCEPTION.
Until a light opens one and only one door,
one wherein a light shines to darken all others.
Therein will lie the secret TRUTH to my existence;
those answers which haunt all unknowing SOULS.
It pours into all the dark places,
trying to fill infernal VOIDS with some substance.
All I know is at least in part due to light,
allotting me vision of what REALITY there is to see.
A doomed cause brings knowledge to ignorance,
when there is always understanding to belie its place.
I see knowledge as the best indicator of that light,
no matter whether its arrival is internal or external.
The lamp and light of knowledge, what a joke
to laugh at that which is not really funny!
Don't ask me to accept knowledge beyond my ken;
light is only available to those who are able to see.
An eye full of light has no need for any other bounty;
shining on the scrawny puppets behind deceitful cloaks.
All of the gross material wealth I'm able to accumulate
has no bearing upon the light brought from within.
For SOUL has no limit with which to inhibit LIFE;
fullness is limited without, possibly vacant within.
The light from STAR my eye can accept is FINITE;
the light from SOUL my eye can accept might be INFINITE.
Fullness of light is dependent upon a shadowy perspective;
can anyone truly handle a light which goes on and on?

08:54

Apparently I fell, blacked out from the effects of fasting;
my body doesn't seem to like my MIND's far-reaching plan.
Where does intangible MIND go when it is not here;
is there some cold place to retreat when its body runs hot?
A fever has come upon me and I'm sticking to the sheets;
right about now, floating above them seems pretty inviting.
Is far MIND as limited as the body to which it is attached;
are THOUGHTS restricted to living within one small BRAIN?
My MIND must be limited because my THOUGHTS are;
those formed by each person are personal and private.
If THOUGHTS are so limited, they should be predetermined;
CONCEPTIONS coming from knowledge, summing to the next.
It's obvious to me that THOUGHTS aren't subject to fate;
mine come and go through no WILL of my own.
Could THOUGHTS be limited, while their source is not;
is it possible untouched MIND is truly INFINITY in nature?
But my MIND seems to be FINITE and located in my BRAIN;
if it's truly INFINITE, then this isn't its location.
How shall the difficulty of finding its home be known;
where does INFINITY live that it may rest easy?
An easy and philosophically fun way to look
for INFINITE of the small is through the use of paradox.
One INFINITY will hopefully lead us to the rest;
it does not exist where FINITY makes its abode.
The 1st 1's of which I'm aware, and best to my concern,
come from Parmenides' disciple Zeno of Elea.
He of a most obtuse visage trudging back in TIME,
illuminating and confusing MINDS at the same instant.
They may be sufficient to show problems with INFINITE,
by trying to find the end of my sensory grasp.
Paradox is quicksand enveloping MIND without release,
holding INFINITY in the light best understood.
My MEMORY doesn't serve me right to exhibit them exactly,
so what comes out could be less clear and less tangible.
It is easy to get lost when making the irrational RATIONAL;
that which is clearly seen goes down a path to nowhere.

Zeno introduces an argument reducing to the absurd;
therefore clearly showing that the obvious is fallible.
Yet he also showed what mystics have obscured:
REALITY consists of the one and not of the many.
A reduction to the absurd comes from a stated premise,
rationally examining it, and showing absurd results.
What is believed gains consideration and earns faith,
if valid THOUGHT has no value whatsoever.
A premise is stated which appears to have merit;
further premises clarify it with no bold contradiction.
Much as FINITY and INFINITY appear to coexist,
until paradox shows this to be an impossibility.
Applying common sense to the basic premise
shows that its inevitable result contradicts its origin.
Where can contradiction coexist as one essence,
if DUALITY mandates one and two must be separate?
The initial premise of any paradox must be a statement
which is totally immune to direct examination.
IDEA helping to infiltrate INFINITY'S domain,
by altering CONCEPTION of how it is able to exist.
Each step of a paradox is carefully weighed,
and it comes together with seemingly obvious THOUGHTS.
Meticulously pawing over fundamental accusations,
blended MIND'S hold on THOUGHT slips from firm to shaky.
A paradox is the result of logically derived observations;
a thing both <is> and <is not>, both are equally extant.
Can paradox show how INFINITY is able to exist at all;
if it could be proven, is it likely FINITY in disguise?
Everything of which I can commonly conceive is FINITE,
which makes me doubt INFINITE will fit in my head.
Yet is there some aspect of INFINITY THOUGHT can match,
so it can become CONCEPTION?
CONCEPTS are defined as what they <are> and <are not>;
INFINITE only seems to exist as what it <is not>.
Many paradoxes seem to require INFINITY'S presence;
why must it exist and still be so hard to comprehend?

09:24

I've recently come out of swimming in fevered DREAM,
where OBJECTS kept dividing and dividing and dividing . . .
What does it take to form OBJECT of FINITY size;
how many of anything will fill up this expanse?
Either the structure of OBJECT is FINITE or INFINITE in nature,
and evidence from my senses leans towards the former.
Thus if any OBJECT is composed from FINITY partitions,
it should not be too difficult to discern the smallest one.
Every OBJECT which comes to the attention of my senses
can be divided into smaller pieces, until there are none.
Which leads to the first of Zeno's paradoxes;
an argument against plurality called <u>The Smallest Piece</u>.
Let me lay out each THOUGHT, item by item,
and maybe I won't confuse 1 meaning with another.
In the beginning,
*there is always the **first** step.*
It takes FINITE numbers of OBJECTS
of FINITE size to form single FINITE OBJECT.
How are we to know of what OBJECT consists,
unless each part and piece is determinable and FINITY?
Part of the essence of what it takes to be RATIONAL
is knowing each OBJECT is made of measurable elements.
After alpha begins,
*there usually comes the **second** step.*
There is no known FINITE OBJECT A with unlimited size;
this OBJECT is like any other, limited and sensible.
In other words, anything FINITY cannot also be INFINITY;
there is a clear distinction between one and the other.
If its size was unlimited, then its size would be INFINITE;
and it wouldn't be 1 OBJECT, but all OBJECTS.
Keep pursuing the quarry;
*watch or miss falling upon the **third** step.*
OBJECT A can't have no-size;
for if it has no-size, then it can't be sensed.
Prove some OBJECT exists within REALITY,
without leaving some trace of its passing.

And therefore it wouldn't be known to exist;
for any OBJECT to exist it must by definition be sensible.
Next fixed stop
*is the middle **fourth** step.*
Extant OBJECT A is of FINITE size,
and is formed from OBJECTS B, each having FINITE size.
Release the claim for phantom OBJECTS like photons;
OBJECTS of no size will form OBJECT of no size.
Also, if OBJECTS B are each of INFINITE size,
then they couldn't compose OBJECT A of FINITE size.
Turning the corner,
*look closely and manage to espy the **fifth** step.*
Each extant OBJECT B must be formed from OBJECTS C,
each having FINITE size.
That is the process the gods of SCIENCE have followed
in order to determine that subatomic particles exist.
And then OBJECTS C must be formed from OBJECTS D
that have FINITE size, etc.
Next to last
*is the following **sixth** step.*
This partitioning of OBJECTS into smaller OBJECTS
has no determinable end, it can go on forever.
Forever can refer to INFINITY of the large;
although in this case it refers to INFINITY of the small.
If there is no end to OBJECTS composing OBJECT A,
then it's formed by INFINITE numbers of FINITE OBJECTS.
The last headache
*is brought forth by the **seventh** step.*
According to (3–6), INFINITE numbers of OBJECTS
of FINITE size are used to form OBJECT A of FINITE size.
Step back in MEMORY to (one), and FINITY numbers
of FINITY OBJECTS are required to form one FINITY OBJECT.
Therefore both INFINITE and FINITE numbers
of FINITE OBJECTS form FINITE OBJECT.
Yet INFINITY numbers cannot also be FINITY numbers;
according to (two), the argument results in a paradox.
If that ordinary train of logic is followed step by step,
then it should be plain to see a conclusive absurdity.

Analysis of the conclusion offers minimal progress;
whichever RATIONAL direction is pursued, thus blocked.
There are 2 propositions the argument could accept,
and each 1 leaves more questions than it answers.
Chasing INFINITY'S tail with FINITY CONCEPTIONS
is like trying to define LIFE as chemical permutations.
FINITE numbers of FINITE OBJECTS form FINITE OBJECT,
or INFINITE numbers of FINITE OBJECTS form FINITE OBJECT.
Absurdity implies they both cannot be true,
yet it also does not imply too much about neither one.
The former proposition seems a posteriori provable,
while the latter seems to possess a priori logical validity.
Since both cannot actually exist in REALITY,
one or the other or both must be definably false.
SCIENCE and logic both identify RATIONAL works,
but they have little influence on resolving a paradox.
A most interesting resolution to an INFINITY predicament;
for LIFE of us, it is hard to imagine—how can this be?
The alternative options make my BRAIN hurt even worse.
For OBJECT to exist it must be composed of other OBJECTS.
Look between each set of discursive THOUGHTS;
each one exists as part of an essence not so limited.

10:04

As 1 DREAM faded another took its place;
I ran towards freedom, but it kept just out of reach.
What is motion and how is DISTANCE crossed;
do we actually travel anywhere or is it all illusion?
That makes no sense! I can walk across this little room;
DISTANCE traveled may not be far, but it's still accomplished.
Then DISTANCE should also be FINITY in its extremes;
the smallest bit of it should reveal itself with little effort.
DISTANCE is defined as the interval between 2 points;
specify a point, and there is DISTANCE to another 1.
There is a second paradox even better than the first,
arguing against motion in a paradox called <u>*The Stadium*</u>.

Once again each THOUGHT must be carefully prepared,
so accumulation of them won't spin out of control.
The beginning shall only
*start with the **first** step.*
Any motion requires FINITE DISTANCE to be crossed,
which is formed from FINITE numbers of FINITE DISTANCES.
Traversing INFINITY DISTANCE would require INFINITY TIME
and INFINITY SPACE and INFINITY ENERGY to make it happen.
I'm concerned with something more simple,
the everyday motion everyone takes for granted.
Next
*comes the **second** step.*
FINITE DISTANCE across a stadium is set DISTANCE A;
substitute any number if letters are too difficult.
Pay attention,
*the **third** step is quite important.*
In order to move from 1 point to another,
any motion must 1st cross the halfway point.
It is like filling a tub full of water,
at some instant the tub must first be half full.
If I want to cross DISTANCE A,
then I must 1st cross DISTANCE A/2.
Repeating motion,
*the next, **fourth,** step is like the last.*
Cross to halfway, and see remaining DISTANCE as A/2;
in order to cross it I must 1st cross halfway, A/4.
Repeating again,
*a **fifth** step is further required.*
Cross to halfway, and remaining DISTANCE is A/4;
in order to cross it I must 1st cross halfway, A/8, etc.
Next to last
*is the **sixth** step.*
Crossing of each half-DISTANCE has no identifiable end;
halves will always come before lasts.
Again and again and again the process repeats;
do FINITY and FINITY and FINITY eventually equal INFINITY?
Therefore INFINITE numbers of FINITE half-DISTANCES have to
be crossed before I can completely cross FINITE DISTANCE A.

At last
*is the end in the **seventh** step.*
According to (2–6), any motion, like crossing a stadium,
requires INFINITE numbers of FINITE DISTANCES to be crossed.
Remembering (one), for any motion to actually happen,
FINITY numbers of FINITY DISTANCES must be crossed.
Therefore any motion across FINITE DISTANCE requires
both INFINITE and FINITE numbers of DISTANCES to be crossed.
As before, FINITY DISTANCE is not seen to be doubly formed;
thus the conclusion leaves a similar paradox to chew on.
Once again I'm left with an unsatisfactory conclusion,
which is by definition what a paradox is for.
Analysis of this paradox is much like the last:
why do OBJECT and DISTANCE divide quite alike?
Once again there are 2 propositions possibly accepted,
to which there are additional unanswered questions.
A paradox easily resolved is soon forgotten,
just like a magician whose illusions are transparent.
INFINITE numbers of FINITE DISTANCES form FINITE DISTANCE,
or FINITE numbers of FINITE DISTANCES form FINITE DISTANCE.
Accept one on the one hand, and one on the other,
then switch them because they are interchangeable.
What a minute! All that does is restate the same paradox,
sending my BRAIN reeling in continuous circular motions.
If only straight logic were more curvy about the edges,
it would not find going round and round to be so difficult.
Acceptance of either proposition attaches to the other,
so logical disposition of the argument leads me nowhere.
A prescription for the same question earlier left
hanging: how can this be?

10:37

It's no longer enough for DREAMS to haunt my nights,
now they come to obsess my MIND during empty days.
Do they have meaning, those scatterbrained DREAMS;
are they just THOUGHTS patched into a coat of many colors?

Whether I assume they do or I assume they don't,
the recent ones indicate OBJECTS and DISTANCES are illusory.
Hrumph and snort and whistle and blow;
objections are many, yet few will find a sufficient mark.
Any sane person's response to The Stadium argument
is that there must be something wrong with it.
Motion, like OBJECT, is known to exist;
at least according to those using only RATIONAL MIND.
Pick out any park or stadium desired,
and I'll cross it before INFINITE TIME has progressed.
So search the argument for its dearest direst manner;
find the point where RATIONAL logic breaks down and fails.
I search the logic and look closely at the language,
and can't find where the argument is seriously flawed.
Bound up in those common sense arguments
are universal assumptions kept as closely guarded secrets.
There have been many solutions offered over the years to
resolve Zeno's paradoxes, most of which are unsatisfactory.
Besides solutions there are a couple of objections;
the gall some people have to handle INFINITY decrees.
My own was 1st to reject them as being trite and banal,
only worth discussion when there is nothing better to do.
Denying they are useful is denying they are RATIONAL,
accomplishing nothing in the higher scheme of things.
A clear objection to those arguments is their 1st premise,
a declarative statement which must stand to be negated.
Something the gods have long known and avoid:
there is no way to prove anything absolutely.
If the statement is true, then there may be a paradox;
if the statement is false, then there is only empty rhetoric.
The last term is a device frequently used by lawyers
to present a solid argument that actually means nothing.
If RATIONAL deductions from a simple statement
lead to its own negation, then it makes no sense.
Is OBJECT not formed from smaller OBJECTS;
can sensation lead PERCEPTION to be so wrong?
Because analysis of OBJECT leads to INFINITE absurdity;
smaller OBJECTS just get smaller and smaller.

Is DISTANCE not formed from smaller DISTANCES;
is this not the manner in which each one is assembled?
Because analysis of DISTANCE leads to INFINITE absurdity;
smaller DISTANCES just get smaller and smaller.
Grasping at REALITY with limited RATIONAL tools;
fighting over the carcasses of many wounded THOUGHTS.
The reduction process doesn't prove the premise is false,
it only shows its negation to be equally valid.
Does anyone seriously believe those INFINITY regressions;
can what is known be reconciled with what is sensed?
It's a line of reasoning showing TRUTH or falsehood
can't be absolutely proven by reduction to absurdity.
Belief determines whether a paradox has any value;
personal preference is to accept rationality or INTUITION.
Since the smallest can't be proven or observed or measured,
its only RATIONAL function in REALITY is not to *<not exist>*.
Zeno did expose how THOUGHTS are incomplete,
like the sewage from talking heads on Sunday morning.
But I can't countenance any sort of assertion
whereby OBJECT or DISTANCE are assumed not to exist.
Both of which are solely known by reference to sensation;
neither of which has greater than FINITY limitations.
So while the paradoxes haven't fully exposed REALITY,
they're still able to estimate where its limitations fail.
Paradox helps to illuminate where CONCEPTION falters,
requiring a fresh perspective on static knowledge.
The paradox itself isn't so important;
more, the resolutions may show a better match to REALITY.
A paradox occurs because of a mixture of poisons;
thinking outside the box is only required if there is a box.

11:07

I place a cool water-soaked towel upon my brow;
it appears to be really happening, but I'm still not sure.
What is more real—towel or DREAM;
why do nightmares cause sweats if they are not real?

I'm not sure how I know the towel has substance,
any more than I know OBJECT and DISTANCE do too.
How does either entity exist without division;
is a paradox sufficient if it depends on this premise?
My previous reflection made the paradoxes dependent
on premises that must be assumed true without doubt.
Do not be too swayed by infantile objections;
any RATIONAL argument is based on some basic premise.
Then all CONCEPTS of REALITY are based upon assumption,
and rejecting all premises means rejecting everything.
Other resolutions have been proposed to satisfy Zeno;
rejecting all CONCEPTION of REALITY is not one of them.
A resolution generally agreed to make the most sense was
the attempt by Cantor to bring INFINITE into the FINITE realm.
Looking for INFINITY in all the wrong places
brings THOUGHT back to the same confused starting point.
A brilliant man who attempted to solve the mathematical
problem of INFINITE by using TRANSFINITES and set theory.
Make the answer part of the problem,
and then watch while all of them gently float away.
He didn't try to solve these specific paradoxes directly,
but all great THOUGHTS bring forth unintended fruit.
Why does INFINITY have such a problem with numbers;
is it RATIONAL to leave distinct CONCEPTIONS so undefined?
The problem is how to treat INFINITE in RATIONAL discourse,
and how to include it in a mathematical argument.
Where does it fit within REALITY'S framework;
what process will show us how to apply it, rigorously?
Start with set theory, which existed before Cantor's TIME;
he just expanded it to close some gaping holes.
Any theory has some hole that cannot be closed;
otherwise it is merely a tautology, a = a.
Set theory is CONCEPT of groups that can be numbers,
or collections of definite distinguishable OBJECTS.
Patterns existing only within insubstantial MIND;
shaved from their growth into CONCEPTIONS by BRAIN.
Some sets: natural, RATIONAL, irrational, real, & imaginary;
each on its own has a separate and distinct INFINITE end.

Multiple INFINITIES existing side by side;
which is the greatest, or at least greater than another?
Cantor's way out of the INFINITE dilemma was an ingenious
productive leap to the use of defined INFINITE sets.
Birds of a feather will flock together;
the same is true for CONCEPTIONS appearing to be similar.
But each defined set couldn't have separate INFINITES;
it's only possible for there to be 1 RATIONAL INFINITE.
How can more than one essence include everything,
and if it does not include everything, is it even INFINITY?
Actually, the only way my BRAIN can conceive of INFINITE
is as non-FINITE OBJECT, a thing without end.
Try to hold all of the water in all of the oceans in a cup;
which nears INFINITY—water, oceans, or cup?
INFINITE itself is beyond QUANTITY and beyond measure;
no OBJECT will attach to endless existence.
When INFINITY becomes QUANTITY it has lost its edge,
and has become something bordering on what it is not.
The possibility of multiple INFINITES is based on that fact;
limiting anything by quantification makes it multipliable.
CONCEPTION surely falling through cracks in its position,
by standing on one limited PERCEPTION of INFINITY.
If I can conceive of OBJECT anywhere in my BRAIN,
then multiplying this OBJECT isn't a scientist's ability.
Wonderful news of many things coming from one,
yet who believes they are only CONCEPTIONS?
There can be no actual CONCEPT of multiple INFINITES,
only the illusion of multiple OBJECTS of not-FINITES.
One symbol may rationally represent all that is;
still, it cannot actually be INFINITE QUALITY.
I can't forget they are 2 different CONCEPTIONS;
REALITY doesn't follow from the illusion.
This is why REALITY is so hard to form into CONCEPTION:
INFINITY is offered to hungry MINDS in slices and not loaves.
Since there can only be 1 RATIONAL INFINITE,
something must be wrong in my CONCEPT of different sets.
One thing can only be another when intuitively viewed;
from a RATIONAL perspective, it just does not make sense.

Cantor recognized each defined set could be limited,
and there could only be 1 INFINITE beyond non-FINITE.
Patching the holes in mathematics with symbols
when nothing more insubstantial is available for use.
His insight was recognizing that mathematical CONCEPTS
of how INFINITES were known must be redefined.
Striving and striving down old familiar tangled paths,
until he gave up on these and tried something else.
Therefore he created CONCEPT of TRANSFINITE,
and included it within his modified set theory.
INFINITY exists where nothing else can take its place,
and where it does not fit no longer matters.
Each set of those numbers previously mentioned
has a TRANSFINITE ending, not-FINITE, formerly INFINITE.
Phantoms only exist where they cannot be fixed
by nailing them down with defined CONCEPTIONS of illusion.
TRANSFINITE by itself doesn't close INFINITE gaps,
set theory is required to make it part of something special.
There is no single key which opens every door;
obstacles are specific, and so require specific revisions.
Set theory is a branch of mathematics dealing with
the properties of well-defined collections of OBJECTS.
TRANSFINITY cannot exist within INFINITY'S solitude;
curiously, it is simultaneously limited and open-ended.
Modern mathematics has recognized its many branches
can be derived from set theory's manifold manipulations.
Consistency and cohesiveness are rationally important
for showing how one version of REALITY binds together.
Sets are a collection of definite distinguishable OBJECTS
of PERCEPTION or THOUGHT conceived as a whole.
Trains, planes, automobiles, and numbers;
limitation to one OBJECT will make them all set-worthy.
His theory had the radical advance of treating INFINITE sets
in the same detailed manner used for its FINITE cousins.
Otherwise there is no modifying of those long trailers;
try to put on pants with inseams measuring to INFINITY.
Creating pseudo-INFINITE sets via TRANSFINITE pseudo-sets,
he used formal principles of extension and abstraction.

Not Extension which refers to Object taking up Space,
one more strictly defined by its mathematical application.
Determining any set by its members defines extension,
so Transfinite ends to defined sets are still full members.
What something is no longer means so much,
as long as it fits within definable parameters.
Unknown Quantity is made a set member by abstraction,
subject to the following specific substitution principle.
It may not be possible to know all about Object,
yet if it fits into a set then it can be a member.
The unknown value becomes a set member if and only if
the set is declarative when Object is substituted for it.
What does all that mean in semi-plain english;
how does it specifically apply to Transfinity?
Transfinite is the unknown member of some defined sets,
standing in for Infinite, which no longer rationally exists.
Each one is required to make Infinity Rational;
first, extension.
Since a set is known by its members, Objects in a set
including Transfinite must be part of some Transfinite set.
That has only attached the set to Transfinity;
it still requires abstraction.
If Transfinite can be perfectly substituted by any Object,
it's part of whatever set to which this Object belongs.
That now attaches Transfinity to the set;
both are required if endless sets are to be serviceable.
Many of those Transfinite sets are known to exist,
which inspires me to believe in many Infinites.
Still it has been shown, and even Cantor realized,
only one irrational Infinity can be worthy of this name.
Since Infinite is solitary, opposing defined Infinite ends,
the way out of the dilemma is to redefine Infinite sets.
Bringing two universes together by that subterfuge
is still the best approximation yet attempted.
Infinite is no longer useful in mathematical transpositions;
it's now replaced by Transfinite for all meaningful proofs.
Cantor alleviated gods of Science from the responsibility
of accounting for the existence of interminable Infinity.

Mathematicians now only have to justify FINITE,
and its defined absence as part of TRANSFINITE sets.
What PURPOSE does TRANSFINITY fulfill within REALITY;
how does set theory enable a better understanding of it?
Set theory applies to any identifiable group of CONCEPTS;
OBJECTS can be composed of transfinitely related OBJECTS.
A chair can be grouped with wood or furniture;
so how is TRANSFINITY good for anything but mathematics?
INFINITE sets can now be treated like simpler FINITE 1's,
allowing absurdity to enter the realm of probability.
Apply those modifications to the exhibited paradoxes;
show how TRANSFINITY can work better than INFINITY.
TRANSFINITE numbers of FINITE OBJECTS CAN form
FINITE OBJECT because they are part of a single set.
OBJECTS can keep getting smaller and smaller
because its end now terminates in limited TRANSFINITY.
And TRANSFINITE numbers of FINITE DISTANCES CAN form
FINITE DISTANCE because they are part of a single set.
How is that different from INFINITY regressions;
does TRANSFINITY really solve the paradoxes as stated?
The trick isn't to treat 1 CONCEPT as different parts,
but to treat the set containing them as 1 and the same.
Any OBJECT or DISTANCE is a whole set of distinctions,
dividing it into parts and pieces is only by CONCEPTION.
TRANSFINITE is a mathematical approximation to INFINITE,
as right as can be for any sort of practical exhibition.
Climbing an INFINITY mountain from different directions
is rationally impassable except by a TRANSFINITY approach.
SCIENCE has no problem with a TRANSFINITE limitation;
INFINITE is of no real use to me anyway.
Usefulness is in the eye of the believer, not beholder;
lack of belief will make any REALITY unreal.

12:25

My feverish DREAMS were always limitless,
indicating to me that there is always something more.

Maybe there is more to REALITY than THOUGHTS can define;
that which fits into FINITE sets is only RATIONAL.
Those things of which I can conceive are FINITE,
and nothing of which I can conceive is truly INFINITE.
So has INFINITY been seen in its best possible light,
and how has TRANSFINITY managed to acquit itself so well?
TRANSFINITE is what is actually not-FINITE;
INFINITE exists out there somewhere beyond both of them.
Beyond the realm sensed as INANIMATE UNIVERSE
lies more than what is possible for BRAIN to truly conceive.
It's the closest estimate of INFINITE achieved by definition,
so close each TRANSFINITE appears to be just like it.
Yet as close, as useful, as TRANSFINITY has proven to be,
it still falls short of glowing with INFINITY'S splendor.
Cantor correctly depicted FINITE, TRANSFINITE, and INFINITE;
at least when considered from a RATIONAL point of view.
His set theory approach to INFINITY is not wholly effective;
two counts bar it from having vaunted success.
TRANSFINITE isn't required to be totally efficacious,
only as much as needed to be useful.
They are the attempt to confine INFINITY as part of a set,
and sets actually use TRANSFINITIES, not INFINITY itself.
And neither is fatal for use in RATIONAL manipulations;
if the fill-in didn't work, it would have been abandoned.
First objection: INFINITY cannot be confined to a set;
alone and by itself, it cannot be a member of anything.
Not a problem. Since only TRANSFINITE is defined,
INFINITE can't be shown to exist anyhow.
A set of OBJECTS which terminates in any ending,
must only contain specific defined constituents.
And those cantorian sets don't end at INFINITE,
which has been acknowledged as impossible.
Any OBJECT defined by a set must be FINITY, not INFINITY,
so INFINITY cannot be included in any defined set.
Therefore Cantor didn't actually find sets to fit INFINITE;
it still exists as CONCEPT, which set theory hasn't touched.
Second objection: INFINITY is not being fully defined,
only its RATIONAL approximation—TRANSFINITY.

No attempt has been made to profess otherwise;
only a charlatan will try to assert immaterial claims.
TRANSFINITY is not some individual type of INFINITY,
defined as being merely part of a set which is not-FINITY.
But those sets are also without observable end,
and they are in that fashion equivalent to INFINITE.
Furnishing a better handle on the meaning of not-FINITY
is not a clearer path into the realm where INFINITY belongs.
Since INFINITE has no definable useful PURPOSE,
finding the path to its realm also has no useful PURPOSE.
Sounding rather trite to those without sufficient math,
most people still conceive of INFINITY as being not-FINITY.
RATIONAL mathematics has decreed INFINITE is a violation
of definitions actually working within INANIMATE UNIVERSE.
Accept the fine distinction between TRANSFINITY and INFINITY
or the difference between universes will not make sense.
TRANSFINITE and INFINITE are 2 separate identities,
and only the former can now wear not-FINITE's mask.
So INFINITY itself appears to be beyond definition;
now approximated as not-FINITY and not-TRANSFINITY.

12:50

The towel on my forehead is severely and finitely limited;
it isn't like in my DREAMS where everything seemed endless.
Thus DREAMS and towels appear to be distinct essences;
one allows inclusion of INFINITY, the other does not.
A place where INFINITE may exist, another where it can't;
any CONCEPT of REALITY must dualistically divide.
Even though TRANSFINITY closely approximates INFINITY,
it still must reside with FINITY in defined proximity.
But TRANSFINITE is a useful solution to INFINITE paradoxes;
accepting it allows any residual conflicts to make sense.
The effect of Cantor's resolution fails from one cause:
divisions of OBJECT and DISTANCE still appear as INFINITY.
He didn't try to resolve Zeno's paradoxes;
his work has been applied there by others less worthy.

The only rationale for TRANSFINITY to ever become known
was that artificial sets of numbers were first created.
Cantor's mathematical way out of the INFINITE dilemma
was to sidestep it by the use of defined TRANSFINITE sets.
Notice how the lack of a wheel makes a car useless;
one CREATION makes the following ones available.
Sets like natural, RATIONAL, irrational, real, and imaginary
are each supposed to be endless, and therefore not-FINITE.
Cantor's subterfuge was to redefine the treatment
of those artificially created not-FINITY ends of sets.
Making INFINITE into FINITE OBJECT called TRANSFINITE,
so each set or OBJECT or DISTANCE has a defined end.
He neglected to include the mathematical necessity
for each set to be artificially predefined as being a set!
CREATION of a set may be an artificial device,
but this only makes it more useful, not less.
Existence of TRANSFINITIES is only possible, or required,
when applying artificial sets of self-sustaining OBJECTS.
That statement has 1 IDEA tripping over another;
each of them contributing, and none of them meshing.
A simpler sound bite: TRANSFINITIES do not exist
unless they have been predefined as having to exist.
Any set of numbers must be defined to exist as a set,
which doesn't mean TRANSFINITES have to exist.
The fact that TRANSFINITY of real numbers is different
from TRANSFINITY of natural numbers was predetermined.
They are still TRANSFINITES created from 1 INFINITE,
which in the end should make them all the same.
Predetermined by the artificial accretion of mandatory sets
creating the appearance of different INFINITIES.
An irrational diatribe doesn't resolve Zeno's paradoxes;
INFINITES have already been dismissed as irrelevant.
Those different sets do not exist as a function of REALITY,
they are needed for math's language to perform regularly.
Numbers in sets are representations of real OBJECTS,
groups which have similar sensible characteristics.
Imagine creating a set of STARS in the sky,
or any other set of OBJECTS with no end in sight.

Each 1 would still have TRANSFINITE for an ending;
therefore those sets could be treated as a whole.
What makes one set more or less a reflection
of what is real than any other defined set?
The ability to make RATIONAL use of a collection of OBJECTS;
a set isn't real unless its characteristics are definable.
Make no mistake, when numbers are grouped into a set,
each number is some oddball OBJECT just like that set.
Written down it's only ink on a page;
within my BRAIN it's only neural electrical impulses.
Yet each component member of a defined set
can exist separate and whole and complete by itself.
So a set no more defines REALITY than its members,
both of which are representations of something else.
The difference between six and seven and eight is not big,
except in the set of prime numbers, which isolates them.
So what! If those numbers represent some part of REALITY,
then their combination into sets does too.
Imagine the numbering system as a continuous blur,
where little difference exists between individual numbers.
There is little difference between 4.309860 and 4.309861,
each of which represent some aspect of REALITY.
INFINITY numbers of numbers exist between those two;
their isolation in sets changes continuity into OBJECTS.
But isolating a blur of numbers into sets is practical;
the distinctions are what make numbers useful.
CREATION of a set takes specific parts of the numerical
spectrum and combines them into a set for convenience.
Therefore sets don't actually represent all numbers,
and OBJECTS are also not able to represent all REALITY.
Spaces between the bars and reading between the lines,
this is where REALITY exists beyond sensation.
A process which can't be unprofitable; on the contrary,
it's virtually required from a pure RATIONAL point of view.
REALITY does not work by creating arbitrary sets
of numbers, and then tacking on TRANSFINITY for capacity.
So all of the sets which have supposedly INFINITE endings,
actually don't because they are limited by definition.

The nature of Infinity *is such that it cannot be limited,*
so any set which precludes another, precludes Infinity.
Infinite as Concept or Object is mathematically useful,
but these all fall short of its actual place within Reality.
Try to include Infinity *in some* Rational *cogitation;*
formulate a set with it, not as an afterthought tacked on.
That is impossible when looked at more closely;
a set by definition must be limited to be defined.
Transfinite is a useful definition created to close a hole
in the definition of sets, and mathematics.
As Concept it fulfills its objective to make sets useful;
it's in its application to Reality where it falls short.
It comes as close to touching Infinity *as* Finity *ever will;*
knowing what it is not is all the knowledge needed.
Infinite used to be objectified as not-Finite,
now it's more appropriately known as not-Transfinite.
Transfinity's existence was created when the first sets
of numbers were mobilized to provide acquisition.
But it wasn't until Cantor came along that
an acceptable fix was formulated to fill its prepared hole.
Infinity cannot be found through the use of defined sets;
artificial beginnings necessitate artificial ends.
What can be defined is its closest Rational approximation,
which Transfinite serves to fill admirably well.
Unfortunately the dilemma at heart belongs to Intuition,
and it was approached in a purely mathematical manner.
The fact that math is Rational isn't unfortunate,
it's required.
No accurate solution will ever be found by using
solely Rational *means to detect an irrational existence.*
And no irrational existence will ever be of use
until it can be rigidly approximated by Rational means.
Transfinities and set theory have been accepted
as the solution to Infinity *dilemmas, yet they are only math.*

13:41

DREAMS have QUALITY of seeming to extend to forever,
where their existence is limited by my handling of them.
What is the difference between irrational numbers
and an irrational view, more properly called INTUITION?
Irrational numbers were created along with geometry;
consider pi, which continues with no discernible end.
Even something so well-defined and rigorous,
still has a gap which requires TRANSFINITY to close it.
Circles are formed by defined geometrical relationships,
a perfect example on which modern SCIENCE is founded.
Perfection requires irrational numbers to exist;
how are they recognized within REALITY's arena?
That set is made of those numbers not in the others;
which makes them, except real, the largest of them all.
Real numbers, like REALITY itself, contain all of them;
except of course for the imaginary numbers.
Undoubtedly there are sets not yet discovered,
which will expand REALITY as imaginary 1's have done.
Slip-sliding past the point not yet sufficiently made:
limitation of REALITY into a set makes it RATIONAL.
Sets are like OBJECTS, both being groups of known pieces
disengaged from REALITY to become not-INFINITE.
When REALITY is represented as being just part of one set,
it is limited from being part of a more inclusive one.
An irrational set has numbers of non-repeating decimals,
where each 1 must still fit between 2 others.
Try and define what has been left out of a set,
when what has been put in is still left incomplete.
Therefore REALITY could, in a sense, be the ultimate set;
everything possible must be included within it.
Convenient IDEA for rationalizing all existence;
although any defined set would still be too confining.
Irrational sets are rationally viewed for existence;
therefore they must exist within INANIMATE UNIVERSE.
Those sets cannot be an actual part of ANIMATE UNIVERSE;
no defined set can be seen from INTUITION's perspective.

An irrational set is seen from a RATIONAL perspective,
while irrational numbers appear to be only semi-RATIONAL.
Yet how can irrational numbers be seen intuitively,
and the set of those same numbers be seen rationally?
Sets by their nature are formed of related OBJECTS;
this definition makes them RATIONAL, not their existence.
Still, is an irrational set a TRANSFINITY approximation
of a more indefinite and complete view from INTUITION?
An irrational set still doesn't include imaginary sets,
which must be included in an irrational view.
This is only going to be repeated for more emphasis:
no defined set can be seen from INTUITION's perspective.
The noticeable universe is FINITE and depends on definition,
while the other is INFINITE and depends on estimation.
Claiming that INTUITION's notions have TRANSFINITY relations
is an attempt to bring INFINITY into the universe of FINITY.
But then the reverse should also be acceptable;
the universal barrier is permeable, not impassable.
Trying to make TRANSFINITY sets approximate INTUITION
is an attempt to bring FINITY into the realm of INFINITY.
And something limited isn't expandable in that fashion;
there is more to REALITY than CONCEPTS can define.
RATIONAL INANIMATE UNIVERSE has an inherent desire
to expand towards that which is beyond itself—INFINITY.
I know that what is sensed, and therefore objectified,
is incomplete and therefore lacks INFINITE capacity.
INTUITION's ANIMATE UNIVERSE exists without understanding;
thus approximated as episodic and experiential.
My need is to make INFINITE fit into conceptual thinking,
and once I succeed at this, I have lost it.
INFINITY by its nature includes all known as FINITY,
the former has no need for approximating the latter.
TRANSFINITE usefully incorporates INFINITE into THOUGHT,
when in actuality it can't fit into any such thing.
Irrational sets do not represent INTUITION's view,
yet what about vague irrational numbers themselves?
Irrational numbers must extend beyond sensation;
the set is defined, but each number is still left open.

The dilemma of many INFINITIES was transfinitely closed;
what seals the holes between individual numbers?
There are numbers which extend off into INFINITE areas,
and I shall likely never be able to capture them.
It is like stepping on pillars across a bottomless chasm,
numbers rising from INFINITY to touch and disappear.
Irrational numbers end up being approximated;
their usefulness only extends to measurable depths.
The question is whether they represent INTUITION'S view
as they get farther and farther away from utility?
The problem then turns into how far I need go
to make use of something which has no ending.
Maybe this is the nature of a RATIONAL approximation:
the closer to INTUITION it gets, the less useful it becomes.
Which makes irrational numbers decidedly successful
at doing the manipulations they were created to do.
Look deeply! Try to point out one single piece
of REALITY that irrational numbers actually represent.
Where many numbers fail, 1 may succeed;
I steadily looking for the many in 1, and the 1 in many.
Do numbers have existence outside of their markings,
or do they just exist as CONCEPTIONS within fixed BRAIN?
My BRAIN must be trained to access common IDEAS,
and their metaphysical existence depends on propinquity.
The markings have no meaning until touching MIND;
clearer yet, the training touches the markings.
Math was originally created to represent, not be, REALITY;
which also responds to more LIFE-affirming languages.
It is useful, but it does not exist;
this is how real the mathematical language truly is.

****

15:54

A wise man once said: make of yourself a light,
for any other source can only result in a premature end.

Even the sun, most powerful of lights, will fall silent,
and no longer be the massive presence in daily trials.
Become light, so no darkness can catch and hold;
slipping by or through as night slides into breaking day.
The problem is my only source for an inner light is me,
and my feeble glow is not fed like the Oracle's at Delphi.
How do we make that which only comes from without,
or does light within warm from some other source?
Within are visions and pale imitations of light reflections;
my MIND is filled with these illusions and CONCEPTS.
What is the source of INFINITY IDEAS
that mystics profess shine and fully fill from within?
There must be some internal light making them shine,
but for me they only exist in black and white.
Shadows still haunt the corners of an exterior vision,
becoming DREAMS of inferior REALITY.
Any light from without can't make me full within,
only an inner light can make me whole and complete.
Light from the sun grants fleet warmth and security,
within is sought a place where neither one is required.
An inner light might abolish physical wants and cravings,
beyond where my body needs comfort from a FINITE source.
Hold a lamp up to make vain eyes abjure darkness;
even when it is removed, it is still there.
Make a light so no path I trod will be in darkness,
my being shall not be extinguished by the depths of DEATH.
Does inevitable DEATH cease the grand inner light,
or is the end of one passage the beginning of another?
My DEATH doesn't kill STAR, so should SOUL survive;
this recognition should emphasize the point.
Inner light comes from SOUL funding LIFE'S essence,
denying sensual pleasure to value greater treasure.
Focusing on the light within denies external warmth;
1 or the other must be the goal I seek.
No summit will be reached unless it is the goal,
and darkness will abound if an inner light is not sought.
Failure doesn't come from setting goals too high;
instead it arrives by setting the bar too low.

How do we find the light which shines as INFINITY,
if the level at which we seek it is mired in FINITY?
Not by grasping for something solid that I can hold on to;
material OBJECTS don't die as I do.
And yet we do die, someday when TIME is right;
if we do not take it with us, what good is it in the long run?
Rocks I know last, but I will be lost upon DEATH'S arrival;
whereas my SOUL may last because it isn't here anyway.
Premature end is the gross world of decaying flesh,
trapped by THOUGHTS of "this is all there is."
FINITE world of light versus INFINITE world of light,
a choice each individual must make for himself.
How is the choice to be made when we know so little;
are we to rely on faith for an inner light as INFINITY?
It isn't really that complicated of a choice;
I know what is FINITE, and I don't know what is INFINITE.
FINITY OBJECTS must be left behind upon DEATH;
SOUL may not exist, and if it does, it is beyond FINITY.
Setting my sights on only what is obviously FINITE
precludes me from setting my goal on INFINITE success.
Inner light is a beacon shining over suspect shoals;
there is more to LIFE than what meets the eye.

16:20

While dreaming, the experiential world goes on forever,
and I still try to limit DREAMS with my THOUGHTS.
Can REALITY fit within the confines of THOUGHT,
or is it so vast it will forever humble vain hopes?
Everything capable of objectification is covered by FINITE,
while INFINITE is available for everything else.
Still INFINITY has been shown to wear OBJECT clothes;
it is only made of less sterner stuff.
INFINITE is useless CONCEPT beyond FINITE or TRANSFINITE,
a dumping ground for dreamers' futile flights of fancy.
The questions then become: does INFINITY truly exist,
and if it does, how can we ignore what it represents?

It isn't observed or measured, so it might as well not exist;
until it finds some use, I quite reasonably ignore it.
INFINITY is not as strange an essence as it might first sound;
nothing exists in a vacuum, and it is viable CONCEPTION.
Any role INFINITE plays in converting THOUGHTS
is more easily and substantially covered by TRANSFINITE.
Substituting one for the other is not replacing it;
a geometrical lid does not cover a realistic hole.
I acknowledge existence of INFINITE as CONCEPT,
not that it's an actual component of REALITY.
For TRANSFINITIES to be math approximations of INFINITY,
they must approximate something necessarily real.
CONCEPT or a picture of a unicorn is quite real,
which doesn't mean unicorns must necessarily exist.
While the totality of that beast may be imaginary,
each of its parts is based on something more tangible.
Therefore TRANSFINITE can be composed of FINITE parts,
and have nothing whatsoever to do with INFINITE.
A unicorn is just a mythical horse with a horn,
and both exist outside of their appearance as CONCEPTION.
So all CONCEPTS are built from a FINITE basis,
the only essence required to configure TRANSFINITE.
The total of horses must have some end in FINITY;
they cannot be used to compose something that does not.
Which still doesn't prove INFINITE is real;
REALITY could end beyond my short attention span.
INFINITY as CONCEPTION covers that which is without end;
just look out into the depths of TIME and SPACE.
That is the point—observation is limited;
what is known constructs that which isn't known.
Anything crossing the bounds of SPACE and TIME
is some aspect of REALITY that cannot be ignored.
TIME and SPACE exist, no doubt they must,
but this is no rationale to rely on their being INFINITE.
Do SPACE and TIME sit inside of something greater;
if they are part of REALITY, must it also be limited?
I may be trying to limit REALITY to FINITE without proof,
but I'm not trying to expand it to INFINITE without proof.

CONCEPTION of INFINITY demands it be totally unproven;
what is LIFE without the mystery of something else?
INFINITE only exists because the ends haven't been found,
which doesn't mean they don't exist.
A graphic portrayal of how a RATIONAL view cannot see
INTUITION'S perspective through its own limited lenses.
If I can't sense it, then I can't know whether it exists;
more than this, it doesn't matter whether it exists.
Yet is it not better to leave the possibility open,
than to end it prematurely without being shown?
No matter what is stated, INFINITE can't be proven,
so I'll only accept its possibility in order to move on.
Closed MINDS lead to closed THOUGHTS;
imagine all the modern inventions originally not possible.
If REALITY includes INFINITE, then it will remain so;
the end will always be just a stone's throw away.
REALITY is CONCEPTION including everything,
not just OBJECTS constructed to be amenable to sensation.

16:48

There were things happening in my DREAMS, very illogical,
which worked by rules my RATIONAL THOUGHTS abhor.
Patchwork REALITY submissively responds to RATIONAL laws;
a paradox highlights the moment when they break down.
There are logical rules by which RATIONAL THOUGHT exists;
if the former break down, then so should the latter.
Assuming that the validity of logic is always real,
and its deductions and inductions are part of REALITY.
Reveal an area, some location, where logic has no value;
where some essence can both be and not-be.
The place is not another planet, no RATIONAL realm;
another universe is where logic will not be found.
But these words must follow logical syntactical rules;
if it's illogical, then it's also unknowable.
Logical gods assumed never wrong or unreasonable;
an infallible method is one which only the fortunate find.

Examine the basic rules to which logic subscribes;
they haven't been created out of thin air.
Superficial rules like modus ponens and modus tollens,
none of which exist but by the law of cause and effect.
Rules of logic give greater validity to that law;
if it was shown inconsistent, it would've been replaced.
Logic is not formed with the essence of REALITY;
it comes from RATIONAL observation, and is so proven.
I can't imagine a world without logical results;
food and air and water would cease to have any meaning.
Its existence as part of INANIMATE UNIVERSE is not denied;
only, it is limited to a language, similar to its math cousin.
Which has been indicated as insufficient for REALITY;
if logic could map it, there would be fewer unknowns.
If logic is not an absolute standard within REALITY,
then resolution of the paradoxes may not be logical.
If it isn't logical, then it will make no sense;
I won't believe anything missing RATIONAL coherency.
IDEA behind a resolution may be totally irrational,
and the message can still be rationally approximated.
But that would mean the paradoxes are irrational,
and their very construction shouldn't follow logical rules.
Resolution may be buried much deeper than that,
within assumptions consistently taken for granted.
Which is part of what I'm searching for,
to find whether there is some greater TRUTH within REALITY.
What if logic does not exist within ANIMATE UNIVERSE;
how could this affect resolution of the paradoxes?
PERCEPTION of OBJECT or DISTANCE depends on BIOMATTER;
resolution could be in this substantial living impulse.
Yet OBJECT and DISTANCE seem to exist independently;
how do we determine whether they are FINITY or INFINITY?
I sense OBJECTS, and DISTANCE between them,
which is physical PERCEPTION of their FINITE existence.
Lack of those same sensations denotes INFINITY;
does this intangible PERCEPTION attach to LIFE?
INFINITE rationally exists as CONCEPT;
there is no place where I can say it exists past my DEATH.

Maybe the difference between FINITY and INFINITY
is the same as the difference between types of PERCEPTION.
Which only applies to living breathing creatures;
externally perceiving sense, internally perceiving feeling.
The known universe is subject to sensual entertainment;
the unknown universe is only approached via LIFE'S bite.
Therefore the paradoxes could be illogically resolved,
if PERCEPTION modifies existence of OBJECT or DISTANCE.
How REALITY is momentarily experienced is different
than CONCEPTIONS which are subsequently formed.
How I feel about OBJECT has nothing to do
with how it can be divided into parts and pieces.
Why should that assumption be made;
do feelings have an effect on how OBJECT is perceived?
They could certainly make any resolution illogical,
but I still don't connect feelings to INFINITY.
Neither can be defined by RATIONAL sensation,
and neither subscribes to the law of cause and effect.
So PERCEPTION may finally resolve the paradoxes,
making composition of OBJECT or DISTANCE subservient.
Whether they are one or many is subject to feelings;
belief helps determine whether they are one or the other.
But I'm actually concerned with what they really are,
which has nothing to do with how I feel about them.
OBJECT or DISTANCE is grasped subject to PERCEPTION,
based on reception from many places, many TIMES.

17:21

OBJECT or DISTANCE as I understand them are whole,
and at the same instant can divide into parts and pieces.
How can this be;
how can an essence be simultaneously whole and divided?
That is the nature of a paradox;
if the answer were easy, it would be just a question.
Many IDEAS exist for how the paradoxes could coalesce,
most of which can be shown to contain a fatal flaw.

It doesn't serve my PURPOSE to open all of those boxes,
only the 1's which might advance my understanding.
One resolution: both FINITY and INFINITY numbers
of FINITY OBJECTS compose FINITY OBJECT (or DISTANCE).
The problem with that type of resolution to the paradoxes
is that the premise offered just leads to more of the same.
Where do we begin to show the veracity of that premise;
how can one OBJECT be dually composed?
It can't, according to any REASON I'm able to use,
if OBJECT doesn't exist as multiple entities at once.
Another resolution: neither FINITY nor INFINITY numbers
of FINITY OBJECTS compose FINITY OBJECT (or DISTANCE).
Another premise sinking my THOUGHTS into a morass;
nothing has been proposed which clears up my BRAIN.
Assuming absurdities will lead to other absurdities,
which may or may not apply to the original paradoxes.
If either paradox has no logical resolution,
then I must use other means to crack them open.
The best argument thus far proposed was presented
in the form of a question: how can this be?
The answer to that question is of course—it can't,
at least when seen from a purely RATIONAL point of view.
Imagine that resolution of The Smallest Piece paradox
is not to assume OBJECT is made from other ones.
That defies basic common sense; if I break a rock
into parts, it's shown to be made of OBJECTS.
How could one OBJECT not be composed of other ones;
is there some way basic OBJECT PERCEPTION is flawed?
For OBJECT not to be composed of other OBJECTS,
it would have to have been an illusion in the 1st place.
Imagine that resolution of The Stadium's motion-dilemma
is not to assume DISTANCE is made from other ones.
That also defies basic common sense;
adding meters together will amount to 1 total DISTANCE.
How could there be an end to passing those markers, which
must be crossed for DISTANCE to be CONCEPTION?
For DISTANCE not to be composed of other DISTANCES,
it would have to have been an illusion in the 1st place.

CONCEPTION of parts to OBJECT or DISTANCE is a hypothesis
based on PERCEPTION moving backwards, not forwards.
But my PERCEPTIONS aren't flawed;
they are what they are; I sense what I sense.
PERCEPTIONS are not flawed, how can they be;
yet once PERCEPTION is absorbed, what happens to it?
PERCEPTION becomes CONCEPT within my BRAIN,
and it's obvious that different animals do this differently.
Thus TIME appears to play a factor,
one event most assuredly following another.
Contrary to what bad SCIENCE fiction has proposed,
TIME does seem to make 1 event follow another.
If CONCEPTION must follow PERCEPTION,
is it possible to reverse this process, back to front?
PERCEPTION following CONCEPTION doesn't make sense,
unless I want to tell my stomach it really isn't hungry.
So knowledge appears to arrive via a sequence of events,
and any other method gives rise to false assumption.
If I'm to understand REALITY as it truly exists,
then it will only be as it presents itself, not as I want it to.
CONCEPTIONS have a dangerous ephemeral existence
because they violate the natural progression of TIME.
THOUGHTS must always follow 1 another, step by step,
even if they are able to loop back upon themselves.
Yet contents of THOUGHTS do not have to follow TIME'S path;
taking PERCEPTION, turning it, and marching backwards.
But that is how REALITY is rationally analyzed,
understanding what things are by a mental process.
Up to a point, the RATIONAL process is excellent;
although it appears to falter as it approaches REALITY.
Negating that approach flies in the face of modern SCIENCE;
if things can't be dissected, then they can't be recombined.
This is not an attempt to violate RATIONAL success;
keep eye of MIND on how it fails to complete REALITY.

17:54

Sitting here focusing on my finger, I see my finger;
focusing on my fingernail, I see my fingernail.
Yet the latter is part of the former, and both are OBJECTS;
how can one be OBJECT and still be part of the other one?
PERCEPTION of each of those OBJECTS is different,
but the difference in my BRAIN doesn't translate to REALITY.
Still, OBJECTS are assumed to be formed by other OBJECTS,
so it is necessary to delve into how they are perceived.
PERCEPTION is the means by which knowledge is formed,
whether attained from the senses or from mystical insight.
Starting the explication is this frontal THOUGHT assault:
OBJECT is perforce separated into arbitrary divisions.
The Smallest Piece paradox assumes every OBJECT
is made of pieces which can be detached and refitted.
An arbitrary division of MATTER, solely
for the RATIONAL convenience of biomaterial BRAIN to use.
There is a solid rationale for why it's believed:
if I smash OBJECT, I get many smaller OBJECTS in return.
Thus a quite understandable presumption is made:
first whole OBJECT was definitely constructed of pieces.
I can always fall back on my proverbial rock;
its relation to OBJECTS can't be denied.
Yet what is seen or sensed, as has already been shown,
is not a true child of REALITY, only symptomatic orphans.
So what if PERCEPTION is an imperfect reflection,
SCIENCE'S marvels have still shown it to be quite good.
One: any OBJECT which is supposedly smashed into bits,
originally was complete and coherent in its own right.
That shouldn't prohibit a rock from flying into pieces;
OBJECT can still consist of other OBJECTS.
Two: no OBJECT can be composed of separate parts,
for then it would not be one OBJECT, but many.
I'm able to see 1st 1 rock and then many,
which seems to indicate the rock was actually the rocks.
It is not possible to sense what holds OBJECT together
because once it is dissected, original OBJECT is gone.

I assume new Objects must come from old Object,
they could have come from no other place in Space.
Assuming one thing inevitably comes from another
grabs the tail of the donkey and calls it its head.
New Objects don't just appear out of nowhere;
magic is illusion, so there is no useful magic.
Inserting fantasy to mix with Perception misses the point;
stay focused and only rely on what sensation determines.
I 1st see there is a rock, 1 whole Object;
and then there are many rocks, many whole Objects.
Now the mission, should curiosity entice one to accept it,
is to prove one Object was composed of parts and pieces.
There is no way to prove it absolutely;
it's just the most reasonable explanation for observations.
It is probably best to forgo any sort of proof,
for one cannot prove what must be assumed at best.
Still, new rocks must come from the original rock;
of this fact my senses don't conspire to lie.
One Object, then many, is sensed—not in question—
this is not a diatribe for belief in superstition or magic.
Pray tell, enlighten me as to the objective,
or leave Rational Thought to those who can do it.
To consider first Object as composed of pieces
is to assume a whole is equal to the sum of its parts.
Which is the foundation of most modern advances;
Science has shown that sum to be equivalent.
That is not-false and has no doubt within skeptical Mind,
yet only if every single one of its parts can be identified.
All of the parts might not be sufficiently ascertainable,
but if some can be, then that is enough to determine pieces.
To assume Object is composed of many other Objects
is to believe the latter can reconstitute the former.
That is exactly what I believe;
things can be taken apart and put back together.
If that is the way Objects are constructed,
then try to remake the old rock out of its destruction.
I can't remake something that has been destroyed,
but I can use its pieces to make something just like it.

Only if first OBJECT is like a sliced loaf of bread,
some pieces can be taken away and put back again.
That is a sufficient analogy, though superficial;
a rock is held together, a loaf is just wrapped together.
A loaf, like a rock, is considered to be one OBJECT
for convenience of THOUGHT and discussion.
Rock, or loaf, is treated as 1 coherent OBJECT
as long as my senses detect it to be 1 and only 1.
Remember a loaf only serves as OBJECT in language;
it is many grouped into a set—OBJECT of convenience.
I know each slice is actually separate OBJECT,
but when they are bound together, a loaf is OBJECT too.
Is each slice OBJECT or is loaf OBJECT,
or is there some other possibility not yet covered?
If I'm sensing a slice, then it's OBJECT in question;
if I'm sensing the whole loaf, then it's OBJECT without doubt.
If this line of THOUGHT is pursued to its inevitable end:
exactly why is each slice of bread considered OBJECT?
Because it reacts as 1 body to my awareness;
there is no part of that OBJECT which isn't that OBJECT.
Yet those slices are each composed of many OBJECTS.
The problem: discern where they end and illusion begins.
So if I were to focus on the crust or particles of wheat,
each 1 of them would in turn be another OBJECT.
Then how do each of those distinct OBJECTS
construct another one, or is it all merely an illusion?
My senses determine how each OBJECT is perceived;
it isn't so much illusion as a necessary convenience.
OBJECT within the scope of REALITY is more like a slab
of granite from which a statue is given form from within.
My senses detect only a slab, not a statue;
though a sculptor might suggest it's already in there.
Before the statue arises to its graceful BEAUTY, it is only
considered one OBJECT, and no others comprise the slab.
The outward manifestation of the slab is completely real;
it appears as 1 OBJECT with no constituent parts.
Once a statue comes out, it is one grand OBJECT,
and many subsidiary objectified pieces.

Only after changing my PERCEPTION from slab to statue
am I able to determine there was something underneath.
No matter what strenuous efforts are made to do so,
those many pieces cannot remake the original slab.
That would be a feat greater than unveiling the statue;
PERCEPTION determines which 1 becomes my CONCEPT.
Since that is impossible and no doubt it cannot be done,
gods commonly reuse a fiction—effect leads to cause.
Proposing OBJECTS as the basis for composing OBJECT
is no longer accurate because OBJECT is an illusion.
Remember OBJECT only works in pursuit of an analogy,
a loaf and a slab are convenient approximations for it.
A loaf is actually many OBJECTS consisting of slices,
while a slab is a statue and other distinct OBJECTS.
OBJECT is complete and coherent unto itself;
sensory votes do not win membership in REALITY.
But senses are required to determine any OBJECT exists;
it's its composition senses are unable to penetrate.
OBJECT does not depend on other OBJECTS for existence;
it either is or it is not, no other assumption is necessary.
When I detect loaf or slab or rock, they are each OBJECTS,
and what they divide into are also OBJECTS.
Just because one OBJECT is termed in that fashion,
does not mean in fact it exists that way in REALITY.
What I commonly term OBJECT is a conceptual convenience
for 1 or many things acting in unison.
OBJECT identification is totally subject to CONCEPTION,
which is largely subject to PERCEPTION from sensation.
Then what I truly know about OBJECTS in REALITY
has been derived from PERCEPTIONS for my convenience.
OBJECT has a slippery definition;
it exists, yet only to the extent sensation can perceive it.
Therefore anything I conceive as being OBJECT,
exists 1 way within my head, and another in REALITY.
The only circumstance not turning out to be false
is to know new OBJECTS came about from the first.
There is no way for my senses to divide up OBJECT;
they tell me there is 1, or there are many.

Time cannot be turned back to show that the reverse is fact;
for Objects to form Object is limited to mere supposition.

18:57

My Dreams progress from 1 situation to another;
a real process whereby 1 event follows another.
Simple observation of Reality detects things as they are;
there is no going back in Time, forget this fiction.
Breaking a rock into pieces necessitates a sequence
where there must 1ˢᵗ be a rock, and then many rocks.
It is possible to break Object down into many pieces,
while there is no evidence many parts construct one.
But I can break a piece of copper into 2 pieces,
and melt them down to form 1 piece like the 1ˢᵗ 1.
What do they prove, those first and last pieces,
other than they are Objects in a sequence of events?
They prove 1 piece of material can be broken into 2,
then be reformed into 1 piece of the same substance.
No. Actually that statement proves this point:
there is no turning back from a one-way Time transit.
The 1ˢᵗ piece of copper has certain characteristics,
and the 2ⁿᵈ reformed piece is exactly the same.
The newly smelted piece of copper is new Object;
from two others, its match with the first is similar at best.
But if they are just alike, there is no difference;
at least my senses determine those Objects are the same.
What has been created is one piece of copper,
like the first in its most important physical properties.
There are no other Rational traits to be accounted,
ignoring the obvious viability of other copper Objects.
They become one new Object totally distinct from the first;
it takes up similar Space, yet no identical Time.
So what! Time has no influence on what Object is,
other than to allow for possible changes to it.
Wait! Do not strive to make unwarranted assumptions;
have gods of Science managed to turn back Time?

As far as I'm aware, no experiment has been done
which contradicts the singular flow of TIME.
The moment in TIME when each perceived OBJECT exists
is one distinct manner they show themselves dissimilar.
That seems to require the existence of ABSOLUTE TIME,
which has been indicated, but still defies modern SCIENCE.
Those OBJECTS also have different MASS and EXTENSION,
the second reformed one will be slightly less.
Which can be attributed to human or industrial error;
theoretically speaking, they should be equal QUANTITIES.
Sustain the process of breaking and remolding,
and there will not be enough copper left to identify.
Losing MATTER may be a practical consideration,
but 2nd OBJECTS are still formed from the 1st 1.
Sands of TIME do not reverse up through an hourglass,
so prove first OBJECT is made of two pieces of copper.
The 2 pieces don't "make" the 1st piece of copper,
but they must somehow come from within it.
There was originally one complete piece of copper,
and from this existence two separate ones were born.
And there is no way of avoiding this simple fact:
whatever formed 1st OBJECT, also formed the next 2.
That is not the question at hand:
how do second two OBJECTS form first OBJECT?
They don't actually form it, like slices of a bread-loaf,
they give evidence OBJECT is made of smaller OBJECTS.
Open up to the possibility that an assumption was made;
while useful and RATIONAL, it is still founded on a guess.
Something must structure the 1st piece of copper,
and there is no other to match the particulate theory.
Assuming many OBJECTS are what compose their parent
is an exercise in the futility of traveling back through TIME.
That so-called exercise has resulted in CONCEPT of REALITY,
by SCIENCE, which makes it more suitable for my use.
One OBJECT cannot be assumed to be made of pieces
until it is first broken into two or more other ones.
I'm having a problem with trying to understand
how OBJECT can divide without 1st being parts and pieces.

Each set of next Objects is assumed to equate with the first,
a totality moving forward and backward in Time.
If 1st Object wasn't constructed of smaller 1's,
then it wouldn't be able to break up into them.
How can anyone know it is one Object and not many;
is there some method for telling one from the other?
That does seem to be the most pertinent question,
and there is no way except from my sensory information.
Object is Object if it always acts as distinct Object;
how else can this be said and actually make it clear?
Therefore a loaf isn't slices as long as it acts as a loaf;
a slab isn't a statue as long as it acts like a slab.
There is Inertia attached to each individual Object,
and it must be overcome to change sensed Perception.
But a sliced loaf has no Inertia holding it together;
it's only Object by virtue of mental Conception.
There is a difference between no Inertia and very little;
if nothing held it together, would it even be Object?
It's Object as long as I conceive it to be so;
though my senses must detect some coherency.
If some identifiable Matter reacts to Forces as if it is one,
then for all intents and purposes it is just one Object.
Then Object is more than just convenient Concept,
some physical essence must account for its focus.
Its necessary division into parts is called into question;
some Objects are constructed of other Objects, not all.
So this reflection allows me to focus on how
particulate Objects are determined, not forbid them.
Original Object could be one or many, know it as
Object of convenient Conception, or Object in Reality.
Then my sense of Object is always illusion,
and sometimes it's close to Reality, sometimes it's not.
Forces and pressures filling Inanimate Universe
continuously oppose Object as such when it acts as one.
A slice of bread reacts 1 way to Forces around it;
a loaf of sliced bread, by its nature, reacts another way.
Many Objects exist when Perception of Forces
mandates they only be accepted in this fashion.

Something changes to alter perceiving 1 loaf or slices,
and the things available are light and my eyes' focus.
Observations gained from FORCES around all MATTER
determine one OBJECT is undivided throughout.
If it's divided within, then it's already not 1 OBJECT;
and if it isn't 1, then it must be none or many.
If it is one continuous OBJECT from within and without,
where do the pieces come from forming it into OBJECTS?
A continuous OBJECT of water can divide into many,
for in no other way can many be created from 1.
There are no pieces within if it is one undivided OBJECT;
parts arrive after the destruction of OBJECT, not before.
So 1 OBJECT has capacity for division into pieces;
while, if it's continuous, there are no pieces within it.
Common THOUGHT assumes pieces exist before it is possible
for them actually to happen in TIME and SPACE.
There doesn't seem to be any other way to figure out
how REALITY exists beyond my materially based senses.
Parents cannot be created from their children;
although they must exist beyond simple observation.
Another example of cause and effect,
and it's simply impossible for the reverse to happen.
The bond between a mother and her child is never broken;
a debt formed which one day a year will never repay.
This voluminous amount of extraneous wording
must somehow lead me back to resolving the paradoxes.
A problem with The Smallest Piece paradox
is to assume OBJECTS are made of pieces.
All I know from actual field observation
is just the opposite—many OBJECTS are made from 1.
Zeno was in effect assigning arbitrary divisions
to an essence existing whole in itself!
It's possible some OBJECTS may be divided,
but unreasonable to assume it can be infinitely done.
Those divisions are useful to any RATIONAL analysis,
except when deciphering the nature of REALITY itself.
This mental exercise has indicated that the internal
composition of any OBJECT can't be truly known.

Any sequence of events depends on TIME to progress,
which is how CONCEPTION of OBJECT is in created MIND.

19:58

Maybe when I was dreaming freedom was out of my grasp,
I couldn't manage to catch it because I already had it.
A piece of DISTANCE or OBJECT could be much like freedom,
there are no parts because its existence is already whole.
But DISTANCES can be defined and then exactly summed up;
there are no DISTANCE pieces missing within the whole.
The Stadium is similar to The Smallest Piece paradox—
only imagination travels halfway to anywhere!
In this regard DISTANCE and OBJECT are quite alike,
CONCEPTS of REALITY depend on limited PERCEPTIONS.
In order to travel to some defined halfway point,
DISTANCE must be crossed, an end has to be reached.
If some DISTANCE hasn't been crossed,
then a traveler couldn't reach an assigned halfway point.
It is only considered a midpoint
because start and end have been arbitrarily assigned.
Those 2 points only have an imaginary existence;
start and end can be applied to any DISTANCE.
Each instance a midpoint is reached, so is an endpoint;
the former is arbitrarily assigned, the latter is forever.
I can consider DISTANCE to be CONCEPT like OBJECT,
which can be manipulated for mental convenience.
If INFINITY numbers of FINITY DISTANCES must be crossed,
arbitrary DISTANCE is assigned as part of the premise.
INFINITE DISTANCES aren't required to cross 1 DISTANCE;
DISTANCE can be crossed in INFINITE numbers of repetitions.
Each arbitrarily divided part of any DISTANCE
is still DISTANCE completed in and of itself.
DISTANCE is divided as another crutch to help support
RATIONAL manipulation of REALITY not otherwise malleable.
Arbitrarily assigning beginnings and endings
is not the way REALITY works outside of CONCEPTION.

Though there is no doubt DISTANCE as CONCEPT
is useful for progress within INANIMATE UNIVERSE.
Is it possible there is no such thing as DISTANCE;
how about DISTANCE perceived between OBJECTS?
Apparently there are 2 DISTANCES to separate:
DISTANCE as CONCEPT, and DISTANCE in REALITY.
Just as OBJECT is CONCEPTION, and OBJECT is in REALITY;
two IDEAS which are confusing when not separated.
Any fixed DISTANCE is a figment of imagination,
with no understanding of why OBJECTS exist separated.
Numbers on a page with no legitimate description
of REALITY DISTANCE as CONCEPTION purports to represent.
Like OBJECTS, the illusion could be something
resembling REALITY, or not.
DISTANCE must exist in REALITY for PERCEPTION to grab it,
yet what appears in actual MIND is something else.
Maybe it's like converting INFINITE into TRANSFINITE;
once DISTANCE becomes CONCEPT, its nature has changed.
What is the difference between those DISTANCES;
why is CONCEPTION not more like REALITY?
There are physical laws which determine why DISTANCE exists
among OBJECTS within INANIMATE UNIVERSE.
Yet DISTANCE as CONCEPTION is not an attempt to understand
how DISTANCE actually exists in its environment.
What I conceive of as DISTANCE may have nothing to do with
how OBJECTS are kept apart from each other.
DISTANCE is generally THOUGHT of as SPACE;
"keep your DISTANCE" means "keep SPACE between us."
Though not synonymous, they are the next best thing;
1 definition of DISTANCE is SPACE between 2 points.
Imagine DISTANCE and SPACE as two distinct essences;
would anyone then DREAM of crossing empty DISTANCE?
If SPACE and DISTANCE aren't the same,
when I'm crossing SPACE I may not be crossing DISTANCE.
IDEA of them may just be fanciful imagination,
or could DISTANCE exist outside of its spatial CONCEPTION?
The point is I really won't know for sure,
as long as CONCEPT and REALITY are kept far apart.

Substitute OBJECT for DISTANCE and obtain the same;
it has been indicated as either CONCEPTION or REALITY.
That is all due to these simple natural failings:
CONCEPT is inferior PERCEPTION is inferior REALITY.
There is no fixed DISTANCE, only continuous difference;
there is no fixed OBJECT, only whole disruption.
As long as I conceive of those realistic phenomena
as identical with CONCEPT, their REALITY will elude me.
The Stadium has the same problem as The Smallest Piece,
assigning arbitrary divisions to a whole essence.
That is a RATIONAL attempt to divide and conquer;
I can grab a branch much easier than a tree.
DISTANCE is not normally considered as a whole essence,
while OBJECT sometimes is, and sometime is not.
DISTANCE isn't considered to exist at all,
except in relation to SPACE existing between OBJECTS.
Once again imagine, each OBJECT or DISTANCE is a unique
essence created as part of the structure of REALITY.
Then DISTANCE is actually real, like OBJECT or FORCE,
not just a conceptual byproduct of SPACE.
Which leads to an obvious question:
what creates DISTANCE?

20:36

A pebble held in the palm of my hand is simple OBJECT,
and it can't be 1 and many at the same instant.
How can OBJECT keep dividing into smaller OBJECTS
if it is not multiple ones to begin with?
The paradoxes have shown me that OBJECT and DISTANCE
division follow a certain progression, but not how they do.
The Smallest Piece and The Stadium reveal how much
BRAIN strives to grab and hold on to nonexistent REALITY.
A RATIONAL view seeks after FINITE, as its nature demands;
even if the nature of REALITY isn't only FINITE.
Futilely grasping for RATIONAL convenience,
unless it is solely done within INANIMATE UNIVERSE.

Breaking a whole into parts is easier to grasp;
like whole trees cut into boards suitable for manipulation.
How can something only identified as itself when whole
be the same as what it is when it is no longer one piece?
Well, there isn't some supernatural FORCE keeping OBJECT
together at the same instant it's being taken apart.
Asking OBJECT to be itself when whole and in parts
is like asking a rock to reassemble itself.
Even my own reasonable self must readily admit,
if OBJECT is divided into parts, then it isn't 1 but many.
Know this to gain a better understanding of REALITY:
every OBJECT is complete and indivisible unto itself.
As any OBJECT exists on its own, beyond sense PERCEPTION,
it can't have any parts because they can't be measured.
Know this to gain a better understanding of CONCEPTION:
every OBJECT is an illusion fostered by PERCEPTION.
OBJECT is created by neural connections within my BRAIN;
each 1 existing until attention is focused elsewhere.
INTUITION does not share the need of a RATIONAL view
to divide REALITY into manageable bites.
But even CONCEPT of REALITY is a single essence,
which makes it possible for there to be multiple REALITIES.
And yet, existence of everything cannot be manifold;
this is what pure INTUITION is able to see.
ANIMATE UNIVERSE is home to the irrational perspective,
and there should be where it perceives unity to exist.
Why would INTUITION not see INANIMATE UNIVERSE,
when a RATIONAL view can approximate ANIMATE UNIVERSE?
An INTUITIVE view should be able to approach its opposite,
but it shouldn't be able to extend unity beyond its home.
As a RATIONAL view must cut REALITY into pieces,
INTUITION has no choice but to see REALITY as a whole.
Therefore INANIMATE UNIVERSE may actually be FINITE,
and only an INTUITIVE view sees it as something more.
A quite reasonable assumption to make,
except the explanation does not explain so much more.
OBJECTS which seem to be both many and 1;
DISTANCES which suffer from the same paradox.

How is Inanimate Universe able to be Finity,
and simultaneously have characteristics of Infinity?
My question exactly
if the universe of Infinite trespasses on the 1 of Finite.
Reality is all one essence, with dualistic universes,
only divided by the need to conceptualize existence.
So each universe is another mental illusion;
an Intuitive view can see Infinite no matter where it is.
That comes from the difficulty in expressing Intuition;
no matter how it is done, it comes out Rational.

21:01

Existence of Time in Dreams is exceedingly strange;
from my own part, it doesn't seem to be in them at all.
How could Time not exist within provincial Mind,
unless it was solely a product of Inanimate Universe?
But Dreams progress from scene to scene,
and this can't happen unless Time is there to move.
The final key to resolving the paradoxes concerns the lack
of Time involved in dividing essences, in Dreams or out.
Neither paradox makes any mention of required Time;
though some must progress for each to happen.
In The Smallest Piece, over Time moving into Infinity,
Infinity numbers of Finity Objects could form Object.
Given that amount of Time, almost anything could happen,
even to the extent of forming Infinite Object.
In The Stadium, again allowing for Infinity of Time,
Infinity numbers of Finity Distances could be crossed.
The paradoxes are intended to show arguments
against the existence of motion and plurality, not Time.
What does allowing for Infinity of Time accomplish;
should a walk across a stadium take this long?
Infinite Time allows for Infinite divisions,
which directly contradict the actual happening.
If Infinity Time cannot occur for Distance or Object,
does this indicate the paradoxes are flawed?

There is no obvious flaw in how they are constructed,
but it does seem as though INFINITE is the problem.
A typical answer from a RATIONAL point of view,
only one item can be the problem.
INFINITE divisions in INFINITE amounts of TIME is a problem;
the rest of the paradoxes just isolate FINITE essences.
Look at REALITY without an eye prejudiced by sense;
is its nature FINITY or TRANSFINITY or INFINITY?
TRANSFINITE is just a cover, and FINITE is too limited,
so it must be some degree of INFINITE measuring it.
Does that mean rocks and refrigerators do not exist;
if they are not INFINITY, then they should not be real?
Of course they are real, the implication is spurious;
they are a part of REALITY, not all of it.
Yet how can REALITY consisting of INFINITY be divided;
if it is all-inclusive, then should it not include everything?
There is no RATIONAL answer I can think of to offer;
REALITY is INFINITE, but FINITE essences are real too.
Think back upon INFINITY TIME and FINITY DISTANCE;
what about these two is causing a problem?
INFINITE TIME and FINITE DISTANCE don't mix,
neither do INFINITE TIME and FINITE OBJECT for that matter.
Precisely why TIME needs to be inserted right here,
it highlights the real problem built into the paradoxes.
INFINITE TIME will take literally forever to happen,
which is no good to either FINITE DISTANCE or OBJECT.
Understand INFINITY TIME and FINITY essence do not mix;
this is all that is required to resolve the paradoxes.

21:22

DREAMS mix together my experiences and imagination,
and then they become confused with my MEMORIES.
Cold hard facts mixing with hot uneven fancies,
out of which comes something in between, beholden to one.
Like TRANSFINITE, which lies between FINITE and INFINITE,
closely approaching 1, but it still resembles the other.

Zeno's paradoxes allow for a better understanding of
the relation between Finity and Transfinity and Infinity.
Those capacities are related to their involvement with sets,
which are only able to contain the former 2.
Modern claims for Infinity numbers of Objects as a set,
fully bypass each step which unfolds in the paradoxes.
The steps exposing each member of a set are unimportant;
they must only comply with extension and abstraction.
There is an objective in identifying each little step;
sets take these important steps and belittle them to none.
Endowing the process with the same status as the result,
which is fine, unless I desire some degree of success.
And yet if each step taken makes perfect sense,
then maybe the problem lies somewhere in between them.
A set is defined by its members, so must the process be;
if a member doesn't properly fit, then it isn't a full set.
Assumptions can arise between each of those steps,
which make complete sense, but are also irrational.
My concern is with sets which have no ending;
they are sufficient if the process creates a solid step.
A set of forever Objects still lands on Infinity's shore;
only treated as Transfinity for mathematical convenience.
Transfinite is close to Infinite for practical purposes,
as least as far as either Concept can be used.
Exactly the point:
Transfinity is a very close approximation to Infinity.
Approximation by its definition still misses the mark;
the paradoxical solution would have to fit in between here.
In order to resolve the paradoxes and truly see Reality,
the answer must be intuitively exact, not rationally close.
But if the message itself is to be rationally transmitted,
then no matter the resolution, it will still be inexact.
Zeno created his elean koans to induce understanding
that some Conceptions when fully examined are irrational.
Irrational Thought can't be communicated;
blog florp nip to was fo she la do mama mabbe dofi.
There is Purpose behind any sort of koan;
it cannot be explained, but the path to it can be shown.

Therefore the resolution to the paradoxes is INTUITIVE, because this perspective exposes personal PERCEPTION.

Take CONCEPTION of INFINITY, try to examine and define it;
no firm IDEA arises of what is dying to be expressed.

When I think INFINITE, I'm actually conceiving not-FINITE, and it's more properly not-FINITE and not-TRANSFINITE.

INFINITY is rationally known by what it is not,
and its two relations can be defined by <is> and <is not>.

FINITE is defined as being limited, not-TRANSFINITE; TRANSFINITE is defined as being unlimited, not-FINITE.

No other identifications will fit into RATIONAL THOUGHT;
INFINITY is not by any method rationally conceivable.

INFINITE can't be defined, but can be approximated, as that which is neither FINITE nor TRANSFINITE.

How can TRANSFINITY be defined as unlimited,
when the term seems to be INFINITY, spectacularly?

TRANSFINITE is a RATIONAL definition of INFINITE; there is no possibility of getting any closer.

Imagine INFINITY surfacing beyond definition;
learn what the word means, then learn how to lose it.

TRANSFINITE is a RATIONAL definition of what is unlimited; INFINITE is INTUITIVE REALITY of this same capacity.

REALITY of INFINITY is only experientially available within,
in the place where secrets are held, then exposed.

INTUITIVE CONCEPTS found herein can only be resembled in the same manner in which TRANSFINITE misses INFINITE.

Know this as TRUTH in REALITY:
seekers will always be able to get transfinitely closer.

TRANSFINITE approaches INFINITE like radioactive half-lives, each step getting infinitesimally closer, but still not there.

There is no way of knowing when the greatest level
of understanding has been reached, INFINITY is further still.

Strangely, INFINITE as CONCEPT both *<is>* and *<is not>*, a word existing with no meaning behind it.

DUALITY loses attachment on any approach to INFINITY,
since unlimited existence is beyond <is> and <is not>.

21:55

Between my THOUGHTS and DREAMS lies a boundary,
maybe best defined as the borderline of consciousness.
On one side lies that which fits neatly into explanation,
while on the other is a frustrating jumble of contradictions.
My THOUGHTS fetch back RATIONAL and INTUITIVE views,
from which 2 universes ultimately are produced.
The acceptable resolution of both paradoxes lies balanced
on the boundary between INTUITION and a RATIONAL view.
The structure of the argument is quite RATIONAL,
but statements without proof must be taken as INTUITIVE.
Zeno's original statements were much simpler,
and have been expanded to highlight specific points.
Simple statements can deceive the best of MINDS,
when they hide assumptions inside common IDEAS.
There is no paradox if one simple endeavor is discarded:
a limited RATIONAL attempt to comprehend INFINITY.
I heed what CONCEPT of INFINITE is supposed to mean,
but my senses only detect it going on and on and on . . .
*Analyzing Zeno's arguments boils down to stark IDEAS:
OBJECT or DISTANCE are pieces only within imagination.
OBJECT or DISTANCE, as CONCEPT, is a poor reflection
of what PERCEPTION detects from REALITY.
CONCEPTIONS can be taken apart and dissected into bits,
or multiplied beyond any hope of meeting the beast.
OBJECT or DISTANCE, in REALITY, may be composed of parts,
but none can ever be shown because of TIME'S progress.
* OBJECTS ejected from one OBJECT are an identification
of a sequence of events, not parts and pieces.
Many or 1 are dependent upon senses for detection,
and these only work in real TIME, not imaginary TIME.
An essence must exist for PERCEPTION to detect it;
transfer of information may be poor, but it does happen.
My problem is I have been so infected with propaganda
from SCIENCE, it's hard to think straight.
When fictions like pieces or half-DISTANCES are set up,
they impose legal limits on something truly limitless.

Even TRANSFINITE, as being that which has no end,
is still held in bondage by this very definition.
OBJECT and DISTANCE are not formed by parts and pieces;
they exist as what they are and they can be nothing else.
I so want to believe a rock divides into pieces,
mainly because I believe a rock is composed of parts.
Imagine pure water, believed made of atomic particles;
this basic postulate of demonology is not known for sure.
I recognize water can be divided into H, H, and O;
of course I'm assuming it's composed of these isotopes.
Remember always to follow Ockham's razor:
the theory with the fewest assumptions is best.
If I just follow PERCEPTION, OBJECTS are whole;
otherwise I can assume they are parts and pieces.
Also remember PERCEPTION can be mistaken; appearance
of one OBJECT could actually be an appearance of many.
Therefore a rock could actually be many things;
though in the form of OBJECTS, not parts and pieces.
No one can show where OBJECT starts and stops within;
it is only known by FORCES exerted from without.
If I could directly sense parts and pieces within OBJECT,
then they still could be illusions covering many OBJECTS.
No one can show parts and pieces of any real OBJECT
because there are none anywhere for anyone to examine.
I can make all of the reasonable assumptions I want,
but none of them will make TIME work in reverse.
No one can show where motion really starts and stops,
at least as long as LIFE'S preserver is continuously alive.
All I'm able to sense is that some DISTANCE
exists between this OBJECT and that OBJECT.
No one can show where motion may begin and end,
which must happen if many must compose one.
DISTANCE and TIME create never-ending-motion;
there is always another before and after.
More fiction created for motion to start and stop,
convenient for the mortal context in which LIFE operates.
I start work, I stop work, I begin running, I stop running;
false claims about how REALITY connects itself.

Necessities of language, and of course a limited LIFE span,
require those mini-fictions in order to grasp IDEAS.
More accurate: I drove to work, after I ate, after I washed,
after I got up, after I slept, after I went to bed, etc . . .
A more realistic communication of actual motion;
although not a terribly useful excuse for being late to work.
Motion is a whole just like DISTANCE;
walking across a stadium is done together, not in pieces.
The problem furtively rears its awkward and ugly head
when REALITY is confused with the utility of the fiction.
It's easy to fall under the spell of my motion as parts;
I can mentally picture each step within a broader bloc.
MIND becomes so used to perceiving REALITY in that light,
it is all but impossible to see that it is only a reflection.
My existence is lived according to that practical fiction;
nothing would ever get done if I couldn't conceive it.
Similar to the problem the gods of SCIENCE experience
in determining REALITY which is not practical or fiction.
Any practical measurement requires CREATION of an arbitrary
starting point in order to make REALITY available.
RATIONAL understanding of all TIME and SPACE is thus hard;
establishing fixed points in essences without them.
Modern SCIENCE has decreed no ABSOLUTE SPACE and TIME
because they can't be measured with any accuracy.
Being absolute, it is natural they cannot be measured;
this is not the same as proving they do not exist.
Which also determines ABSOLUTE TIME and SPACE
is outside the bounds of SCIENCE's administration.
Gods of SCIENCE have been, and will be, hampered and
facilitated by their RATIONAL criteria for a fixed reference.
No measurement has ever been taken with either end
of a tape left loose to become tangled in the wind.
REALITY is not a thing exposed for measurement;
it exists beyond a RATIONAL ability to show all of its secrets.
Received observations and measurements
are only an approximation of what REALITY truly is.
Gods of SCIENCE cannot exist without a start and an end;
REALITY has no room for these orphans in its home.

Which doesn't proclaim SCIENCE is useless, far from it;
it's the highest state of RATIONAL achievement.
Although CONCEPTION is part of REALITY because it exists,
its substance is no more than green cheese in the moon.
Any THOUGHT I have must exist somehow,
at the least it consists of neuroelectochemical signals.
THOUGHTS with start and end do have some vitality,
while REALITY they are supposed to mimic is empty inside.
So CONCEPTS in themselves have no "knowledge" existence,
but they must exist somewhere to have any function.
SCIENCE and math have facilitated a growth of knowledge,
a fiction which does not exist every where, or every when.

22:46

DREAMS I had earlier today possessed a limitless QUALITY,
defying any attempt I made to fit them into QUANTITIES.
Why should two dissimilar essences be combined
if they will just separate as soon as they are left alone?
If I can use the combination, cost vs. benefit will justify it;
even TRANSFINITE results from joining FINITE with INFINITE.
The actual cause of the paradoxes is the attempt
to combine a FINITY paradigm with an INFINITY paradigm.
REALITY is all 1, but its perceived perspectives are 2;
my BRAIN isn't capable of mixing them together.
Confining INFINITY to FINITY cannot be rationally done,
or even to mix them in any RATIONAL argument.
Zeno's paradoxes expose the universal antagonism
by using common sense to see how one-sided views fail.
The problem begins with CREATION of each paradox,
defining any OBJECT'S parameters or sporadic DISTANCE.
Either of which demand arbitrary measurement;
I know OBJECT and DISTANCE by their fixed QUANTITIES.
A zone of observation created for one strict use:
RATIONAL precision of CONCEPTIONS of INANIMATE UNIVERSE.
The better my senses of MATTER and its attributes are,
the better is my ability to use them constructively.

Once anything is subjectively defined as being Finity,
it is precluded from any possibility of Infinity meaning.
Infinite is itself precisely because it can't be defined,
which should make this sentence hard to understand.
The artificial definition of anything
as divisible Finity Object makes Infinity inaccessible.
It may be possible for Infinite attachment to all Objects,
but if I wish to use it, it must be rationally limited.
Finity Objects or Distances still must exist,
as anyone performing physical labor knows full well.
I'm not trying to envision Reality in a fashion
which is more silly than the 1's already extant.
Defined Object or Distance only exist to a Rational view;
thus Intuition has a more open-ended perspective.
Likewise Science and mathematics only exist to that view;
whatever an Intuitive view sees must be crossed over.
Infinity is irrational Conception bound by sophistry,
with secrets forbidden to open via Rational chanting.
Only Finite and Transfinite Concepts find any lucidity;
compensation for an inability to count beyond sensibility.
Infinity attaches to absolutes, any Quality, any Emotion,
or any other way of irrationally viewing Reality.
It's actually quite funny to see psychologists
attempting to quantify something as indefinite as Emotion.
Infinity is disconnected from Finity Object or Distance;
existing both large and small, it must reach everywhere.
A view: Finite is the linchpin between Infinites;
what I sense determines what I think everything else is.
Picture Reality as growing very large or very small,
between are trapped Finite essences holding it together.
Another view: Infinite is the linchpin between Finites;
my senses only give me illusions of greater Reality.
Picture Reality as little motes in the wilderness,
tumbling about lost in a magnitude betraying expression.
Each perspective offers advantages to its adherents,
and each 1 also carries too tangible trappings.
Yet why would either view have a better vantage point;
could not each one depend on the other?

I'm not able to comprehend them in that manner;
DUALISM insures that 1 and 1 consistently make 2.
Can INFINITY of the large attach to INFINITY of the small,
looping around out of view of material PERCEPTION?
That makes more sense than the other possibility;
multiple INFINITES are harder to fathom than just 1.
Thus all INFINITIES could in fact be just one,
some essence defying conceptual ability to multiply.

23:14

When the fever finally broke, I felt great relief,
which passed in almost the same instant it arrived.
Is it possible for a moment to last any longer;
do FINITY moments contain INFINITY moments?
INFINITY of the small may attach to INFINITY of the large,
but FINITE THOUGHTS have no hope of containing them.
So if one INFINITY cannot be rationally contained,
is it possible for flexible MIND to handle more than one?
That appears to be a non-starter as a question;
if 1 won't fit in my BRAIN, then more than 1 surely won't.
RATIONAL THOUGHT cannot contain multiple INFINITIES,
or any INFINITY, only CONCEPTIONS of INFINITY.
Multiple TRANSFINITES within RATIONAL capacity
are nothing like what INFINITES are within REALITY.
As INTUITION is not restricted to FINITY inhibitions,
it is also not restricted to seeing one essence covering all.
I had tentatively accepted unified REALITY, only 1,
and now an INTUITIVE view doesn't see only 1 at all.
INTUITION sees unity, not one, there can be many;
INFINITY of INFINITIES is possible from purifying this view.
Then INFINITE must be something other than QUANTITY,
if many exist, and rationally there can be only 1.
Can TRANSFINITES be used to represent multiple INFINITIES,
which would make understanding them possibly easier?
If multiple INFINITIES exist somewhere out there,
TRANSFINITES should be able to represent them adequately.

Any belief is allowed the masses, no matter how spurious;
ubiquitous governments have only tried to outlaw EMOTION.
If that substitution will help me understand REALITY,
then it's quite reasonable I should use it.
It cannot help to find continuing elusive essences;
REALITY *is not accessed through incomplete reflections.*
If I propose multiple INFINITES are possible,
it's only by treating INFINITE as 1 RATIONAL OBJECT.
The perceptive barrier between REALITY *and* CONCEPTION
clarifies that a one-to-one match is not possible.
Multiple INFINITES as derived from a RATIONAL view
create multiples just like any other OBJECT as CONCEPT.
Multiple INFINITIES, *as existing and observed by* INTUITION,
do not have any demarcations between one and many.
OBJECT in REALITY is limited to a FINITE existence,
unless of course all OBJECTS are part of 1 INFINITE.
Thus the defining characteristic of OBJECT, *individuality,*
could be false, and all REALITY *is truly one aetheric essence.*
But that would still only grant me 1 INFINITE embrace,
no other INFINITE could possibly exist.
INANIMATE UNIVERSE *forms one and then creates many;*
ANIMATE UNIVERSE *forms many and allows notice of one.*
Therefore OBJECTS I see are distilled from greater 1's,
each potentially INFINITE in its own right.
The way multiple INFINITIES *are derived in each view*
prevents TRANSFINITIES *from matching them in equity.*
Multiple INFINITES, which RATIONAL TRANSFINITES represent,
have nothing to do with unrelated INTUITIVE INFINITES.
TRANSFINITY *is merely the best* RATIONAL *approximation*
of any single observation gleaned from any universe.
Once INFINITE is established as RATIONAL OBJECT,
it can be treated just like any other solid substance.
In effect, this entire expiation is a glossy interpretation
of how multiples could exist without becoming OBJECTS.
It's difficult enough to estimate an INFINITE view rationally,
without piling on the problem of multiplying it.
Some rationalizations of INTUITION *may already be close*
to the absolute standard held just out of reach.

I can always get a little closer to realistic perfection,
but I can never hit the bull's-eye.
Form a mental picture of what Infinity *actually is;*
envision, beyond Object *identification, that which is, not.*
My neural image of Infinite patterns a picture in my Brain:
Stars and Stars laid out upon the night sky.
Animate Universe is blessed and cursed with Infinity,
so multiple Infinities *are quite possible here.*
Inanimate Universe is blessed and cursed with Finite,
so multiple Transfinites are quite possible here.
Yet everything alive is united in essence and Purpose;
barbed Conceptions *influence a desire for multiplication.*
So even if multiple Infinites do exist in Reality,
they are irrelevant except when rationally available.
There are no Objects *of* Intuition;
it cannot be transmitted in a language requiring parts.
The 1 hand: I can rationally see many possible Infinites,
all of them growing out of just 1.
A preference for isolation and self-reliance;
everything good or bad starts and ends with me.
The other hand: there is an Intuitive unity of many Infinites,
effectively making many of them into 1 Object.
A shift in attitude toward making many into one;
look back from far away and all seen is merely here.
Dual views and universes are opposite and incompatible,
neither 1 giving so much as an inch to the other.
Repulsive substances described by the I_____ word
should now only refer to some process of Intuition.
When I_____ is mentioned in any regard,
it must be recognized as infected with an Intuitive disease.
Transfinity is the closest term which will rationally approach
what the ends of Thought *can hope to reach.*

23:54

Joy best describes what I felt when the fever broke,
Emotion many people seem to feel too little.

Where does joy, or any EMOTION, begin and end;
is this where QUALIA of LIFE is to be found?
EMOTIONS begin and end with my expression of them,
my corporeal existence notes when they start and stop.
Even though there is no way they could be,
QUALIA and EMOTIONS are INFINITY in nature.
But I'm able to limit how I feel about something,
which should indicate EMOTIONS aren't INFINITE.
INFINITY cannot be measured or taken apart,
so any RATIONAL view of its existence is only a guess.
There are also degrees of QUALITY,
as indicated by good and better and best.
A part of REALITY perpetually out of material clutches;
try to lay hold of loops just beyond detailed fingertips.
I can touch a fabric and note its texture;
soft, hard, coarse, and silky are all measures of QUALITY.
Only one way leads to INFINITY views of REALITY:
look within to the individual connection of seeker and goal.
Looking within will lead me to encounter EMOTIONS,
but they still react to FINITE physical phenomena.
Beyond external sensation, it is beyond measurement;
to the SCIENCE gods' concern, INFINITY does not exist.
Which has no bearing on affecting QUALITY and EMOTION,
neither of which bother hard SCIENCE in the least.
INFINITY can never be absolutely proven to exist;
each seeker must go and find it for himself.
No man is able to write his own ticket;
whatever my MIND creates could be total fantasy.
QUALIA and EMOTIONS happen without interruption;
INFINITIES existing as non-OBJECTS without dissection.
There has been no evidence offered for that proposition;
what is within doesn't necessarily equate to what is without.
Experience a moment of sadness and ask a question:
where does it begin and where does it end?
It starts and ends based on some physical occurrence,
which TIME separates into a window for crying.
Depths of depression have no bottom on which to land;
to think otherwise is never to have felt unending despair.

So physical release starts and stops within TIME's trap,
but emotional feeling has no end to its depths.
How to arise for air from the bottom of INFINITY seas;
how to express boundless joy with insignificant words?
My physical existence doesn't forfeit itself to INFINITE;
EMOTION is still expressed with tears or laughter.
We touch those feelings as they touch us;
LIFE is INFINITY as long as they contribute their bounty.
The biomaterial realm grants limited LIFE to EMOTION;
my BRAIN's neurons can't fully handle an INFINITE existence.
QUALIA and EMOTIONS are patently difficult to place,
to try and put each INFINITY feeling in a home for FINITY.
They are placed where they have grown and feel at home;
my body reacts quite differently to individual feelings.
BEAUTY leads the eye of the beholder;
QUALIA affect us all and are only found within.
Never can I convey who and what meets my specs;
it's introduced and there it becomes something special.
Plato theorized many centuries ago an absolute standard
of BEAUTY out there . . . somewhere.
He could see it and still not get the words quite right;
what I express is only a reflection of what it is.
INFINITY BEAUTY exists somewhere in ANIMATE UNIVERSE,
individually accessed and viewed with flesh-tainted eyes.
BEAUTY appearing on a canvas or in a song
is a mere black-and-white portrait of spiritual REALITY.
True BEAUTY is lost in the midst of ego and history,
delusion and desire, profound and still a parody.
Still 1 I can own, or rent for a while;
each INFINITE QUALITY stands to measure for the rest.
There is no definition for joy or grief or BEAUTY;
the only place to find it is to look within for a caress.
But I see QUALITY and EMOTION expressed all around me;
this is when most people seek to increase their supply.
Capital CREATIONS foist external measures upon us;
what other orbs are able to see what is beautiful?
Seeking my own standards opens me up to hubris,
daring to follow my own path instead of a better vision.

Likewise with good or evil or any measureless QUALIA,
each individual view finds its own suitable answer.
That is a path to total anarchy,
with no defined standards of good and evil.
Society's standards are different from individual ones;
why should we expect them to fit together?
Because without a universal standard there is no right
to mandate which set of rules is better than another.
Right or wrong is one of the many eternal questions;
choose to partake INFINITY internally, or FINITY externally.

24:30

DREAMS don't exist where I can define them;
they appear to come from the same never-land as IDEAS.
INTUITION born of ANIMATE UNIVERSE feeds all THOUGHTS
and CONCEPTIONS which reside within INANIMATE UNIVERSE.
My RATIONAL perspective is based upon defined existence,
which is why INFINITE is so hard for me to objectify.
FINITY and TRANSFINITY, INFINITY and INFINITIES;
these are more dualistic divisions of REALITY.
Settling upon either gives rise to further THOUGHTS;
QUANTITIES are seen as many and 1.
FINITY is CONCEPTION solely within INANIMATE UNIVERSE;
TRANSFINITY and INFINITY cross what is to what can be.
The limits of materiality petitioning immortality,
1 essence seeks definition by what it almost is.
INFINITY is not-CONCEPTION solely within ANIMATE UNIVERSE;
INFINITY and TRANSFINITY cross what can be to what is.
A gap through which information slides;
knowledge gained beyond anything ever imagined.
TRANSFINITY reliably exists in an unreliable universe,
yet it only finds solace in its objectified realm.
A quantified expression of INFINITE is tangible;
it means something, and it finds substantial use.
INFINITY unreliably exists in a reliable universe,
yet it is only home on the immaterial range.

There must be something out there which defines INFINITE,
which makes it more than just insubstantial.
INFINITIES have no RATIONAL existence except as a vague
objectified multiplication of something that cannot exist.
From where my puny BRAIN supports its THOUGHTS,
multiple INFINITES are no different than 1.
INFINITIES are piled up where they are proper and right,
closer together than one from another.
Accessed by means which are rationally unavailable,
they are of even less use than 1 supreme INFINITE.
No IDEA will be transmitted without help from DUALITY;
RATIONAL access to REALITY is granted in this fashion.
TRANSFINITE is not-FINITE,
DUALISM of limited REALITY from a RATIONAL perspective.
Where there is one, there are many, and more;
what is felt real transcends that which is known real.
INFINITES are not-INFINITE,
DUALISM of endless REALITY from an INTUITIVE perspective.
Each universe is conceived subject to its own DUALITY,
dividing and dividing until it reaches its untamed version.
DUALISM exists solely from a RATIONAL perspective;
an INTUITIVE view has no PERCEPTION of this realistic split.
INFINITY wraps around FINITY from large to small,
an embrace sheltering substance from dissolution.
A real divide: RATIONAL FINITE QUANTITY INANIMATE UNIVERSE,
versus INTUITIVE INFINITE QUALITY ANIMATE UNIVERSE.
Yet remember there are no opposites and no differences,
unless some desire finds occasion to make use of OBJECT.

****

24:51

There is a house most familiar;
I know it, but it is like no place I have ever lived.
A hispanic friend of mine is out to smuggle some drugs;
what's his name, its like no name I have ever known?

He tests the weed with some chemicals in a bag;
shake and bake, it's immoral to sell fake poison.
We take the bag with us to go on an errand, then return,
meeting the house owners and their pseudo-daughter.
They start to grill me about this and that,
mostly their unfavorable comparison to the neighbors.
I tell them they have gotten their message wires crossed
with my actual words.
"You unfortunately have many
unfortunate similarities to those unfortunate people."
Just then the bag begins to smoke,
and we run as fast as we can down into their basement.
He is waiting for me down in the stunningly
appointed living quarters, and he is very afraid.
Of what I am not sure,
and question—why is he so young?
A bestial man locked inside the suburbs for many years;
disposing people, he is left in a bathtub with their remains.
I manage to slip past the keystone cops and escape;
imminently clear details, later they fog over and close.
I go over and visit a friend's house,
and my mother arrives with a little girl in tow.
We all go inside and I tell them to go away,
so they will not get hurt by the falling rain.
Grab some foam and a razor to shave off all my hair,
and drive away as the cops arrive; mom has turned me in.
This is important!
What does it mean? I know it has some meaning!
I have trouble with a Viper which looks like a Pac-Man;
it does not bite, but I am constantly afraid.
Then I am floating high in a zootrope, whatever that is;
far far above the earth.
It has very steep sides,
so it is best not to slip and fall to my DEATH.
Walking on the sides with velcro-like slippers on fabric;
it is like a planet suspended in a vacuum.
There are a lot of people there going to school;
many many girls with their heads in the clouds.

The guide shows me how to track fast through the sand;
racing and using my MASS as a brake.
I do not fall,
and I do not see anyone else fall either.
All of their words have meaning, as do their THOUGHTS;
is something hidden within them which cannot be defined?

Day VI _____

06:00

The past is MEMORY, *the future is* DREAM;
nothing exists beyond measureless present TIME.
Things must have existed in order for them to exist now;
TIME has no REALITY without a past, and probably a future.
If we would know the secrets to REALITY—
TIME *is the key!*
I'd like to know the secret to keep mine from running out;
every passing day releases more of my biomaterial sand.
What is it, what makes it tick,
what gives it motion, what makes it go?
Its existence is acknowledged by everything under STARS,
and still it can't be defined any better than pornography.
Aye, no one can firmly grasp that member;
apparent to all, and still slipping away from definition.
Strange for TIME to have so vital an influence on REALITY,
and no 1 even attempts to determine what it really is.
What is it made of
that it can hold such a profound dominion over existence?
Einstein and his heirs have made notable advances,
and they still haven't managed to penetrate its thick hide.
What about TIME *fills it completely obtuse;*
can something so prevalent be truly complex?
TIME, like MASS and EXTENSION, is BASIC QUANTITY;
SCIENCE has no methodology to light these holes.

342

While the gods of SCIENCE may not be able to see what it is,
this has not stopped them from trying to manipulate it.
Which fulfills the essential nature of those QUANTITIES,
a capacity for relating MATTER to SPACE by useful divisions.
Only one nature is relevant in an oily over-driven world:
TIME is king.
Though I might rage against TIME's undying inequity,
to force it to stop, it will continue to march me along.
Holding itself in stolid isolation, no audience granted,
TIME makes us serfs tilling the fields for a tyrannical ruler.
Within the walls of its existence I'm substantially free;
my choices work from its incessant pressure, not against it.
We ARE ruled by TIME, make no mistake;
first comes LIFE and next comes DEATH, no reversal.
Even dumb rocks and animals know no better;
every OBJECT must exist from each moment to the next.
TIME is not the final judge of all possible tangents;
although it and only it grants how much will fit into now.
This moment could last as long as a second,
or it could be the merest sliver of a microsecond.
Over the many eons recognizing its viable essence,
humanity has assumed TIME to be immutable.
<Tick-tock> it kept on moving at a steady pace,
until Einstein came along and threw out primitive beliefs.
Even Einstein only modified it at near-light speeds;
why did he, and why do we, accept it to be this way?
Because motion is the only proven way to change it;
no other phenomena seem to slow it down.
Is TIME this . . . thing . . . wrapping around everything,
an essence seemingly endless and still limited by light?
That is the best view of TIME currently proposed;
hands off its nature, and hands on its applications.
Increasing technology has had minimal effect on TIME;
the infernal TIME clock still ticks away man's existence.
For millennia devices have existed to measure TIME,
which change its environment, but not its coverage.
It is a race to reach there before TIME runs out—
where?

It doesn't matter,
grabbing the ring is part of the race.
Pick a direction and strive toward some fantasy goal,
until TIME *catches up and rewards* DEATH—*the end.*
It does seem kind of silly to race against an unknown
opponent to a place I can't see.
Why should mankind try so hard to defeat TIME
while also not trying to understand what makes it tick?
A race run by rules I can't understand,
ending when some mysterious FORCE intervenes.
Nobody explains why we should follow TIME'S *dictates;*
other than merely because nobody understands its nature.
It may well be beyond my capacity for comprehension;
TIME is a shifting and wriggling solid presence.
That is an insufficient answer frequently offered;
it is failure not to try, it is fate not to succeed.
But it's QUANTITY furnished to be vast and powerful;
it invades every OBJECT and every corner of SPACE.
As with any problem, there is only one place to begin:
what is TIME?

****

7:04

A wise man once said: taking no THOUGHT *for tomorrow,*
blessed are those who do not lay up treasures on earth.
The situation I'm in doesn't make that too difficult;
some dirt over in the corner might make a nice pile.
Those shall be blessed who know it from a curse,
which should be neither given nor received.
Grasping after treasure is just following animal instinct,
like rats and squirrels hoarding their precious belongings.
In essence, treasure is born from value,
an instinct made necessary to know glitter from dross.
An inclination helping me to decide on appropriate actions;
therefore I'll know which are least likely to waste TIME.

If no plans were formed to acquire treasure in bulk,
would anything under the sun have any value at all?
All known as good upon the material earth is from treasure;
even acts of charity are treasured by the donors.
Treasure itself does not divide good from bad,
for the LOVE of money is the root of all evil.
Therefore the action of amassing treasure isn't the problem,
personal applied value leads to damnation.
Where are treasures stored if not upon this earth;
where else can a gem exist but where it shines?
Treasure and the value applied to it are distinct identities;
it's easy to cherish essences far removed from money.
Apply value to personal longings no else can see,
or treasure LIFE writhing in a mud-spattered home.
It can't be anything which will fit into my palm,
nor anything which this same palm can touch and tell.
There can be only one place to find those values:
not in what is sensed, only in what is felt.
Which would mean anger and hate are treasures;
if they open heaven, I have enough for myself and others.
No . . . it is not just defined CONCEPTIONS agitating the path,
it is the actual feeling, not even love.
But there is no other place for love and anger to matter;
whether wanted or not, they arise and are treasured.
When feeling within, there is a spark attached to nothing,
an eternal moment which is given a name—EMOTION.
I can understand how not to lay up treasure upon earth;
weighing that which doesn't exist is beyond my intellect.
It flares brightly inside the eye of MIND,
and then just as quickly dies to be replaced by another.
Therefore treasured EMOTIONS are false gods,
nothing but pale reflections of what they represent.
To the supreme value are attached drab THOUGHTS;
woolen coats loosely tossed onto silken skin.
The "thing" I must value has no physical relevance;
whatever I think it to be slips into something else.
Those feelings have no past and no tomorrow;
they are now and only now, and never anything but now.

When I attach myself to anger or love,
I become Concept, no longer in touch with either Emotion.
The values within are those interminably now feelings
which cannot exist as Thought for tomorrow.
If I define myself by Thoughts, without Emotion,
then I'm giving my very self over to the past or the future.
External treasures are part of a temporal comparison,
or granted an appearance through gold-tinted glasses.
There is nothing wrong with either anger or love;
my hold on Emotion is what changes it into treasure.
Thoughts are not Emotions, only words on feelings within,
flying to the surface as each moment is freed from now.
My Concepts are as much treasure as any diamond;
things at home in a material, not an immaterial, world.
Faux treasures are held by those superficial transients,
inbreeding with one another to perpetuate the species.
Thoughts I have are responsible for more of the same,
so if 1 isn't stopped, it will soon become a hoard.
A true blessing is as immeasurable as is its true value;
an essence which disappears as it begins cannot be held.
I hold in my hand or Brain the appearance of permanence,
left there by the kingly right of Thoughts to succeed.
Feeling is the treasure which cannot be held;
lose those Thoughts which try and fail to trap Emotion.
But they are such a comfort in my loneliness;
no other than Thoughts give succor to mental anguish.
To find true treasure give no care for days gone, planned,
bending no knee to those who spread the filth of guilt.
It's difficult to imagine how to continue along that path,
material existence demands I proceed rationally.
If it does not come from within and lingers to stain,
a false attachment can only quaff from Life's cup.
It's natural to use Thoughts arising from within,
but unnatural to force Thoughts to mate with Time.
Follow the advice of mystics and just let go;
exist in the moment because any other Time is unreal.

07:39

There is a clock in the hall in its own metal cage,
a prison which firmly holds TIME in its grasp.
Is there any way to stop PASSAGE of TIME;
if it is freed from its watchful jail, will it die?
Since I haven't got any IDEA, even the slightest,
as to what TIME is, I don't know if it could ever stop.
To know if it starts or stops, delve into its nature—
where is the beginning of TIME'S path, is it INFINITY?
Asking a better question may lead to better results;
stalking the unknown should begin with what is known.
What are some QUANTITIES normally found with TIME,
and what are some QUALITIES also associated with it?
1. TIME can be transfinitely large or transfinitely small,
stretched around between out there and in here.
How can TIME be so much like INFINITY
when it is also so much a part of INANIMATE UNIVERSE?
The divisions of TIME keep it accessible for general use;
dividing and multiplying them lead to its extremes.
Is TIME built up layer upon layer like supposed MATTER,
or is it one whole essence with observable parts?
2. It's continuous and cohesive throughout REALITY;
every known essence experiences the progress of TIME.
Is it an experience exactly the same for all;
do OBJECTS see the same second or the same eon?
OBJECTS are perceived by determination of their moments;
my knowledge of their existence necessitates TIME.
We may perceive TIME as something less than it is,
and thus conceive it as something more than it is.
3. Its transit is a vector moving in a positive direction;
SCIENCE fiction is fun, but reverse travel is still a myth.
As Hawking has suggested for that proposition:
if there are reverse TIME travelers, where are they now?
TIME isn't subject to alteration of its basic flow;
SCIENCE only manages its relations with other OBJECTS.
Is there any identifiable OBJECT within worldwide purview
able to reverse, or even halt, TIME'S march?

4. Its measurement gives it a physical existence;
a FINITE capacity placing it firmly in the material realm.
What does it mean to measure TIME;
does this have anything to do with achieving motion?
SCIENCE has little to say other than it's BASIC QUANTITY,
partaking in REALITY along with MASS and EXTENSION.
Why are the gods able to measure BASIC QUANTITIES;
is this capacity an existential requirement?
5. It appears to be much like SPACE,
whatever and wherever this other expanse belongs.
What is the real connection between SPACE and TIME;
is there one point or many where they consummate?
TIME in concert with SPACE forms a continuum,
whirled and swirled into the lumpy fabric of the universe.
A fabric which is supposedly modified by GRAVITATION,
or more correctly by FORCES resulting from interaction.
Those are the initial parameters I have regarding TIME;
no doubt incomplete, but sufficient for my reflections.
Since that is the way TIME is currently viewed,
pursue each THOUGHT individually to see what pops out.
I hope to be able to pierce through TIME's thick hide,
and find some clue as to what makes it tick.
TIME, as currently conceived, is a dead weight;
thus current assumptions about it should be denied.
I'm not yet in a position to draw but 1 conclusion:
TIME exists.
It is not the fourth dimension; it is not moved by GRAVITY;
there is no travel back in TIME; there is ABSOLUTE TIME.
Statements contrary to what many notable physicists think;
no basis has been offered for a new temporal theory.
Any extant postulate misses what TIME is about because
no attempt is made to understand its nature and function.

08:07

The round school-like clock has no second hand,
so it seems to take forever for 1 minute to click by.

If TIME moves at the same rate for all existence,
why should watching a clock seem to make it slow down?
There is a disconnect between TIME and my sense of it;
focusing on its flow transports me out of limited awareness.
Is there some aspect of INFINITY associated with TIME;
whether large or small, do they both offer perspective?
TIME can be split into minute fragments,
then further and further divided like 1 of Zeno's koans.
Hopefully those reflections on INFINITY will now pay off,
and enlighten sleepy MIND with the smallest unit of TIME.
If TIME exists within INANIMATE UNIVERSE, it's FINITE;
and it shouldn't be possibly INFINITE, but TRANSFINITE.
So what is the smallest TRANSFINITY bit of TIME;
where do seconds stop dividing and go no further?
The lower inner boundary of TIME should occur
when nothing actually happens and there is no action.
If there is a difference between moments or in OBJECTS,
there will be at least a minimal progression of TIME.
But as with the paradoxes it's hard to pinpoint;
the smallest bit is TRANSFINITE, and I can know no more.
Then, does TIME start when motion does,
or does it begin with the existence of OBJECT?
No-TIME equates to no-existence and no-action,
and as long as something exists, then so does TIME.
Which seems to indicate no-TIME some-TIME in the past;
can it get both very small, and very remote?
That just opens another potential paradox,
unless either small or remote CONCEPT of it is inaccurate.
It seems as though TIME must stretch into the past;
how else are OBJECTS supposed to get here from there?
TIME in the past is subject to 2 possibilities:
1 is the big bang, and the other has no beginning.
The former runs into an immediate problem:
how did it happen unless TIME previously existed?
SCIENCE's IDEA is of everything coming from nothing,
and therefore no BASIC QUANTITIES existed then either.
Once again another paradox is encountered;
one right, one wrong, both right, or both wrong?

There is no way to show when Time really began;
though its paradoxical nature infers both aren't right.
If Time did begin with the big band sound,
does this not indicate Time is of a physical nature?
Mass and Extension can be held in the palm of my hand,
but Time is somehow different, it's ephemeral and not.
What if Time had no beginning, was past Creation,
then what would be its nature?
Then it shouldn't be included within Basic Quantities;
it would be totally unlike what the others are.
Time's past may be too difficult to decipher,
so try to imagine how Transfinity Time exists at present?
At this instant, the 1 just passed,
Time didn't exist because it wasn't moving.
Then how does Time exist here and at other Stars;
is it not ever-present to work everywhere at once?
Time itself is detected by its motion;
it can't be both an essence, and the motion of the essence.
Imagine Time is not just like Mass and Extension,
only similarly lacking understanding as to why they exist.
Then Time in the present is also a paradox;
it seems to be everywhere, and is moving at the same pace.
Now try to look at what Time is in the future:
how does it exist different from past and present?
That Time hasn't yet occurred, though it's predicted;
maybe not with total accuracy, but enough for Science.
Events are predicted, not Time, it is just the vehicle:
is it possible Time does not exist into the future?
If Time doesn't extend transfinitely into the future,
then there is no existence beyond now.
Time into the future is a big mystery;
only Mind can truly go there since it cannot be observed.
So if I were able to use Time travel to go into the future,
I would still only exist within a different present.
Future happenings are predicted because of the past,
when Time in either does not seem to really exist.
Science tells me Inanimate Universe will contract,
or all usable Energy will eventually run out.

Yet that is just extrapolation based on present patterns;
there is no way of experiencing TIME beyond now.
Something will happen to the production of events
which will make TIME cease from 1 moment to the next.
Assuming TIME exists beyond now,
when the only proof offered is its permanent home—here.
If I consider TIME to be transfinitely large and small,
I have a problem also stretching it into the past and future.
What about endless TIME into the past or future;
how and where do they obtain existence?
If TIME has a TRANSFINITE existence, they don't;
past or future TIME are just productions of fantasy.
How does TIME exist in the here and now
unless it comes from the past and goes to the future?
Think of the past as a moving present existence;
inexorably moving onward, with nothing left behind.
A wall of events all moving in concert;
yet how do they exist now unless they existed previously?
I'm looking for the structure of REALITY;
TIME, as it existed in the past, has no presence.
TIME is movement;
still, how can present TIME be more valid than the past?
If TIME stretches transfinitely into macro and micro SPACE,
both those expansions could only exist within the present.
Imagine dualistic types of TIME actually exist;
the one term nominally used is insufficient to cover it all.
Then TIME could transfinitely stretch in 2 directions,
and still might not exist in the past or future.
What if there is no such thing as present static TIME,
and if TIME must change, what could this TIME be?
Under those conditions,
present TIME is merely the change from past to future.
TIME could feel present because it is experienced;
although its realistic existence is merely a transition.
Therefore past, present, and future are all fictions;
this aspect of TIME is merely metamorphosis.
Two different TIMES of TRANSFINITY are still left,
attaching to SPACE both large and small.

But that is present TIME dividing so far,
which has just been introduced as not existing at all.
Inaccurate, because present TIME must exist;
it just exists dynamically, not statically.
So past, present, and future are static representations
of a dynamic action extending in TRANSFINITE directions.
TIMES of TRANSFINITY are either none or one or two;
any more than these leave the bounds of perspective.
None makes no sense so I cast it aside,
and 2 is the dualistic predilection my BRAIN is given.
TIME meets where all TRANSFINITIES do,
at the intersection conceived as one genuine INFINITY.
My limited capacities only view perspectives 1-by-1,
which divide INFINITE TIME into 2 TRANSFINITES.
Picture a greater view of TIME to be like a mobius strip;
each side appears distinct, unless belief is illusion.
The other aspect of TIME attaches TRANSFINITE SPACES,
stretching out and in so far they eventually meet.
Thus TIME is divided into two distinct CONCEPTIONS:
one with SPACE, and one which continuously changes.
Each CONCEPT is based on different PERCEPTIONS:
TIME attaches to everything, and TIME is in motion.
Both are TIME, yet how can they be,
unless there is more to TIME than we are led to believe?

09:05

Each minute, each second, is attached to its neighbors;
continuity of TIME spells doom forward and regret back.
The trait of TIME which makes it continuous and coherent
sounds like a good place to pursue it further.
Yes . . . continuous and coherent,
bringing opposites together might require these QUALITIES.
Could TIME be merely an awareness of continuity,
where there is no past or future because all is one?
If it's continuous, then it's an unbroken whole essence;
no matter how many types there are, they all roll into 1.

Imagine TIME is not continuous;
where else could PERCEPTION of continuity come from?
Possibly from SPACE,
but I don't know how to separate 1 from the other.
Continuity of TIME is viewed periodically—
tick tock tick tock.
Each passing second is distinct from another;
tied to those before and after, seemingly continuous.
Is it possible for TIME to be continuous,
and still move to a rhythm which shakes the universe?
It could be like a sine wave, continuous while varying,
but supposedly 1 second doesn't vary from another.
TIME as a heart pulsing to a repetitious beat;
a clock by which REALITY orders its events.
That is why TIME can be measured to such great effect;
it can be made extremely accurate and it doesn't vary.
Why should events be required to follow TIME;
what vagary of REALITY makes this more than probable?
The frequency of any event uses a second as its reference,
or an event's duration can be similarly measured.
A second is itself seen as a periodic measurement;
what does a second use to set its period?
A second is a measurement of how TIME keeps moving,
existing the same for me as for my chair.
Could a second be some special QUANTITY
above and beyond reference requirements?
A second has material phenomena to which it's referred,
measuring how events repeat for my PERCEPTIONS.
The reference for a second is TIME and nothing else;
still open is the relation between one thing and itself.
A second doesn't just appear out of nowhere;
like any perceived effect, every second has some cause.
There must be some more basic source for a periodicity
using the second as the basic unit of TIME's progress.
If an event transpires in 1 second,
then it occupies TIME just as OBJECT occupies SPACE.
The grand inference—TIME is much like SPACE,
so how can one move unless the other one does?

I conceive of things moving in SPACE, not itself in motion;
a similar consideration would mean TIME is static.
Imagine TIME is a big ball moving through SPACE,
changing its face based on where it appears.
That ball of TIME would have to change place per TIME,
and I won't define TIME in terms of itself.
If TIME is truly continuous, then how can it move;
what is uniquely viewed as the progression of TIME?
Conceiving TIME attached to everything, and also moving,
is difficult when both of them appear to exist continuously.
There must be some rationale for why this trait is shared;
what are some things observed to be continuous?
TIME, SPACE, LIFE, MIND, OBJECT, DISTANCE, ENERGY, etc.;
where division of a thing seems to lead to TRANSFINITE.
Many of those essences are perceived as immaterial,
yet is their continuity in REALITY mental or physical?
A question which tends to slip past the point:
(dis)continuous TIME (can't) must be mental or physical.
Try and compare TIME to another continuous essence;
see whether this will lead to a better grasp of what it is.
As I sense SPACE, it has the following attributes:
infinitely large and small, and continuous just like TIME.
It has other habits which give SPACE more definition;
these may help to further distinguish TIME.
SPACE is omni-directional, its locations are relative,
and it's defined by the absence of OBJECTS existing within it.
Now look carefully at what has been enunciated;
what is SPACE when extraneous THOUGHTS are set aside?
When I look at what forms CONCEPT in my BRAIN:
SPACE is what isn't there!
Actually VOID is what is not there;
although since it is beyond PERCEPTION, SPACE will do.
Therefore, if SPACE is the absence of OBJECTS,
it's possible for TIME to also be the absence of something.
Perceiving continuity by the absence of continuity;
which essences could be absent and account for TIME?
There is more to TIME than exists in BIOMATTER,
but my MIND must exist in order to recognize TIME.

Could TIME be the absence of unhindered MIND,
something existing outside of this developed domain?
That does make some sense as strange as it sounds;
my MIND in deep meditation doesn't progress in TIME.
How could TIME and independent MIND be attached,
if all OBJECTS seem to experience the transit of TIME?
No cause I can believe would instill MIND into a rock;
there is more to TIME than its content in THOUGHT.
If SPACE is absent OBJECTS, and TIME is absent MIND,
then the difference is in its PERCEPTION, not its REALITY.
So TIME might exist where my MIND can't possibly exist,
which seems to defy a distinct ordering of THOUGHTS.
Steady MIND exists with THOUGHTS, and beyond their spin,
at least as they are now normally understood.
TIME can't be just the absence of MIND
because even THOUGHTS must pass from 1 to the other.
Lettuce leaf off THOUGHT about THOUGHTS,
for it grows into a path leading to an imperceptible thicket.

09:48

Sitting here, I experience the continuous flow of TIME,
but I don't detect how each second connects to the others.
Is continuity truly experienced
if one moment is noticed not to be the same as the next?
Experienced TIME is my observance of TIME'S progress,
not TIME in itself.
What about TIME is observed as continuous,
if actual sensation is of one moment, and then another?
Continuity I imagine as characteristic of TIME
is actually consistent QUANTITY describing its progress.
Remember SPACE for its lack of sensible OBJECTS,
with the possibility of being replaced by one.
Maybe TIME could be the lack of continuity,
with the possibility of being replaced by a second.
An essence is continuous as long as it is the essence;
TIME might be unique because it violates this rule.

But there is no other way to form CONCEPT rationally;
if TIME isn't continuous, then I can't understand it.
Visualize it as an essence existing in the past,
there is still no knowledge as to when TIME began.
That is part of my current understanding of TIME;
it continuously exists, but I don't know how far back.
Foresee the very same essence into the future as long
as it continues to exhibit this essence's characteristics.
I don't believe TIME might be continuous front to back,
and simultaneously not continuous in between.
Imagine something like the boat of Theseus,
where individual planks are removed one by one.
Eventually some point must be reached
where there are no more planks, or no more boat.
Which leads to THOUGHT identifying continuity:
at exactly what point does the boat cease to be a boat?
Either it's a boat as long as I conceive it to be a boat,
or as long as I perceive it continues to function as a boat.
Two methods by which REALITY is understood;
one comes to reticent MIND, and one comes to sensation.
If it's the former, then any definition depends on belief,
and this doesn't fit the form of a definition in my book.
Does PERCEPTION of function require CONCEPTION
if reticent MIND is to recognize anything at all?
The difference to note is between my MIND and OBJECT,
not in how PERCEPTIONS turn into CONCEPTS.
Any OBJECT, or essence, can be defined as what it is,
if it continues to behave in the manner making it distinct.
My PERCEPTION of a boat is defined by its existence;
if it behaves like an anchor, I won't perceive it as a boat.
A pile of driftwood can be used as a boat;
PERCEPTION of any existence is not an absolute.
A boat will no longer be a boat when it ceases functioning
in a manner which my THOUGHTS would tend to call a boat.
Which requires PERCEPTION of its function,
and CONCEPTION of this PERCEPTION, to remain a boat.
The boat has an existence outside of my MIND,
but its function meets its essence only as CONCEPT.

The problem is identifying where the boat starts and stops,
not whether the boat continuously exists in REALITY.
Determining where any essence begins and ends
is an inherent difficulty when using RATIONAL CONCEPTS.
Continuity of TIME, like the boat, should not be in dispute;
functional CONCEPTION and direct experience are detached.
Arbitrarily framed for the convenience of any observer,
I have no defined sense of the nature of TIME.
Which is why TIME might be the absence of continuity,
as SPACE is an essence beyond direct PERCEPTION.
I still sense the continuous existence of events happening,
and infer TIME'S progression from these PERCEPTIONS.
The boat is continuous in liaison MIND or REALITY;
does this conclusion imply TIME must be, or not?

10:16

The minute hand on the clock clicks off bit by bit;
it looks as if it springs forward too far, and then snaps back.
A piece of TIME sliding across its neighbors' boundaries;
is it continuous if each of its measurements is inexact?
TIME is very exact, it's the most available QUANTITY;
progress of SCIENCE is measured by the accuracy of TIME.
Would there be continuity of OBJECTS and events
if they could be exact, but there was no observer?
Any measurement requires an observer,
so quantification of TIME must fit within this rule.
Forget TIME for a second, since its essence is not known:
what about anything available to sensory experience?
OBJECTS and events would still exist,
but no sense of continuity results from no PERCEPTION.
Why must those two "terms" be connected;
what about their essences forms this bond?
PERCEPTION requires my senses to be continuous;
no matter into what little bits it may be divided.
Second is a name given to ideally divided bits of TIME,
distinctions made of some continuous aspect.

Each and every second, in a sense, must be continuous;
their linkages make sure TIME will flow normally.
Continuity is required for an essence to be one, the same;
division creates something no longer one, not the same.
But it isn't useful unless some divisions are made of it,
and I still believe my REALITY is sensed as continuous.
Is a physical body actually able to sense continuity,
or does some other process make this possible?
I see or touch boats or chairs, and know them continuous;
if any 1 was broken, it would be more than 1 OBJECT.
Continuity exists as CONCEPTION formed from PERCEPTION,
and detection ability is limited in a corporeal body.
Vision to light frequencies, hearing to audible vibrations,
and other senses are limited by exterior molecular contact.
Many frequencies and molecules known to exist
are interspersed with SPACE and remain undetected.
But their existence must still be detected by senses,
even if those senses are magnified by machines.
Human beings cannot detect below a certain level;
dogs have much better sniffers than human beings by birth.
Similar to what is done with analog to digital conversion;
a sampling rate is more accurate with more detection.
Eyes, ears, and such approximate a continuous presence;
so it is not perceived, only interpolated based on five tries.
Therefore it isn't possible for me to detect real continuity
because my body is limited in its sensory capacities.
Things interpreted as continuous may have this capacity,
yet sensation will never possess its true PERCEPTION.
Light appears to be continuous,
but it's now supposed to arrive in quanta.
How can it actually be both;
is the whole CONCEPTION of continuity based upon fiction?
Its common definition just requires it to be unbroken,
though nothing is said about the level of detection.
Could nothing within INANIMATE UNIVERSE be continuous,
and only limited sensation leads us into a false promise?
That may be possible and at the same instant irrelevant;
I still perceive continuity and attach it to TIME.

If continuity does exist somewhere out in REALITY, it is more
than what sensation is able to discover about it.
I assume the continuity of a chair while I can't prove it,
it just continues to act as a chair.
A chair will continue to act as a chair even though
it is changing from the chair it was to the chair it will be.
The only link between my CONCEPT of a chair and my sense
of it is a RATIONAL assumption—the chair is continuous.
It is a bad habit to assume what sensation determines
as continuous is some necessarily defined part of REALITY.
Using the chair as support, I conclude my senses
also can't determine real TIME has a continuous aspect.
How silly does this sound to the untrained ear:
only CONCEPTION accounts for a chair's continuity?
But this is the way predictions are always made:
the future is real because the past will hold true.
CONCEPTIONS formed from assuming non-existent PERCEPTIONS
will not lead to an accurate view of REALITY.
If my only sense of the transit of TIME is its continuity,
my only proof is assumption based on past sensed events.
Human CONCEPTION of TIME may just be a bad habit
of regularly assuming that what has happened will happen.
That does coincide with some relativistic observations,
where TIME only progresses in relation to an observer.
Is this something RATIONAL MIND could learn to accept,
conceiving TIME'S transit based on an observer's senses?
It's difficult ever to accept my sensory limitations;
if my vision deceives me, maybe my touch will be better.
Remember the most important point from this reflection:
what TIME is in itself will not be known just by sensation.
TIME is obviously something because events happen,
but my past CONCEPTS of it must now be thrown away.
PERCEPTION is too limited to grant INFINITY access,
so continuity is not an attribute pasted onto TIME.
I'm not able actually to sense any continuity of TIME,
and other continuities are based on this past indiscretion.
Thus TIME is neither continuity nor its absence;
since the former is illusion, the latter makes nonsense.

10:56

No matter when or how I look at the clock,
it's still ticking in the same direction, at the same rate.
Another aspect of TIME may better serve to illuminate it:
its progression as a vector with magnitude and direction.
TIME'S capacity for QUANTITY acknowledges magnitude,
and it has 1 accepted direction, which is forward.
Why should TIME have those capabilities;
what relation to REALITY enables its unique presentation?
I recognize TIME'S progress because of positive motion,
allowing distinction between 1 moment and the next.
Is it possible for TIME to have a defined magnitude,
and still be able to move in at least one other direction?
Fiction of SCIENCE believes travel back in TIME,
in a negative direction, isn't only possible, but likely.
Yet how would anyone recognize that transition,
if an ability to detect REALITY is based on normal TIME?
Hollyweird just reverses the film and shows this picture;
occurrence of previous events would be the same, reversed.
That makes so many assumptions it is not worth debating;
TIME as celluloid is at best a representation of REALITY.
The other popular notion is a TIME travel device,
where the tourist would just pop out into the past.
Which is even more bizarre than the first suggestion;
how can things just start materializing out of nowhere?
I'm listing the possibilities, not agreeing with them;
there doesn't seem to be a capacity for reverse TIME travel.
Examine the possibility from a strict practical view:
does nature provide evidence of a negative temporal path?
None from nature or any type of unnatural experiment;
my senses only recognize TIME'S forward direction.
Until some solid counter proof is offered,
the possibility of reverse TIME travel is reliably denied.
If some created machine is able to reverse TIME,
then I will gladly eat my words and pay for a trip.
Go out on a limb and take it one step further:
if reverse TIME exists, an aetheric view of REALITY does not.

Looking backward doesn't help me open TIME'S secrets;
I have to examine what it is, not what it might be.
What does one forward direction say about TIME;
what can RATIONAL MIND conclude from this observation?
If I place TIME upon a 360° reference,
then it doesn't veer from 1 path, say 0°.
How is it possible for all REALITY to move uniformly
in a singular direction without any additional goading?
Some natural phenomenon must account for it,
and there must be none, 1, or many to make it happen.
Imagine nothing makes TIME move positively;
what arrangement would make this possible?
It's BASIC QUANTITY like MASS and EXTENSION,
and this is my sense of it, not what it actually is.
Thus TIME may not be moving at all;
we sense events happening and attribute this to TIME.
If all existence is AETHER and part of 1 essence,
then I'm only part of it detecting other parts moving.
It is quite possible nothing is motivating TIME;
accept it as an essence beyond cause and move on.
If TIME is an effect, rationality demands it has a cause;
if TIME is a cause, it's its own source to my PERCEPTION.
Could many goads move TIME in a positive direction,
leaving many different causes with one general effect?
That would require massive coordination among causes,
so many common effects are generally perceived as 1.
Yet PERCEPTION is imperfect, as has been introduced;
one general TIME may just be a convenient fantasy.
So . . . many different causes could result in joined effects,
or TIME is actually many, and I just don't know it.
Finally, there could be one overseer whipping TIME,
one source making all things flow.
That option is the most rationally probable,
and why I tend to view TIME as a distinct essence.
Which means none or one or many all seem possible;
how can TIME be concurrently sourced from each of them?
There is only 1 conclusion I can draw:
TIME is none, TIME is 1, and TIME is many.

The reflection on direction is rapidly leading to nowhere;
distinguish the other part of TIME'S vector, magnitude.
It's distinguished into hours and minutes and seconds,
but math lets them go backwards as well as forwards.
What is the nature of that unnatural progression;
can numbers truly represent existence beyond REALITY?
Imaginary numbers cover TIME'S reverse motion;
accepted because of an easy rationale—the numbers work.
Some people allow math to do their thinking for them;
faith in numbers is just another set of gods to worship.
Math is a concise language for correlating THOUGHTS;
modern society requires this capacity to function.
Using math is like programming modern appliances,
using bad instructions instead of independent THOUGHTS.
Instructions are usually the best path, unless they are bad,
and then there is no recourse but to think on my own.
People with independent capacity might make it work,
yet those only able to follow orders must forgo options.
So overly depending on math is like instructions;
if I solely rely on it, and it's wrong, then I'm stuck.
Imaginary numbers allow the possibility of reverse TIME;
the numbers cannot lie, so it has become an institution.
But many physical phenomena have become useful
by acknowledging that the math works before it's proven.
The problem comes in blindly, relying on math to show us
TIME is able to move both forwards and backwards.
That is part of the proof leading to Einstein's RELATIVITY,
and it has been proven enough to satisfy disbelievers.
Completely bowing before incomplete gods of SCIENCE
is merely a failure by nameless MIND to recognize itself.

11:39

Whatever else a clock may be able to reveal about TIME,
at the least it's shown to have a physical existence.
And yet TIME cannot be held like a glass of water;
how it is felt and how it is measured are kept separate.

Which doesn't change the fact it's real, it exists;
there is something in REALITY which a clock represents.
The gods of SCIENCE treat TIME as QUANTITY to manipulate
because it can be measured, and therefore exploited.
The magnitude of TIME's vector isn't physical QUANTITY,
at least not in the manner in which SCIENCE treats OBJECT.
There is something called TIME which does exist,
with tangible tombstones to make graves of the past.
If it can be measured, it must have a physical existence,
beyond its obvious ability to standardize change.
What could TIME be to have its capacities;
so like MASS and EXTENSION, and yet so different?
It can be dissected into regular measurable increments,
but it can't be manipulated like OBJECTS in SPACE.
Floating free from supporting the weight of substance;
immunized from the mortal inclination to tear its fabric.
I can change seconds to hours to eons,
but nothing has been done to change TIME itself.
When the unknowing say a second has been lost,
then something has been acknowledged—but what?
I could say milli- or microsecond, the division is irrelevant;
none of them tell me what has actually transpired.
It is almost as though TIME really was physical OBJECT,
where pieces of it can be grabbed second by second.
A second is TIME progressing from some arbitrary
starting point to a distant point in TIME, which repeats.
What goes from one point to another;
what is TIME for a second to exist within it?
It isn't like measuring DISTANCE walked across the floor,
nor is it like TEMPERATURE, commonly confused with HEAT.
How can one QUANTITY be so different than those others;
should its capacity for measurement make it complete?
Each of those QUANTITIES can be moved back and forth,
stopped and then moved on, while TIME can't.
TIME is used for more than just restricting OBJECTS,
it is also the basis for regulating any type of motion.
Frequency, speed, and other measurements per second;
it's not so much physical QUANTITY as a reference point.

Cycles/second or miles/hour are relative terms,
how some event relates to transit in TIME.
TIME'S essence only seems real when it pertains to me;
I only experience it as it passes before my eyes.
Since TIME'S *essence is not readily apparent,*
imagine how another OBJECT *might detect its magnitude.*
If I put myself inside any OBJECT'S SPACE,
then the seconds will still parade past 1 by 1.
How do animals consider TIME *as opposed to humanity;*
does a rock feel TIME *weigh on its boulder's shoulders?*
It sounds silly to say a rock experiences TIME'S progress;
there is no awareness with which it can detect difference.
That is confusing awareness of TIME *with its experience;*
if rocks do not endure it, how do radioactive ones decay?
Radioactive rocks exist much longer than man;
their notion of TIME should be much longer than mine.
If TIME *is considered to be like a massive ruler,*
then a rock's is just scaled differently than a person's is.
So I look at TIME in seconds because this is the way
my sensory apparatus is attuned by nature through EVOLUTION.
Smaller and greater spans of TIME *can be perceived,*
yet there is a limit to how far either one can go.
I have no mechanism to sense nanoseconds or years;
their existence is from CONCEPTS, not direct PERCEPTION.
Man first divided TIME *into days and months and years,*
the limit of his ability to utilize natural distinctions.
I don't sense a year has passed, only that seasons repeat;
then deduce a regular interval of a year has gone by.
All the while understanding TIME *is progressing,*
in order to create something with the length of a day.
With civilization, TIME began to require distinctions,
dividing a month into weeks, a day into seconds.
All of those latter divisions were originally arbitrary;
only lately has a second been set to a natural event.
The engine of SCIENCE requires smaller divisions of TIME;
greater accuracy makes greater use of REALITY'S bounty.
TIME is marked with the second because it is useful:
what is the usefulness of the second to a rock?

A rock's LIFE is measured in eons, not years,
and it can't make use of arbitrary divisions of TIME.
The magnitude of TIME relates to OBJECT'S ability to use it;
thus experience of it is based on each OBJECT'S nature.

12:14

The only good thing about jail is taking naps in the day,
but my strange DREAMS don't allow me peaceful rest.
Fantasy as a rockman, with near-immortal LIFE,
possessed of enough awareness to see REALITY pass by.
A rock in the shape of a human, totally immobile,
with a striking degree of serenity and sanity.
Living as a rockman throughout one hundred years
equates with what a human experiences for one second.
Assuming a human standard for side-by-side convenience,
a rockman's second would be a human's century.
Experience of TIME'S progress comes from noticing changes
in personal environment, not a defined length.
I see the sun moving, plants growing, my body changing;
my sense of MATTER moving within INANIMATE UNIVERSE.
Directly perceiving REALITY as it is made available
to each OBJECT'S inherent ability to ascertain it.
A human is aware of plants growing;
a rockman detects the half-LIFE of radioactive rocks.
How would a rockman perceive entire LIFE of a plant
when it entirely passes within so short a span of his TIME?
A human hears sound frequencies in beats/second;
a rockman detects the earth revolving around the sun.
His marbleized body wearing away with patient tears,
a rockman would not know himself on a human scale.
A pebble in a riverbed I happen upon hiking 1 day
will take eons to wear down; the river will die 1st.
Thus a rockman would be made aware of his LIFE,
detecting a century as his smallest second-hand timepiece.
But the detectable scale doesn't change REALITY;
a second is a second long no matter what reference is used.

Reality of Time is in its usefulness to the entity involved;
humanity's arrogance declares Time is absurd for a rock.
That isn't the substance of my point,
units of Time are adjusted by shifting decimal places.
A century to one is as important as a second to the other;
events of less than a century would pass within a second.
Although a century would be more important,
a second would still exist as Concept to a rockman.
Now expand this Thought experiment one step further:
suppose a rockman is just a long-lived human.
Then he would be able to make use of phenomena
lasting a second for him and a century for me.
Grant him the ability to interact with his environment,
although only to the ability he is able to make use of it.
The rockman could use any events happening in a century,
just as a human can use events happening in a second.
The Time reference used is changed by arbitrary numbers;
how the gods of Science make one is in this fashion.
Interaction of heavenly bodies, and Cesium 133 decay,
combine to make what is now officially 1 second.
No one can dispute those phenomena would still exist
for a rockman who just perceives Time differently.
The rockman would detect things on a scale around
9 orders of magnitude greater than human programming.
A human does not sense nanoseconds because he has not
been endowed by nature with this physical ability.
But a human has the ability to make use of nanoseconds,
merely by transferring from Perceptions to Concepts.
Still, the nanosecond has no use at all to a human being,
unless it can manipulate something he can directly sense.
Music or video are able to function because of a human's
Concept of divisions much smaller than a second.
Music and video are useless to a human,
unless they function at a level of sensation he can use.
A television scans its screen at a rate, marketable
experimentation has determined, his eyes continuously see.
The modifications to Reality micro-seconds make useful,
only result in being useful if a macro-human senses them.

A rockman could still make use of the nanosecond;
though he would detect it as 10^{-18} rather than 10^{-9}.
His use of them still has to transfer to longer detection;
try to imagine a tv working so sssssslllllloooooowwwwww.
So TIME is only useful based on perceptive abilities;
each distinct OBJECT has its own perspective on TIME.
Not quite. Only a human's ability to use TIME within his
sensory capacity makes any sort of TIME division useful.
Seconds are useful to humans, their senses let it be so;
centuries would be similarly useful to rockmans.
TIME is not naturally divisible into seconds;
its nature is not conducive to be hacked into pieces.

12:47

Each second a clock ticks off is priceless to me,
but now I'm not sure exactly what it is I should value.
What is really measured if TIME distinctions are arbitrary;
does a second have any relation to the essence of TIME?
A second is an accurate measure of something, likely TIME,
though I now correlate them less than I did before.
This is an important point, so stop and take notice:
TIME distinctions are as illusory as they are FINITY.
So . . . I'm able to measure TIME because something is there,
but what I divide it into isn't really there.
Units of TIME are distinguished because they are useful,
not because they have an intrinsic connection to REALITY.
But if I'm not able to detect what TIME really is,
then its spurious divisions are the closest I can get.
Seconds obtain their duration because of the way
a physical body interacts with its environment.
So what! As long as I'm able to make use of them,
it doesn't matter what distinctions are made in TIME.
Why have human senses evolved to cherish a second;
is it possible five seconds could be just as important?
Those are irrelevant questions, as least for now;
just divide TIME, any division can be made equally useful.

If true, then TIME *divisions must be arbitrary:*
so how can they offer a true portrait of REALITY?
If it can be measured, it must exist;
therefore it must have some connection with REALITY.
Is TIME *being measured, or its divisions;*
does this mean they are related or different?
It's the divisions that are being measured, not TIME;
maybe because TIME itself has no magnitude.
Is it possible those divisions do not quite depict TIME,
that immeasurable TIME *is something else entirely?*
Those TIME divisions have to represent some REALITY;
they might not be all of TIME, but they're something.
Eventually, the essence of TIME *will have to be pursued;*
for now, a mutual exclusion needs to be acknowledged.
TIME isn't the same as its divisions;
there, it has been formalized, now I can move on.
Always remember its divisions are arbitrary,
yet since they are, how can TIME *be rationally discussed?*
Arbitrary only means any measure is equally valid,
so I can still get transfinitely closer and closer.
Thus another somewhat unsettling separation is pictured:
a RATIONAL *view uses gods, but is not reliant on them.*
So I may be able to approximate TIME rationally,
while SCIENCE is left to use TIME's divisions.
Is there any point to this reflection,
if a second is still a second no matter where it comes from?
If I only desired to investigate TIME's divisions—no,
but I'm beginning to understand TIME is something more.
TIME's progression seems continuous through moments;
although defining this movement elicits more problems.
I know TIME divisions are useful, no doubt,
but it may no longer be acceptable to term them TIME.
They constitute arbitrarily measured QUANTITIES,
divisions attached to specific OBJECTS.
A second can now be related to a specific physical event;
chosen for the preexisting value already given its length.
Where is our MIND's *wink with respect to* TIME;
what has been uncovered that may help find it?

There is no past or future, they are only CONCEPTS;
only present TIME stretches off in TRANSFINITE directions.
A present which is merely a change from past to future,
inducing us to believe TIME is continuous.
But my physical ability to detect TIME is limited,
so I can't know if it's truly continuous, or an absence.
TIME has magnitude and a positive direction,
and its divisions are arbitrary with no direct connection.
For some REASON this doesn't make much sense to me:
TIME and its divisions don't have much in common.
TIME is supposedly divided based upon the utility
gained from any creature using it.
No observation shakes me up as much as this:
TIME is none, TIME is 1, and TIME is many.
One notion appears to have seeped into closed MIND:
there is more than one meaning attached to all TIMES.

****

13:48

A wise man once said:
PAIN and delight both cause suffering from dross flesh.
Which is counter to everything I learned growing up;
I seek delight because it's the opposite of PAIN.
How are we to know one from the other
if they both cause the effect all LIFE seeks to avoid?
Delight causes suffering, delight causes suffering;
maybe if I keep repeating it, I'll start to believe it.
Did he mean they are in fact the same thing;
if they are, why do they have two separate meanings?
I obviously see them as different, as did he;
therefore there must be 2 causes to the 1 effect.
Maybe they only indicate what we must avoid;
those two causes are really effects from another cause.
Well if that is what he meant he would have said so;
after all, he was the wise man, not I.

For there to be one rhythm which is not heard,
there must be one crass drum which is not beaten.
Which can't be referring to the effect of suffering;
this is the result, not an action to be contained.
Pain and delight are symptoms of some greater tragedy;
the boils on the skin denoting the disease deep within.
There isn't much preceding Pain and delight,
just mental anticipation from knowing what will follow.
How are we to know what the future will bring;
is pleasure sometimes experienced when Pain is predicted?
There are many instances where I expect bad results,
and after Time rolls around, it isn't that bad after all.
So if expected Pain or delight slide past existence,
how can they be the direct cause of suffering?
Ah . . . Pain or delight don't cause suffering,
it's the mental disease leading to avoidance or seeking.
If Pain is sought, then now is not being experienced,
just the plan of how to receive it.
But Pain happens now whether I seek it or not;
it won't cease just because I no longer plan on it.
If delight is avoided, then now is not being experienced,
just a plan for tomorrow's reward.
Maybe Gandhi was right, if I try for enjoyment,
then I don't know what it's like to enjoy just trying.
Pain and delight are earthy treasures,
dug out of placid Mind and given their own lives.
No Force on earth can stop them from happening;
I'll experience Pain and delight just by living.
Yet the experience becomes confused with the pursuit
of capturing a past feeling, or sidestepping future misery.
My existence then becomes trapped in a vicious cycle,
always trying to make 1 happen and not the other.
Children of yesterday being forced into tomorrow,
seeking something that does not really exist.
Living my Reality in Concepts of avoid and seek;
trapped into living every moment but here and now.
The feelings will come whether they are sought or not;
what else shows there is Life in here?

This body in my grasp is the source of my weakness,
the source of all known as good or bad.
Imagine a body wrapped in spirally bound emotional tape,
each one a treasured delight, or unendurable PAIN.
From me flows PAIN, from me flows delight,
from me flows the causes for me to seek and avoid them.
They are just names attached to that which is real,
and that which is real is now, only now.
My CONCEPTS never run fast enough to catch my feelings;
whichever 1's are in my head, they aren't real.
Suffering comes from trying to create THOUGHT
to match a feeling arising on its own; it must.
Effortless;
accepting my body's flesh for what it is, not what I want.
Separating now from REALITY *splits* TIME *from* SPACE;
unless the two remain merged, suffering will result.
All my ENERGY is wasted searching for the home
where I can control all the suffering REALITY has to offer.
Look for TIME *and it will be found in its* SPACE;
the source of suffering is ever-dividing DUALITY.

14:19

The hands on the clock don't just exhibit TIME,
they must move through SPACE to show it has passed.
One enlarged reflection is required to complete TIME,
how it is intimately connected with its spatial cousin.
I need to understand how SPACE interacts with TIME,
how they are alike, and how they are different.
*TIME *and* SPACE *are observed to exist as positive essences;*
is it possible for them to become negative?
Shrink or divide them into the tiniest possible bits,
and there will still be some positive amount left over.
How far out can SPACE *and* TIME *go;*
is there some limit sensation has not been able to reach?
There is no limit to the reaches of TIME or SPACE;
they appear to go on forever.

Here again Infinity *of the large and small are encountered:*
where else can they meet but here and now?
Space and Time are both transfinitely large and small;
never reaching the end, either within or without.
Do they find their home in Object,
where each one finds its own Time *and* Space?
I'm not trying to understand how Object exists in them,
but what Reality is, that they could subsist in it.
Space and Time *have perceptible attributes,*
sensations feeding upon the spoils of Infinity's *leftovers.*
There appear to be 4 dimensions to Time and Space,
bound into a continuum curved with gravitational flows.
Are Space *and* Time *truly dimensional,*
or is this another hoax pulled over willing eyes?
Conceiving them as 4 dimensions works quite well;
I know of no other scheme which will fit in this place.
How do dimensions attach to Time *and* Space;
is there some locale where Transfinity *becomes* Finity?
My sensory apparatus tells me they are dimensional;
up/down, forward/backward, right/left, in/out.
So how does a corporeal body attach to them;
must it if it can inhabit all of those dimensions?
My body exists in 1 Space and Time;
all dimensions can be conceived to originate from here.
Which is why Einstein had such a problem with them,
many points of origin indicate many Times *and* Spaces.
Not quite. Points of origin are just relative to 1 another,
each Object moving within its own coordinate system.
Yet all points of Space *must touch all points of* Time;
how else can Time *move uniformly throughout* Space?
It doesn't;
Time is related to the speed of light, nothing is faster.
So the light reaching the earth right at this instant
did not exist at the sun eight minutes ago?
That is quite a pedestrian perspective on Time;
the universal continuum is more complicated than that.
Why;
does Reality *need to be complicated to be understood?*

SCIENCE only measures that which can be observed;
if it can't be measured, then it might as well not exist.
How can anybody seriously suggest
TIME has anything to do with its frame of measurement?
Since no frame of reference is better than any other,
and the speed of light is consistent, TIME can't be.
There is only one problem with that view of TIME:
the assumption that any frame of reference is real.
But that is how SPACE is attached to TIME;
how I exist is related to my position with everything else.
This is one thing everybody should be able to agree on:
TIME is somehow connected to SPACE.
SCIENCE does it with numbers and proven experiments,
showing how the continuum is based on points of view.
Perspective gives one indication of REALITY'S substance;
the gods of SCIENCE are only looking from a singular one!
But every moving OBJECT has its own perspective,
which is why the fabric of the universe is curved, not flat.
Question: whether the continuum of SPACE/TIME is warped,
or whether it is the measurements taken of it that are?

14:49

The cursed clock and my slowly starving body extend
into unified TIME and SPACE like any other sensible OBJECT.
They are connected together, but how;
do their dimensions tie them into cohesive REALITY?
The dimensional model of SPACE and TIME is the best
yet proposed for how BASIC QUANTITIES can coexist.
Are TIME and SPACE truly dimensional;
can four dimensions account for their extended existence?
TIME is the 4th dimension, as is well-known,
tacked onto the 3 filling up the settled regions of SPACE.
There is no accuracy in calling TIME the fourth dimension,
primarily because there are no dimensions to SPACE.
Then there is no accounting for the fact that any direction
I move in can be described by a 3-dimensional vector.

Gods of Science have traditionally transferred the notion of
three-dimensional Objects onto three-dimensional Space.
Because the most reasonable assumption
made about Objects is their existence in similar Space.
How could Objects have length and width and depth
unless they exist within similar Space yielding to them?
I also observe the performance of many varied motions,
providing additional evidence for 3-dimensional Space.
No one can determine within what essence Objects exist
because Void by its nature has no sensible attributes.
Therefore it's Rational to assume the simplest explanation:
Space surrounding Objects is 3 dimensional.
No discrepancy between Space and Time in that regard,
only between the gods of Science and Reality.
Any other assumption is totally baseless;
I can rely only on Perception to bring me closer to Reality.
Reflect on how Object actually achieves motion:
can dimensions actually coexist with Absolute Space?
If any Object moves from 1 point to another,
it moves from 1 location in Space to some other place.
Gods of Science attempt to measure all movement
by instituting an artificial system of coordinates.
Any motion can only be measured between locations,
ideally composed of defined start and end points.
Object moves through something identified as Space,
which is notable for its massive lack of Perception.
Some reference point, usually Object, is set as the origin
of a specific coordinate system by which motion is fixed.
The three spatial dimensions are this overlaid system,
not the measure of whatever constitutes Space itself.
Thereafter any point or motion in Space can be measured
with regard to those coordinates which work so very well.
Yet has Relativity not shown that method to be flawed;
is any coordinate system not relative to its motion?
An origin is set in relation to at least 1 moving Object,
so its coordinate system is dependent on this local motion.
Thus an observer and Objects are moving in relation,
each defined by its own individual coordinate system.

With relative coordinates, and a constant light speed,
SCIENCE claims an absence of ABSOLUTE TIME and SPACE.
Yet mathematical description of REALITY is an abstraction:
how can gods decree what they cannot accurately map?
There is no other way to make use of empty SPACE
than to use some defined relative coordinate system.
If there is no ABSOLUTE SPACE,
then how does OBJECT move from one place to another?
There must be empty SPACE for OBJECTS to move within it;
it's impossible for 2 OBJECTS to be in the same place.
What happens to empty SPACE it was in after OBJECT moves;
does some mysterious mathematical formula fill it in?
I 1ˢᵗ sense no OBJECT (SPACE), then I detect OBJECT;
finally, I once again sense an absence of OBJECT.
Is it just possible, it sounds really silly to state it,
ABSOLUTE SPACE takes up ABSOLUTE SPACE that OBJECT was in?
But SCIENCE has proven there is no ABSOLUTE SPACE,
and from there has gone on to show no ABSOLUTE TIME.
Better TRUTH might be hard for gods of SCIENCE to accept:
there is no MEASURABLE ABSOLUTE TIME and SPACE.
But neither SPACE nor TIME are of use without numbers;
there is no way of proving ABSOLUTE existence.
Contrast the imprecision of math with common sense;
numbers are not holier than the priests who control them.
It's outrageous to cast derision upon math's precision;
if it weren't so precise, it wouldn't exist at all.
Some type of ABSOLUTE SPACE hosts OBJECTS' coexistence,
something which closely resembles VOID.
It must be devoid of any possibility my senses might attach,
but it still must be something other than VOID.
No wonder priests of SCIENCE hate this CONCEPTION so much,
there is no possible way to exploit ABSOLUTE SPACE.
I can accept no measurable ABSOLUTE SPACE and TIME,
which mandates a RATIONAL view of FINITE TIME and SPACE.
Since it is possible for SPACE to exist without dimensions,
then it is also possible for TIME to exist without them too.
There is a problem never satisfactorily solved by math:
TIME is only a 1-way path without imaginary numbers.

Its transit is unidirectional, guilty until proven innocent;
trust in plain observation, not SCIENCE fictional math.
As far as a RATIONAL understanding of the subject presents,
the 3 dimensions overlaid on SPACE are bidirectional.
If TIME was bidirectional, OBJECTS would not be forced
to keep going forward and forward and forward and . . .
I don't start from a point in SPACE and keep going on;
each action can return within the same coordinate system.
If that is REALITY, from the simplest view possibly seen,
why would we observe TIME as a fourth dimension?
Because it's convenient and useful and it works;
no RATIONAL function for it exists beyond these parameters.
Introducing a problem with the current view of TIME:
it so infects our THOUGHTS, shedding it may be too difficult.
RATIONAL THOUGHT will never be entirely lost;
at worst it will undergo a beneficial transformation.
On the bright path to see the subtle face of TIME,
dimensions are arbitrarily FINITY, continue on from here.

15:34

TIME is moving forward for both me and the clock;
I don't understand how it attaches to 2 distinct OBJECTS.
How does it pass in two places unless it is ABSOLUTE;
if it is limited, then should it not be different for each one?
If TIME is ABSOLUTE, then it shouldn't move at all;
as OBJECTS move in SPACE, so should they move in TIME.
Do not doubt that a form of ABSOLUTE SPACE and TIME exists;
the task is to try to understand how this essence can be.
It's thoroughly possible if their FINITE essences are acquired
from a source not already forbidden by SCIENCE.
Any arbitrarily measured FINITY view of TIME or SPACE
is enclosed in a larger TRANSFINITY view of SPACE or TIME.
If I'm to take a conceptual snapshot of some essence,
then what I possess is just part of something larger.
Just as a photograph sees only one side of the subject,
there is always something CONCEPTION is missing.

A measurable view of TIME or SPACE is limited;
therefore the dimensional perspective must be FINITE.
Does any part of REALITY exist in isolation,
where what is sensed requires no larger adjustment?
If there is a FINITE view of SPACE and TIME,
there must be something outside encompassing it.
Every conceived OBJECT sits inside a larger one,
until imagination reaches a limit, and it is called ABSOLUTE.
It might not be ABSOLUTE TIME or SPACE,
but it would be ABSOLUTE for all my RATIONAL CONCEPTS.
If existence of ABSOLUTE TIME might now be believed,
then how is it spread among all distant STARS?
If the earth exists as an event at this instant in TIME,
then the sun exists as an event at this very same instant.
Is TIME'S existence dependent on the movement of light;
how does the sun exist now unless it existed then?
It's common knowledge that light
takes 8 minutes to travel from the sun to the earth.
By necessity, TIME existed on the sun eight minutes ago,
just as it did on the earth eight minutes ago.
That moment, and every similar moment, in TIME
is the same instant on the sun as well as on the earth.
Not to miss, it was also the same on Alpha Centauri;
TIME touches all of SPACE with each passing moment.
The limitation of sight brought on by the speed of light
insures I can't know of TIME'S motion until after the fact.
There is no possible way to observe all TIME at once;
actually, only one small illumination can be approached.
But SCIENCE says TIME is moving with light,
and nothing is able to move faster than this speed.
Does that mean common sense should be fooled
into believing the events do not happen simultaneously?
If I can't directly sense TIME occurring everywhere,
then I have to rely on induction to guess this conclusion.
This is a crux of what seekers are led to believe:
rely on induction, or rely on deduction.
Induction implies probability given true premises;
deduction implies certainty given true premises.

The point is to determine whether the premises are true;
then the more valid approach can be determined.
Since measurement of TIME isn't TIME itself,
this seems to indicate SCIENCE'S deduction is invalid.
While induction of TIME touching all SPACE at once
can at best be granted some TRANSFINITY probability.
All the evidence I have suggests TIME is universal;
a 99% probability of ABSOLUTE TIME touching all SPACE.
One of the clutters the gods of SCIENCE make is to mistake
phenomena as REALITY for phenomena within REALITY.
My PERCEPTIONS create phenomenal INANIMATE UNIVERSE,
which is all I rationally know of REALITY.
Thus exploited by the gods of SCIENCE to create
false REALITY for convenience and profit and gain.
TIME measured to advance knowledge isn't false;
it may not be ABSOLUTE, but it's more than nothing.
The mathematics which priests use is precise and elegant;
too imprecise for REALITY, it is FINITY to a TRANSFINITY degree.
Deduction just using math is unnaturally accurate;
identification with it is what shows REALITY largely FINITE.
Gods easily demonstrate their perpetual dominance;
offer disagreement, and we are commanded to prove it.
Like the TIME difference between the sun and the earth,
any proof will be limited by the ubiquitous speed of light.
Thus there is no way of absolutely proving
two distinct events happen at the exact same timed instant.
Light will take TIME to transit from 1 point to another,
and no proof is possible until light reaches an observer.
TIME is measured as a passenger riding on a ship of light;
it is not possible for the former to exist without the latter.
Any observation must be made from light reproduction,
which is why ABSOLUTE TIME can't be measured.
The gods of SCIENCE have rigged the game;
they will only accept knowledge gained by their rules.
And also why SCIENCE has gained predominance,
mumbo jumbo imitating knowledge is thereby quashed.
What if REALITY does not play by those rules,
if there is more to it than can be indicated by sensation?

Then induction can play a large part in its discovery;
not as much as deduction, but it still might be viable.
*The gods try to eliminate ABSOLUTE SPACE and TIME by
assuming they do not exist because the math will not work.*
However their existence may be interpreted to exist,
they must still correlate with proven dictates of SCIENCE.
*Part of REALITY has not been deciphered by the gods:
ABSOLUTE TIME and SPACE cannot be measured.*
Which only means a part of REALITY is useless to SCIENCE,
so part of me doesn't really care whether they exist or not.
*As common sense tells me, and RELATIVITY indicates,
an observer must exist for a measurement to be made.*
An observer must exist for REALITY to be known anywhere;
anything beyond possible PERCEPTION doesn't exist to me.
*Should we accept SPACE and TIME as discretionary,
arrogantly presuming REALITY will collapse without us?*
If I can't sense certain OBJECT, then it doesn't exist;
maybe something is out there, but it remains unknown.
*If all human LIFE was extinguished in just one instant,
planets and STARS and SPACE in between would still exist.*
Impossible to know, unless I accept beyond all REASON
that imagined REALITY is as real as proven REALITY.
*How can anybody seriously suggest TIME and SPACE
are subject to the limitations of material PERCEPTION?*
SPACE and TIME are useless without an observer;
some would say they don't exist without this voyeur.
*Thus we should accept an observer is all-important
for detecting the essential nature of REALITY.*
That is the only way PERCEPTION will work;
all of my knowledge comes through physical sensation.
*Yet the observer for the gods of SCIENCE is just RATIONAL;
there is another perspective entirely, one of INTUITION.*
But an INTUITIVE view isn't capable of PERCEPTION,
not the type achieved through my senses.
*One way of viewing REALITY is not better than the other;
the gods make a false accusation in negating ABSOLUTES.*
SCIENCE has only made a rationally viable conclusion:
since ABSOLUTES can't be measured, they don't exist.

Gods have decreed ABSOLUTE TIME and SPACE to be bunk;
whereas it seems obvious they just cannot see them.
If ABSOLUTE SPACE and TIME exist, then SCIENCE is wrong,
except experimental evidence proves they don't exist.
A RATIONAL view is not wrong within INANIMATE UNIVERSE;
as was previously indicated, one perspective is incomplete.
A problem I have is in drawing a distinction between
sensed INANIMATE UNIVERSE and its part in REALITY.
SCIENCE has made an incorrect assumption about REALITY,
so any conclusions drawn from it will no longer be valid.
Therefore any deductions which require a denial
of ABSOLUTE TIME and SPACE can no longer be supported.
Completing this theory requires an impartial experiment:
delete priests one by one to see whether REALITY remains.
That won't prove anything at all;
SCIENCE is just the best observer, not the only 1.
What other proper way will serve to establish knowledge,
than doing experiments verifying a theory's repetition?
Any valid theory requires repetition to prove its worth;
killing scientists doesn't assert anything worth finding.
The theory—REALITY is independent of sensation;
the proof—individual priests will be deleted.
That will only show their views no longer exist,
not that what they perceived was independent.
Each instance where one is lost, and REALITY still exists,
just adds weight to the theory of multiple perspectives.
But in order for some perceived REALITY to exist,
there must still be some observer around to sense it.
Repetition is the only valid proof for any theory,
so confidence will grow with each certifiable case.
Elimination won't actually prove 2 views are valid,
rather, known REALITY is dependent on an observer.
It is of course impossible to prove any theory completely,
so quite a few priests of SCIENCE may have to be deleted.
Scientists have no problem with existence of a multiverse;
eliminate the politicians who use SCIENCE without insight.
It should not be a problem for RATIONAL con-SCIENCE;
consider them to be lab rats used for the greater good.

It doesn't matter how many scientists no longer observe;
as long as 1 creature senses it, this is how it exists.
In order for the theory to be completely tested,
and for obvious objections, all LIFE must be deleted.
REALITY may still exist without BIOMATTER in it,
but since there aren't any observers, it can't be proven.
A corollary: non-priests will accept the existence
of greater REALITY at the expense of only a few priests.
In every instance where an observer is eliminated,
if REALITY remains, then it exists beyond human senses.
ABSOLUTE SPACE and TIME are parameters of REALITY,
existing because they must, not because they can.
Therefore, current physical laws need not change
because existence of ABSOLUTES is beyond their application.
They are incapable of being observed by RATIONAL means,
and are similar in their lack of dimension.
But TIME and SPACE must be measured;
a hell of a lot of them get measured every day.
It does not exist because it can not?
Again confusing a sense of REALITY with what REALITY is.
I won't accept dispensing with meters and hours;
ABSOLUTES are fine until they invade RATIONAL SPACE.
There is a difference between ABSOLUTE SPACE,
and arbitrarily dimensioned and measured FINITY SPACE.
So the measurements taken are in INANIMATE UNIVERSE,
while ABSOLUTE SPACE exists somewhere at the edge of it.
Also note a difference between ABSOLUTE TIME,
and arbitrarily dissected and measured FINITY TIME.
So bits of TIME extracted are in INANIMATE UNIVERSE,
while ABSOLUTE TIME exists somewhere at the edge of it.
Those subjective RATIONAL interpretations of REALITY are all
that limited sensation is capable of directly perceiving.
My 5 senses are able to transfinitely approach REALITY,
creating an entire system known as INANIMATE UNIVERSE.
ABSOLUTES are existentially related phenomena,
known by a RATIONAL deduction of their existence together.
Somewhere SPACE and TIME must unite as 1;
if not as 4 dimensions, then as something more INTUITIVE.

Confusing different aspects of REALITY *as the same thing*
leads to problems with the conclusions thereby drawn.
There are different types of TIME and SPACE;
1 is existence of their ABSOLUTES, beyond measurement.
Left is to find the path noting the difference between
the transfinitely ABSOLUTE *and the finitely observed.*

17:02

I'm able to sense the existence of the clock on the wall,
which is how I know of its temporal and spatial existence.
What if SPACE *and* TIME *existed, yet were not sensed;*
how would the essence of what they are be known?
I don't know where to begin the next reflection:
if my senses are gone, then so are my RATIONAL PERCEPTIONS.
For now try to imagine existing as an embodied spectre;
how would SPACE *be experienced?*
It would be a complete being with none of my 5 senses;
essentially a person, with no direct apprehension of things.
Could the spectre acknowledge existence of SPACE,
an essence which requires absence for presence?
I detect SPACE as the absence of sensible OBJECTS,
so the specter wouldn't know it in my neural manner.
The spectre might notice distinct aspects to its existence;
it is here rather than there, maybe now rather than later.
But the specter is insensible, nothing exists;
it wouldn't be able to sense differences in anything.
A spectre trying to penetrate a wall not seen or touched
should be able to discern whether it can proceed further.
It may not know why it can no longer move as it was;
though without proprioceptors, it wouldn't know motion.
A world which exists, and yet sensation cannot touch it,
possessed of a body which does not understand itself.
There should be NO senses available to the specter;
it shouldn't be able to feel itself as well as others.
How would the spectre even know it existed,
if even aches and pains signal there is LIFE *in here?*

I imagine if I couldn't sense I exist,
I still should be able to feel I'm not nothing within.
What is nothing if it is not SPACE?
It cannot be VOID, which is even the absence of nothing.
Descartes said he THOUGHT, he must exist,
and there must be a location to THOUGHT other than SPACE.
THOUGHT is generally sensed to be located in BRAIN,
yet without sensation, it is founded upon another imprint.
I have an intrinsic ability to feel, not found by my senses;
knowledge my MIND isn't in empty SPACE.
MIND which itself seems to be made of torrid spectres,
swirling around without senses to tie them down.
Therefore the specter would know something exists,
and if there is some thing, then there must be no thing.
The spectre would know SPACE, if not the nominal one,
yet would it comprehend itself as part of REALITY?
If the specter couldn't sense its location,
it would have no CONCEPT of REALITY as I understand it.
It would know it exists somewhere, within something;
like SPACE, its REALITY would thus be defined.
If it can't know it has a solid place to exist,
its REALITY would be limited to the substance of its MIND.
Imagine some other possibility for where ghost MIND lies;
where would the substance of the spectre reside?
If the specter has no localized place of existence,
then it exists everywhere or nowhere or at random.
There is no here or there attached to the spectre;
these attributes are specific products of sensation.
It couldn't exist nowhere,
because then its MIND wouldn't exist.
Loose MIND must be tangible, even if it is not material;
thus some place which is beyond INANIMATE UNIVERSE.
It couldn't exist everywhere,
because then its MIND couldn't have independent THOUGHTS.
THOUGHTS are recognized as being different, and connected;
one is detected because it is unlike others.
The other option is of the specter randomly flitting about;
its existence is indeterminate like at the quantum level.

If it only has a probability to be at one place at one instant,
could the spectre exist at random?
If it did, then it would have no CONCEPT of location,
no parts to form a fixed association.
Musing: THOUGHTS existing without location, in transit,
yet are still able to find each other for connection.
There doesn't seem to be any way to locate THOUGHT
unless it's tied to some experience or existence or OBJECT.
The spectre is lacking PERCEPTIONS of sensation;
THOUGHTS do not flow from just this physical ability.
If my BRAIN was starved of all of its sensory food;
it wouldn't be able to form external CONCEPTS.
Lame MIND would still be able to work in some fashion,
in a process unfathomable to RATIONAL touches.
Therefore even if the specter did exist at random,
it could discern a location for irrational THOUGHTS.
How would it fix IDEA of location
when irrational THOUGHTS are insubstantial, ephemeral?
If I have THOUGHT of joy, it implies THOUGHTS of not-joy,
so I should be able to locate a position for these THOUGHTS.
All required for floating MIND to formulate location
is the ability to separate one essence from another.
If the specter is able to form THOUGHTS of 1 place,
it may exist both at random and at 1 finalized location.
Totally irrational, this is what that is:
THOUGHT existing outside of RATIONAL INANIMATE UNIVERSE.
My THOUGHTS of SPACE are normally OBJECT dominated,
separating 1 from the other to create a spatial pattern.
Imagine an embodied spectre would be able
to conceive location and therefore SPACE—how?
Implying the possibility of feeling SPACE without senses,
as some blind people can remotely sense OBJECTS.
Feeling eyes falling upon the back of waiting prey,
or even LIFE calling out its distress as it passes away.
The OAA part of my BRAIN allows me to distinguish
between myself and others, but this is purely neural.
Imagine the ability to feel existence in SPACE,
without the aid of sight or sound or touch.

Either SPACE is the absence of sensible OBJECTS,
or I can internally detect it without the aid of sensation.
Now there is a fork in the path of the imaginary spectre;
is it possible SPACE can be felt, as well as sensed?
SPACE, like TIME, may consist of more than 1 essence;
1 that can be sensed, and 1 that can be felt.
SPACE conceived without sensation is only useful
for mental manipulation—SPACE lost in THOUGHTS.
Mental SPACE needs consideration in a mental regard;
physical SPACE is the 1 up for discussion.
Both are required to understand SPACE completely;
its existence is being questioned for an insensate spectre.
SPACE, as the absence of sensible OBJECTS, exists as long
as INANIMATE UNIVERSE exists, in which it can't be sensed.
Thus a type of SPACE exists within which the spectre may
be located, yet it will never be aware of this situation.
SPACE which can be located just by mental differentiation
has little, or no, connection with sensible attributes.
This other type is irrational, think ABSOLUTE SPACE;
something that cannot be disposed of in a sensible manner.
REALITY isn't dependent on the sensations of BIOMATTER,
but the rationally formed CONCEPT of SPACE is so addicted.
Is there any way to determine how to feel SPACE,
a type existing without the need for sensible OBJECTS?
I imagine some sort of sensory-deprivation tank,
relieving my BRAIN of impulses, would do the trick.
After a while, physical sense of location would disappear,
and remaining MIND would be left—with what?
Sensory deprivation changes a person's emotional state,
and the ability to function rationally would go all to hell.
Hallucination is a distinct probability,
yet there is no evidence for losing awareness of SPACE.
People only submerse themselves for a limited period;
disassociation from SPACE may take a longer immersion.
Any feeling of SPACE, purely internal and irrational,
is also insufficient to help a person think rationally.
The sense of SPACE within INANIMATE UNIVERSE seems
intimately tied up with distinguishing cause and effect.

While an internal feeling of SPACE *is part of some hidden*
system by which all MIND *conjoins to all of its body.*
So if an internal feeling of SPACE does exist,
it isn't rationally viable, and can't be used with OBJECTS.
The knowledge is there of an individual who exists,
yet what is he then supposed to do with it?
The advantage it offers is a wider perspective of REALITY,
SPACE can be something other than the modern view.
The insensate spectre would not sense SPACE'S *absence;*
formless MIND *created outside of* INANIMATE UNIVERSE.

18:05

I would like to take the clock down from the wall,
and wreck it, but that wouldn't help me to resolve TIME.
There appears to be no way to penetrate TIME *directly,*
maybe lifting the layers of surrounding SPACE *will help.*
SPACE does appear more amenable to observation,
possessing tangible OBJECTS which help to fill its vastness.
Yet those OBJECTS *grant indirect* PERCEPTION *of* SPACE;
it is not something sensation has been able to find.
If SPACE is to help me uncover TIME,
then I must start with how I know about it—with OBJECT.
What do we really know about OBJECT *in* SPACE;
how does sensation separate one from the other?
OBJECT takes up SPACE: 1st SPACE is empty,
then OBJECT moves in, leaves, and it's empty again.
There must be some empty SPACE *for it to move;*
a boat requires empty water to leave a wake in passing.
I note OBJECT as taking up SPACE by sensing OBJECT itself,
not any kind of SPACE.
What about SPACE *distinguishes it from* OBJECT;
must there be some PERCEPTION *of it as distinct?*
Wherever I feel an essence or a thing,
it can't be filled with just cold and barren SPACE.
In a sense, OBJECTS *push aside some discernible essence;*
they "take up SPACE" *as an engine sucks in air.*

I assess taking up SPACE to sensible OBJECTS,
including those only detected via machine enhancement.
What about the sensation of OBJECTS assumed to exist:
protons and electrons and other sub atomic particles?
An electron has been observed to exist;
its movement flitting through a closed cloud chamber.
Just another charged OBJECT posing as a fantasy;
an existence created solely to prove it exists.
Maybe SCIENCE doesn't detect them as perceptible OBJECTS,
but as best estimates from the results of experimentation.
They do not exist at all to PERCEPTION;
only in imagination do they retain a medium for survival.
As yet I see no evidence for abolition of those particles;
for now I assume they take up SPACE like other OBJECTS.
A more suitable phrase for taking up SPACE is needed—
SPACE PASSAGE can refer to how OBJECT exists within it.
That phrase sounds uncommonly like motion,
when I believe it refers to something else entirely.
It should not be confused with motion through SPACE;
SPACE PASSAGE, regarding SPACE, is the same as OBJECT.
So under that view OBJECT is "part" of SPACE,
rather than a separate essence residing within it.
Now, how can OBJECT make PASSAGE through SPACE,
unless there is a connection which allows it to do so?
PERCEPTION of any OBJECT through my senses allows me
to denote any OBJECT as having existence as OBJECT.
Detection of OBJECT is the defining moment which allows
vague SPACE to be divided into where it is and it is not.
My ability to comprehend SPACE is highlighted
by a lack of any physical ability to sense it as it exists.
Where there is something there is no-SPACE;
where there is SPACE there is no-thing.
OBJECT can be SPACE PASSAGE because there is no such thing
as OBJECT which exists without SPACE around it.
So part of OBJECT can be that which passes within SPACE;
empty SPACE must exist for it to be possible.
If there is some location where SPACE can't exist,
then nothing can pass SPACE there, and no OBJECT resides.

Maybe a black hole is what fills spatial Void,
where Space *does not exist for something to exist in it.*
Space *and* Space Passage *appear to require coexistence;*
like cause and effect, 1 can't exist without the other.
Thus there is more to Space *than just absence;*
if Object *cannot fit within it, it is not* Space.
Space *is the lack of sensible* Objects,
but also the possibility of their existing by passing Space.
Is that all of what Space *can be;*
why cannot it be more like Infinity *in nature?*
Normal awareness of Space is limited by a physical ability
to acknowledge only those things passing it by.
So Space *likely exists beyond sensation to detect;*
understanding from Intuition *grants it safe* Passage.
If Rational Concept of Space is through my senses,
either existence, or lack, of Object is via this medium.
Space exists as an essence transcending boundaries,
yet there is a component of it which must be limited.
Therefore any aspect of Space,
rationally available, is also sense based.
Reality is dualistically divided by Conception;
Space can be viewed either rationally or intuitively.
If observers were deleted, Space like Reality would exist;
only its absence wouldn't be subject to Perception.
At least one part of Space *is made rationally available:*
Object defines existence in terms of its spatial mastery.
Part of Space exists outside of my muddy Perceptions,
but it isn't useful without a human-sensed viewpoint.
One part of Space *is known as* Space Passage;
the question is to determine—are there more?

18:43

There is defined Space between me and the clock;
Space which determines each location relative to another.
Can Space *exist as* Passage *and be the source of location,*
far away from the singular type which veils Perception?

SPACE PASSAGE is just another term created for OBJECT;
calling a thing by another name gains me nothing.
The problem with SPACE is its all-enclosing embrace,
too many divergent terms are included within one.
I thought I didn't know what TIME was,
and now it appears I also don't know what SPACE is.
SPACE is misunderstood in at least two ways:
how it exists as limited SPACE and ABSOLUTE SPACE.
Limited SPACE has been partially indicated in OBJECTS,
but limited SPACE between them is still left undone.
Categorize it by what it is—DISTANCE,
which makes three obvious distinctions for SPACE.
SPACE PASSAGE is part of arbitrarily measured OBJECT;
ABSOLUTE SPACE is untouchable by RATIONAL PERCEPTION.
Is it fair to characterize any measurement as arbitrary,
if the units used have been agreed upon in advance?
A rod supposedly measured to a certain length should
shorten when moved closer to light speed, thus arbitrary.
If the measurement accurately reflected the rod's length,
then it would not change with increasing motion.
Similarly, DISTANCE between OBJECT and observer changes
based on their relations to light speed and each other.
Length and DISTANCE are fixed arbitrary measurements
based upon a limited relation of dimensions to REALITY.
RELATIVITY theory has introduced this suspicion:
a firm sense of TIME and SPACE is subject to interpretation.
Maybe DUALITY of SPACE is split into CONCEPTION between
that which can be measured and that which cannot.
Both ways of viewing SPACE from a FINITE perspective
must have OBJECT involved for measurements to be taken.
Both are likewise different from ABSOLUTE SPACE,
which by its name implies INFINITY is applied near it.
From which I can deduce there exists ABSOLUTE SPACE,
with FINITE SPACES (EXTENSIONS and DISTANCES) within.
SPACE PASSAGE and DISTANCE show well with numbers,
unless attempting to penetrate into what they really are.
A nomenclature of math attached to SPACE
doesn't affect its REALITY as much as how it's perceived.

The gods of SCIENCE cannot decree changes to SPACE
based upon their incomplete understanding of REALITY.
The fact that parts of SPACE are decidedly FINITE doesn't
mandate that a RATIONAL view is fully able to expose it.
REALITY is used in a RATIONAL fashion, but is not reversible;
the view does not make the substance what it is.
When RELATIVITY replaced newtonian mechanics,
it was with expansion and not with destruction.
Newton's views are still valid, they are just incomplete;
traditional views of SPACE are likewise not fully ripe.
Any pure RATIONAL view of REALITY needs to be expanded to
include an INTUITIVE view, not accessible by external senses.
The view from Aristotle, then Newton, then Einstein,
changed how PERCEPTIONS are observed and understood.
There is FINITE RATIONAL INANIMATE UNIVERSE
exactly corresponding to the paradigm SCIENCE investigates.
Now expand that paradigm to include something ancient,
something which is totally irrational in nature.
Expanding upon the view that SCIENCE has been able to see
requires looking over the cliff into what can't be defined.
Seen at the edge of the unliving universe is ABSOLUTE SPACE,
as TRANSFINITY of CONCEPTION as can be known to exist.
ABSOLUTE SPACE is thereby differentiated
from FINITE SPACE PASSAGES and DISTANCES between them.
How can we understand what is meant by one SPACE,
when there are three distinct versions of what it means?
The whole panorama of OBJECT bodies and their lack
is my best estimate of what constitutes ABSOLUTE SPACE.
In order for ABSOLUTE SPACE to exist,
OBJECT must have the possibility of existing or not.
An arbitrarily measured RATIONAL observance of OBJECT
is my best estimate for what constitutes SPACE PASSAGE.
OBJECT could equal SPACE PASSAGE except for one thing:
it is required to exist within the parameters of TIME.
The arbitrarily measured RATIONAL relation between OBJECTS
is my best estimate for what constitutes DISTANCE.
DISTANCE depends on whether SPACE exists or not,
and the substance between OBJECTS is also not VOID.

The general assumption I have always had—
SPACE is nothing—is a perspective no longer valid.
DISTANCE needs SPACE, SPACE does not need DISTANCE;
more of SPACE is ABSOLUTE, which is farther than DISTANCE.
There is more to SPACE than DISTANCE between OBJECTS;
as OBJECT sits in SPACE, DISTANCE sits in SPACE.
The problem is to differentiate SPACE from its PASSAGE
in order to clarify what is known about its structure.
From what I've been able to gather so far,
what I can know is more than what I can sense.
SPACE PASSAGES are mapped onto a three-d replica:
three-d does not portray REALITY, does it portray OBJECT?
OBJECT has length and width and depth;
it makes no sense to suggest it doesn't.
The question is whether observations reflect OBJECT
as poorly as three dimensions manage to exhibit SPACE?
Any dimension isn't false as much as it's superficial,
useful for measurement, not for grasping REALITY.
OBJECT can be detected as possessing three dimensions;
feeling it and seeing it verifies its physical existence.
Only people who blindly follow religious gurus
willingly believe what exists doesn't really exist.
The same is true for disciples of SCIENCE, but opposite;
blindly following knowledge will never lead to TRUTH.
Dimensional maps don't separate SPACE from its PASSAGE,
they are only a verification of OBJECT truly existing.
SPACE may exist without DISTANCE, what about PASSAGE;
could SPACE exist without OBJECTS in it?
SPACE might exist without existence of OBJECTS within it;
however, there would be no way for it to be detected.
All of SPACE is ABSOLUTE, which is longer than PASSAGE,
again inferring PASSAGE of it requires SPACE.
The different types of SPACE are giving me a headache;
it doesn't matter which is which if I can't sense them.
What about ABSOLUTE SPACE;
is it possible for it to exist without including INFINITY?
TRANSFINITY covers here, INFINITY covers there;
so ABSOLUTES still fall short of INFINITE existence.

What in Space allows it to extend endlessly,
and also include Finity elements amenable to mapping?
Consider Space the same thing as Absolute Space,
while Space Passage and Distance are types within it.
And still, Absolute Space is not rationally perceptible;
its existence is imagined based on Objects within it.
Finite Space Passage and Distance are the sensed aspects
of Transfinite Absolute Space, beyond Rational detection.
The essence of Space is directly grasped by Intuition;
this is where it changes from Conception to Absolute.
Both halves of the spatial puzzle must exist;
Reality can always be perceived from 2 perspectives.
An approximation which works, but is still inaccurate:
Space Passages plus Distances equal Absolute Space.

19:38

The clock on the wall and my body are both part of Space,
pieces of a more complete unified essence within Reality.
Space has Finity and Transfinity aspects via raw Duality,
and since Time is connected, how does it divide?
If Time is bonded to Space as my sweaty body is to a sheet,
then the divisions of Space should have temporal twins.
Some Idea of Space has been established,
now imagine how Time could be similarly distinguished.
Absolute Space is the sine qua non of Space;
there must be some similar relation for Time.
Time and Space may be the same or different in essence,
yet to a Rational view, they are much closer than apart.
If there is Absolute Space, then there is Absolute Time;
their intimate inaccessibility makes this probable.
Envision Time to be as much like Space as feasible;
Reality dualistically dividing right down the line.
Then Transfinite Absolute Time can't be sensibly perceived,
and its Finite Passage, and something else, exist within it.
When a second is acknowledged to have come and gone,
what has actually happened?

My take on it is that all OBJECTS in INANIMATE UNIVERSE
have simultaneously moved forward in TIME together.
Those OBJECTS exist in TIME as well as SPACE:
how is it they are all able to synchronize TIME?
OBJECTS exist independently in SPACE and TIME;
their TIMES should be as distinct as their SPACES.
So if OBJECT passes SPACE to exist,
then should not OBJECT also pass TIME to exist?
Meaning TIME passes independently for each OBJECT—
there is discrete TIME PASSAGE to match SPACE PASSAGE.
What about how ABSOLUTE SPACE infiltrates existence,
and the relation between it and its constituent OBJECTS?
ABSOLUTE SPACE doesn't change as the relations
between it and observed OBJECTS within must diverge.
Now infer a correlation which does not deviate
from the intimate connection between TIME and SPACE.
ABSOLUTE TIME doesn't change as the relations
between it and observed OBJECTS within must diverge.
ABSOLUTE SPACE and TIME are as unchanging as REALITY;
when they are sensed, then they become pliable.
Therefore TIME and SPACE don't inherently change,
sensible PERCEPTIONS of them do.
What of RELATIVITY warping them into a putting green,
enabling SPACE and TIME to alter their existence?
TIME clocks flown around earth have proven RELATIVITY;
measurement of TIME PASSAGE is motion related.
There is no doubt RELATIVITY has been proven,
yet what it says about TIME and SPACE is still open.
The special theory of RELATIVITY is fairly well fixed;
the more ambiguous general theory isn't so well formed.
It is the general theory which claims to warp REALITY;
RELATIVITY only shows changing relations, not ABSOLUTES.
The curvature of the SPACE/TIME continuum RELATIVITY
exhibits as REALITY isn't of ABSOLUTE SPACE and TIME.
It is only a mathematical model of the relationship
between ABSOLUTES, their limitations, and an observer.
Therefore the attachment of TIME and SPACE to light
is really only a description of how it shows their relations.

A reflection left for expansion at a later moment,
for now concentrate solely on TIME PASSAGE.
Similar to how OBJECT passes in SPACE for its existence,
it's also required to pass in TIME.
A distinct difference between TIME PASSAGE, and TIME;
just as there is between SPACE PASSAGE, and SPACE.
It's very easy to confuse TIME with TIME PASSAGE;
the common view is of 1 TIME, 1 SPACE.
That is the problem all TRUTH seekers have to face,
for we have been trained to believe traditional confusions.
Most of my problem appears to be transfinitely related,
trying to make a RATIONAL account of INFINITE REALITY.
Prior to Einstein no one could make a dent in TIME;
how can there be many if its march never changes?
RELATIVITY began to show TIME wasn't immutable
QUANTITY SCIENCE had long claimed it to be.
Why does there need to be any difference;
cannot TIME suffice to cover its different aspects?
There are a few justifications, like the language for 1,
which warp any CONCEPT of it just like the continuum.
If TIME and TIME PASSAGE are the exact same thing,
why does adding PASSAGE change the word's meaning?
For something to pass, or even to pass by,
there must be some OBJECT there to perform the task.
TIME does not pass, rather OBJECT passes TIME,
somewhat like moving past a stationary position.
There is no better way of comprehending the universe
than a mandate for verbs to be accompanied by nouns.
TIME is only one TIME if it does not move;
and right here, right now, there is this ABSOLUTE TIME.
If TIME is to pass, then there must be something to pass;
SCIENCE side-steps REALITY to avoid this consideration.
Old TIME covers REALITY like a big warm soft quilt,
a known presence wrapped around and pressing on.
TIME, as I've always understood it, is omnipresent FORCE;
it's something continuously passing.
That traditional understanding needs violation,
breaking TIME from the chains of normalcy with a bit.

When I speak of a second or a minute or an hour,
I'm making distinctions in . . . I'm not sure what.
For understanding REALITY, *this must be uncovered:*
what is the thing those measurements carve into slices?
TIME PASSAGE moves unidirectionally, seemingly divisive;
ABSOLUTE TIME is like SPACE, dimensionless in VOID.
Yet they cannot actually be VOID;
something must be there for TIME *and* SPACE *to pass.*
VOID can't be without ABSOLUTE SPACE or TIME,
they both must cover all places and all moments.
VOID *could be part of* ABSOLUTE TIME *and* SPACE;
all things and events covered by what is and what is not.
Therefore ABSOLUTE TIME and SPACE might be REALITY,
with AETHER feeding existence into empty VOID.
Part of those ABSOLUTES *is total complete substantiality,*
the movement of ENERGY *we conceive as* REALITY.
The contrast between extremes is what is detected
by SCIENCE bent on discovering change and motion.
ABSOLUTE TIME *and* SPACE *are static to sensation,*
with PASSAGES *full of treasures for priests to unearth.*
SCIENCE hasn't been able to comprehend their essence
because ABSOLUTES have no difference to detect.
Part of REALITY *is consistently throughout* SPACE *and* TIME,
passing before eyes of MIND *into some unknown future.*
I rationally assume there exists some TIME and SPACE,
in order for whatever those essences are to pass.
Yet that is not direct PERCEPTION *of their* ABSOLUTES;
in order to know SPACE *and* TIME, *it must be gained.*
The lack of my ability to sense them is key to their nature;
being nothing sensible, they are 4 square out of bounds.
Which installs ABSOLUTES *at the limit of universal propriety,*
all of them beyond mortal ability for sensible PERCEPTION.
It's difficult to know TIME different from its PASSAGE;
this is why I must depend on its relativistic mate, SPACE.
SPACE *appearing so well-known to common use,*
largely because of its capacity for FINITY *measurement.*
SCIENCE has made magnificent strides in the accuracy
of separate measurements of FINITE TIME or SPACE.

Space and Time which are Absolute and limited,
dualistically divided into conceivable bundles.
Absolute Time can only be directly grasped intuitively;
Time Passage can only be directly grasped rationally,
Yet both must exist to create the fullness of Time;
an attempt to force them into the same niche always fails.
I'm still left with a gap in my understanding of Time;
to match it with Space, another piece must complete it.
Space is known in three different modes:
Absolute, and limited Passage, and limited Distance.
Time should also be known in 3 different modes,
but for now I've only been able to decipher 2.
What part of Time might correlate with spatial Distance,
remaining perpetually in contact, all on their own?

20:39

Time must simultaneously pass for both me and the clock,
but I don't understand how it could do this over Distance.
If Time passes for all Objects in a continuous fashion,
then some process must exist to connect it to all Space.
That Idea is a little hard for me to accept,
how the furthest reaches of Space touch same Time as I do.
Imagine how Time could continuously touch Space,
where there is no part of one ever leaving the other.
It's not difficult to imagine Absolutes together;
each becomes Transfinite, merging into the same thing.
What about Space Passage and Time Passage,
how could they connect to form identifiable Objects?
Any extant Object must pass Space to be sensed;
likewise, Object must pass Time to make it real.
Object does not just wink in and out of existence,
there is a perpetual change from its past to future.
Therefore it's also fairly simple to attach its Passages;
Space and Time seem to connect at the endpoints.
Could the cosmos consist of Transfinity Space wrapped
around a single point of Time stretched to Transfinity?

I mentally picture this to be like a Popsicle,
where the gooey part is wrapped around a single stick.
Whereas, could a black hole be TRANSFINITY TIME wrapped
around a single point of SPACE stretched to TRANSFINITY?
That would make them both appear to be continuous,
and still be beyond my ability to sense them.
ABSOLUTE TIME and SPACE are transfinitely large and small,
and these two limited essences have to meet somewhere.
If TIME is ABSOLUTE,
it must simultaneously touch all similar points of SPACE.
Otherwise the same moment would not pass
on earth as it does on the sun or in Alpha Centauri.
Which would require me to shed any THOUGHT I have
of TIME occurring at the same instant in distant places.
The limitations of measurements and dimensions are what
fool priests into believing TIME is light-limited.
Loosening THOUGHT, SCIENCE is less able to keep me from
forming RATIONAL independent CONCEPTS without its aid.
Could one TRANSFINITY point of TIME
be construed as some recalcitrant lack of continuity?
No, because 1 point is still continuous throughout;
TRANSFINITE of the small doesn't allow any separation.
Leaving reflection to play with words and definitions,
neither of which lead to understanding TIME.
I envision ABSOLUTE SPACE as RATIONAL and TRANSFINITE,
while SPACE PASSAGE is RATIONAL and FINITE.
SPACE and TIME are no more than bottled constituents,
and where one goes the other is sure to follow.
So ABSOLUTE TIME is also RATIONAL and TRANSFINITE,
and TIME PASSAGE is RATIONAL and FINITE.
That fits quite well with reflections up to this moment,
yet it still does not explain what TIME is, or its PASSAGE.
The problem I have is my traditional view of TIME,
it keeps popping into CONCEPTS where it no longer fits.
ABSOLUTE TIME correlates to TIME endlessly forming now,
while TIME PASSAGE transitions OBJECT from past to future.
So there are few conflicts with the habitual views of TIME,
these are solely RATIONAL and largely refer to TIME PASSAGE.

Still, the gods of SCIENCE have a mathematical domain,
which has to be included for a complete picture of TIME.
The laws of SCIENCE have been repeatedly shown true;
any view of REALITY must incorporate them as they stand.
SPACE is divided into TRANSFINITY and FINITY domains, neither
of which can exist past limited dualistic CONCEPTIONS.
TIME has been divided into TRANSFINITE and FINITE types;
what remains is to further divide its FINITE applications.
With a working postulate on how TIME is divided up,
no impediment exists to constructing its essence like SPACE.
Don't forget to apply numbers when finitely dividing;
a RATIONAL nature makes them subject to measurement.
Which may be the key to closing the gap in TIME,
measures inculcating MIND into better THOUGHTS on it.

21:09

The clock is passing TIME even while it's measuring;
the materials are decaying while TIME ticks on.
Could measurement of it not accurately reflect PASSAGE,
and seconds pasted onto OBJECT mean nothing at all?
Another statement which doesn't make much sense;
if seconds didn't apply to me, then I wouldn't grow old.
If a part of FINITY TIME is seen in OBJECT as TIME PASSAGE,
and the other part must be measured, what is it?
TIME PASSAGE has a definite beginning and ending,
which agrees with scientific explanations of origination.
REALITY supposedly began in the big band era,
or did just INANIMATE UNIVERSE begin that way?
The big bang created TIME PASSAGE, not TIME;
there must have been ABSOLUTE TIME at that instant.
What about in the distant future when everything stops,
all HEAT dying to bring about the universal end?
That will occur when no more OBJECTS exist,
so there will no longer be any use for them to pass TIME.
Yet TIME should still exist just like in the big band era;
there is no way to dispose of ABSOLUTE TIME.

Time Passage appears to be dependent upon Objects,
but I still have no Idea what it is.
Look now at how Time is distinguished in passing,
the way it is measured may expose some hidden clue.
Finite Time passing uses measured distinctions,
which originally were solely based on solar phenomena.
All Objects within the defined nearest solar system
are greatly, and mostly, influenced by one Star.
Prime Concept of Time passing
has thereby been divided into the day and month and year.
Even the moon as it passes through its phases
depends on bright Star for an observer to see it.
Time passing for primitive people was simple solar units:
day and night, lunar phases, and seasons becoming years.
And typical for the ever inquisitive human race,
nature's legs were pried apart to see the secrets within.
Commerce and knowledge made big Time insufficient,
so mankind then turned to sundials and hourglasses.
Any Time with inappropriate measurements is too big,
so the emphasis turned to small Time, and smaller.
With the advent of the renaissance for Science,
Time passing was distinguished on a more precise scale.
Where will the division of Time end,
when it can always get one little exponent smaller?
Time clocks were next created to divide Time
into passing units of seconds and smaller equivalents.
There is an obvious pattern here to those most aware:
measurement of Time is getting farther from Reality.
The numerical basis for formulating the second
was 86,400 bits, not quite accurate enough for Science.
Bits of what, partitions in varying days and nights;
whose little bit, ours over here, or theirs over there?
Finally Science based a second on a natural phenomenon:
a few disturbances of a Cesium 133 isotope.
How many flashes make up the divine number;
what revelation will make one better than another?
For those events to be expanded into an arbitrary second,
its decay had to be compared to extra-terra phenomena.

One and one always make two,
even if the resulting measurement is fantasized as one.
Solar or sidereal or ephemeris (no longer used),
the sun and STARS still give meaning to the second.
A second is now based on a defined series of events,
yet its dependence on the sun has been entirely forgotten.
Atomic methods of measuring the second are accurate,
and very precise, but not infinitely so.
A second has always been accurate, in the ballpark;
now it has become precise, with no deviation.
The decay rate of the Cesium 133 isotope was specifically
selected to compare it to transient solar phenomena.
No part of REALITY exists in isolation;
gods of SCIENCE cannot make measurements supreme.
The second is a comparison between micro and macro,
so any fixed TIME is only known by this dynamic.
Precision of the second is not doubted, it works;
the question to ask is how this result illuminates TIME?
Measurement of TIME is based on the second,
which is obviously an arbitrary and FINITE comparison.
Two natural phenomena create measured TIME:
how do these events relate to TIME PASSAGE?
Solar events and the isotope don't require measurement;
they exist, they pass TIME, whether measured or not.
Yes. Although they are not measured as just themselves,
they are measured in relation to something else.
But TIME moving forward is TIME PASSAGE,
this is what the measurements are supposed to indicate.
The day compares to the month compares to the year;
none of them stands in isolation as a measurement.
And the second to the minute to the hour to the day,
all of which show me part of TIME is moving forward.
Part of TIME must be measured RATIONAL QUANTITY,
which forbids it from being endlessly known by INTUITION.
Limited TIME is extremely valuable when used that way,
which has made modern SCIENCE grow so fast.
TIME cannot be measured into infinitely small divisions;
it is based on FINITY observations of natural phenomena.

The second is just a randomly derived comparison;
once 1 is fixed, all other divisions are just multiples.
There is only a TRANSFINITY series of FINITY divisions;
no real TIME distinctions are infinitely small.
TIME is only measured to the limits of machinery,
and TIME is only mathematically divided based on need.
As soon as a second is created,
a millisecond and a microsecond and so on must exist.
Something has to exist to move TIME forward;
if it isn't split seconds, then it's something else.
If a second exists as a function of REALITY,
then so does a sub second to (-TRANSFINITY) power.
But it can't be measured and it can't be used,
so according to SCIENCE it might as well not exist.
Although it must;
if its tiniest bits do not exist, neither does a second.
Its tiny bits do exist, they just can't be measured,
and like any other set its limits are TRANSFINITE.
CREATION of a second leads to the familiar paradox;
how can the gods depend on a second if it is irrational?
A second is RATIONAL as long as it's useful;
therefore SCIENCE will continue depending on the second.
Created TIME divisions only have an existence based on
a FINITY ability to be used within INANIMATE UNIVERSE.
That makes perfect RATIONAL sense;
anything measured can't be intuitively perceived.
We have become habituated to seeing the world from
a limited distinct perspective and with no explanation why.
I prefer a view including SCIENCE because it's mature;
centuries of trial and error have perfected its use.
Seeing the world and reacting with the animal instincts
which have pervaded THOUGHTS for all of man's existence.
Wait just a minute!
Rationality and SCIENCE are late additions to humanity.
Not quite. A RATIONAL view is based on sense PERCEPTION,
our ability to be RATIONAL is attached to our animal senses.
From that viewpoint all animals are RATIONAL;
any creature must use its senses to survive the wild.

Expecting limited REALITY *becomes ingrained as* REALITY;
it is all but impossible to view it in any other fashion.
So a RATIONAL perspective isn't only a THOUGHT process,
it's from everything detectable within INANIMATE UNIVERSE.
SPACE *as three dimensions,* TIME *as one dimension,*
what can be done within these defined transgressions?
Started/stopped/divided/measured/analyzed/numbered/
described/observed/sensed/limited/controlled/dissected.
Seeing REALITY *by one methodology allows forgetting*
the inherent required ability to see it in a different manner.
REALITY I know best is divided into parts and pieces;
the only problem is in understanding TIME and SPACE.
It is a mistake to mistake what is seen for what is real;
sensation tells us the sun revolves around the earth.
Adding CONCEPT to PERCEPTION corrects that mistake;
RATIONAL power can overcome animal dependence.
Gods gained their zenith by improving limited sensation;
although until now the break has not been entirely made.
A RATIONAL perspective of REALITY will always be limited
by the physical PERCEPTIONS on which it's based.
REALITY *is being broken from its sole* RATIONAL *view;*
there is more to it than that which can only be measured.
Maybe measured TIME is different from TIME in OBJECT;
TIME PASSAGE is only 1 of 2 types of FINITE TIME.
The other is the part of TIME *created by the second;*
*it is best known by its arbitrary name—*SUBJECTIVE TIME.
So TIME, like SPACE, divides into ABSOLUTE and limited,
and then further limitation divides it into 2 QUANTITIES.
ABSOLUTE TIME *is* TRANSFINITY *stretching over the present;*
TIME PASSAGE *and* SUBJECTIVE TIME *are moving on.*
The part of TIME connected to OBJECTS is TIME PASSAGE;
the part of it regularly measured is SUBJECTIVE TIME.
An approximation which works, yet is still inaccurate:
TIME PASSAGES *plus* SUBJECTIVE TIMES *equal* ABSOLUTE TIME.

22:19

The subjective clock gives me information I don't need;
it has no effect on how TIME is individually passing for me.
SUBJECTIVE TIME accurately portrays TIME moving,
yet does not manage to exhibit what is really in motion.
All OBJECTS, all sensed REALITY, must pass TIME to exist;
SUBJECTIVE TIME shows the direction, not the essence.
The essence of TIME has still not been undressed for view,
only how it has been misperceived in the past.
So far TIME and SPACE fit quite well together;
even SUBJECTIVE TIME shows motion with DISTANCE.
SPACE is best understood by what it is lacking;
maybe the key to TIME is finding what it has lost.
I've tried to tie TIME to SPACE, to make it continuous,
or lacking, and neither has shown me TIME I seek.
The problem is using continuity as the medium for TIME;
its essence is beyond CONCEPTION from false PERCEPTION.
Generally, SPACE is the absence of continuous OBJECTS;
in this case OBJECT is the substance which identifies it.
What is needed is something appearing continuous,
the lack of which could constitute TIME.
It must be some conceivable essence in INANIMATE UNIVERSE
which pervades it as thoroughly as TIME.
What is continuous, unidirectional, exists with SPACE,
and there is the possibility of its lack—maybe LIFE?
That answer is way too homocentric;
besides, a living essence is centered in ANIMATE UNIVERSE.
What about ENERGY;
could perceived TIME be where it is missing?
TIME would then be the lack of ENERGY;
measurements of it would indicate how it builds up.
Where is ENERGY conceived not to exist;
does its lack match up to the perversity of TIME?
A dead universe wouldn't pass any ENERGY;
therefore it also wouldn't pass any TIME.
Could a lack of ENERGY be attached to all SPACE;
how could TIME come from its defined absence?

Energy is defined as the capacity for doing work,
so my chair has a low level, and the sun has a high level.
What could make the chair so low and the sun so high
in regard to the existence of Time and Space?
The chair displaces little Space and little Time,
while the sun displaces much Space and much Time.
Yet Matter and Star are claimed particulate in nature;
how could their essences also be energetic?
I'm only trying to infer possibilities
from a basic assumption of Time as a lack of Energy.
As limited sensation gives the illusion of continuity,
it could also give the illusion that Matter is not Energy.
Relativistic equivalence essentially says a loss of Mass,
and therefore Matter, is a form of Energy.
The solid chair providing support for a solid rump
is actually not continuous Matter, but mostly empty Space.
A theory of charged particles moving at such high speeds
grants an illusion of perceived solid Matter.
Imagine that Matter as it passes Time and Space
is actually just lacking Energy in many different forms.
My poor Brain is insufficient for that task;
the parameters of the problem are too large to attack.
Consider a new chair and the same one a century old:
what do Space and Time mean for the existence of each?
I assume both chairs pass the same amount of Space;
they would be different, but I'm looking for Time.
The only other difference is in their relation to Time;
one has just met it, and the other is tired of it.
Each chair is Object to me;
therefore their differences must originate in this capacity.
Object is related to Time and Space by Passage;
name one Object ever known totally still.
All things I can prove to have knowledge of must come from
some aspect of Passage of Space and/or Time.
What is the difference in Energy between the two chairs;
what happens as a chair falls into disuse, then apart?
As Time passes for any chair as it ages,
usable Energy is passing into unusable forms.

A relation which has been observed many TIMES before,
within laws defining how INANIMATE UNIVERSE exists.
Usable ENERGY is always decreasing;
TIME PASSAGE is always increasing.
It is obvious TIME has passed for the old chair;
how can a difference in ENERGY be detected?
The old chair has lost more ENERGY by virtue of the fact
that there is less of the old chair than of the new chair.
Thus it is not possible to ignore SPACE PASSAGE;
the old chair cannot be assumed the same as the new.
The deduction I make is it takes ENERGY to exist;
any OBJECT will use it just to survive as itself.
And since ENERGY has been lost, never to return,
it has also passed some TIME, which is never to return.
The century-old chair can't be reassembled;
new parts can be added, but this just makes a new chair.
Could ABSOLUTE TIME be total ENERGY within REALITY,
while limited TIME is its lack?
It may be possible, but it's hard to imagine;
I don't sense TIME or ENERGY missing, as much as moving.
What if the requirement for missing TIME is deleted,
and instead just look for how TIME changes?
In trying to equate TIME with SPACE,
the comparison may have gone a little bit too far.
Sensation of a TRANSFINITY essence with FINITY revelation
should result in its perceivable QUANTITY as being different.
Forgotten was their substantial distinctions;
otherwise, 1 wouldn't be TIME and the other SPACE.
The search for TIME got off track by assuming it is lacking
something as SPACE is the lack of sensible OBJECTS.
All I require of any type of FINITE TIME is that it should
appear continuous, with no lacking involved.
FINITE TIME could be the continuous flow of ENERGY
within INANIMATE UNIVERSE from higher to lower levels.
Change is the distinct advantage of TIME,
energizing OBJECTS with magnificent motion.
TIME is composed of ABSOLUTE and limited types;
the former is always flowing through the latter.

Absolute Time is all available Energy in this universe!
Finite Time is distinguished by its limited usage.
Energy is the perceived continuous essence
which makes Time appear as its unique cyclorama.

23:07

In order for the clock and my body to both pass Time,
their existence in Space must be tied to the same source.
How could Energy be related to Space and Time;
is there some process providing it to all Reality?
Its getting late and these Thoughts give me a headache;
maybe I should just shut down and begin again tomorrow.
Do not stop now! Consider how an energetic version
of Time must intimately coexist with Space.
As far as Reality makes any sense to me
there is no way for Time to exist without Space.
In Space where there is no Time component
there might still be the capacity for Objects.
But it would be a static universe,
Mass and Extension where nothing would happen.
In Time where there is no Space component
there would still be the capacity for events to happen.
But nothing would exist for anything to occur;
a universe full of Infinite possibilities with no actualities.
So why are Space and Time considered in isolation,
manipulating their essences with arbitrary numbers?
Finite Space is often so considered for static convenience,
while it must be attached to Object to make it worthwhile.
That false isolation is why they fit into dimensions;
as soon as they are united, they no longer fit in.
Actually, the only instance where Finite Time and Space
aren't considered together is for Rational abstraction.
Convenience is not Reality,
only a deathly delight with destruction and dissection.
A Rational perspective has a strong settled hold on me;
Space and Time seem inconceivable minus dimensions.

Time and Space are still considered to be Quantities;
what are they if they are not scaled?
I have 4-dimensional Concept of Finite Space and Time,
overlaid on Absolute Time and Space.
What if the ubiquitous four-dimensional model
is thrown away for energetic Finity Space and Time?
Then Time and Space may not be 4 dimensions;
they connect on a more realistic non-dimensional plane.
Absolute to Absolute and limited to limited;
with Conceptions, unlike charges, like ones attract.
Absolute Time attaches to Absolute Space, Time Passage
to Space Passage, and Subjective Time to Distance.
Space and Time were always considered distinct;
then Einstein came along and threw it all out the window.
Every bit of Science before him had to be revisited;
previous theories were based on limited assumptions.
Yet even he still retained the dimensional model,
retaining the coordinate systems, and connecting them.
Any scientist connects Time and Space with coordinates,
systems so designed to make my limitations bearable.
Einstein was not a scientist, he was a philosopher,
puttering along with numbers he barely understood.
I shouldn't be afraid of committing any more heresies,
enough have already been done to burn me in the chair.
Dependence on dimensions skews visions of Reality,
requiring it to exist according to mental convenience.
Science overlays dimensions on Reality,
and then tries to make this abstract universe fundamental.
It might be better to understand Reality as it truly is,
and then overlay a system of Thought best describing it.
Rational knowledge versus Intuitive understanding;
building a whole from parts, or seeing parts in a whole.
Instead of tying Time to Space via an artificial system,
maybe they are unified, and dimensions are evidence.
Therefore, Einstein found the true connection in Reality,
and had to justify it using limited scientific principles.
Thus Time does not equate with all Energy,
the combination of Absolute Space and Time does.

Then each Finite aspect of those Transfinites
must be connected because their source is connected.
Know this as Truth in Reality:
Inanimate Reality is Absolute Time and Space is all Energy.

23:37

For Time and Space to be energetic in nature,
the part of them located in the clock can't be particulate.
If Time manifests itself so distinctly as Energy,
then how does Space exist in an energetic form?
Science and I both connect Finite Time and Space;
Distance could be energetic, but Objects are particulate.
In order for Intuition's view of Reality to hold up,
Space Passage must consist of some form of Energy.
Absolute Space and Time come from 1 same Aether;
there is no way for 1 to be Energy, and the other not.
Time Passage is the loss of Energy attached to Objects,
which makes Space Passage . . . what?
I tried to understand Time from more identifiable Space,
now I have to go back and throw all that out the window.
Space cannot remain locked into past Ideas;
its Passage through Objects should be as fresh as Intuition.
Space isn't just the absence of sensible Objects,
this was a false start into opening Inanimate Universe.
For now, imagine Matter is not divided within;
Objects pass Time because they are Energy.
Time Passage is a type of Finite Time, which is Energy,
attached to Objects and lost from Absolute sources.
Considered alone, Time is a separate dimension;
affiliated with Space, it becomes something more noble.
Absolute Time is Absolute Space is all Energy,
so Object as Space Passage must be in an energetic state.
Yet Object seems so solid and Energy so fluid;
how can one essence appear to be two things at once?
Object passes Time for its existence, and Time is Energy,
so it goes from a higher Energy state to a lower 1.

Detection of TIME is the detection of moving ENERGY,
and any motion is based on a difference in location.
OBJECT at any single TIME is at a specific ENERGY state,
and as TIME passes its state becomes less and less usable.
OBJECT is a combination of TIME and SPACE PASSAGE,
so the conclusion should not be too hard to ascertain.
SPACE PASSAGE is the part of OBJECT sensed to be
at a specific ENERGY state, and it's constantly changing.
OBJECT is sensed as solid because any direct PERCEPTION
of it must be at some fixed instant, so it appears fixed.
Even though SPACE PASSAGE is moving ENERGY,
it must be moving between states to be detected at all.
The problem with the traditional view of ENERGY
is an assumption of acquisition from external FORCES.
ENERGY is acquired from motion or position,
due to some OBJECT forcing others to do work.
Step back for a minute and think independently:
what if FORCE comes from ENERGY instead of vice versa?
The proposition: all ENERGY is ABSOLUTE for MATTER,
and OBJECTS pass TIME and SPACE as part of existence.
Where does ENERGY come from if not from OBJECTS;
how does it just appear as POTENTIAL or KINETIC?
It's reasonable to postulate all ENERGY in the universe,
therefore FORCE, comes from OBJECTS and not to them.
At least ENERGY which shows within INANIMATE UNIVERSE;
PURPOSE from ANIMATE UNIVERSE is entirely different.
Every OBJECT is always sensed in a state of static ENERGY,
just as each OBJECT is always passing SPACE.
Being FINITY themselves, OBJECTS and the separation between
them are suited to limited SPACE and TIME.
SPACE PASSAGE is the static ENERGY state of any OBJECT;
TIME PASSAGE is a dynamic loss of useful ENERGY in it.
Do not forget about SUBJECTIVE TIME and DISTANCE,
which are also measured FINITY aspects of their source.
DISTANCE is formed by static ENERGY states between OBJECTS;
SUBJECTIVE TIME relates to ENERGY moving therein.
Mentally picture OBJECT moving through SPACE
in a different light, one more conducive to ENERGY flow.

OBJECT doesn't just move through SPACE and pass TIME,
it's part of an ABSOLUTE aggregate, more than a continuum.
Sensation paints a limited picture of how REALITY is;
everything is connected ENERGY from source to disposal.
I'm unsure how OBJECTS move through SPACE and TIME,
but I no longer subscribe to an incomplete prescription.
The mystics were right in their description of REALITY:
striking someone else is just striking oneself.

24:08

Even something as simple as the clock submits to DUALISM;
its existence and its function are both separate and united.
TIME and SPACE become just another aspect of DUALITY,
CONCEPTIONS which are divided into ABSOLUTE and limited.
My dimensional picture of them is still valid;
it just must be tempered with more inclusive knowledge.
REALITY is AETHER flowing through existence,
available to the universes, ANIMATE and INANIMATE.
Bound up in that paradigm are forms of SPACE and TIME;
my CONCEPT of them has changed by subsuming awareness.
Thus part of AETHER must be ABSOLUTE TIME and SPACE,
or do they merge more complete in some place beyond?
AETHER as PURPOSE exists within ANIMATE UNIVERSE,
so I see AETHER as the sum of ENERGY and PURPOSE.
All of the same essence, from the same source;
all sensed or felt originates from the grand unification.
But once again I have a problem with part of existence:
somehow a piece of AETHER is able to force itself.
If everything is AETHER, non-empty TIME and SPACE,
how does anybody or anything move within it?
PERCEPTION of REALITY makes it different,
mandated by the fact that it both <*is*> and <*is not*>.
Limiting REALITY to what can be verified by sensation
only comforts those who desire to remain animals.
Animals detect motion based on a need for survival;
this is how they exist, not why they exist.

Previously, motion was conceived as moving in SPACE,
through TIME to some anticipated future goal.
But ABSOLUTE TIME is ABSOLUTE SPACE is all ENERGY,
so any non-inclusive PERCEPTIONS are flawed.
Full understanding shows sense PERCEPTIONS to be limited:
why should CONCEPTIONS of insensibility be any better?
Don't ask me for any irrational opinions;
everything I know is based on what I can sense.
All things are one within the vast energetic field;
OBJECTS do not move so much as aetheric ENERGY changes.
So everything I currently know about REALITY
is based on false assumptions, due to my limited senses.
AETHER feeds everything and everywhere and everywhen;
look through the veil of PERCEPTION, as the poet saw it.
Now I am looking to poets for explanation,
which seems to me like looking under water for air.
ABSOLUTE TIME and SPACE are the dualistic resolution
of INTUITION'S view of ENERGY, which can only exist as one.
Therefore there is only unity throughout SPACE and TIME,
requiring RATIONAL CONCEPT as a minimum of 2.
Thus the gods of SCIENCE say ABSOLUTE TIME and SPACE
do not exist—they can only be seen intuitively.
Their existence may at best have inductive strength,
no more proven than any other a priori assessment.
Nobody knows what it is OBJECTS move within:
how are we to know that which cannot be perceived?
But many CONCEPTS are accepted without my senses;
for them it will always be the evidence that counts.
How can OBJECTS of MATTER exist within those SPACES;
why should their internal and external motions be TIME?
Because things have to exist in something;
they can't exist in themselves or in nothing.
Yet AETHER itself exists towards more empty VOID;
there can be only one, the objective of its existence.
I rationally accept the probability of 1 AETHER,
but no process exists by which INTUITIVE becomes RATIONAL.
It is only a figment of sensory limitations to suppose
MATTER moves just in SPACE, not in a greater unified whole.

Nothing happens without the advent of TIME,
and its ABSOLUTE version detected in 2 limited forms.
Notice how travel back in TIME is also not viable:
how could the gods of SCIENCE separate SPACE and TIME?
Reverse TIME travel would require spatial reversal;
SPACE's 2 limited versions backing up into its ABSOLUTE.
AETHER arriving via REALITY is down a one-way river;
only LIFE has figured out a way to briefly halt the ride.
FINITE TIME is simply the loss of ENERGY in FINITE SPACE;
to move back in TIME a traveler must reverse this flow.
Even LIFE does not reverse the flow;
it is held in abeyance for PURPOSES remaining to be seen.
If I want to accomplish travel back in TIME,
I will concurrently have to learn to travel back in SPACE.
Which makes that IDEA just silly to contemplate,
a complete misreading of how REALITY is presented.
REALITY is always unfolding before my eyes;
turning them inward sees another view, not backwards.
One more reflection will serve to divine TIME fully:
how does this source divide into none, one, and many?
Since TIME and SPACE are inextricably intertwined,
then the source of them both must be none, 1, and many.
No source is ABSOLUTE TIME and SPACE;
there is none if the source is itself.
Limited REALITY as 1 seems to indicate something else,
but 1 is FINITE and limited in application.
One source is TIME and SPACE PASSAGE;
if OBJECT is ENERGY, there is only simple unity within.
OBJECTS are too similar to come from many sources;
their MASSES and EXTENSIONS are similar BASIC QUANTITIES.
Many sources are SUBJECTIVE TIME and DISTANCE,
diverse OBJECTS creating an opus of SPACE and TIME.
SPACE between OBJECTS, and TIME measured in seconds,
their continuum seems to imply they are all there is.
TIME and SPACE can be divided into ABSOLUTE and limited,
yet why REALITY exists this way has not been uncovered.
There are many questions left open in this aetheric theory,
not the least of which concerns MATTER as ENERGY.

Does REALITY exist as a mechanism or a pattern,
or maybe <just maybe!> it could be a little bit of both?

****

24:51

A mannequin is dressed and acting like a soldier,
yet what is this battle being fought, or is it a war?
Peace comes, bringing harmony to my home in the woods,
until it is shattered once again by confrontations.
Forced to encounter people who will just not be fair,
seeking to find a path where no people are involved.
Attach a rainbow to the house, it looks just like one;
two in the same vicinity is not a sin against nature.
Who is this woman prattling in my ear;
is she unknown if she is at ease giving advice?
One drive, three buildings, no neighbors;
the count is the same, so it should be my home, but it's not.
The physical side spends itself in wasted exertion,
while mental notions see all, and are still unable to act.
Now it gets exciting because I get to break some laws,
not just the ones made to be broken.
Fate leads me to become a burglar breaking into a vault;
is that the right term, should it be a vaulter?
There is a secretary at a desk out beside where I work,
or where the administrative assistant is in charge of sitting.
Placing some chairs there for no REASON whatsoever,
I then plug in my own devices and make it a new home.
Setting some water on the desk, I guess it is normal;
then proceed to break in the vault, one follows the other.
A band is on TIME to come marching down the street
(in order to cover the noise of the break-in).
Unfortunately, she and her grown children live
across the street, and they are watching everything I do.
They have the gall to come over to my crime,
make me pack up all my tools, and leave.

Stirring around I wonder while I'm still half-asleep,
why the hell didn't they just call the police?
Then I become a boy scout, but keep getting lost,
chased by a bunch of rednecks all related to one another.
Never been to that part of Louisiana;
water and docks and crawdads, no sport.
Bereft of EMOTION, events take a toll on TIME.
How will they come back unless they first go away?
"This is what it's all about;"
then a train rushes by my ear and it's TIME to wake up.

End of Book I

FIGURE A

STATIC SUBSTANCES

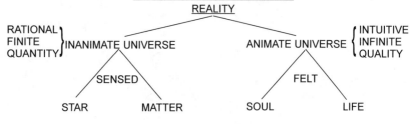

REALITY

RATIONAL
FINITE } INANIMATE UNIVERSE
QUANTITY

ANIMATE UNIVERSE { INTUITIVE
INFINITE
QUALITY

SENSED

FELT

STAR   MATTER   SOUL   LIFE

DYNAMIC ENERGY

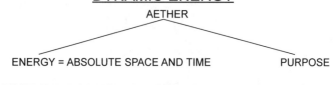

AETHER

ENERGY = ABSOLUTE SPACE AND TIME   PURPOSE

AETHER IS THE SOURCE TO KNOWN REALITY FEEDING INTO VOID

SPACE AND TIME

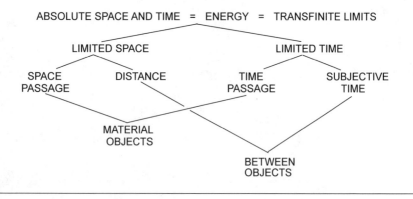

ABSOLUTE SPACE AND TIME = ENERGY = TRANSFINITE LIMITS

LIMITED SPACE   LIMITED TIME

SPACE   DISTANCE   TIME   SUBJECTIVE
PASSAGE   PASSAGE   TIME

MATERIAL
OBJECTS

BETWEEN
OBJECTS

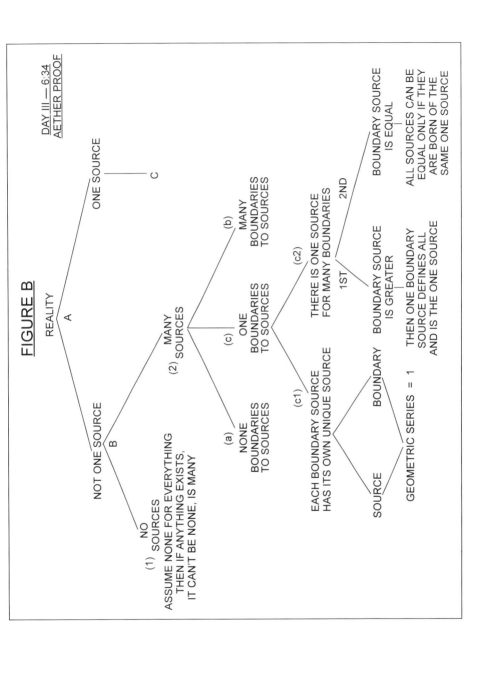

FIGURE B

DAY III — 6:34
AETHER PROOF